Praise for S[illegible]
and The Lakeshore Chronicles

"Superb. Wonderfully evoked characters, a spellbinding story line, and insights into the human condition will appeal to every reader."

—*Booklist* on *Summer at Willow Lake*

"Empathetic protagonists, interesting secondary characters, well-written flashbacks, and delicious recipes add depth to this touching, complex romance…"

—*Library Journal* on *The Winter Lodge*

"Wiggs's uncomplicated stories are rich with life lessons, nod-along moments and characters with whom readers can easily relate. Delightful and wise."

—*Publishers Weekly* on *Dockside*

"Wiggs is at the top of her game here, combining a charming setting with subtly shaded characters and more than a touch of humor. This is the kind of book a reader doesn't want to see end but can't help devouring as quickly as possible."

—*RT Book Reviews*, Top Pick, on *Snowfall at Willow Lake*

"An emotionally gripping tale centered on family. Wiggs is back in top form."

—*Booklist* on *The Summer Hideaway*

"Wiggs delights…the evolution of Darcy and Logan's relationship makes enduring love believable."

—*Publishers Weekly* on *Candlelight Christmas*

Also by Susan Wiggs

CONTEMPORARY ROMANCES

Home Before Dark
The Ocean Between Us
Summer by the Sea
Table for Five
Lakeside Cottage
Just Breathe
The Goodbye Quilt

The Bella Vista Chronicles

The Apple Orchard
The Beekeeper's Ball

The Lakeshore Chronicles

Summer at Willow Lake
The Winter Lodge
Dockside
Snowfall at Willow Lake
Fireside
Lakeshore Christmas
The Summer Hideaway
Marrying Daisy Bellamy
Return to Willow Lake
Candlelight Christmas

HISTORICAL ROMANCES

The Lightkeeper
The Drifter
The Mistress of Normandy
The Maiden of Ireland

The Tudor Rose Trilogy

At the King's Command
The Maiden's Hand
At the Queen's Summons

Chicago Fire Trilogy

The Hostage
The Mistress
The Firebrand

Calhoun Chronicles

The Charm School
The Horsemaster's Daughter
Halfway to Heaven
Enchanted Afternoon
A Summer Affair

Look for the newest Lakeshore Chronicles novel
Starlight on Willow Lake
coming soon from MIRA Books

SUSAN WIGGS

Marrying Daisy Bellamy

ISBN-13: 978-0-7783-1771-5

Marrying Daisy Bellamy

For questions and comments about the quality of this book, please contact us at CustomerService@Harlequin.com.

www.MIRABooks.com

Printed in U.S.A.

This book is dedicated to my readers.
When Daisy Bellamy first sneaked into
Summer at Willow Lake years ago, a sullen teenager with a
chip on her shoulder, she was meant to just pass through
the series. Instead, you kept her in your hearts,
book after book, patiently waiting for her story to be told.
You've helped me stay motivated to write "Daisy's story"
for years. Many thanks for inspiring me
to send this character on her own journey.

Marrying
Daisy Bellamy

Part One

One

The bridegroom was so handsome, Daisy Bellamy's heart nearly melted at the sight of him. Please, she thought. Oh, please let's get it right this time.

He offered her a brief, nervous smile.

"Come on," she said in a barely audible whisper, "once more with feeling. Say *I love you,* and mean it. Show me what you're feeling."

He was a storybook prince, in his dove-gray swallowtail tux, every hair in place, adoration beaming from every pore. He stared intently into her eyes and, in a voice that broke with sincerity, said, "I love you."

"Yes," Daisy whispered back. "Got it," she added, and lowered the camera away from her face. "That's what I'm talking about. Good going, Brian."

The videographer moved in to capture the reaction of the newly minted bride, a flushed and pretty young woman named Andrea Hubble. Using his video camera as an extra appendage, Zach Alger gently coached the couple with a word or two and soon had them talking intimately about their love, their hopes and dreams, their happiness on this glorious day.

Daisy took a candid shot of the couple as they leaned

in for another kiss. In the background, a loon beat skyward from Willow Lake, droplets of water sparkling like stars in the glow of early twilight. The beauty of nature added a sheen of romance to the moment. Daisy was good at capturing romance in her camera frame. In life—not so much.

She longed to feel the joy she saw in her clients' faces, but her own romantic past was a series of mistakes and missed chances. Now here she was, a screwup trying to unscrew her life. She had a small son who didn't realize his mom was a screwup, a responsible job and an unadmitted yearning for something she couldn't have—that shining love her camera observed through its very expensive lens.

"I think we're done here," Zach said, checking his watch. "And you guys have a big party to go to."

The bridal couple squeezed each other's hands, their faces wreathed in smiles. Daisy could feel the excitement coming off them in waves. "Biggest party of our lives," said Andrea. "I want it to be perfect."

It won't be, thought Daisy, keeping her camera at the ready. Some of the best shots happened at random, unplanned moments. The flaws were what made a wedding special and memorable. The glory of imperfection was one of the first things she'd discovered when she'd started working as a wedding photographer. Every event, no matter how carefully planned, had its imperfections. There would always be a groomsman facedown in the punch bowl, a collapsing pavilion tent, somebody's hair on fire when they leaned too close to the candles, an overweight, fainting auntie, a wailing infant.

These were the things that made life interesting. As a single mother, Daisy had learned to appreciate the unplanned. Some of her life's sweetest moments came when she least expected them—the clutch of her son's tiny hands, anchoring her to earth with a power greater than gravity. Some of the most awful moments, too—a train pulling out of the station, leaving her behind, along with her dreams—but she tried not to dwell on that.

She suggested that the newlyweds hold hands and hike across a vast, pristine meadow at the edge of Willow Lake. During the World War II years, the meadow had been the site of a communal Victory Garden. Now it was one of Daisy's favorite settings, particularly at this golden hour of the day, when time hovered between afternoon and evening.

The meadow was suffused in the last pink and amber of the sun's rays. This moment, for Andrea and Brian, *was* perfect. The bride led the way, walking slightly ahead of him with her chin held aloft. The groom's posture was protective, yet he exuded joy from every angle of his body. The breeze kicked up her gown so that the shadows connected the two of them like a delicate dark web, the unrehearsed drama of the movement coinciding with the firing of the camera shutter.

Checking the viewfinder of her camera, Daisy suspected this might be an iconic shot for this couple.

Except…she zoomed in on a small spot on the horizon.

"Damn," she muttered.

"What?" Zach asked, leaning to look over her shoulder.

"The Fritchmans' dog, Jake, got loose again." There he was in high-resolution glory, silhouetted against the sweeping sky, taking a crap.

"Classic," Zach remarked, and went back to coiling his cables and organizing his gear for the wedding reception.

Daisy pushed a button to tag the photo for later retouching.

"Ready?" she asked Zach.

"Time to party on," he said, and they followed the bride and groom along the lakeshore path to the main pavilion of Camp Kioga, where the reception would take place. The couple made a pit stop to freshen up for their grand entrance, and Daisy prepared to document the festivities.

She'd liked the bride from the start, and she had always loved the setting of Camp Kioga. The serene lakeside resort was a historic landmark on Willow Lake, and it belonged to Daisy's grandparents. Tucked into the wildest corner of Ulster County near the town of Avalon, Camp Kioga had been founded as a retreat for the elite of New York City, a place where the well-heeled could escape the steamy summer heat.

These days, the camp had been transformed into a luxurious resort by Daisy's cousin Olivia. Last year, the reinvented retreat had been featured as a destination wedding venue on www.Iamthebeholder.com, and bookings were steady.

To Daisy, Camp Kioga was more than a beautiful setting. She had spent some of her life's most joyous—and most painful—moments here, and the entire landscape had shaped her aesthetic as a photographer.

The firm she'd worked for since finishing college, Wendela's Wedding Wonders, was a local institution, and Daisy was grateful for the job. The work was steady, the hours crazy and the income adequate, if not lucrative. There would never be a shortage of people wanting to get married. And okay, she did dream of branching out from weddings and portraits, because her deepest love was something she termed narrative nature photography.

At heart, she was a storyteller. Her photos offered intimate glimpses through her lens. She captured the fragile, ephemeral nature of the world around her with pictures that haunted her heart, arousing deep emotions from the simple grace of trees dipping their branches in the water, the abundance of a green-shadowed forest in springtime, the epic shape of granite crags above a gorge. In college, she'd always been under deadline pressure because her subjects would not be rushed—tadpoles transforming themselves, a fawn finding its way through a meadow, the stillness of a heron as it waited in the marshy shallows for its next meal.

Photography was where she'd found her artist's voice and a passion for the work. The fascination had begun with the gift of a Kodak camera on her eighth birthday. She had captured a shot of her grandma Bellamy learning to hula hoop that day, experiencing a moment of such satisfaction that it felt like a benediction. It was a moment that would never again be repeated; she had frozen it forever in time and memory, and despite the fact that it featured her own grandmother, there was something universal in the shot that anyone could understand.

That was the moment she'd discovered the power of photography. She often wished for more time to produce fine art with her camera, but even fine artists—and their small sons—had to eat. For a single mom, steady work trumped high art every time. And the photo snobs seemed determined to overlook a key fact. In the midst of a wedding, opportunities abounded for finding a transcendent moment. A good photographer simply knew where to look for them and how to capture them. At a wedding, you could find people at their most real. The same story played out in endless ways and infinite variety, and for Daisy, it held a kind of fascination.

She was intrigued by the mysterious alchemy that drew a couple together and compelled them to embark on a journey through life together. A camera, properly wielded, could tell the story, over and over again in all its manifestations.

Perhaps this was because Daisy longed to understand it for herself. Perhaps if she became the world's foremost expert at capturing life's happiest moments, she would figure out a way to find her own.

The wedding wasn't perfect. In the middle of the toast, Andrea Hubble's mother became tongue-tied and dissolved into tears. The bar ran out of champagne in the first hour, and the DJ blew a speaker. One of the bridesmaids broke out in hives from something she ate, and the five-year-old ring bearer went missing, only to be found fast asleep under a banquet table.

Daisy knew that within hours, none of this would matter. As the DJ broke down his set and workers disassembled the tables, the blissfully happy couple headed off in the night for the Summer Hideaway, the resort's most secluded cabin. Her final shot, lit by the moon and her favorite off-camera strobe flash, showed them walking down the path toward the cabin, the groom lifting his arm and twirling the bride beneath it. No question the night would go well for them, Daisy thought, putting away her things with a restless sigh.

The wedding guests occupied Camp Kioga's other lodgings—old-school bunkhouses, A-frame cabins or luxurious rooms in the main lodge.

In the work van on the way home, Zach cracked open a can of Utica Club purloined from the bar and held it out to Daisy.

She shook her head. "No, thanks. It's all yours." Contrary to her demographic—recent college grad—she wasn't much for drinking. Truth be told, drinking had never done her any favors. In fact, the reason she'd become a mom at nineteen had everything to do with drinking. If Charlie ever asked her where babies come from, she would have to find a way to explain that he'd come from an abundance of Everclear punch and a weekend of supremely bad judgment.

"Here's to you, then," said Zach. "And to Mr. and Mrs. Happily Ever After. May they stay together long enough to pay off the wedding."

"Don't be such a cynic," she chided him. In his own way, Zach Alger had had a rough go of things, too. They made a good team, though. He was more than an assistant and videographer to her. He was one of her favorite—though reluctant—subjects to photograph, with strong, angular features and unusual Nordic coloring, so pale he was sometimes mistaken for an albino. He was totally self-conscious about his white-blond hair, the kind that seemed to absorb color from other sources. Daisy had always thought it was cool. Some of the images she'd shot of him had been picked up commercially. Apparently his look—the pale coloring and wintry eyes—was popular in Japan and South Korea. Somewhere in the Far East, his face was selling men's cologne and cell phone minutes.

Not enough to pay the bills for either of them, however. He was just out of college, too, skilled at high-tech media. What she liked most about Zach was that he was a good friend—nonjudgmental, easy to talk to.

"I'm just saying—"

"Don't worry about it," she said. "You're such a worrier."

"Right, like you're not."

He had her there. Daisy didn't see any way around being a worrier, though. Having a kid tended to do that to a person.

"Maybe if we pool all our worries," she suggested, "we'll generate enough energy to fuel the van."

"I only need enough to make it to the end of the month." Zach guzzled the beer, belched and fell quiet, staring out the window at the utter nothingness that was the town of Avalon late at night. The locals joked that the sidewalks rolled up by nine, but that was an exaggeration. It was more like eight.

She and Zach didn't need to fill the silence with chit-chat. They'd known each other since high school, and they'd both endured their share of trials. While she became a teenage mom, Zach had been dealing with his dad's financial meltdown and subsequent incarceration on corruption charges. Not exactly a recipe for serenity.

Yet somehow they had each muddled through, a little worse for the wear but still standing. Zach was methodically working his way through a mountain of student debt. And Daisy had made a series of bad choices. She felt as if she were living life backward, starting with having a kid while still a teenager. Then came school and work, and all that was swinging into balance, but one thing eluded her. It was the thing they photographed nearly every weekend, toasted and celebrated by her ever-changing array of clients. Love and marriage. These things shouldn't matter so much. She wished she could believe her life was just fine, but she'd be kidding herself.

It was a challenge to avoid looking back and second-guessing herself. She could have had a shot at marriage. A surprise Christmas Eve proposal had come at her out of the blue and sent her reeling. Even now, months later, the very thought of it made her hyperventilate. Thinking back about a night that might have changed her life, she flexed her hands on the steering wheel. *Did I make the right choice? Or did I run away from the one thing that could have saved me?*

"So, is Charlie with his dad tonight?" Zach asked, breaking the silence.

"Yep. They're the dynamic duo." She slowed the van to avoid a small family of raccoons. The largest of the three paused, turning glittery eyes to the headlamps before herding the two small ones into the ditch.

Charlie's father, Logan O'Donnell, had been as messed up and careless as Daisy herself was, back in the teen years. But like Daisy, Logan had been transformed by parenthood. And when she needed him to take Charlie for the night, he gladly stepped up.

"And what about *you* and Logan?" Zach pried.

She sniffed. "If there's anything to report, you'll be the first to know." Things between her and Logan were complicated. That was the only word she could think of to describe the situation. Complicated.

"But—"

"But nothing." She turned a corner and emerged onto the town square. At this hour, no one was around. Zach lived in a small vintage walk-up over the Sky River Bakery. As teenagers, they had both had jobs there. Now a new generation of kids managed the giant mixers and proofing machines in the wee hours of the morning. Hard to believe, but Daisy and Zach weren't the kids anymore.

She swung into a parking spot. "I'll be in the studio by ten tomorrow," she said. "I promised Andrea a sneak peek by next Saturday."

"Jeez," he groaned. "Do you know how many hours I shot?"

"Actually, I do. It's only a sneak peek. I like this bride, Zach. I want to make her happy."

"Isn't that the groom's job?"

"She has four younger sisters."

"I know. They couldn't stay away from the camera." He shouldered open the passenger-side door and stepped down. The glow of the streetlights turned his hair to amber.

"Maybe they couldn't stay away from you," she suggested.

"Yeah, right." He was probably blushing, but in this light, she couldn't tell. Zach had never been much for dating. Though he'd never admit it, he'd been carrying a torch for Daisy's stepsister, Sonnet, since preschool.

"'Night, Zach," she said.

"See you tomorrow. Don't stay up too late."

He knew her well. She was usually pretty wired after an event and couldn't resist loading the raw files. She liked to post a single, perfect teaser shot on her blog to give the bride a taste of things to come.

Her own place was an unassuming small house on Oak Street. She took her time letting herself in. One of the worst things about raising Charlie with a guy she didn't live with was that she missed her son like mad when he was with his father.

She locked the door behind her, and the all-pervasive silence took her breath away. She'd never been very good with all-pervasive silence. It made her think too hard, and when she thought too hard, she worried. And when she worried, she made herself insane. And when she went insane, that made her a bad mom. It was a cycle that refused to end.

Maybe she should get a dog. Yes, a friendly, bouncy dog to greet her at the door with swirls and yips of delight. A funny, nonjudgmental dog that would completely distract her from the things she didn't want to think about.

"A dog," she said, trying out the concept aloud. "Genius."

Wandering into the study nook, she took out a small deck of memory cards from the wedding and watched the images load, one by one. Some were familiar, shots she took at every wedding, because they were expected—the first dance, with the couple silhouetted dramatically against the night sky, the parents of the bride and groom sharing a toast. Others were unique, a pose or a look she'd never seen before. She'd caught the bride's grandmother cross-eyed as she slurped down an oyster, the groom's uncle making a rapturous face during a song, one of the bridesmaids visibly ducking to avoid catching the bouquet. And then there was one shot, the one she'd expected, that turned out to be transcendent.

It was the last-minute frame of the bride and groom hiking across the meadow, hand in hand. It told a story, it said who they were, it expressed them as a couple. Two together, linked by a handclasp that looked eternal.

Minus Jake, she reminded herself, opening the editing program. The pooping dog in the background would have to go. As she busily cleaned up the photo, she studied the gleam of light on the bending fronds of grass, the distorted reflection of the couple in the water, the unfurling emotion in the bride and the joy shining from the groom. The shot was good. Better than good. Entry-in-a-photo-competition good, that's what it was, she thought.

As the notion crossed her mind, her gaze flicked to a folder in the tray on the desk. That was where she was supposed to file her entries to the photo exhibit contest for the Museum of Modern Art in New York. The top entries each year would be placed on exhibit in the MoMA's Emerging Artists section. The competition was the fiercest in the industry, because being selected would open doors and launch careers. Daisy was dying to submit her work.

However, the tray was woefully empty, the file folder like a barely cracked-open door showing only blankness inside. All the good intentions in the world, all the lofty ambitions, could not give Daisy the one thing she needed to complete the project and submit her materials. The gift of time. Sometimes she caught herself wondering when her life was going to finally be *her* life.

Pushing aside the frustration, she refocused on the bridal photo and quickly posted it on Wendela's company blog, titling the entry, "Andrea and Brian sneak peek."

Sitting back and gazing at the shot, Daisy indulged in a private cry. She didn't want people to know the sight of happy couples made her cry. She didn't want anyone to see her need, her desire, her knife-sharp longing. Alone in the small hours of the night, she cried. And then she shut down her computer.

By then it was one o'clock in the morning, and she needed to get to bed. As she went around turning off the lights, she noticed a few envelopes on the floor below the mail slot of the front door. She bent down and went through the small stack. Fliers and junk mail. Solicitations, notices about neighborhood meetings. Coupons she would never use. And…a cream-colored envelope, addressed in a very familiar hand.

Her heart skipped a beat. She ripped open the thick envelope.

> You are hereby invited to the commissioning of Julian Maurice Gastineaux as a Second Lieutenant in the United States Air Force ROTC, Detachment 520 at Cornell University on Saturday 14, May, at 1300 hrs in the Statler Auditorium.

On the back, scrawled in that same familiar bold script, was the message, "Hope you'll come. Really need to talk to you. J."

So much for sleep.

It was nuts, realizing a simple name on a piece of paper could send her spiraling through a past filled with what-ifs and paths not taken. Because Julian Gastineaux, soon to be Second Lieutenant Julian Gastineaux, was her own personal path not taken.

Two

Camp Kioga, Ulster County, New York
Five years earlier

The summer before her senior year of high school, the last thing Daisy wanted to do was stay in a musty lakeside cabin with her dad and little brother. She had to, though. They were making her do it.

Although neither of her parents said much to her and Max, their family was in the process of breaking up. Her mom and dad couldn't keep up the pretense of being a happy couple, even though they'd been trying for years. Her dad's solution was to retreat from their Upper East Side home to the Bellamy family compound—historic Camp Kioga on Willow Lake—and act like everything was dandy.

Well, nothing was dandy and Daisy was determined to prove it. She'd packed her bag with a summer's worth of hair products, an iPod, an SLR camera and a goodly supply of pot and cigarettes.

Though determined to ignore the mesmerizing beauty of the lakeside camp, she felt herself being unsettled by the deep isolation, the pervasive quiet, the haunting views.

The last thing she was expecting, out here in the middle of nowhere, was to meet someone. Turned out a boy her age had also been sentenced to summer camp, though for entirely different reasons.

When he first walked into the main pavilion at the dinner hour, she felt a funny kind of heat swirl through her and thought maybe the summer was not going to be so boring after all.

He looked like every dangerous thing grown-ups warned her about. He had a tall, lean, powerful body and a way of carrying himself that exuded confidence, maybe even arrogance. He was of mixed race, with tattoos marking his café au lait skin, pierced ears and long dreadlocks.

He sauntered over to the buffet table where she was standing, as if drawn to the invisible heat coursing through her.

"Just so you know," said the tall kid, "this is the last place I wanted to spend the summer."

"Just so you know," Daisy said, making herself sound as cool as he did, "it wasn't my choice, either. What're you doing here, anyway?"

"It was either this—working on this dump with my brother, Connor—or a stint in juvey," he said easily.

Juvey. He tossed off the word, clearly assuming she was familiar with the concept. She wasn't, though. Juvenile detention was something that happened to kids from the ghetto or barrio.

"You're Connor's brother?"

"Yep."

"You don't look like brothers." Connor was all clean-cut and WASPy, a lumberjack from the wilds of the North, while Julian looked dark…and dangerous, alternative's alternative.

"Half brothers," he said nonchalantly. "Different dads.

Connor doesn't want me here, but our mom made him look after me."

Connor Davis was the contractor in charge of renovating Camp Kioga to get it ready for the fiftieth anniversary of Daisy's grandparents. Everyone was supposed to be pitching in on the project, but she hadn't expected to encounter someone like *this*. Even before learning his name, she sensed something fundamental about this boy. In the deepest, most mysterious way imaginable, he was destined to be important to her.

His name was Julian Gastineaux, and like her, he was between his junior and senior years of high school, but other than that, they had nothing in common. She was from New York City's Upper East Side, the product of a privileged but unhappy family and a tony prep school. He was from a crappy area of Chino, California, downwind of the cattle lots.

Like moths around a candle flame, they danced around each other through dinner; later they were assigned cleanup duty. She didn't raise her normal objection to the manual labor. An intimate camaraderie sprang up between them as they worked. She found herself fascinated by the ropy strength of his forearms and the sturdy breadth of his hands. As they were hanging up their dish towels, their shoulders brushed, and the brief encounter was electrifying in a way she'd never felt with a guy before. She'd known her share of guys, but this was different. She felt a weird kind of recognition that both confused and excited her.

"There's a fire pit down by the lake," she said, searching his strange, whiskey-colored eyes to see if he sensed anything, but she couldn't tell. They were too new to one another. "Maybe we could go down there and have a fire."

"Yeah, we could hold hands and sing 'Kumbaya.'"

"A couple of nights without TV or internet, and you'll be begging for 'Kumbaya.'"

"Right." His cocky smile quickly and easily gave way to sweetness. Daisy wondered if he realized that.

She found her dad as he was leaving the dining room. "Can we go make a fire on the beach?" Daisy asked.

"You and Julian?" His suspicious eyes flicked from her to the tall kid.

"Duh. Yeah, Dad. Me and Julian." She tried to maintain her attitude. She didn't want him to think she was actually starting to like it here, stuck in this rustic Catskills camp while all her friends were partying on the beaches of the Hamptons.

To her surprise, Julian spoke up: "I promise I'll be on my best behavior, sir."

It was gratifying to see her dad's eyebrows lift in surprise. Hearing the word *sir* come from the mouth of the Dreadlocked One was clearly unexpected.

"He will," Connor Davis said, joining them and passing a look to his brother. The stare he fixed on Julian showed exactly which brother was in charge.

"I guess it's all right," her dad said. He could probably tell Connor would kick Julian's ass if the kid stepped out of line. "I might come out to check on you later."

"Sure, Dad," Daisy said, forcing brightness into her tone. "That'd be great."

She and Julian were both pretty lame at making a fire, but she didn't really care. They used a box of kitchen matches down to the final one before the pile of twigs finally caught. When the breeze wafted smoke right at her, she happily wedged herself snugly against Julian. He didn't put the moves on her, but he didn't move away, either. In fact, simply being near him felt amazing, not like making out with guys from school, under the bleachers at the athletic field, or at the Brownstones at Columbia, where she lied about her age in order to get into a college party.

Once the flames were dancing nicely in the fire pit, she saw him studying the reflection on the black surface of the lake.

"I was here once before," he said. "When I was eight."

"Seriously? You came to summer camp?"

He laughed a little. "It's not like I had a choice. Connor was a counselor here that year, and he was stuck watching me that summer."

She waited for a further explanation, but he stayed silent. "Because…" she prompted.

His smile faded. "Because there was no one else."

The loneliness of his words, the thought of a child having no one but a half brother, struck her in a tender place. She decided not to press him for details, but man. She wanted to know more about this guy. "So what's your story now?"

"My mother's an out-of-work performer—sings, dances, acts," he said.

What, did he think she was going to let him off the hook? "That's your mother's story. I was wondering about yours."

"I got in trouble with the law in May," he said.

Now that, she thought, was interesting. Fascinating. *Dangerous.* She leaned forward, pressing even closer. "So what was the incident? Did you steal a car? Deal drugs?" The minute she said the words, she wanted to die. She was an idiot. He'd think she was racial profiling him.

"I raped a girl," he informed her. "Maybe I raped three."

"Okay," she said, "I deserved that. And I know you're lying." She looped her arms around her drawn-up knees.

He was quiet for a bit, as if trying to make up his mind whether or not to be ticked off. "Let's see. They caught me using the high dive at a public pool after dark, skateboarding down a spiral parking lot ramp…stuff like that. A couple of weeks ago, I got caught bungee jumping off a highway bridge with a homemade bungee cord. The judge ordered a change of scenery for me this summer, said I had to do something productive. Trust me, helping renovate a summer camp in the Catskills is the last thing I want to do."

The image she had of him did a quick one-eighty. "Why would you go bungee jumping off a bridge?"

"Why *wouldn't* you?" he asked.

"Oh, let me see. You could break every bone in your body. Wind up paralyzed. Brain-dead. Or plain dead."

"People wind up dead every day."

"Yeah, but jumping off bridges tends to hasten the process." She shuddered.

"It was awesome. I'd do it again in a heartbeat. I've always liked flying."

He'd given her the perfect opening. She reached into her pocket and took out an eyeglasses case, flipping it open to reveal a fat, misshapen joint. "Then you'll like this."

With the glowing end of a twig, she lit up and inhaled. "This is *my* kind of flying." Hoping she'd succeeded in shocking him, she held it out to Julian.

"I'll pass," he said.

What? Pass? Who passed on a hit from a joint?

He must have read her mind, because he grinned. "I need to watch myself. See, the judge in California gave my mother a choice—I had to leave town for the summer or do time in juvenile detention. By coming here, I get the bungee-jumping incident wiped off my record."

"Fair enough," she conceded, but kept holding out the joint. "You won't get caught."

"I don't partake."

Ridiculous. What was he, some kind of Boy Scout? His reticence bothered her, made her feel judged by him. "Come on. It's really good weed. We're out in the middle of nowhere."

"I'm not worried about that," he said. "Just don't like getting high."

"Whatever." Feeling slightly ridiculous, she added a twig to the fire, watched it burn. "A girl's got to find her fun where she can."

"So are you having fun?" he asked.

She squinted at him through the smoke, wondering if she'd ever asked herself that question. "So far, this whole summer has been…weird. It's supposed to be a lot more fun. I mean, think about it. It's our last summer as regular kids. By this time next year, we'll be working and getting ready for college."

"College." Leaning back on his elbows, he gazed up at the stars. "That's a good one."

"Aren't you planning to go to college?"

He laughed.

"What?" She let the joint smolder between her fingers, not caring if it went out.

"No one's ever asked me that before."

She found that hard to believe. "Teachers and advisers haven't been hounding you since ninth grade?"

He laughed again. "At my school, they figure they're doing a good job if a kid makes it through without dropping out, having a baby or being sent up."

She tried to imagine such a world. "Up where?"

"Sent up means doing time at juvenile hall or worse, prison."

"You should change schools."

Again, that joyless laughter. "It's not like I get to choose. I go to my closest public school."

She was skeptical. "And your school doesn't prepare you for college."

He shrugged. "Most guys get some crappy job at a car wash and play the lottery and hope for the best."

"You don't seem like most guys." She paused, studying the bemused expression on his face. "What? Why are you looking at me like that?"

"I'm nobody special."

She didn't believe that for a second. "Look, I'm not saying college is, like, nirvana or something, but it sure as hell beats working at a car wash."

"College costs all kinds of dough I don't have."

"That's what scholarships are for." She flashed on the year-end assembly that had taken place a few weeks earlier. She would have skipped out, except the alumni magazine had needed her to take pictures. Some military guys had given a presentation on how to get paid to go to school. She'd zoned out during the presentation, but the topic had stuck with her. "Then get into the ROTC. Reserve Officers' Training Corps. The military picks up the cost of your schooling. Earn while you learn, that's what they said."

"Yeah, but there's a catch. There's always a catch. They send you to war."

"They'd probably let you do more than bungee jumping."

"What are you, a recruiter for these guys?"

"Just telling you what I know." She didn't really care whether or not this kid went to college. For that matter, she didn't really care whether or not *she* got into college. Pot tended to make her chatty. She put the now-cold joint into a Ziploc bag to save for later. Maybe to save for somebody who wanted to get high with her. The trouble was, she really only felt like hanging out with Julian. There was something about him. "It must be weird to go to a high school where no one helps you get into college," she said. "But just because no one's helping you doesn't mean you can't help yourself."

"Sure." He tossed another dry branch on the fire. "Thanks for the public service announcement."

"You've got a chip on your shoulder," she said.

"And you've got your head in the clouds."

Daisy laughed aloud, tilting back her head as she imagined the notes of her voice floating upward with the sparks and smoke from the fire. She felt wonderful around him, and it wasn't the pot. She liked him. She really, really liked this guy. He was different and special and kind of mysterious. He didn't touch her, though she wanted him to. He didn't kiss her, though she wanted that, too. He simply sat back and offered a subtle, slightly lopsided smile.

Those eyes, she thought, feeling a peculiar warmth shudder through her. She looked into them and thought, Hello, other half of my soul. It's good to finally meet you.

Present Day

Daisy pondered her history with Julian far more than she should, especially at times like this, the middle of the night, when she was all by herself, her body aching for a human touch. If her life had followed a movie script, everything would have been simple after that first unlikely, electrifying meeting. The music would swell, the birds would sing, and that would be that. Go directly to happily ever after. Do not pass go, do not collect $200. Just go.

It was a lot of baggage to lay on the first meeting of two teenagers, she acknowledged. The wilderness camp had been the ideal setup for a summer romance—two star-crossed kids, attracted to each other against all common sense…forced apart at summer's end by families who didn't understand them. *Perfect.*

Except things hadn't played out that way. Instead, Daisy and Julian had done the impossible. Resisting the heady rush of revved up hormones, they had spent the summer in an agony of yearning, and by some miracle they hadn't hooked up. It wasn't really a miracle, but Julian's self-restraint. He'd made a vow to his brother to stay out of trouble, and it hadn't taken her long to realize he was a man of his word. At summer's end, they had gone their separate ways, resigning themselves to circumstances.

She should have realized they never had a chance to be more to each other than a summer memory. Back in Manhattan that fall, Daisy went a little nuts at the start of her senior year in high school. She'd made an incredibly bad decision that had resulted in an incredibly precious gift—Charlie, born the summer after graduation. But just because she'd had a baby didn't mean she could forget Julian. She never had. She kept waiting and hoping their time would come. But she had a kid, and Julian had a dream of his own to follow.

She tried to read between the lines of the invitation to his commissioning ceremony, a futile endeavor, since it was printed, like all the others had been. The words on the back could be interpreted in a variety of ways. Did he really want to see her, or was he simply being polite?

She didn't know, because she was in a weird place with him, like always. Despite a mutual, undeniable attraction, she tried to stay resigned to the fact that she and Julian were destined to go their own ways. He was a graduating senior at Cornell, focusing on school and on his ROTC program, as well he should. She lived in Avalon now, a place that had seemed as bleak as Siberia when she'd first seen it that first summer at Camp Kioga. These days, she called it home because it was close to family, the best place to raise Charlie.

There didn't seem to be any way for her and Julian to be together without one of them sacrificing everything. Some things, she told herself often, simply weren't meant to be. Still, she couldn't help but dream, and in the deepest, most sleepless hours of the night, she caught herself wondering if her time would ever come, if she'd ever experience the searing joy of love her camera captured, wedding after wedding.

A small inner voice reminded her that she'd had her chance, not so long ago. There had been a ring, a proposal...but she'd been too scared and confused to even consider it. She'd opted instead for half a year of studying abroad with Charlie, which ultimately proved to her how very much she needed her family.

Oh, Daisy, she thought. *Figure out your own heart. How hard could it be?*

Torn and restless, she set down the invitation and walked away, her chest already squeezing tight with emotion. Julian had always had that effect on her, from the first moment they'd met as teenagers.

Yet in spite of the diverging paths their lives took, their connection persisted. During their college years—she at SUNY New Paltz, he at Cornell—they managed to see each other on rare occasions. Whenever their school holidays synched up and didn't bump up against his ROTC training and duties, they stole time together. And on each occasion, the yearning that had begun all those summers ago flared, more intense than ever. It seemed to grow despite all the life events that intervened. They continued to seek each other out, but it was never enough. She didn't understand it, tried to rationalize it away, because being with a guy like Julian seemed so impossible. Their lives kept leading them away from each other. He had the ROTC and Cornell, and she had Charlie, work and...

Charlie's dad. No wonder things had never worked out for her and Julian.

Sometimes when Daisy fantasized about being with Julian, she tried to imagine him and Charlie together, like father and son.

But the painful fact was, Julian seemed adamant about *not* taking on that role. He was nice enough to Charlie, yet she could see Julian keeping his distance. She recalled a time when Charlie had slipped and called Julian "Daddy." Julian had winced visibly and said, "I'm not your daddy, boy."

Little had he known the remark would give rise to a nickname. From that day onward, Charlie had dubbed Julian "Daddy-boy."

When you were a single mom, Daisy reminded herself, your life was dictated by the needs of your child. Charlie needed a *dad*, not a daddy-boy.

Against all expectations, Logan was a pretty great dad. Like Daisy, he'd earned his degree from SUNY New Paltz and settled in Avalon. He had bought an insurance agency from a guy who was retiring. Business was brisk. Despite hard economic times, people still needed to cover their asses in case something happened. Daisy didn't know whether or not he felt passionate about his career, but he was totally devoted to Charlie. So far, their unconventional arrangement was working out.

Sometimes she caught herself wondering if this was really supposed to be her life.

She sighed, picked up the invitation once more, and turned the reply card over and over in her hands. The commissioning ceremony sounded important. It *was* important. Everything Julian had done since high school was important. With no money, nothing but brains and ambition, he had done exactly as she'd suggested that summer. He had qualified for ROTC to finance college. It was the only time she'd given advice and it had actually worked out. In exchange for his Ivy League education, he owed the next four years of his life to the air force, longer if he later qualified for pilot training.

This service incursion meant he might be sent anywhere in the world.

Anywhere but here, she thought, thinking about the place she called home—impossibly small, impossibly quaint Avalon, of absolute zero strategic value to the military.

She double-checked the date of the event.

Yes, she was free that day. Wendela's Wedding Wonders employed several photographers and technicians, and Daisy wasn't scheduled for anything that weekend. She could ask Logan to watch Charlie, and she could go to the event in Ithaca, camera in hand, to document this most auspicious moment.

She wanted to go. She *needed* to go. She needed to find some serious private time with Julian. After years of yearning for him, years of stumbling toward each other, only to be pulled apart by circumstances, she finally saw her chance.

Once and for all, she would do what she should have done long ago.

It was time to get real with Julian, with herself. She would have to be completely honest. Finally, after all this time, she was going to tell him exactly how she felt. Judging by his cryptic note on the back, she suspected he might be thinking the same thing.

Three

Falling through thin air at a speed of 150 mph, Julian Gastineaux exulted in the way the g-force of the wind seemed to enter his very essence. It ripped at every seam of his jumpsuit, filled his nose and mouth, turned his face into a nightmare visage of distorted features. He felt caught up in a power that was greater than any man, and it was the ultimate trip.

Kind of like being in love.

Unlike love, this was an optional training exercise. Although in his opinion, when offered a chance to jump out of a plane, a guy's only option was to go for it. His work in the field was done, but he'd never been one to say no to a jump. He might be crazy but he wasn't an idiot who'd turn down the opportunity. He loved the feeling of weightlessness and knowing that beneath him there was nothing but sky. He could see the patchwork countryside of middle New York State—undulating hills, river-fed farmland, a spectacular array of long lakes gouged out of the landscape as if by giant claws.

His altimeter vibrated, signaling that it was time to quit admiring the scenery. He loosed the pilot chute into the airstream.

A wind shear swooped in at the worst possible moment. As the bridle of the pilot chute was supposed to be pulling out the deployment bag of the main chute, control was torn from him.

And just like that, the optional training exercise turned to a nightmare. He was sent careening off target—way off target, way too fast, at the mercy of the stream. Grinding out curses through clenched teeth, he managed to wrestle the deployment bag out. The lines were supposed to release one stow at a time, but they were a tangled mess. The main chute was lopsided, out of control. He worked the toggles to slow the wind as the stream rushed him toward a dense thicket of trees.

He signaled Mayday, let out another string of violent curses and said a prayer.

The prayer was answered, sort of. He hadn't slammed into the ground at 150 mph, turning himself into a pancake of blood and gristle. Instead, he'd managed to navigate a little and slow down. The landing wasn't quite what he'd been aiming for, though.

Hanging upside down in his parachute harness, he surveyed the world from a unique vantage point. Pliant branches, covered in new leaves, bobbed up and down with his weight. He could see nothing but green and brown, no sign of civilization anywhere.

Damn. This had been the final exercise of his training here, and it was supposed to go well.

He forced himself to be slow and deliberate as he considered what to do. Blood trickled from somewhere on his face. He hurt in a lot of places; nothing felt broken, though his shoulder flared with fire. It might be dislocated. His goggles were completely wrecked. Just reaching for his utility knife caused him to slip too fast toward the ground, so he went still, trying to plan his next move. Breaking his neck right before commissioning would bc the lamest of moves, for sure. And Daisy—he didn't even want to think about what it would do to his plans for her and hoped like hell this mishap was not a bad omen.

He was still pondering his options, noting the strange feeling in his head, when a crashing noise sounded somewhere in the woods. A few minutes later a small figure in a jumpsuit appeared.

"You're a damn maniac, that's what you are," railed Sayers, one of his training partners. She was a no-nonsense girl from Selma, Alabama, and she reminded Julian of some of his relatives in Louisiana. Except that unlike those relatives, Tanesha Sayers was duty-bound to give aid and assistance to her fellow officer in training.

"Fool," she blustered, "you're damned lucky your beacon worked. Otherwise you'd be swinging here till you turn purple in the head and die. Hell, I ought to let you turn purple."

Julian let her yammer on. He made no excuses for himself; no sense blaming the wind shear. Besides, Sayers was basically harmless. She had an uncanny ability to berate a person roundly and simultaneously get things done. Slated for commissioning, same as Julian, she would make a good officer. She chewed him out, all the while hoisting herself up into the branches where he was caught and using a utility knife to cut him free.

"You got your own knife," she pointed out. "Why the hell didn't you get yourself down?"

"I was going to. Wanted to make sure I didn't cut the wrong strap and land on my—" He plunged to the ground, slamming against the forest floor. He felt the impact despite his helmet.

"Head," he finished. "Thanks, Mom." In the unit, Sayers's nickname was Mom because, although she fussed and bossed everyone around, she cared about each one of them with the fierceness of a mother bear.

"Don't thank me, fool," she said. "Just you hold still while I put a field dressing on that wound."

"What wound?" He gingerly touched his forehead, feeling a warm slickness at his hairline. Great.

She jumped down, landing with a grunt, and radioed the base.

He wiped his hand on his jumpsuit, and that was when he thought about the ring. He'd carried it around for a long time. Even during the jump, he had kept it in a pocket next to his heart, layers deep, zipped up tight.

When the ring was offered to Daisy, it wasn't going to be like last time, in the midst of a fistfight on a train platform, for Chrissake. This time…

He ripped open the Velcro collar tab at his throat and plunged his hand inside, fingers grappling with a zipper closure on his shirt.

Sayers knelt down in front of him. "What's the matter?"

"Just checking for—ah." Julian went limp with relief as his hand closed around the ring box. He pulled it out and flipped it open to reveal the prize—a certified non-conflict diamond in a warm gold setting, engraved on the inner curve with "Forever." He angled the box so Sayers could check it out.

She studied it thoughtfully. "Sorry, Jughead," she said, using his nickname, "but I don't love you in quite that way."

"Sure you do." He snapped the lid shut and tucked the box away. "You're on your knees, baby."

"Mmm." She ripped open a blister pack of sterile wipes. "It's your wounds I love. I swear, Jughead, you are a walking, talking crash test dummy. I *love* that about you."

Sayers wanted to attend medical school one day. She was obsessed with blood and guts, the gorier, the better. Julian, with his penchant for going to extremes, had provided her with more than his share of abrasions, sprains, bruises and bleeders during their training.

She cleansed the gash and clamped it shut with a few butterfly bandages. As she worked, she said, "What are you doing, carrying that damn ring everywhere you go?"

"I don't know what else to do with it," he said. "Shoving it in the back of my underwear drawer seems a little... well, that's where I used to stash my—never mind." He didn't want to go there with Sayers. "Sad to say, campus theft happens."

Unspoken was another truth they both understood. If the jump had proved fatal, the presence of the ring box would've been a silent final message to the woman he loved, the woman he wanted to love forever.

"I figure I'll keep it handy and I can pop the question when I know the time's right."

Sayers shook her head in disgust as she touched gentle fingers to the row of butterflies. "A word to the wise," she cautioned. "Make sure the poor girl is present when you whip it out."

"That's the plan. I invited her to our commissioning ceremony, so if she comes for that—"

"Wait a minute, *if?* There's some question?"

"Well, things have been a little weird for us," he said. *Understatement.*

"Oh, now there's a fine basis for a lasting relationship," she said, putting away her gear and grabbing his hand. She yanked, helping him to his feet.

He shook out each limb, schooling himself not to wince at the pain. His nerve endings had nerve endings, but pain was only a feeling. Everything was in proper working order—that was the key. Despite the fiery aches, he was sure they hadn't overlooked a break or sprain. Nope, he was good to go.

"See, here's the thing," he said, wading up the chute. "With Daisy and me—we've been like a moving target. Nothing is ever simple. She's got this kid, a great kid, but he complicates things. She's going in one direction, and I'm going in another, and we can never get on the same page."

He and Sayers started hiking out of the woods. His heart sped up as he thought about Daisy. "I'm nuts about her, and I know she feels the same. Getting engaged is going to cut through all the extraneous crap and simplify everything."

Sayers stopped walking and turned to him, putting her hand on his chest. "Oh, honey. Can you really be that stupid?"

He grinned. "You tell me."

She studied his face, her expression reflecting concern, exasperation and barely suppressed compassion. "My mama once told me never to underestimate the thickness of a man's skull. I think she was right."

"What? She's nuts about me, too," Julian pointed out. "I know she is."

"That makes two of you, then."

It took a while to get back, make a full report, tag and submit the chute for a safety study.

Julian ignored a deep twinge of soreness in his shoulder as he returned to campus, stopping off at the student center to check his mail. He sorted through the small stack as he hiked back to the residence hall. He tried not to let the commissioning ceremony mean too much to him. It was a personal milestone, his achievement to own, and if nobody but his half brother, Connor, showed up for it, Julian would be okay with that.

Then again, he was probably telling himself that, preparing for disappointment.

Others in his detachment were planning on half the civilized world to show up. Julian simply didn't have a ton of people in his life. His father, a professor at Tulane, had died when Julian was fourteen. Julian's aunt and uncle, in Louisiana, had lacked the means and the space to take him in. With no other options available, Julian had gone to Chino, California, to live with his mother.

It wasn't the kind of personal history that gave rise to a host of adoring relatives. Could be that was why he was so at home in the service. The people he trained with and worked with felt like family.

As usual, his mind wandered to Daisy. She came from a big extended family, which was one of the many things he loved about her, yet it was also one of the reasons he had trouble imagining a future with her. His duties meant she'd have to tell them all goodbye. It was a hell of a lot to ask of someone.

Flipping through the mail, he came to a small envelope, pre-addressed to him. He ripped into it, and his face lit up with a grin.

Everything fell away, his worries about the ceremony, the pain in his shoulder, the fact that he had a presentation due tomorrow, everything.

He stared down at the simple reply card: "Daisy Bellamy_✓_ will__ will not attend." At the bottom, she'd scribbled, "Wouldn't miss it! Bringing camera. See you soon.—XO."

He was in a great mood by the time he got back to his room. Davenport, one of his suite mates, took one look at his face and asked, "Hey, did you finally get laid, Jughead?"

Julian simply laughed and grabbed a bottle of Gatorade from the fridge.

"You must have finished your presentation, then," said Davenport.

"Barely started it."

"What's the topic again?"

"Survivable Acts in Combat."

"Which means it'll be a very short list, eh? No wonder you're not worrying."

"You'd be surprised what disasters a person can survive," Julian said.

"Fine. Surprise me." Davenport swiveled away from his computer screen and waited.

"Parachute mishap, if you can find a soft place to fall," Julian said, rotating his sore shoulder.

"Ha-ha. Give me a rocket-propelled grenade over that, any day."

"A grenade can be survivable."

"Not to the guy who throws himself on top of it to save his buddies."

"You want to throw the thing back where it came from, ideally."

"Good to know," said Davenport.

Julian wasn't worried about the topic. The hard part of life did not involve physical tasks and academic achievement. He could do school, no worries. He could run a marathon, swim a mile, do chin-ups one-handed. None of that was a problem.

He was challenged by things that came easily to most other people, like figuring out life's biggest mystery—how love worked.

That was about to change.

There was no textbook or course of study to show him the way, though. Maybe it was like getting caught in a wind shear. You had to hang on, navigate as best you could and hope to land in one piece. That was kind of what he'd always done.

February 2007

Julian stared at the cover letter from the United States Secretary of the Air Force. He couldn't believe his eyes. Three different ROTC detachments had admitted him, and now he had confirmation of his scholarship. Crushing the formally worded notice against his chest, he stood in the middle of a nondescript parking lot and looked up at the colorless sky over Chino, California. He was going to college. And he was going to fly.

Although bursting with the news, he couldn't find anyone to tell. He tried to explain it in rapid-fire street Spanish to his neighbor, Rojelio, but Rojelio was late for work and couldn't hang out with him. After that, Julian ran all the way to the library on Central Ave., barely sensing the pavement beneath his feet. He didn't have a home computer, and he had to get his reply in right away.

The author John Steinbeck referred to winter in California as the bleak season, and Julian totally got that. It was the doldrums of the year. Chino, a highway town east of L.A., was hemmed in by smog to the west and mountain inversions to the east, often trapping the sharp, ripe smell of the stockyards, which tainted every breath he took. He tended to hole up in the library, doing homework, reading…and dreaming. The summer he'd spent at Willow Lake felt like a distant dream, misty and surreal. It was another world, like the world inside a book.

To make sure the other kids didn't torture him at his high school, Julian had to pretend he didn't like books. Among his friends, being good at reading and school made you uncool in the extreme, so he kept his appetite for stories to himself. To him, books were friends and teachers. They kept him from getting lonely, and he learned all kinds of stuff from them. Like what a half orphan was. Reading a novel by Charles Dickens, Julian learned that a half orphan was a kid who had lost one parent. This was something he could relate to. Having lost his dad, Julian now belonged to the ranks of kids with single moms.

His mom had never planned on being a mom. She'd told him so herself and, in a moment of over-sharing, explained that he'd been conceived at an aerospace engineering conference in Niagara Falls, the result of a one-night stand. His father had been the keynote speaker at the event. His mother had been an exotic dancer performing at the nightclub of the conference hotel.

Nine months later, Julian had appeared. His mother had willingly surrendered him to his dad. The two of them had been pretty happy together until his dad died. Julian's high school years had been spent with his mom, who seemed to have no idea what to do with him.

He didn't have a cell phone. He was, like, one of the last humanoids on the planet who didn't have one. That was how broke he and his mom were. She was out of work again, and he had an after-school job at a car dealership, rotating tires and changing oil. Sometimes guys gave him tips, never the rich guys with the hot cars, but the workers with their Chevys and pickups. His mom had a mobile phone, which she claimed she needed in case she got called for an acting job, but the last thing they could handle was one more bill. Their phone service at the house was so basic, they didn't even have voice mail.

At the library, he could surf the web and access his free email. He quickly found the ROTC site and used the special log-in provided in his welcome packet, feeling as though he'd gained membership to a secret club. Then he quickly checked his email. That was how he kept in touch with Daisy. They weren't the best at corresponding, and there was nothing from her today. He had school and work; she'd recently moved from New York City to the small town of Avalon to live with her dad. She said her family situation was weird, what with her parents splitting up. He felt bad for her, but couldn't offer much advice. His folks had never been together, and in a way, maybe that was better, since there was no breakup to adjust to.

Email only went so far, though. He wanted to call her with his news. And to thank her for reminding him college wasn't out of his reach. Her suggestion, made last summer, had taken root in Julian. There was a way to have the kind of life he'd only dreamed about. In a casual, almost tossed-off remark, she had handed him a golden key.

The apartment he shared with his mother was in a depressing faux-adobe structure surrounded by weedy landscaping and a parking lot of broken asphalt. He let himself in; his mom wasn't around. When she was out of work, she tended to spend most of her time on the bus to the city, going to networking meetings.

Julian paced back and forth in front of the phone. He finally got up the nerve to call Daisy. He wanted to hear her voice and tell her in person about the letter. The call was going to add to a cost he already couldn't afford, but he didn't care.

She picked up right away; she always did when he called her on her cell phone because nobody else called her from this area code. "Hey," she said.

"Hey, yourself. Is this a good time?" he asked, thinking about the three-hour time difference. In the background of the call, he could hear music.

"It's fine." She hesitated, and he recognized the song—"Time of the Season" by the Zombies. He hated that song.

"Everything all right?" It was weird, he hadn't seen her since last summer, but her *It's fine* struck him as all wrong. "What's up?" he asked.

She killed the music. "Olivia asked me to be in her wedding."

"That's cool, right?" Julian was going to be in the wedding, too, because his brother was the groom. He'd never attended a wedding before, but he couldn't wait because it was going to take place in August at Camp Kioga. Suddenly it occurred to him to check his ROTC schedule to make sure he was free that day.

"It's not so cool," Daisy said, her voice kind of thin-sounding. "Listen, Julian, I've been trying to figure out how to tell you something. God, it's hard."

His mind raced. Was she sick? Sick of him? Did she want him to quit calling, make himself scarce? Did she have a boyfriend, for Chrissake?

"Then tell me."

"I don't want you to hate me."

"I could never hate you. I don't hate anybody." Not even the drunk driver who had hit his dad. Julian had seen the guy in a courtroom. The guy had been crying so hard he couldn't stand up. Julian hadn't felt hatred. Just an incredible, hollow sense of nothingness. "Seriously, Daze," he said. "You can tell me anything."

"I hate myself," she said, her voice low now, trembling.

The phone wasn't cordless, so his pacing was confined to a small area in front of a window. He looked out at the colorless February day. Down in the parking lot, Rojelio's wife was bringing in groceries, bag after bag of them. Normally, Julian would run down and give her a hand. She had a bunch of kids—he could never get an accurate count—who ate like a swarm of locusts. All she did was work, buy groceries and fix food.

"Daisy, go ahead and tell me what's going on."

"I screwed up. I screwed up big-time." Her voice sounded fragile, the words like shards of glass, even though he didn't know what she was talking about. Whatever it was, he wanted to be there, wished he could put his arms around her, inhale the scent of her hair and tell her everything was going to be all right.

His mind scrolled through the possibilities. Had she started smoking again? Was she failing in school? He waited. She knew he was there. He didn't need to prompt her anymore.

"Julian," she said at last, a catch in her voice. "I'm going to have a baby. It's due in the summer."

The words were so unexpected, he couldn't think of a single thing to say. He kept staring at Rojelio's wife, now on her second trip with the grocery bags. Daisy Bellamy? Having a baby?

At Julian's school, pregnant girls were pretty common, but *Daisy?* She was supposed to have, like, this privileged life where nothing bad ever happened. She was supposed to be his girlfriend. It was true, they'd parted ways in the summer having made no promises, but it was an unspoken assumption between them.

Or so he'd thought.

"Julian? Are you there?"

"Yeah." He felt as if he'd been punched in the gut.

"I feel really stupid," she said, crying now, sounding scared. "And it can't be undone. The guy…he's somebody from my school in New York. We weren't even, like, together or anything. We got drunk one weekend, and… oh, Julian…"

He had no idea what to say. This was not the conversation he'd imagined when he'd picked up the phone. "I guess…wow, I hope you're going to be all right."

"I pretty much changed everything for myself. I told my parents, and they're, like, in shock and everything, but they keep telling me it'll all work out."

"It will." He had no idea if it would or not.

"Julian, I'm so sorry."

"You don't need to apologize."

"I feel terrible."

So did he. "Look, it is what it is."

"I wouldn't blame you if you never wanted to see me again."

"I want to see you."

She breathed a sigh into the phone. "I still want to see you, too."

"I guess we will at the wedding."

"Right. So…enough about me." She gave a weak laugh. "How are things with you?"

It didn't feel right to share his news with her now. All the energy had been sucked out of him. He couldn't stop thinking about the fact that she was pregnant…and what she'd done in order to get that way.

"Everything's fine," he said.

"Good. Julian?"

"What?"

"I miss you."

"Yeah," he said, though he didn't know what he missed. "Me, too."

Four

"Hey, buddy," said Daisy, perching on the edge of Charlie's sandbox. "Guess what?"

Her son smiled up at her, green eyes twinkling in a way that never failed to catch her heart. "What?"

"You're going to have a sleepover with your dad."

"Okay."

"Does that sound like fun?"

"Yep." He went back to the trench he was digging in the sand.

The afternoon light filtered through the new leaves, glinting in his fiery red hair. "Silly question," she said, pushing a toy truck along one of the roads he had paved. "You and your dad always have fun together, right?"

"Yep." He filled a dump truck with sand. The backyard sandbox was elaborate, a gift from his O'Donnell grandparents for his third birthday. Charlie loved it. His grandpa O'Donnell claimed this was because shipping and transport—the O'Donnell family business—was in his blood, same as his red hair and green eyes.

He looked so much like Logan that Daisy sometimes wondered what part of her their son carried in him. Looking at Charlie felt like peering through a strange lens that took her back across time, to Logan as a child. Before she knew it, Charlie would be starting kindergarten; he'd be the same age Logan had been when Daisy had first met him. That was freaky to contemplate.

Logan's mother, Marian, loved showing Daisy pictures of Logan at Charlie's age. "It's uncanny," she would say. "They could be twins. Logan was always such a happy child," Mrs. O'Donnell often added.

A happy child who had nearly ruined his life by the age of eighteen. Daisy suspected Logan had grown up under enormous pressure from his parents. He was the only boy of four kids, and his family was very traditional. Much had been expected of him. He was supposed to excel at academics and sports in school, and he had done so. He and Daisy had attended the same rigorous Manhattan prep school, where she'd watched him swagger through the halls with a twinkle in his eye. He came from a privileged background, and he'd been groomed to carry on the tradition—an Ivy League college, or at the very least, Boston College, his dad's alma mater, followed by a position in the family's international shipping firm.

Daisy looped her arms around her knees and watched Charlie, who was lost in a world of play. Why did parents saddle their kids with expectations, instead of letting the kid become whoever he wanted to be? Didn't they know it made kids want to do the opposite?

It was a sports injury that precipitated Logan's descent into drug addiction. A soccer championship was on the line, and Logan had suffered a knee injury. He discovered if he swallowed enough painkillers, he could keep playing.

Hide your pain and keep on playing. It was the O'Donnell family way.

Daisy pushed her son's toy truck over a plastic bridge and silently vowed never to pressure him about anything.

Ever. She wondered if her own parents had made that same vow about her. Didn't every generation promise to be better parents than their own parents had been? How come it never worked out that way?

"Good, it's all settled, then," she said to Charlie. "A sleepover with your dad."

"Because you're working?" Charlie asked, scooping out a hole with a yellow plastic shovel.

That was the only reason she ever left him. To work. This time was different.

She paused her truck at the end of the bridge and took a breath. "This is not for work. I'm going to see Julian."

Charlie didn't stop digging and he didn't look up. "Daddy-boy," he said quietly.

"Okay?" she asked.

No response.

"Julian's got something important to do called a commissioning ceremony." It was the moment Julian would actually be given his officer's commission, and she couldn't imagine missing it. "It's a really big deal to be an officer in the air force," she added, wondering how much of this Charlie was absorbing. She stuck a plastic gas station by the side of the sandbox road and pushed her truck into the bay to fuel up. "They're going to tell every body where he has to go for his job. He could be sent anywhere in the world, from Tierra del Fuego to the North Pole."

"Where Santa lives," Charlie said, his face lighting up.

"You never know."

She shook off a wave of melancholy, thinking about how hard it was going to be, seeing him go off somewhere to start his life as an officer. She was determined not to show her sadness. This weekend was about celebrating Julian's incredible achievement, not about lamenting the chance they'd never had.

"Tell you what," she said to Charlie. "Let's go grab some lunch and you can pick out three toys to take to your dad's."

"Four toys," he said, always pushing for more.

She was pretty sure he didn't know what four was, but that wasn't the point. You didn't bargain with a little kid. "Three," she said. "And they have to fit in your Clifford bag."

Charlie was sound asleep in his car seat when Daisy drove up to Logan's place. She spotted him up on the roof of the house he'd bought last fall, pounding at something. The house was old and graceful, from the 1920s, on a tree-lined street prized for its vintage architecture and quiet ambiance. The neighborhood was a haven for the upwardly mobile, close to schools and the country club. It didn't appeal to Daisy in particular—her taste ran to funky lakeside cottages—but Logan had embraced home ownership with his usual tenacity.

Like all older homes, the house had issues. He insisted on doing many of the renovations himself, even though he could probably afford any contractor he wanted. It was as if he had something to prove. Born to a wealthy family, he'd never had to do home repairs. With his new place, he embraced the challenge. It was a steep-roofed two-story house surrounded by overgrown rhododendrons and hydrangea bushes, with a big hickory tree in the front. He must have heard her drive up because he paused in his work and lifted his arm to wave.

He lost his balance and wheeled his arms, and his feet came out from under him. Gathering speed, he skidded down the steep slope of the roof. It was like something out of a nightmare. Daisy opened her mouth in a voiceless scream and clamped both hands over her mouth. A part of her understood that this would be a really bad time for Charlie to awaken—in time to see his daddy fall to his death.

Logan grabbed for a purchase, hooking onto the eaves. The old metal tore away. He tumbled to the edge and dropped like a sack of mail, crashing down on an old rhododendron bush.

Daisy leapt out of the car and rushed over to him. He lay by the broken bush, motionless. His eyes were closed, his face chalk-white.

A sense of unreality fell over her. *No.* These things didn't happen. They weren't supposed to happen. He looked dead. He *was* dead. Just like that.

She couldn't catch her breath. She sank to her knees beside him. "Logan, *no,*" she said. "Please."

A terrible sound came from him as he sucked in a breath. "Please…what?" His eyes fluttered open, and he groaned.

She cried harder, from joy now. "Are you all right? I thought you were dead."

"Hey, *I* thought I was dead. Completely knocked the wind out of me."

"Should I call 911?"

He pushed himself up, plucked a rhody branch from his hair. "Sorry to disappoint you, but the emergency is over." He moved his head from side to side. "No broken neck. Extremities all intact."

A thin, livid scrape slashed across his cheek, and his hand was bleeding.

"Are you sure you're okay?"

"Okay enough, I swear." He wiped his hand on his shirt.

"You shouldn't have been up on the roof all by yourself. Couldn't you have called someone?"

"Now you're sounding like my mother."

"Sorry."

He offered a lopsided grin. "Maybe the fall knocked the silver spoon from my mouth. Here, give me a hand."

She pulled him to his feet and looked into his eyes, making sure the pupils matched. "Did you hit your head?"

"Nope. Fell on my ass." He laid his arm around her shoulders. He smelled of sweat and broken greenery. "I should lean on you, though. You know, just in case. Where's my boy?"

"Asleep in the car."

"I got plans for us this weekend," said Logan. "My soccer team's got a big match."

She cast another worried look at him. "You might be really hurt."

He stepped away from her, spread his arms wide. "Look, I'm fine, okay? I took a spill—"

"From a two-story roof."

"And lived to tell the tale," he said. "Quit worrying. Charlie and I'll be fine. Perfectly fine."

"What were you doing up there, anyway?"

"Fixing some loose shingles. A regular home handyman."

"Do me a favor. No ladders, no roof repairs while you're in charge of Charlie."

He raised his right hand. "Scout's honor." He unbuckled Charlie's seat and pulled it out. Charlie stirred but didn't wake up, so Logan carried the whole rig into the house. Daisy followed with the Clifford bag and Charlie's weekender.

"I could call Sonnet," she suggested. Her stepsister was Charlie's favorite babysitter. After finishing her studies and internships in Germany, Sonnet was back in Avalon for a few months. In the fall, she would start work at the U.N.

"Or either of my parents could help out—"

"Enough, okay? I didn't get hurt. I'm perfectly capable

of taking care of my own kid." He spoke quietly, but his voice had an edge. Because of his past as an addict and drunk, people tended to tiptoe around him or assume he was inadequate. Just the suggestion of help brought out his defensiveness.

"I know you're capable. But you just fell off a roof. You're not Superman."

He grabbed a Nehi soda from the fridge. "Sure, I am." He offered her a sip.

She shook her head. "All right. Instead of getting another sitter, I could cancel." Thus proving once again how easily life interfered with her and Julian.

"Nope," he said quickly. "No way."

This startled her. Logan knew she was going to the commissioning ceremony, and he couldn't stand Julian. In Logan's mind, Julian was the one thing that stood between them, preventing them from having a deeper relationship. Which was so wrong, but that was a different conversation. Still, she didn't get why Logan seemed to want her to go to Ithaca.

He must have read her mind. "You need to see him get his commission. Maybe it'll be, I don't know, closure for you."

"Closure?" She hated the sound of that word.

"You need to see that the air force is his life." Logan spoke kindly. "You'll never be first with him. Maybe after this weekend, after he gets sent to Timbuktu, that'll finally be clear to you."

It irked her that Logan assumed that was the way things would play out. He spoke as if he had some kind of crystal ball.

"Great, now you're my relationship analyst." God, how did I get here? she wondered. Sometimes she looked around her life and asked herself that. How was it that she was getting relationship advice from the father of her child, a guy who had come into her life through an act of bad judgment, and stayed through sheer determination.

"Logan—"

"I want you to know, I'm here. I'm not going anywhere, not to Timbuktu or the Pentagon or North Dakota or Cape Town. Here, Daisy. You know what you mean to me."

She did know. If she ever needed a reminder that this was true, all she had to do was remember what had happened the Christmas before last. The day had started out innocently enough. She and Charlie had been invited to spend the holiday with the O'Donnells, which meant taking the train with Logan from Avalon downstate to the city. She remembered feeling so torn that day, knowing Charlie deserved equal time with his paternal grandparents, yet realizing it would mean spending the holiday away from her own family. For Charlie's sake, she'd put on a brave face, packed her bag and met Logan at the station.

At the last minute, Julian had come to town to surprise her. His train had arrived shortly before hers was scheduled to leave. He'd come bounding over to her platform with his usual exuberance, which deflated visibly the moment he'd spotted Logan. She hadn't known they would both be there. It was never comfortable having the two of them in the same vicinity.

Predictably, and to her complete mortification, it had all gone wrong in a flurry of angry words and accusations. Like a couple of rutting animals, Julian and Logan had gotten into a fistfight right there on the train platform. A *fistfight*. Between two men who both claimed they cared about her—Logan, the passionate family man she'd known all her life and the father of her child, and Julian, the guy she hadn't been able to get out of her heart since they'd first met.

In the midst of the altercation, things had flown from pockets, littering the platform—change, a Swiss Army knife, keys…and a small velveteen jewel box. It had hit the pavement, popping open to reveal the unmistakable glint of a diamond ring. She'd been so shocked, she could barely think, but she'd blurted out, "Oh. You dropped something."

And God help her, she couldn't be certain who had brought the ring.

Most women dreamed of a romantic marriage proposal offered on bended knee with soft music playing in the background. In Daisy's case it had been a nightmare enacted in public before a crowd of people. A far cry from a tender moment to remember and savor with misty-eyed fondness, it had been one of those occasions that had left her wishing the ground would open up and swallow her whole.

Instead of a sweet recitation of love and devotion, the occasion had started with a fight. What happened next still made her cringe. A babble of spectators. Strangers pressing in, drawn by the drama. There had been a moment, a split-second leap of hope, when she imagined the ring had popped out of Julian's pocket. But no. Marriage was discouraged for ROTC candidates.

Seconds later, with one eye swelling shut and a trickle of blood coming from his lip, Logan had snatched up the box and said, "I meant to surprise you with this, but that son of a bitch forced my hand. I want you to be my wife."

Julian had made a sound of disgust and stalked away from the platform. More passengers gathered in close, intrigued. Daisy had prayed for a swift, merciful death.

She had refused to see either Julian or Logan that Christmas and had spent the next semester and summer studying photography abroad. After several months in Germany, where her stepsister Sonnet had been living and working, Daisy had returned, as confused as ever.

"The offer's still open," Logan said now, and she knew exactly what he was referring to.

"My answer is the same."

Logan smiled a little. "Your lips are saying no, but what you really mean is, not yet."

"No means no," Charlie murmured, waking up with a drowsy smile. It was one of those phrases Daisy tended to say to him…a lot.

"Hey, buddy." Logan hunkered down and freed the little boy from the car seat. "I've been waiting to see you all day."

"Dad." Charlie clung to him like a monkey and they kissed.

Daisy watched, caught by fondness and exasperation both. Complicated. That was the word for her life. How simple everything would be if only she could believe she was supposed to be with Logan. The three of them together—a family. What was wrong with her? She and Logan had made this amazing child. Why couldn't they be happy together?

Five

The officer in the mirror stared back at Julian with a sense of grave purpose. Who was this intensely serious guy? He didn't even recognize himself. Was that him?

Like so much of officer training, this was a deliberate strategy on the part of the air force. Through all the drills and preparation, the individual was taken apart and remade, perhaps reborn in a way. This suited him fine, dumping a past he couldn't change for one he could control. He was learning to look the part—an officer. A leader. A warrior.

"My, my," said Davenport, letting loose with a wolf whistle. "Aren't you as sweet as honey?"

"Screw you." The man in the mirror grinned, appearing a little more familiar now. Then he checked the time. "I'm ready to get the show on the road."

"Have a seat. We've still got a half hour."

"Can't," said Julian.

"Can't what?"

"Can't sit down. Do you know how long it took me to get these creases right?"

"Hours and hours," Davenport said with a laugh; then he sobered. "Dude, you look like a million bucks. Or at least like you've earned the commission you're getting today."

Julian had no idea if his suite-mate was right. He'd worked his ass off, but given the nature of his first assignment, whether or not he was prepared could be anybody's guess. The most frustrating thing about the news was its top secret classification. He couldn't tell anybody the details. He didn't even know most of the details himself. For the past year, he'd been groomed to be part of a special team, a highly unlikely designation for someone at his level. Although he knew his base assignment, he could tell people only that he'd been commissioned for active duty.

He shook hands with his friend, and Davenport resumed his jocular air. "I might advise you to go for a short walk to clear your head, but that would be a bad idea."

"Why?"

"You are way too pretty in full dress uniform. You'll end up going through the whole ceremony dragging along an entourage of drooling women."

"Right. And how many women do you know who get turned on by the sight of brass buttons and epaulets?"

"I guess you're about to find out."

Julian checked out his service dress uniform again, making sure every detail was right. Ribbons, devices, badges, insignia—all present and accounted for. Stuck in the side of the mirror was a five-year-old photo of him and Daisy, standing side by side, laughing at the camera. He remembered the exact instant it had been taken, with the shutter on timer. She'd made him laugh by saying, "Okay, pretend you like me," knowing full well they were totally into each other.

He was glad he remembered because otherwise he might not even believe the kid in the picture had ever existed. That tall, skinny kid with waist-length dreadlocks, assorted tattoos and piercings and a bad attitude was a stranger to the clean-cut officer in the mirror. Julian had been a punk—an adrenaline junkie with not much going for him except an unexpectedly stellar academic record and test performances. And of course, his status as a minority. He didn't want people to assume race was the reason he'd been admitted to an Ivy League school and an elite training program, so he made sure he outperformed everyone else.

Taking pains not to mess up his uniform, he slipped his hand into his inner breast pocket and touched the ring for luck.

His phone buzzed, and he picked up. "Gastineaux."

"Hey, Mr. Almost-second Lieutenant," said his brother, Connor. "We're outside. Come on down."

"I'll be right there."

Connor and Olivia had driven from Avalon with Daisy. His nerves jangled with excitement. He turned to Davenport and was startled to see all five of his suite-mates gathered at the exit. They had shared quarters all year long. They'd fought and laughed and partied and competed and helped one another. Now the five of them formed a gauntlet at the door.

"Good luck, Jughead," said Williams. "We wish you the best."

The solemnity of the moment was broken by Del Rio, who played the air force hymn on a kazoo.

Julian saluted them with all the smartness and respect he would afford a superior officer. "Thanks, guys."

He made one last check of everything. Tie, perfectly knotted. Shoes, gleaming. Hat, well-placed on his shorn head.

He was ready. He was so damn ready. He took the elevator because the stairwells tended to be dusty. He emerged into the small lobby of the residence hall and headed for the door, which opened onto a shady courtyard. In search of his visitors, he strode outside, his heart beating a mile a minute.

When he saw Daisy, he could feel himself smile out of every pore of his body, if such a thing were possible. She was wearing a yellow dress with white dots, white sandals with heels. Toenails painted pink. And a smile he saw every night in his dreams.

"Julian!" She ran over to him but brought herself up short. A shadow of something—uncertainty, bashfulness?—flickered in her face. "Is it okay to hug you?" she asked. "I don't want to muss your uniform."

He laughed and held his arms wide. He didn't care if she smeared lipstick all over his formal blue shirt, truth be told. She looked like a fantasy to him; staring at her was like staring at the sun too long. So bright, she hurt his eyes.

"Girl, you can mess me up anytime you want," he whispered into her silky blond hair.

"I might take you up on that," she said, but then she stepped back, smoothing her hands down his jacket sleeves. "You look incredible. Just so you know."

His heart hammered against the ring stashed in his pocket. He almost did the deed right then and there, but forced himself to wait, take a breath, try to think a coherent thought.

He greeted Connor and Olivia, and Zoe in her stroller. Julian's half brother, Connor, was also his best friend. If Connor hadn't stepped in when Julian was an exploding teenager en route to juvey, things would have turned out very differently for him.

Olivia and Daisy were cousins, though they looked enough alike to be mistaken for sisters. There was definitely a Bellamy family resemblance—blonde, classy, but not too full of themselves. More than that, they both seemed to be the type of women who inspired thoughts of forever.

"We have a surprise for you," Daisy said, leading the way to the paved footpath, crowded with families headed toward Statler Auditorium.

"What kind of surprise?" He wasn't expecting anything

"This kind!" She brought him around a corner of the walkway. In the shade of a budding chestnut tree stood a slender woman in a blue dress and high-heeled sandals.

"Mom!" Julian couldn't believe his eyes. His mother? Here?

She had sent her regrets several weeks ago, saying she couldn't get away from work this weekend. These days, she had a job on a cable series filmed in L.A., and was in the middle of taping a new season of episodes.

But here she was, beaming at him. "Well, look at you," she said. "My lord, but you make me proud."

"Me, too," said a deep, sonorous voice Julian hadn't heard in years. Three others arrived from the direction of the parking lot.

"Uncle Claude! And Tante Mimi. Remy!" Julian laughed aloud. "I feel like I'm seeing things."

Uncle Claude was the brother of Julian's late father. When he died, Claude and Mimi had offered to take Julian in, but there was no room and no money in their tiny, southern Louisiana house. Remy was their youngest of four and developmentally disabled.

He and Julian were the same age. As kids, they used to be fast friends. "Hey, Remy," he said, completely elated. "Remember me?"

"'Course," said Remy, "I got me a book full of pictures of us." He still sounded like the cousin Julian had known, speaking slowly and hesitantly, as always. The speech impediment was muted now, and his voice rang with a deep resonance, like his dad's.

When the two of them were young, Julian had gotten into many a fight, defending his cousin from the teasing of other kids. Fully grown, Remy looked like an NFL linebacker, and it was doubtful he suffered from teasing anymore.

"I'm real glad you're here," Julian said. He turned to his brother. "Is this your doing?"

"You can thank my lovely wife. She made it happen. I think she might have been a genie in a past life."

Julian gave Olivia a hug. "You're the best."

He glanced at Daisy and caught her eye. Other than Connor, she'd never met any of his family. She didn't know the world he'd come from, how different his upbringing had been from hers. She seemed at ease with them, however, walking alongside Remy as they made their way to the auditorium for the ceremony.

"You'll have to tell me stories about you and Julian, growing up," she said to his cousin.

"I got stories." Remy offered a bashful grin. "I can tell you stories 'bout me and Julian, for sure."

"We're going to dinner after the ceremony," said Connor. "He can fill you in then."

Even with the extra family members, they were one of the smaller groups to attend the commissioning. He spotted Tanesha Sayers with her mother and a whole entourage of aunties and cousins, a colorful garden of black ladies wearing fancy hats. A beaming Sayers waved at him from across the yard. "Good luck, Jughead," she called.

"Same to you." Where she was going, she'd need it. To her disappointment, her plan to attend med school had been deferred because the air force needed her elsewhere. The good news was, she was headed to a posting in the

Pentagon to work in protocol. With that sharp tongue of hers, it would be a challenge.

"Friend of yours?" Daisy asked.

"Sayers is in my detachment." He was dying to figure out if Daisy was jealous. He kind of wanted her to be, because of what that would mean.

"She calls you Jughead." She laughed. "I like it."

"Hey, how about some family pictures before we go in," Connor suggested.

"I'm on it," Daisy said.

Julian's family didn't resemble anything people pictured when they thought of "family," but they were all connected, and it meant the world to him that they had come. Daisy took photos of him and the others in every possible combination. They were definitely a picture of diversity. Connor, whose father was white, looked like Paul Bunyan in a new suit. Their mother, who these days called herself Starr, was as blonde as Olivia and Daisy, while his aunt, uncle and cousin had the same fine ebony coloring as Julian's late father. Julian himself was a mixture of dark and light, and was sometimes mistaken for Latino. Which, where he was headed, was not necessarily a bad thing.

He was dying to tell Daisy what he could of his news, to really have a chance to talk to her, but now was not the time. Likely the same thought had occurred to her; she was doing that thing she sometimes did, lifting her camera up, like a shield between her and the world.

"She's a famous photographer," Connor told Uncle Claude as she crouched down for a shot of a manicured campus garden with Remy and Mimi in the background.

"Get out," said Daisy, her face flushed. "I'm not famous."

"She's a professional," Julian explained, happy to contradict her. "She's one of the youngest photographers ever to be published in the *New York Times*."

"Your work was in the *New York Times?*" Julian's mom perked up. Anything having to do with fame and image generally intrigued her.

"It was one assignment," she said. "I had a lucky break involving a local baseball player."

"Everybody starts somewhere," his mom said. "I'd love to see the pictures."

"You're going to love this even more." Daisy positioned Julian and his mom side by side, with Cornell's clock tower behind them. "The light's really pretty here."

Starr glanced back at the tower. "Looks like the set of a sniper movie I was in a few years ago. The shooter was up on the ledge surrounding the clock, and we had to figure out a way to escape."

"And did you?" Julian asked.

"Yep. As I recall, I set something on fire and created a smoke screen. Who knows, now that you're going to be a hotshot in the air force, you'll be doing things like that for real." She turned her gaze up to Julian, and he recognized a rare flash of pride in her regard. His mom knew so little about his life. In a way, that saddened him, but in another way, it was very liberating. She never had any expectations for him to live up to, so he had no trouble exceeding them.

"Has anyone ever mentioned you look like Heidi Klum?" Daisy asked.

Julian could feel his mom's gratification in her posture. "You think?"

"Sure." Daisy took several shots.

"I like this girl," said Julian's mom. "Where'd you find her?"

His eyes met Daisy's, and he read the question there. No, he'd never explained Daisy to his mother. In the first place, Starr was too self-absorbed to actually care. And in the second place, his relationship with Daisy often seemed to defy explanation.

Since Starr had asked him a direct question, he went with the digest version. "We met the summer before our senior year of high school. Remember, the summer I spent at Willow Lake."

Looking back, Julian now realized he'd been saved in more ways than one that summer. Camp Kioga and the Bellamys had been a revelation to Julian. He met not just Daisy, but a whole group of people who were nothing like the *cholos* he hung out with in his industrial town east of L.A. The people he'd met that summer saw life as filled with promise, not a dead end, even for a kid like him. He simply had to pick his path and do what he needed to do in order to get where he wanted to be. Despite its simplicity, this was a concept that had not occurred to him before.

"You've been together since high school and you never told me?" his mother chided him.

"Um…" Daisy looked uncomfortable and lifted up her camera again.

"Mom, check it out." With perfect timing, Connor interrupted, pushing the baby stroller into her path. "Zoe just woke up, and she's ready to see her grandma."

The little two-year-old eyed her glamorous grandmother with cautious interest. Absorbed with her life in L.A., Starr had only seen the tot one other time, soon after Zoe was born.

"Of course she wants to." Starr clasped her hands, beaming at the pretty, yellow-haired child. "But 'grandma' sounds so…so old. We'll have to come up with some alternative, won't we, Zoe?"

The awkward moment passed, and Julian's mood was buoyant by the time they reached the imposing, concrete-and-glass auditorium.

He took his place with the other cadets and midshipmen; all service branches were represented. A brass band played a couple of standards, and the glee club sang "America the Beautiful."

The school president's address was a balance of idealism and realism. "Today we honor you. Your numbers are few but your commitment is great. The call to serve one's country is heard and heeded only by a select cadre of individuals, and our nation is fortunate indeed that the likes of you will join the ranks of our greatest heroes. And to the families—we honor you as well, because you are about to let them go now."

At that, Daisy pushed a wad of Kleenex against her face. Julian winced, feeling her pain echo through him. He wished he could tell her it wasn't going to be that way, that nobody had to let anything go. But he'd be wrong. The price for this career was steep, in terms of relationships. Damn. He hoped she understood. He needed this. He needed the purpose and the pride of being an officer in the air force. And God knew, he needed the money. His education had not cost him a cent. Now he would repay the debt with a chunk of his life. Back when he'd signed up for ROTC, it had seemed a fair enough exchange.

One by one, the candidates crossed the stage, raised a right hand and spoke the oath that would seal admittance into the military's most elite class of commissioned officers. Each man or woman stood proudly as family members pinned the rank or bars onto each shoulder. Julian's mother played her role with gusto, managing to project intense emotion as she stood on one side of Julian, while his father's brother stood on the other.

Julian earned a citation for physical performance and engineering. It was the engineering prize that nearly did him in, right there in front of everyone.

His father had been a rocket scientist. It had always

been a family joke that Louis Gastineaux's passion for work surpassed his passion for life itself. He'd led an unconventional life, but Julian had always felt safe and protected. Sure, he'd wished for a mom, but his father had explained her absence without bitterness or recrimination. "It's something she's called to do," Louis had told his small son, whenever Julian had asked about her. "Just like me and physics."

"But you're with me," Julian would argue.

"How could I not be?" his dad would gently ask. "Tell me that, honey. How could I not be with you?" That had been before tragedy had struck, before the car accident that had paralyzed Julian's father and eventually caused his death.

At the podium, Julian held the plaque of commendation. Thanks, Dad, he thought. I love you.

He didn't know what kind of life his father had dreamed of for him. But today, he thought maybe this might be it.

Afterward, there was a dinner at Cornell's hotel school restaurant. Julian was still dying for some time alone with Daisy, but it wasn't to be. The mixed blessing of a family demanded that he attend to all of them. He told himself he'd waited a long time, and another few hours wouldn't matter.

Everyone wanted to know about his orders. Where would the future take him? What would he be doing? How many in his command? The questions buzzed around him, as they had these last few weeks. People in his detachment had been swapping their news and speculation for several weeks. Plenty were going on to be pilots or navigators, but the chain of command had a different plan for Julian.

Due to the nature of the mission, he wasn't able to say much. "It's an active-duty assignment," he said. "A cooperative international venture. I'll be doing tactical and operations training."

"What's that?" asked Remy.

"Just…doing my duty."

"Duty. You're good at that stuff, Jules," said Remy.

"Where will you be stationed?" asked Connor.

Julian paused. His gaze flicked to Daisy, who sat beside him. He could feel her holding her breath. There was only so much he was authorized to share.

"Colombia," he said. "There's a newly upgraded base there called Palanquero."

His uncle let out a low whistle. "Man. Colombia."

Julian could practically feel Daisy wilt with disappointment, but she kept her smile in place. "That's exciting, Julian," she said. "You'll get to use your Spanish."

He couldn't tell her, but he'd been groomed specifically for this one-of-a-kind assignment. His training had been multifaceted, including attendance at the Inter-American Air Forces Academy in Texas and undergoing rigorous security evaluations to make sure he was fit for covert ops.

He had first encountered Colonel Sanchez, the head of the operation, during a field training exercise two summers ago. He hadn't known it then, but Sanchez had been combing the rosters, identifying personnel for the team. Julian fit the bill. He had the physical qualifications, the language skills, the technical and tactical skills. At first he hadn't realized he was actually being scrutinized for high-risk operations. He later learned his reputation for being an adrenaline junkie had made him an early favorite.

These days, the troubles in Colombia didn't tend to make headlines. The rebel FARC and other antigovernment paramilitary organizations had diminished, and news from the Middle East and even Mexico tended to overshadow Colombia, although the mountainous nation still produced eighty percent of the world's cocaine. What the press generally failed to mention was that in the wake of the paramilitary demobilization, criminal groups had arisen and filled the niche, like opportunistic infections. The drugs kept coming. And in recent times, something sinister had developed—ties between the drug cartels and terrorist organizations. That, combined with a base closing in Ecuador, had spurred the U.S. to action. The idea behind the action coalition was to disrupt the activities of the drug and weapon operations, and cause their organizations to fall apart.

"All I know about Colombia is the coffee," his mother admitted. "And stories about scary drug lords."

Julian didn't say any more. He couldn't; it was strictly classified. Those scary drug lords were the reason he was being sent to South America.

Six

Staying in a hotel was a treat for Daisy. Sometimes while on a wedding assignment, she stayed at the venue, but that was work. Unfortunately, all the luxury in the world could not translate into a good night's sleep when she was working.

Nor could it when she was worrying. And on this night, she was worrying. She paced the floor. Stared out the window at the moonrise as it tracked imperceptibly across the night sky. And paced some more.

Colombia. It was half a world away; she'd checked it out on Google maps. She and Julian hadn't managed to get together while living in the same state. Now that he was going to be on a different continent, what hope did they have?

Julian was about to start a different life, as an officer and a gentleman. A striver, a patriot. A man with a duty to his country, about to embark upon the adventure of a lifetime. But all she could think about was that his duties were going to take him far away from her into an unknown and dangerous world.

Be happy for him, she told herself. Everything is as it should be.

Had she been fooling herself all along, thinking there was a chance for them? Now, more than ever, she needed to have a difficult, honest conversation with him about the two of them. Their relationship was a series of encounters filled with a burning chemistry that thus far, had led only to yearning and frustration. Whenever she even thought of him, she felt a longing so fierce it hurt. Still, all the longing in the world didn't add up to any kind of future together. For that matter, they'd never even declared their love aloud. They'd never had time or space for anything to grow and develop, knitting them together.

They were stuck in the magic stage; they idealized each other, not knowing for certain if they were truly meant to be together. Maybe they had habits that would eventually annoy one another. Maybe they were sexually incompatible; she wouldn't know, because they'd never slept together. Maybe they were on different paths and destined to stay that way.

But in her heart of hearts, she wished this didn't have to be the case. She loved him with so much of herself that she couldn't imagine any other way to feel. To stop loving him would be to stop breathing the air.

Still, all the love in the world couldn't change the fact that she was tied to home, to Charlie and his dad, while Julian was bound for adventure. The only practical thing to do was to make their peace with reality. She tortured herself with the very real possibility that in his travels, Julian might meet someone, a woman who was free to follow him to the ends of the earth. For the briefest of moments, she fantasized about what it would be like to be that woman, unfettered, nothing keeping her from striking out on an adventure. Then she thought of Charlie and immediately felt guilty. How could she even imagine a life without Charlie?

Somehow, she managed to steal a few hours of sleep.

In the morning, they all gathered for breakfast. She sat next to Julian, watching him methodically eat his way through the buffet—an omelet, pancakes, cereal, fruit—like a starving man.

"You always did have a big appetite, boy," Tante Mimi said fondly.

"'Member when we had that pie-eating contest?" Remy asked.

"Sure," said Julian. "I was the winner."

"Yeah, but you had a bellyache all night." Remy leaned forward to catch Daisy's eye. "Me and Jules, we went camping at the state park. What we call that park, Mama?"

"I don't remember," said Tante Mimi. "It was by Lake Pontchartrain."

"Yeah," said Remy, "with our scouting group, and we had the eating contest. Learned stuff, too." He handed Julian a plastic matchbox. "'Member this? I made it for you."

"Thanks, Remy." Julian slid open the box. "Strike-anywhere matches, a water purification tablet… It's everything I need to survive in the wilderness." He took out a small wire. "I don't remember what this is for."

Remy beamed, clearly delighted to be the authority. "You rub it on your hair and set it on top of some water, and it'll always point north." He frowned at Julian. "You got enough hair for that, Jules?"

Julian burst out laughing. "I guess I'd better check." He demonstrated the makeshift compass on his water glass. The tiny filament swung gently toward Remy. "Look at that," Julian said. "You're my true north, Rem."

"Even in Colombia?" Remy asked.

Julian's smile stayed in place, though Daisy sensed the tension ramping up. "A compass works differently south of the equator," he said. "Still works, though. Thanks, Remy."

His New Orleans relatives and his mother had a long

day of travel ahead of them. Daisy would be driving back to Avalon with Connor, Olivia and baby Zoe.

Soon, Daisy would be back with Charlie and the life she'd made for herself. A few times, she caught herself thinking, *I wish...* And then she would rein herself in. Let him go, she thought. Let him go.

After breakfast, she returned to her room to get her bag, pausing to check her hair and makeup. For some reason, it seemed important to look nice when she told him goodbye.

In the lobby, she was surprised to find Julian there by himself.

He was dressed in civilian clothes, loose cargo shorts and a pink golf shirt. It didn't escape Daisy's notice that every woman who passed by checked him out, yet he seemed oblivious to the attention. He had no idea how amazing he looked, at the peak of fitness, his posture perfect even when he was relaxing. The minute he spotted Daisy, his gaze never wavered, focusing on her with laserlike intensity.

So much had changed for them both, but one thing remained constant—this pull of emotion that drew them together. It felt particularly present this morning, and Daisy discovered she was not the only one who felt that way.

"Morning," he said in a low voice that sounded intoxicatingly sexy. "I thought you'd never get here."

This was not, she reminded herself, the way she had scripted the conversation in her head. She was supposed to have a talk with him, tell him their lives were taking them in different directions and figure out how they were both going to deal with that.

"Where is everyone else?" she asked, trying to get her bearings.

"They all took off for the airport. They said to tell you goodbye."

"Connor and Olivia?"

Julian picked up her overnight bag. "Already headed back to Avalon."

"What?" She stopped in the hotel doorway. "But what about me?"

"I'll get you home."

Her heart skipped a beat. "You're driving me all the way to Avalon?" It was a long drive. The idea of having him all to herself was almost too much to bear.

"I'm not driving you," he said.

"Then how—?"

"You'll see."

They boarded a campus-to-town bus marked Cayuga, the name of the narrow, forty-mile-long lake that stretched from Ithaca to Seneca Falls.

She looked around nervously at the other passengers. "Don't tell me we're—"

"Hush." He gently put a finger to her lips, and his touch made her shiver despite the warmth of the day. "You'll see."

She tried to steel herself against his charms but instead settled into a sense of delicious anticipation. Their heart-to-heart could wait a bit longer. "I do love surprises," she said.

"Then I guess you'll love this."

At the lakefront he led the way past a busy marina, bobbing with sailboats and runabouts. There was a boat-house, with kayaks and canoes stacked on racks. At the end of a long, L-shaped dock were a couple of float planes.

When Julian started down the dock, she balked. "Really, Julian? Seriously? You're flying?"

He grinned, his eyes bright with excitement. "You okay with that?"

Unable to hold herself back, she set down her camera bag and raced toward him, leaping into his embrace and wrapping her arms and legs around him. "What do you think?" she demanded.

He held her as if she weighed nothing. "Cool. We'll be back in Avalon before Connor and Olivia."

"I'm in no hurry," she said. "I mean, I miss Charlie. I always do when I'm away overnight, but—"

"It's okay." He brushed his knuckles over her cheek.

He knew her well. He knew that having a good time without Charlie around was a struggle for her. She and her little boy were a pair, even when they couldn't be together.

The float plane was a single engine two-seater that had been painted fuchsia. It belonged to the local flying club, which Julian had joined as soon as he'd matriculated at Cornell. He'd been taking flying lessons all through college, exchanging mechanical and maintenance labor for instruction, flight hours and fuel.

Before boarding, he went through a safety and readiness checklist with methodical precision. She knew the reckless boy was still inside him, the guy who jumped rows of barrels on a motorcycle and tackled the worst technical rock climbs without batting an eye. Now she watched that restless energy channel itself into intense focus and concentration.

She stood back on the dock, admiring the assured efficiency of his movements as he worked. Like a child's toy, the moored plane bobbed in time to the lapping of the water. "I can't believe we're doing this," she said.

He flashed a smile that managed to be at once boyish and sexy. "I've always wanted to take you flying." He loosened the mooring ropes, holding one in his hand.

"I feel like I already am," she said, then flushed because that sounded so lame. Still, she could not help smiling. It was a magnificent day, the sky cloudless, the water flat and calm. The surrounding hills wore mantles of new green growth. Everything in sight seemed swollen with abundance, and anything seemed possible.

Daisy knew she would soon be telling him farewell for good, or at least for the foreseeable future. But how could she do that now, when he was taking her flying, for heaven's sake? She didn't let herself dwell on it. Instead, she focused on the undeniable splendor of this day and felt grateful to be spending it with Julian.

He jimmied the change in his pocket, seeming oddly nervous. "As a matter of fact, I was planning to—"

"Julian, the plane!" She jumped to the edge of the dock. "It's getting away."

Without hesitation, he leaped onto a pontoon, causing the small aircraft to bob wildly. He tossed her a rope. She grabbed it and pulled him back to the dock.

"Thanks," he said, "I almost lost you before I even had you."

"You should be more careful."

"I had my head turned. It's not like I get to spend every day with the girl of my dreams."

"*What* did you call me?" Her heart was racing now.

"The girl of my dreams. It's cheesy, I know, but that's how I feel."

There were many ways to think about what he'd said. She knew he meant it in the best possible way, but she parsed the words, a habit of hers.

Even the word *girl*. She hadn't been a girl since the day she'd stared in horror at a home pregnancy test wand and realized her entire life was about to change. And being someone's dream sounded all well and good, but in actual fact it turned her into a concept, an ideal, and she didn't want that. She wanted him to know her on the most real level possible.

"Julian—"

"Ready?" he asked, unlocking the plane and flipping

open the surprisingly flimsy door. "Climb aboard. I'll load your stuff after."

She felt a thrum of excitement in her chest. The interior of the plane was like that of a middling sports car. Vinyl bucket seats, regular seat belts. The view out the front, over the sloping nose of the plane, was certainly different, though. The lake rolled out before them, reflecting the endless sky.

Julian shoved off the dock and climbed into the cockpit. "Put on your headset. It's going to get noisy in here."

She gamely donned a bulky headset. "Roger that." Her voice sounded tinny and artificial. "How do I look?"

"Like Princess Leia, with those big things on the sides of your head."

He did some more checking of the panel and gauges, and spoke on another frequency to a tower somewhere.

The single engine started, sounding like a lawn-mower motor. Daisy did not have a single reservation about his flying. She knew she was safe with him.

He slowly navigated the plane out of the marina, and the whine of the motor crescendoed to a powerful drone. The shoreline flickered past with ever-increasing speed, and then they were swept aloft with a breath-stealing lift of power. The treetops seemed close enough to touch, and the long curved finger of Lake Cayuga beckoned with flashes of silver reflecting the sun.

Daisy leaned back in her seat and laughed aloud. The day was glorious, and life was good.

To most of the world, "New York" meant Manhattan—gridlock traffic, skyscrapers, Times Square, the Statue of Liberty. The rest of the state got little attention. Most people would be surprised by the vast wilderness and variety of the landscape. The brilliant scenery rolled out before them. There were towering hills and river-fed forests, rock formations and cliffs and gorges. They soared over Cherry Ridge Wild Forest and the Catskill Wilderness, overshooting Willow Lake for a view of the famed Mohonk Mountain House, a historic resort. Daisy had gone there with her mom and brother one winter, when their mother was still in the midst of picking up the pieces of her life after divorce.

The thought of her parents' divorce no longer felt like a fresh, bleeding wound to Daisy. She would always mourn the loss of her family, but if she was being completely honest with herself, even when all four Bellamys lived under one roof, they weren't quite a family. From her earliest memory, there had been a deep chasm between her parents. She hadn't understood it then, but she did now. As hard as it had been to accept, her mom and dad simply weren't meant to be together, no matter how hard they tried.

The breakup had not been easy for either parent, but the rewards were uncountable. Her father had remarried first, turning Daisy's best friend, Sonnet Romano, into her stepsister. Later, Daisy's mother had settled in Avalon and joined a law firm. Against all expectations, she'd fallen in love with the local veterinarian and couldn't be happier.

Daisy sighed with contentment and looked over at Julian. He must have felt her gaze because he turned, too. In high-tech aviator shades, he looked incredible, Top Gun in a pink golf shirt.

The plane swooped down over the Shawangunks, a rocky ridge gouged by deep fissures. This particular wilderness area marked a special time for them both.

"Remember?" he asked, indicating the dramatic striated rock formations above the river. A few rock climbers, looking like four-legged spiders, clung to the sheer faces. Julian had taken her climbing there the first summer they'd met. She had railed and resisted the climb with almost as much force as she had railed and resisted his friendship—at first.

At that time in her life, she had not allowed herself to trust anyone, and that included Julian, even though she was completely intrigued by him. Challenged by him to climb, she had balked, but he'd simply been patient, knowing even then that she would come around. He was the only person she'd ever met who recognized her appetite for adventure. When everyone else dismissed her as another overprivileged city girl destined for a life of shopping and lunch, Julian had challenged her to want more, to be more.

At the summit of the climb, lying exhausted in the powdery red dust, she had done something life-changing. She had taken out what became her last pack of illicit cigarettes and with Julian as witness, made a small fire and burned them all. She never smoked a cigarette again after that day.

It would have been nice if that special, healing day had somehow inoculated her against future bumps and bruises, but it was not to be. At summer's end, she'd gone back to her senior year at prep school, where she'd managed to screw up a lot more.

A whole lot more.

Julian flew the plane over a waterfall at Deep Notch, where they'd gone ice climbing one winter, another place wrapped in memories of a day like no other. Ice climbing. Who but Julian would think it was a good idea to scale a wall of ice? And who but Julian could talk her into following him? So many of the things she'd done with him involved climbing and striving, embarking on dangerous pursuits, trying extreme sports. The funny thing about following Julian on impossible adventures was that she always seemed to succeed.

Getting to the top of the wall of ice had its own reward, but that was not what she remembered about that day. What she remembered was that, sitting at the frozen summit, shaking and sweating from the treacherous climb, she and Julian had finally shared their first kiss. Before that moment, she'd already known she loved him. What she had learned that day was that she would probably never stop.

"And how about this place?" he asked, his voice thready over the headset.

She wasn't even going to pretend to be coy. "I remember every minute."

"Me, too." He headed for their destination—Willow Lake. From the sky, the small lakeside town of Avalon looked both familiar and crazily different, like something generated by computer animation, perhaps. The town square and lakefront park were dotted with people out enjoying the day. She spotted the Avalon Meadows Golf Course and Country Club, where she'd shot many a wedding, and the Inn at Willow Lake, owned and operated by her dad and stepmom.

She looked straight down at the cataract known as Meerskill Falls, draping a plunging gorge like a bride's veil. At the top, almost indistinguishable, were hills and cliffs punctured by the famous ice caves, another place she and Julian had explored.

She was tense, thinking about the past, and so she shifted gears, aiming her thoughts to the present moment.

Finally, they came to the most familiar, most beloved landmark of all—Camp Kioga.

She reached over and touched Julian's arm. "It's so beautiful," she said.

The gardens and sports courts were pristine. Window boxes with flowers in bloom decked the cabins, bungalows and bunkhouses clustered at the water's edge. The grand pavilion dominated the landscape. A few kayaks were paddling around Spruce Island, a small green atoll crowned by a gazebo. A catboat skimmed by, its sail flying, offering a welcome glimpse of summer.

"Want to take the controls?" asked Julian.

"Are you kidding? Show me what to do."

He had her grip the controls. "The key is to have a light touch. No sudden movements, don't try to force anything."

"Got it." Very gently, she eased back and the plane climbed. She felt the way she imagined a kite would feel, or a bird with wings spread wide, riding the very air itself. I love this, she thought. I could do this forever.

"I'll take over for landing," Julian said after a while. He guided the plane into a downward glide toward an isolated area of the lake designated for float planes. The touchdown was smooth and exhilarating, and within minutes, they were tied up at the dock.

Daisy put her arms around him and jumped up in another full body hug. It felt so good to be held by him. "That was magical," she said. "Thank you so much." Every nerve ending tingled as he set her down on the dock.

"What's that face?" he asked, breaking in on her thoughts.

"What face? I don't have a face."

"Right."

Her heart sped up. Time to speak up—that difficult conversation she'd imagined this morning hovered on the edge of her consciousness. This was her first opening. It might be her only chance before he was sent off to Timbuktu. She took a deep breath, and the words rushed out: "I love you, that's what."

He froze, staring at her.

She couldn't believe what had come out of her mouth. It was supposed to be *I can't let myself love you, our lives are leading us too far apart, there can't be any future for us.* Instead, she'd spoken from a place where the stark truth dwelled, a truth she couldn't escape, even though it defied common sense.

She wondered if the words had shocked him. She couldn't read his expression, and that scared her. "I've never told you before," she said. "I didn't mean to blurt it out." She'd really blown it now, deviating from the script that had seemed so sensible in her hotel room this morning.

Even though it felt as reckless as one of Julian's stunts, she couldn't stop herself. "I'm glad," she rushed on foolishly. "I'm glad I said it, because I mean it. I've felt this way for a long time, *forever* and I keep waiting for it to go away, but the opposite is happening. It's only getting worse."

He still hadn't said anything, and she still couldn't make herself shut up. "I can't stop thinking about you. When I went away to Germany, I expected to get over you. To get over *everything.* Instead, I ended up missing you so much it hurt. Seriously, it hurt like I'd been stabbed or something. And when I got back, I loved you just as much—no, more. It doesn't make any sense. It doesn't seem right, but—"

He strode forward with a look on his face she'd never seen before. It was as intense as rage but different. She still hadn't figured it out when he caught her against him, stopping her with a kiss. A long, searching kiss that was tender but commanding, all-consuming, leaving her breathless. His lips were softer than she remembered, his taste sweeter. They had kissed before, but there was something different going on here, a peculiar emotion that grabbed at her heart with a special intensity. She curled her fists into his arms, feeling the rock-hard muscles shaped by relentless and rigorous training. He tasted like something wild, like raw honey, maybe, and in that moment she was so caught up that her ears rang.

A breakup wasn't supposed to start with a kiss.

Although technically, she wasn't breaking up with him, because she'd never been…with him.

Finally he pulled back, but only far enough away to say, "I love you, too, Daze. I always have. I'm sorry I didn't say it first."

She felt dizzy, as if she were still flying. "I'm not sorry." She sank against his chest, feeling exhausted, as if she'd run a mile. It was one of those flawless days on Willow Lake, the water perfectly still down to its mysterious depths, and the wind so quiet, she could hear both their hearts beating. Being here with him made her feel safe and protected, as if no harm could ever come to her.

They kissed some more, their mouths lazing and lingering like wordless promises. Daisy was filled with a soaring sense of liberation at having spoken her truth—and the stunning joy of knowing he returned her love. She wished the moment could last forever, but slowly, inevitably, he pulled back. Placing a tender kiss on her forehead, he whispered, "What time are you supposed to pick up Charlie?"

Charlie. Her beloved reality. "Logan's flexible," she said. "Why do you ask?"

"I'm not ready to share you yet," he said, "not even with my favorite rug rat."

Her thoughts flickered to the conversation she was supposed to be having with him. "Then I'm all yours for a while longer."

"Good." He took an insulated green bag out of the cargo bay. "I brought lunch."

"Julian!"

He laughed. "I know, right? Romance at its finest."

"Did you, like, look this up online, under 'how to organize the perfect date'?"

"What, you don't think I could've thought of this on my own?"

"The plane, yes. But a picnic?"

"Okay. I had help with that."

"Help?"

"I kind of became a favorite of the dining hall ladies. They like guys who eat a lot."

"Then they must be totally in love with you. I've seen you eat, Julian. It's…epic."

He set the bag in a skiff that was moored to the dock. Then he took her hand and helped her in.

"I assume you have permission to use the boat."

"Ma'am, I'm an officer in the United States Air Force. Stealing is no longer an option."

"You planned this."

"Yeah. Didn't want to leave anything to chance today."

There was a feeling she always had around him, something she'd never found with any other person. It was a sense of complete and utter joy, mingled with freedom. There were many people she loved in her life, but no one she loved like this. A part of her wanted to explain it to him, to share that, but not now. One day, maybe.

The trouble with her and Julian was that "one day" for them was hard to pin down. Impossible, really. That was the conversation they needed to have. She didn't want to say it and spoil this perfect day.

She shook off the thought and settled in the bow of the boat, facing backward. She didn't know where they were headed. Didn't really care. Bracing her arms behind her, she tipped back her head and shut her eyes to enjoy the soft warmth of the sun on her face.

"I feel like Cleopatra."

"Yeah? That worries me. Romance didn't really work out for her," Julian pointed out.

"Did you say romance? Is that what you're doing—romancing me?" Daisy sat up straight and watched him row. She was mesmerized by the powerful build of his shoulders, the easy extension of his muscles, reaching back and forth as he propelled the boat through the water.

"I'd like to think we've evolved since the days of Cleopatra. And I'd definitely like to think I don't have her quirks."

"Quirks?"

"Okay, her personality flaws."

"You don't have any flaws, Daisy."

"Right."

"Except maybe bad timing."

She fell silent. Here was an opening, then. "Um, about that. My timing. Our timing. Julian, I meant what I said earlier. I love you. I always have, but I'm scared."

"Of what?"

"Scared we'll never get a chance to be together."

His rhythmic strokes didn't falter. "Never is a long time."

"Just trying to be realistic."

"Were you being realistic when you said you loved me?"

"I was being completely honest. I can't help myself. Still, it doesn't change the fact that you're going far away—"

"That's temporary."

"How temporary?"

"I can't say."

"I can. When you're done in Colombia, they'll send you someplace else."

"Active duty doesn't have to mean continual deployment. Air force families move from posting to posting. The system works. It just takes some planning."

"That's easy to say, but I have to think about Charlie." She hugged her knees to her chest. "My little boy is my whole world."

"I understand that. I know how hard it's been for you, raising him alone."

"Do you?"

"My friend Sayers once told me air force training is a tea party compared to being a single mom. She was raised by a single mom."

"It's hard, but…in a different way." She wondered if the direction of the conversation had ruined this magical day. Julian was clearly in a romantic mood, and bringing up the topic of her son by another man might put a damper on things. But they should be able to talk about Charlie and not feel like the entire day was ruined.

"Charlie's great," said Julian. "I'm in love with the kid. Always have been."

The statement caught her off guard. "You love him?"

"Sure. What, you don't believe me?"

"I want to. But it's just…you seem to hold back, when it comes to Charlie."

"Kids latch onto people, and they hurt when those people go away."

"Are you talking about Charlie, or are you talking about yourself, when you were a kid?"

He didn't contradict her. "I know what it feels like to have a broken family. Charlie should never have to feel that. So I don't want to give him mixed signals. When I was little, growing up with my dad, I used to want a mama so bad, I'd fantasize about every woman my dad even looked at—a bus driver, a grocery checker, the crossing guard—if she said even two words to him, I was ready for him to pop the question. And I was disappointed every time. You have to understand how much it hurts a kid to want a traditional family. How much hope he hangs on the slightest encouragement. So maybe I've been too careful about Charlie, but that's my take on it. I never wanted to make him a promise I couldn't keep. That doesn't mean I don't love him."

Unexpected tears stung her eyes. "You never told me you loved him."

"Daisy. He's your son. He's never asked for anything except to be loved. How can I not love that?"

Her heart turned to mush; she loved hearing him talk this way.

"He can't help it if his father's a douche—"

"Julian." She knew he was still thinking of the fight on the train platform, the night everything had fallen apart. The fight had not caused the problem. The fight had been the culmination of the problem. The mushy part was over, clearly.

"I'd never say that in front of the kid, but come on. And honestly, no matter what I think of Logan, I'd never let on to Charlie. And I'd never want to interfere with that relationship. I had a great dad. He wasn't perfect, but I thought the world of him. So yeah, I get that Logan has to be part of Charlie's life. A big part."

"I'm glad you understand. There are a few things in my life that are completely certain," she reminded Julian. "The most important is my son. Every choice I make is dictated by what's best for Charlie."

"I understand."

"Another constant is Logan. He is Charlie's dad, which means he'll always be part of my life, no matter what."

"Is he still in love with you?"

She could still hear Logan's voice in her ears, loud and clear. *I'll always love you, Daisy. I'll wait as long as it takes.*

She ducked her head to hide her expression, but apparently she wasn't quick enough.

"I see," said Julian.

"I don't think you do. I can't tell you what Logan is thinking. Persistence is his middle name. I swear, I don't encourage him. You know that. I want… God, Julian. I want this to be simple. Why is it so hard?"

The rowboat bumped against the mooring bulkhead at the tiny island. Julian pulled a rope around a cleat. Then he extended a hand and helped her to the dock.

He sat on the weathered wooden planks and drew her down beside him. "Have a seat. This might take a while."

"It might?"

"I've got a lot to say to you."

Something in his tone made her shiver despite the heat. "I'm listening."

He steepled his fingers together and stared into the lake for a long moment. The still water was a mirror of dark glass. "It's *not* hard. I'm not saying I hold all the answers. God knows, I didn't have much to go on when I was a kid. My dad was all about intellect and process and the scientific method. My mom was focused on her acting career, her image, herself. I've spent the past few weeks wondering if I even have the emotional hardware for the kind of relationship I want with you."

She was stunned speechless to hear him talking like this. Maybe her silence was a good thing, because he was being more honest with her than he'd ever been before.

"And I wondered why danger and risk feel good to me. Maybe it's because whenever I took a risk and put myself in danger, people paid attention, sometimes just to yell at me. Even Connor—the sole reason we had a relationship at all was that he had to take charge of me when I got into trouble. But you, Daisy. You're the first person who didn't pay attention to me because I was doing something dangerous. You paid attention because…hell, I don't know, but I know it felt different. Everything about you is different, the way you look and smell, the way you feel in my arms."

They weren't even touching, yet Daisy had never felt closer to anyone than she did to Julian at this moment. She didn't dare move or speak because she sensed this was hard for him and didn't want him to stop.

"I was seventeen years old the first time I met you," he said, still staring into their reflection in the water, "and I wish I'd paid more attention then to the way you made me feel. Maybe I would've had the sense to find a way to stay close to you, after we parted ways that summer, instead of watching you head off to a bad situation. When I found out you were pregnant, I thought it was a sign that you'd taken another path. A path that didn't include me. And all through college, I guess I felt like I had to prove myself to you. You know, the beautiful rich girl. And any way you cut it, I'm from the wrong side of the tracks. It's ridiculous to think about me and a Bellamy, for Chrissake. I didn't see how you and I would ever connect. We come from totally different worlds."

She held her breath. Was he saying they were incompatible, that love wasn't enough? "Julian—"

"Hang on, I'm getting to the point. Where we come from doesn't have to matter. I'm not going to worry about what other people will say, the color of our skin and what our kids might look like. What matters is…it's us. Our hopes and dreams and what we want our lives to be."

He kissed her swiftly, his warm lips lingering against hers, his breath gusting over her cheek. "Whew," he said. "That's, like, the longest speech I've ever given. Sorry if I rambled."

She could listen to him talk like that forever. "You didn't ramble."

"I've been practicing what I wanted to say. In my head. God, don't think I was walking around campus, spouting stuff about hopes and dreams. But I meant every word." With that, he got up and grabbed the picnic bag, bringing it to the steps of the gazebo, built some years ago for her grandparents' golden anniversary. She followed, still entranced by the things he'd said. There was no one around. The gazebo was broadcasting music from somewhere. She recognized the old classic, "Wonderful Tonight" by Eric Clapton.

"Whoa," she said. "Is someone here?"

"We are now." Julian set down the bag. Turning to face her, he paused for what felt like a full minute and studied her face. She did the same, seeing love and pain in the yearning in his eyes.

"Thanks for coming here with me," he said at last, bending down to kiss her again.

"Thanks for bringing me," she said, feeling drunk from the taste of him. "It's been an awesome day."

"We're just getting started." He took out a bottle of champagne and two glasses.

When he uncorked the champagne with a loud *thwok,* Daisy felt a surge of excitement. "Julian?"

"Hang on," he said, putting his arm around her. "You okay?"

"I'm kind of shaking." The Eric Clapton song was perfect, romantic and true. He was a guy from an older generation, but his music told the stories in her own heart.

She didn't drink the champagne. She was too nervous; she might upchuck on herself and ruin everything.

"I wanted to say this here because I know it's a special place to you."

She nodded. "Sacred ground. To the Bellamy family, anyway."

"I'm glad I got to meet your grandparents on their fiftieth anniversary. I'd never met anyone who'd been married that long."

It had been the most special of days, not only for her grandparents but for all the Bellamys. Daisy had been in enormous emotional pain that summer, yet she could still appreciate the wonder of a love that had endured for half a century.

"It gave me hope," she said.

"It gave me a dream." He took both her hands in his and turned to face her. "I want what they have, Daisy. I was a kid back then, we both were. We're adults now, and the dream hasn't changed, not for me anyway. It's only grown stronger."

His kiss was gentle, searching, full of yearning. She felt so emotional, she thought she might fly into a million pieces.

"All those places we flew over today," he said, "they mean something to me because of what we shared there."

"They're special to me, too," she said, her throat aching with the words.

He nodded, swallowed hard, as if gathering his thoughts. "I have to go away soon. I have a job to do, a duty…it's what I signed up for. Life is unpredictable, so I have to do this while I have the chance."

"Do what?" Somewhere in her heart she knew already, and her pulse raced almost out of control.

"My service in the air force is not forever. I'm saving 'forever' for you, Daisy. I don't want to live my life without you."

With that, he sank down on one knee before her.

Everything stopped. Time, breath, reality, the world on its axis. Even the wind seemed to quiet. She could feel the sweet air on her skin, and birdsong rang in her ears, mingling with the music from the hidden speakers. At the center of it all was Julian, looking at her with love shining from the deepest part of him.

She wanted to say something, she didn't know what, but her voice felt trapped, frozen in her throat. She wasn't able to utter a sound, which was probably a good thing, because for some inexplicable reason, she hovered on the verge of tears. She couldn't believe this moment was happening to her.

"Daisy Bellamy, I've loved you since our first summer at Willow Lake," he said. "I swear, I'll never stop. Will you marry me?"

Though this was something she'd dreamed of, fantasized about, hoped for in a secret place in her heart, she was unprepared for the emotion that jolted through her, almost violent in its intensity. *Will you marry me?*

Her thoughts reeled. She knew she should think about all the reasons she couldn't be with him, the dangers and drawbacks of giving herself and her young son to a man like Julian. Charlie needed security and stability. She needed…she needed… The tears fell and her heart spoke before her brain could object. "I would love to marry you, Julian Gastineaux. With all my heart, I would love it."

He laughed aloud and took a ring from his pocket, a simple diamond solitaire on a slender gold band. "They knew your size at Palmquist's," he said, slipping in on her finger.

For a split second, she flashed on a memory of Logan's Christmas Eve proposal, that humiliating night she could never quite get out of her head. Logan had gone to the same jeweler.

"It's perfect," she said, distancing herself from that memory. "It fits perfectly."

"Really?" He stood and picked her up with him, as though she were as light as air.

"Really," she said, kissing him and brimming over with a happiness so intense, it felt like a kind of pain.

He set her down, and they held each other for a long time. She pressed her cheek to his chest and listened to the throb of his heart. The past few minutes had changed her life. She was going to marry this man. It was unbelievable.

"I didn't know I'd be asking you today. I've been waiting for the right time. When you told me you loved me, I figured it was a sign."

She pressed her cheek against his chest, listening to the powerful throb of his heart. This was not the conversation she thought they would be having today. This was…a dream come true. "I couldn't keep it in any longer."

"I know what I'm asking, because of my job," he said. "But I also know we're going to make this work, I swear."

"Yes," she said and kissed him again, feeling giddy with elation.

She set her camera on timer and leapt into the frame with him, eager to mark this precious, precious day with a picture together. The viewfinder showed them on the dock with their arms around each other, the late-afternoon sun suffusing the scene with a golden glow. In her professional life, Daisy had taken many photos that were technically superior and more sophisticated than this shot. But never, ever had she captured a more joyous moment.

A sense of wonder held the world at bay and kept reality from intruding. For now, she savored the sweetness of knowing their love had a future. How could a feeling this powerful be wrong? It was a palpable thing. Nothing could stand in their way.

Seven

Daisy sat for a moment in Logan's driveway, collecting her thoughts. Only yesterday when she'd dropped off Charlie, she never could have imagined this moment. Julian wanted to marry her. She'd said yes. So simple. She knew it wasn't, but she had to believe they could make it happen.

She flexed her left hand on the steering wheel. The brand-new diamond glinted in the sun. *Surreal.*

She got out of the car and could hear laughter coming from the backyard. Her heart lifted at the sound of her child's voice, and she hurried around the side of the house.

Logan and Charlie were playing monster, a game they'd invented. It had intricate, unwritten rules only they understood. The play involved Logan hunkering down like an ogre, making threatening noises as he stalked Charlie around the yard. Once caught, Charlie was subjected to loud, smacking kisses all over his bare belly, which never failed to cause him to shriek with glee.

The two of them were beautiful together, so alike as they threw themselves into the fun, given to moments of joy that consumed them both. For a few minutes, they were lost in their hilarity and didn't notice her, standing at the garden gate.

Without really letting herself think about why, she slipped off the ring and stashed it deep in the pocket of her jeans.

"Hey, you two," she called.

They fell apart, sprawling on the ground. "Mommy!" Charlie yelled and picked himself up, staggering toward her, drunk with laughter. "I missed you."

"I missed you, too." Her spirits were buoyed by her son, like always. The sweet sound of his voice, the smell of his skin, the sturdy weight of him in her arms, reminded her that he was her reason for living. He was an unasked-for blessing, precious beyond imagining. Since the moment he was born, she had never had a thought or made a decision without his interests in mind. Her entire life had been fashioned around what was best for Charlie—the college she'd chosen, the path of her career, the town where she lived, the friends she chose. Her pathetic lack of a love life—until lately.

Already, a short time after saying yes to Julian, she realized something. Charlie was not at the center of this decision.

"Thanks for keeping him," she said to Logan.

"No problemo."

"Let's go inside and get his stuff."

Awkward, she thought. This was a circumstance most books on etiquette and protocol didn't seem to address. How do you tell the father of your child you just got engaged to someone else?

Particularly when the father of your child had already proposed and been turned down?

Maybe Logan sensed something weighing on her mind. He gave Charlie a juice box, put him in front of the TV and turned on *Dora the Explorer*. "What's up?"

"Um, something *has* come up," she said.

He groaned. "Not the dog thing."

She gave a startled laugh. "What?"

"Yeah, Charlie told me you were talking about getting a dog."

She hadn't expected the conversation to go that way. "Actually, I was. This summer, in fact. I haven't figured out exactly when, but I'd like to take him to the rescue shelter and pick out a dog."

"Why would you want to do that?" Logan broke out a bundle from the laundry service and extracted several items that belonged to Charlie. To Daisy's knowledge, Logan had never done laundry in his life. Though determined to take on the manly chores of home repair, he couldn't abide housework. It was the way he'd been raised—you sent your laundry out to be done or hired someone in. She personally had no love for doing laundry, and on the surface Logan's aversion seemed like a harmless enough quirk. Yet Daisy made sure that at her house, Charlie was learning the simple basics of doing laundry. She couldn't quite put her finger on why it was important—but she sensed that it was. A kid needed to learn responsibility, starting small.

Which brought her back to the matter of the dog, an easier topic to tackle than the real issue—she'd just agreed to marry a guy Logan couldn't stand. "Why wouldn't I want to get a dog? It's a great thing to do for a kid. Taking care of a pet teaches him all the important life lessons—empathy, duty, gentleness, compassion—"

"Dogs die," Logan said bluntly. "No matter how well you take care of them and how much you love them, they die and take your heart with them. You never outlive a dog. It's a biological fact. So by getting a dog, you're basically handing the kid a tragedy to deal with, something that could mess him up for the rest of his life."

His vehemence took her aback. "Whoa, where is all this all coming from?"

"Simple common sense, that's where. You get him a dog now, and it'll become his best friend. That's what kids and dogs do. They become best friends."

"Exactly. So…"

"So you're setting him up to experience the death of his best friend. Hell, maybe he'll even be the one to have to euthanize the animal. You ever read *Old Yeller?* I don't know about you, but I'm guessing most kids do fine without having to put their pets to death."

"Wow, Logan. You have some strong opinions about this. I had no idea."

"Now you do."

She wondered if one day he'd explain what was behind his dark view of the subject. Meanwhile, she refused to let him keep Charlie from having this kind of joy in his life. "I have opinions of my own on the subject. And I don't choose to see every pet as a tragedy waiting to happen to an unsuspecting little boy. I see it as a huge chance for love and joy, memories to cherish for a lifetime. Losing a pet doesn't ruin a person's life. It simply doesn't work that way."

"Sounds like you're going to do what you want," he said.

"It's something I want for Charlie," she said. "And for me. I never had a dog growing up, and I always wanted one."

"Yeah, well, I did have a dog."

"I never knew that, Logan."

"Because I don't talk about it."

"You can, you know. Talk about it."

"Thanks, I'll pass. Reliving the death of my best friend was not on my agenda today."

"Logan. I'm sorry."

He waved away her concern and went back to sorting Charlie's laundry.

She cleared her throat, trying to calm the flutters in her stomach. "When I said something came up, I wasn't really thinking about the dog." She spoke in low tones, and that caught his attention.

"Okay," he said. "So, what's up?"

She kept her gaze steady as she regarded Logan, seeing him in all the phases of his life, from a mischievous boy in grade school to the man he was today. He was a good dad, and they cared for each other deeply. A feeling of sadness undercut her joy. Taking a breath, she found herself wishing for a way to soften the news; she hadn't even said this aloud yet, it was so new. "I'm going to marry Julian."

Logan turned to stone, right before her eyes.

She could feel the silent hurt emanating from him. *Oh, Logan.* "I'm telling you first because you're so important to Charlie. I'm going to explain it to him as best I can. The main thing I need him to understand is that he's still going to have his mom and dad, same as ever."

"Right. And how will you explain the stepfather?" Logan demanded.

It felt strange to hear Julian referred to as a stepfather. "Lots of people have stepdads," she pointed out. "Including me. My mom's husband, Noah, is incredible. I adore him, you know that. He'll never replace my dad, but I feel really lucky to have them both in my life."

"When did you turn into such a bullshit artist?" Logan demanded.

She inhaled another breath. Easy does it. She could hardly expect his blessing. "It's all really new. It just happened and there isn't a concrete plan at the moment. I'm not going to do anything rash or impulsive. I've loved him for a long time." It was almost a relief to say the words aloud.

"You love an illusion, Daisy. A dream. It isn't real." He held up a hand to stop her objections. "Hear me out. I kind of hoped I wouldn't need to say this. We've never had a formal arrangement about Charlie because we haven't had to. But if you marry this guy, move halfway around the globe, that changes things. Like that time you took Charlie to live overseas," he reminded her, conveniently forgetting the reason for her departure. "Those months apart about killed me."

Her blood chilled. Logan had been incensed when she'd taken off, despite the fact that he'd been the very cause of the Christmas Eve disaster. He had even engaged a lawyer to assert his paternal rights.

"We'll make it work," she promised. "I've always tried to make it easy for you and Charlie to be together, you know that."

He stared at her for a long time, his eyes reflecting a world of hurt. "It's never been easy," he said.

Julian paced the dock, feeling the sun beat down on his bare back. He couldn't believe it was finally happening—he was marrying Daisy Bellamy.

She had gone to pick up Charlie from his dad's. The plan was for the three of them to spend the rest of the day together here at Camp Kioga. The afternoon was on fire with unseasonable heat, so a swim in the lake was on the agenda.

First, they would have the big talk with Charlie. He was too young to fully understand, but they didn't want him hearing things peripherally and feeling confused. Today, they would explain as best they could in terms he would understand that they were going to get married and the three of them would be a family.

The idea made Julian's heart expand. He was elated, excited, on top of the world. The decision felt so right he couldn't sit still, so he paced the dock some more, watching the sunlight glint on the lake. He knew full well this was not going to be a cakewalk, but he was going to make this work if it killed him. It was what he wanted, what he'd always wanted—to love Daisy and make a life with her.

At last she arrived, parking near the dock.

"Look who came to see you," she said, beaming at Julian as she helped Charlie out of his car seat.

For a moment, the glare of the sun came from behind Daisy. Julian could only see her in silhouette, the woman he loved, holding an equally beloved child. Then she stepped into the light, and reality intruded.

Charlie was another man's son, with the lily-white skin and flame-red hair to prove it.

Julian knew he'd have no trouble loving this kid. But loving the fact that Logan would always be in the picture? More of a challenge, for sure.

"Hey there, my buddy," he said.

"Hey there, Daddy-boy."

"How you doing?"

Bashful, Charlie rubbed his eyes, then tucked his face into the crook of Daisy's neck.

"Now, there's a boy who loves his mama," Julian remarked. He bent and kissed Daisy's cheek, then the top of Charlie's sun-warm head. "I love your mama, too," he added.

"Mom said I could swim," Charlie informed him. "We already got our suits on."

"Me, too," said Julian.

"Let's go down by the lake," she suggested.

They headed to a grassy area where the water lapped gently at the shore. "Can we swim now?" asked Charlie.

She'd warned Julian that the kid had the attention span of a fruit fly, so he figured he'd better get down to business.

"Hey, super-Charlie," Julian said. "Your mom and I are going to get married." He paused. Charlie plucked at a blade of grass.

"Married," Julian repeated. "Do you know what that means?"

Charlie offered a tiny smile that could mean anything.

"It means we're going to be a family," said Daisy.

"Mom, Dad, Charlie," said the kid.

Julian and Daisy locked eyes. The boy was clear on who the members of his family were.

"In this new kind of family," Julian said, "there will be three of us—Charlie, mom and me, er, Daddy-boy."

"And Dad," Charlie said reasonably.

"Your dad will still be your dad," Julian said. "That's not going to change."

"Okay." Charlie strained toward the water. "Let's go swimming."

Daisy turned to Julian. "That went well."

"Did it?" He wasn't so sure.

"Come on!" yelled Charlie.

"Come on, yourself," Julian said. He raced to the end of the dock and launched himself off the end, limbs flailing to make as big a splash as possible. The water was cold but exhilarating. He dove deep, his chest brushing the gritty bottom of the lake. He surfaced to find Daisy standing at the end of the dock, holding Charlie's hand.

Charlie was wearing a tiny flotation vest. Daisy peeled off her Yankees jersey to reveal a bikini that made Julian glad the water was so cold, taming his involuntary reaction.

"I'm gonna jump," Charlie yelled.

"Ready, set, jump," said Daisy.

Charlie snatched his hand away. "I'm scared."

"I'll hold your hand, and we can jump together," Daisy said. "And Julian will catch you."

Julian treaded water, holding up both hands, palms out. "I got you, buddy."

"No," the little boy reiterated. "You jump, Mom."

"You don't want to do it with me?"

"Scared."

"It's okay to be scared. Nobody's going to make you jump."

"But I *want* to."

She shook her head. "Then…"

"You jump," Charlie repeated.

"Fine. It's really easy and fun." Daisy jumped. Julian could hear her gasping for breath as she hit the water. She surfaced, laughing. "Come on in, Charlie! I'll catch you."

"No," he said, dancing from foot to foot. "Julian."

"Whenever you're ready, my buddy." Julian observed the war between longing and apprehension in Charlie's face.

Charlie turned away. "Don't want to jump today," he said.

"That's cool. Maybe another day," Julian said.

Daisy glided to the ladder and climbed out.

If there was something sexier than Daisy Bellamy in a pink flowered bikini, dripping wet with slicked back hair, Julian couldn't imagine what that might be. Her toenails were painted the color of seashells. She was wearing little gold earrings, two in one ear, one in the other.

"Did you say something?" she asked, grabbing a towel.

He hoisted himself out of the water. "That," he said, "was a moan of pure frustration."

"Yeah?"

He put his arm around her as they walked, letting his hand trail down her goose-bumped skin to her butt. "Really."

"I want to jump off the dock," Charlie said.

Julian forced himself to see the humor in the situation. "I thought you'd changed your mind. Are you saying you want to try again?"

"Okay."

"You want to jump with me or do you want me to go first?"

"With you."

"Cool, let's do it." Julian had never understood fear of physical danger. It simply wasn't part of his makeup. The things he tended to fear were hard to pinpoint and far less rational.

Charlie went with him right to the very end of the dock. He stopped there, his toes curled over the weathered plank on the very end. "Ready, Daddy-boy?" he asked.

"Ready, Charlie boy," Julian replied. "We have lift-off. On three."

The kid bent his knees and swung his arms back and forth, screwing up his face in anticipation of impact.

"One…two…no!" Charlie turned and ran to his mother, and his face crumpled.

Daisy sent Julian an apologetic look. "Maybe next time," she said.

"Sure. Maybe."

Charlie stared at the dock. He nudged a weathered plank with his toe.

"Don't worry about it." A bit awkwardly, Julian patted the boy's head. "I taught my cousin Remy how to jump in the water, back when we were kids," he said. "Remy is the same age as me, but he didn't like jumping," Julian explained.

"I like to jump," Charlie protested. He wandered away to play in the shallows.

Julian and Daisy glanced at each other. "Not exactly

a conventional way to spend the day we got engaged," she said.

He slid his arms around her. "Sweetheart, if I could, I'd sweep you away to a five-star hotel and make love to you all night long."

A shiver of pleasure rippled down her spine. "And if *I* could, I'd let you."

Charlie gave a shout, splashing among the reeds and coating himself with mud. "Lookit, a frog! I caught a frog!" The small creature leapt from between his cupped hands, back into the reeds, and he laughed and went after it.

"Are you sure you're up for this?" Daisy asked Julian.

"I've never been more sure of anything." He gave her a kiss, broke away and joined Charlie on the frog hunt.

Eight

Daisy's news surprised no one. She hadn't been expecting that. She thought the whole world believed she would eventually settle down with Logan. They'd made Charlie together, after all. Logan had moved to Avalon for the sake of their son and had started a business here despite his family's objections. They both worked hard to be good parents. She figured people anticipated that they'd get together one day.

She couldn't have been more wrong about her friends' and family's assumptions.

"It's wonderful," said her mother, hugging her close. "I'm so happy for you."

Even her brother, Max, a high school jock and no fan of hugging, gave her a hug. "That's awesome," he said. Then, in typical practical male fashion, he thought of logistics. "Not to slip a turd in your punch bowl or anything, but how's that going to work, with him being in the air force and all?"

She winced at his turn of phrase, but he did bring up a good point. "We have a lot to figure out." After the lake, she and Julian had gone to her house, where they'd talked long into the night, dreaming, fantasizing, planning and hoping. She'd yearned for him to stay, but for Charlie's sake, they reluctantly parted ways, and Julian went to stay at his brother's.

"We considered eloping—Mom, I said *considered,*" she quickly explained before her mother had a fit. There were compelling reasons to marry before deployment, Julian had pointed out. He'd enumerated the benefits—increased basic housing allowance and family separation pay, and survivor's benefits if he was killed.

The moment he'd mentioned that, she'd shut him down. "Don't you dare," she'd whispered, clinging to him. "Don't even go there." To her mother, she said, "We both want a small, traditional wedding."

"Have you set a date?" her mother asked.

"First Saturday in October. He can get a one-week furlough from his mission. We want to get married at Camp Kioga. I hope you don't mind."

"Mind? I was married there myself, once upon a time."

"Yeah, but that didn't work out so well for you and Dad, did it?"

"Immaterial," her mother said. "It's a beautiful place, so special to all the Bellamys."

"Thanks for understanding. I want a cake from Sky River Bakery and Julian wants Cajun food. Do you think that will be a problem?"

"Sucking the heads off crawdads?" She shrugged. "We'll deal. What about flowers?"

"Julian says daisies. I have no preference."

Truth be told, all she cared about was marrying him. "Mom, I never dreamed I'd be sitting here with you, planning my wedding. It just didn't seem like something that would happen to me."

"Oh, baby. You're still so young. All of life is in front of you."

Daisy felt a welling of emotion. "Thanks, Mom."

"I'm glad you're waiting until fall. You'll need the time to—" She stopped, her gaze shifting away.

"What?" asked Daisy.

"Let's enjoy your news, that's what. We can talk about details later."

She knew exactly what details her mother meant.

Daisy sailed through each day, spreading the news like fairy dust wherever she went. "I'm being totally obnoxious," she told her stepsister, Sonnet, during one of their marathon phone conversations. "I can't help myself. It's a wonder people don't run the other way when they see me coming."

"Everybody's happy for you," Sonnet assured her. "They've all wanted this for you for a long time."

"As many brides as I've photographed, I never quite understood why they seemed…I don't know. Apart, like they live in a special world you can only inhabit when you're a bride. Now I get it. I'm a basket case, in the best possible way, walking around with this teary lump of joy in my chest."

"Enjoy every minute of it, okay? Where's Prince Charming now?"

"With Charlie. They're having some man-time together, no girls allowed. God. I can't stand the thought of him leaving. I'm going to miss him so much."

"You'll stay busy getting ready for the wedding."

"I feel so clueless. Working in the industry, I thought I had it all figured out. It's kind of overwhelming."

"Weddings are supposed to be, at least that's what I've heard."

Daisy hung up with a goofy smile on her face. She felt lucky to have such great friends and family. She picked up Julian's framed service portrait, which she kept on her bedside table. Technically, the photo was only workmanlike, even cookie-cutter. Yet in his dress uniform, beside the flag, he looked so proud and handsome it brought tears to her eyes.

"What a life we're going to have," she said, knowing she'd have many imaginary conversations with him in the months to come. "You're a one-man adventure, that's for sure."

"Mom! Mom!" Charlie's voice shrilled from the back door. "Come see what we did."

Oh boy, she thought, hurrying downstairs. She found them in the kitchen, their faces alight with joy. It was a joy she shared…until her gaze fell on the small, scruffy brown creature standing between them, stubby tail wagging furiously.

"Blake!" Charlie exclaimed. "Her name's Blake! We can keep her if she does real good."

"I explained to Charlie we've only got her out on trial," Julian said quickly.

"On trial." She felt torn between exasperation and gratitude. Sure, she'd been wanting to get a dog for a while, but not like this. She didn't want Julian to bribe his way into the little boy's heart.

"That means we gotta give her back if it's not a good match," Charlie explained soberly. He sank down and sat back on his heels, gently petting the little terrier's head. She gazed up at him with worshipful eyes.

"You couldn't have checked with me first?" she asked Julian, trying not to melt at the sight of her little boy and the adoring dog.

"We wanted to surprise you."

"Manipulate me, you mean," she said.

"But in a good way," he said, grabbing her around the waist and giving her a quick, hard kiss. "She belonged to a serviceman who couldn't keep her after he got back from a deployment."

"Blake needs us," Charlie said.

"We'll see."

"Yes." Charlie held up a hand in a victory salute.

"I said we'll see."

"That's what moms always say when they don't want to say yes right off the bat," Julian explained.

"Hey," said Daisy.

"I love her," Charlie said, draping his arms around the dog. "I can't help it. I do."

Daisy got down on the floor and smoothed her hand over the terrier's warm, bony head. Her rough brown coat felt substantial, a coarse counterpart to the doe-soft eyes. "Dogs have a way of doing that to people," she said.

"The dog's in the bed with him," she said to Julian that night.

"Is she keeping him awake?"

"No, just the opposite. He fell asleep faster than ever." She'd been completely charmed by the sight of Charlie and Blake, relaxed and cozy, curled together like the yin and the yang.

"That's a good thing, then," he said.

"I still say you should have talked to me about it first."

"You would've said to go for it." He drew her down next to him on the sofa. "If I thought it was going to be a problem, I wouldn't have brought the little rascal home."

"It was incredibly sweet. Thank you." She settled into his shoulder, feeling a wave of contentment. If they spent every evening like this for the rest of their lives, she'd have nothing to complain about.

"You're keeping her," Julian said.

He almost never asked questions. She hadn't noticed that about him before. "Tell me about Blake's former owner."

"I did—a guy who was in the service."

"Details, Lieutenant. He came back from deployment and what? Why can't he take care of his dog anymore? Did he get hurt?"

"I don't know him personally. Didi Romano, down at the Humane Society, said he was going through some personal problems after he got back. Taking care of a dog was too much for him."

She sensed he was evading her. "Too much? I don't understand."

Julian drew her closer, pressed his lips to her forehead. "He came back with PTSD. Tried to take his own life."

A chill slid through her, despite the warmth of his embrace. "Oh, God."

"There's a lot of support for military personnel with mental health issues. That hasn't always been the case, but it is now. He gave up the dog for good, though."

She turned in his arms and took his face between her hands. "Promise me," she said, her voice harsh with intensity, "promise me you're going to be all right, no matter what you see or do, no matter what happens to you."

"Babe. I promise."

He should have been a politician. He had the voice, the sincerity. She had more faith in him than she did in the rising sun. "I just love you so much," she whispered against his mouth, but the words weren't nearly enough. With a soft sigh, she leaned back, peeling her shirt up over her head. She needed to show him. To feel him, at last, all barriers down. His hands spanned her waist, pulling her down again as he kissed her. Finally, she thought, half dizzy with joy and desire. *Finally.*

"This couch isn't big enough for the two of us," he murmured against her mouth, as if reading her thoughts. They made their way to the bedroom, closing the door quietly but firmly.

After all the times she had imagined making love to

him, she should have been prepared for the breathless pleasure of being free to touch him, to love him with every part of her. She wasn't, though. Every moment exploded with surprise and delight. Her hands made discoveries that left her light-headed with wonder, and her heart was caught up in the joy of being, at long last, in a place she had only ever truly dreamed about. His muscles, honed by the best military training in the world, felt rock hard but alive with warmth beneath his smooth velvet skin. She loved that he seemed so strong and tender at the same time. But more compelling than the feel of him under her hands was the way he touched her, with an intensity that hovered somewhere between eroticism and reverence.

For the first time in her life, she understood the power of a loving touch. When he reached for her, his hands shook, yet he showed no hesitation as he explored, bringing to life sensations and emotions so powerful she was almost afraid. Almost, but not quite.

He pinned her hands up above her head, making her vulnerable to him, and it was thrilling because she felt nothing but blind trust. She let herself be lost in him, drowning in feeling, nearly weeping from the shattering sweetness that crested through her, leaving her weak and mindless with happiness.

It was raining the next day when Julian left. He had further training and briefing at a facility in Georgia, and from there, he would travel to Colombia to take up his duties, which he was forbidden to talk about. Daisy took Charlie and Blake to Logan's house. Logan was clearly not pleased about the dog, but he held his tongue, for which she was grateful.

Julian was already at the train station, waiting to say goodbye. She approached him quietly. Last night, everything had been said between them, though she didn't recall many words exchanged, only touch. They'd made love for hours, kissing and holding each other with a tender desperation that filled every cell of her body. Now all that was left was to say goodbye.

She sat with him on a bench under an awning. The rain battered down, creating a curtain of mist between them and the outside world. Cars trolled sluggishly through town, some turning into the parking lot, splashing through puddles as they went. A few pedestrians huddled under umbrellas or hurried along, hunched into hooded raincoats.

She clung to both of his hands. He had big hands, filled with strength, but they were infinitely gentle as they cradled hers. The engagement ring glinted on her finger, a tiny sparkle of light in the gloom. She felt strangely fragile, and sweetly sore in places that reminded her of last night.

"You look incredible," she told him, eyeing the uniform. "An officer and a gentleman."

He smiled, brushed a wisp of hair from her forehead and kissed her brow. "Right, that's me."

"I'm going to miss you so much," she said for the hundredth time. "We should be used to this, right? We've been apart before. But I've never been this scared."

"Don't be." His hands closed around hers. "This isn't supposed to be scary."

She swallowed a lump in her throat. "I don't understand how it's possible to be so happy and afraid at the same time."

"Focus on the happy part."

She nodded. "Next time we see each other, we'll be getting ready for our wedding. I can't believe it's happening. Our *wedding*." She leaned against his shoulder, inhaled his warm, familiar scent. Oh, she wanted more time with him. More time to savor all the little things she loved about him—the way his eyes shone when he looked at her, the lightning quick smile that lit his face at the slightest provocation. His enormous appetite, the sound of his laughter, the way he tended to whistle tunelessly through his teeth when he was concentrating on something.

He checked his watch, craned his neck to view the tracks coming into the station. He seemed almost impatient.

He'd been meticulous, almost chilling in his attention to the details of leaving. He'd drafted a will, joking that his beater car and collection of books weren't even worth the filing fee. He'd stored his stuff at his brother's, written private letters she prayed she'd never read, canceled his phone service.

Taking in a long breath, she mustered a smile, letting her heart show in her eyes. She didn't want to lose herself in tears and fears. In preparation for his departure, she'd studied all the literature she could find on being in love with a military man. It was uncanny, how spot-on the articles were. Over the past few days, Julian seemed to go away in his head sometimes, creating a subtle sense of detachment. It was normal, she reminded herself. And it was also normal for her to be filled with such an intense emotional need for him that she could barely concentrate on anything else.

Be here now, she reminded herself. Be here in this moment.

She fought the part of her that wanted to claw at him, beg him not to go. One of the things she'd gleaned from the military spouses she'd already met was a peculiar dignity that was somehow more piercing than tears and hysterics.

A train whistle sounded. Julian looked at his watch again. "I'd better get up to the platform," he said.

Daisy's heart beat fast as she walked with him under the awning, then up the stairs to the platform. After all the waiting, the slow, agonizing seconds leading to this moment, everything had sped up.

She could only focus on Julian. He set down his duffel and took her in his arms, kissed her for a long time. Their last kiss for five months, she thought. How could she make this seem different, more special, more memorable? How could she turn this into something that would sustain her the whole time he was gone?

"Take care," he whispered against her mouth. "Promise me."

"I promise," she echoed. "I'll think of you every minute."

"Be sure you think about how much I love you. I tried to show you last night. It's only the beginning."

She cried but managed to keep from sobbing herself into a pool of despair. Her heart was breaking, but she dug deep and unearthed a certain quiet stoicism she never knew she possessed.

They separated, stepping away from each other, hands clinging, then fingers, then nothing but air between them. He picked up his bag and headed for the train, melting into the small cluster of people who were boarding.

She felt empty, like someone who had just been assaulted, as if some violence had been done to her. Why hadn't they held each other longer, shared one more kiss?

As the train pulled out of the station, he appeared in the opening between two cars. Over the clash and hiss of the train, he yelled, "Daisy, I love you!"

"Yo, Daisy," yelled another passenger nearby, "he loves you!"

"He loves you, Daisy," called yet another unseen stranger, and several more joined in the refrain.

She laughed through her tears and called back, "Julian, I love you!" By then he probably couldn't hear; the train whistle shrilled, drowning her voice.

"Oh," said Sonnet. "No no no no no." Daisy's stepsister bustled into the house and walked in a circle around Daisy, who was getting ready for her first meeting of the ROTC friends and family group.

One thing about the military, Daisy had quickly learned, was that there was a support group for everything. She was getting ready to attend a meeting of people who were dealing with the issues of having a loved one in the service. Members of the ROTC tended to get engaged and married this time of year, so groups were mobilizing.

Sonnet, whose natural father had made a long and successful career in the military, was pretty familiar with the subculture. Daisy had asked her to come over and help her get ready.

"What do you mean, no?" Daisy asked, holding her hands out to her sides. "Something wrong with my outfit?"

"You look like Jackie Kennedy," Sonnet said with a toss of her corkscrew curls.

"And that's a bad thing?" Daisy smoothed her hand down the pencil skirt.

"Not if you want to look like a stewardess." Sonnet grabbed her hand and led the way to the bedroom, pausing to peek at Charlie, who was napping peacefully in a bed shaped like a dinosaur. Sonnet was going to babysit him while Daisy went to the meeting.

"Maybe I shouldn't go," Daisy said.

"You're going. You need to get used to doing stuff like this, meeting other fiancées and spouses. Being in the service demands so much from everybody. The women you meet in these groups are going to be your lifeline sometimes, you mark my words."

"Then they won't care what I've got on, right?"

"You need to look like you," Sonnet said, trolling through the closet. "What's with all the black and beige?"

"Work clothes," said Daisy. "I have to wear stuff that helps me fade into the background when I'm photographing. And I always need lots of pockets."

"Today is not a workday. You need something that looks like you. Not you trying to look like someone else." She took out a dress with a ruffled neckline, then put it back. "Cute, but too fussy." The next couple were "boring," and others were "loud." Daisy was starting to get a complex and was a little worried she would run out of clothing.

"Aha," Sonnet said, snatching a dress and holding it under Daisy's chin. "I think this is it, and in your signature color, too."

"I have a signature color?"

"Yellow. It's dynamite on you."

"Aw. Sonnet, that's so nice of you."

"We don't have time for nice. Put this on. I'll find you shoes and a bag."

Ten minutes later, Daisy felt a surge of confidence as she checked herself out in the mirror. "I don't know what I'd do without you."

"You don't have to do without me. That's what sisters are for."

Daisy grinned at their images in the mirror. "Do you think we look like sisters?"

Sonnet was Italian and African-American to Daisy's blond hair and pale skin. "A matched set. Look at us. When we were back in high school, and our parents were just getting together, I never pictured our future. It seemed like bad luck to do that."

In college, Sonnet had spent most of her time studying abroad. She'd done prestigious internships at NATO and SHAPE. Soon, she'd be working at the United Nations for UNESCO. She was the smartest, most ambitious person Daisy knew.

"I have something to ask you," she said.

"You want to borrow my Kate Spade bag?" Sonnet asked. "It might look great with that outfit."

"No, nothing like that. I wanted to know if you'd be my maid of honor. In the wedding."

Sonnet took a step back. "Seriously?"

"Of course, seriously. Don't act so surprised."

"Okay, but you have, like, this whole flock of girl cousins, so I figured you'd pick one of them—"

"I want you. You're the best friend I've ever had, and you're Charlie's aunt, and it would mean so much if you would do it."

"Of course I'll do it," Sonnet said.

A thrill rippled through Daisy, the way it did every time she thought about Julian and the upcoming wedding. She couldn't keep the grin from her face. It was almost embarrassing, how happy she was. She gave Sonnet a hug and said, "I'm so excited, it's ridiculous."

"That makes two of us. But right now, you have to get through this meeting. I can't believe you're going to be an air force wife."

"I can't believe I'm going to be any kind of wife at all," Daisy said. "I miss him so much already, Sonnet. Maybe someone at this meeting will tell me how to deal with missing him."

"How can you not miss the love of your life?"

"Julian and I have had a lot of practice being apart. I thought I was prepared for being separated from him now, but it's different, somehow. Now that we're engaged, everything just…I don't know, *matters* so much." She looked around the house she'd made into a home. One day soon, she would be making a home somewhere with Julian. She didn't know where, didn't know his likes and dislikes. There was so much to discover, but when would they ever have time?

"Sonnet, am I signing on to have an absentee husband?"

"It's only temporary. His service commitment is four years, right? That's how long it takes to become a doctor."

"There's a huge flaw in your logic, but I get what you're saying." She checked herself one more time in the hall mirror. "It's the weirdest thing, almost magical. We've managed to fall in love and stay that way while never even living in the same town. He knows me in ways no one else does even though…some things are still… mysterious. In a good way," she added quickly.

Sonnet shooed her out the door. "Charlie and I will be fine," she said. "Don't even think about coming home before dinner."

The people at the meeting were mostly female, mostly young. All shapes and sizes, all races. The one thing they had in common was that everyone had recently married or was about to marry an officer. A good many of the attendees came from a military background, and they tended to speak in code, rattling off acronyms for every possible eventuality—would she be in the OWC or the EWC? When can you expect the CACO at your ADU?—until Daisy felt her eyes glaze over. She forced herself to listen attentively and make notes.

During the question-and-answer period, the questions ran the gamut, from how the on-base housing system worked to establishing a career of one's own while following the spouse all over the globe.

Daisy felt lucky in this respect. Her camera made for a portable career. After she and Julian married, she would be a freelancer. The prospect was a bit daunting after the relative stability of Wendela's Wedding Wonders. She thought about the empty in-box tray at home, sitting on her worktable in silent accusation. She really did need to get to work on her submission to the MoMA competition. Earning a spot in the exhibition was a long shot, a risky one, but everything worth having was risky.

She was drifting, her thoughts wandering to some idyllic place, when one of the spouses—a guy—raised his hand. "Rudy McBean," he said. "My wife's a second lieutenant in the army, and she was deployed last week to Afghanistan." He looked around the now-silent room. "Sorry to bring this up," he said. "I know it's easier to talk about stuff like the difference between the base dispensary and the commissary, and who to call about banking and health care and so forth. Those are all important things, I'll allow that."

Murmurs of agreement drifted through the room.

He stared at the floor, steepled his fingers together. "What I need to know, what nobody's explained to me yet, is what you do with the worry. Every time I turn on the TV or open an internet browser, I'm bombarded with bad news about the war. How do I get through the day, knowing my wife is in the thick of the danger?"

His anguished query threw a pall of silence over the room. Daisy's lungs felt cold from holding her breath. Looking around at the others, she realized the guy had spoken for many of them, herself included. Julian was on a special mission he wasn't allowed to talk about, but there was one thing he didn't need to tell her—he was exposed to danger on a regular basis. She could not fool herself about that.

"That's why groups like this exist, and we're everywhere. You can always find someone to talk to. It helps to remind yourself that every single job in the world carries risks. Soldiers, sailors and airmen, sure. But also mailmen and bank clerks, and hell, runway models."

Daisy studied the woman speaking. She was more like a girl, with a name tag that read "Blythe." She looked even younger than Daisy.

The guy who had asked the question chuckled. "Somehow I think I'd worry less about the runway model getting maimed or killed."

"Choose not to focus on your worry," Blythe said. "Choose to focus on the joy."

"Easy to say," he pointed out. "But can anyone actually do that?"

She got quiet for a moment. Then she said, "I did."

No one moved. Her use of the past tense was very pointed. She said, "I was eighteen when I got married. Nineteen when Manny was killed. And it was like…it was like going to hell. The only thing that saved me was focusing on the love and joy we had, however brief. Now I'm in love again." Her face softened. "He's a pilot. Probably more at risk than your average mailman. But I love him, and that's what I'll focus on. Every day."

Daisy didn't want to believe her ears. She wanted to run from the room, and she suspected a lot of the others felt the same way. But this girl, younger than Daisy herself, was a cold blast of reality in all the idealistic talk.

"I wanted to bring your attention to these brochures here," said the hostess in desperation. "If you're interested in continuing your education, you have a lot of options…"

Somehow, equilibrium settled in again. Daisy helped herself to several pamphlets and brochures, and she sat listening politely to the conversation. Nearby, two women were trading comments. "She's right about the risk," one said. "The average person has a greater chance of being in a car accident than a combat soldier has of getting killed."

In her head, Daisy was already composing her next email to Julian. *Why didn't you tell me about the risk,* she would say in an ironic tone.

The fact that he had a risky job was completely consistent with the Julian she'd always known—the rock-climbing, bungee-jumping, adrenaline junkie determined to wring every drop of excitement out of every moment of life.

It was part of what made him Julian. It was part of what made her love him.

Nine

Near Puerto San Alberto, Colombia

Dangling from a rope several hundred feet above a river gorge, Julian spoke into his shoulder-mounted radio. "Just do it the way we did in training drills. Piece of cake." He looked over at Francisco Ramos, his Colombian counterpart. Ramos was on a rope several feet away. His face, spackled with camo paint, flickered with uncertainty, and his widened eyes clearly begged to differ.

There were a few hundred treacherous feet between them and their destination, a hidden drug operation. Julian and Ramos were charged with installing surveillance gear to monitor the activity. The unit had run through drills until they'd seen every detail in their sleep. Julian had practiced every possible move, from rappelling out of trees to simulate a helicopter exit to employing a new computer program designed to jam or decode signals.

"I don't like heights," Ramos said.

"You couldn't have said something before now?"

"It would not have mattered. I do as I'm told."

"We all do," Julian conceded. Ramos, who was in the Colombian Air Force, was as well-trained and dedicated as his U.S. counterparts. The success of the ops depended on it. "We'll be done before you know it. Let me check in."

"Talk to me, Angel," he prodded the COM specialist at the base of operations. "We're almost there." Angel de Soto was the glue of the procedure, and he seemed to hold more details in his head than a computer's hard drive. He was miles away at Palanquero Air Base, coordinating the efforts of the Americans and Colombians in the cooperative covert operation. The mission, planned for months, was about to be executed by a top secret team.

"The chopper is waiting," said Angel. "The other team finished. Install the gear and get your asses back to the chopper. Over."

"Gastineaux, out." Julian lowered himself with quick, assured movements. Through gaps in the trees, he could make out what amounted to an entire armed city surrounded by a towering forest of mahogany, cinchona and evergreens twined with exotic vines. He could only pray like hell the men on patrol wouldn't see him and Ramos as they installed the high-powered, weatherproof surveillance system. Suspended like a couple of spiders against the sheer rock face, they were at huge risk for being spotted. And when the enemy was armed with full-auto AK-47s, former Soviet RPGs, hand grenades and even some American light antitank weapons—you definitely didn't want to be spotted.

"Some view, eh?" he said to Ramos.

His partner flashed a nervous grin, revealing his signature gold front tooth. He'd once explained that his father insisted the dentist use gold rather than porcelain, to prove to the world he could afford dental work for his family.

Through his scope, Julian scanned the strategically located camp at the estuary of the river. With its busy docks and warehouses crammed with ordnance and bricks of cocaine, its airport and system of private roads, its private army and infrastructure, the drug lord's compound seemed to run like a machine. It was better financed than any government entity, thanks to investments from overseas terror organizations.

The ultimate goal was to take out the operation and with it, Don Benito Gamboa, one of the richest and most dangerous men in Colombia, lord of an empire of soldiers and criminals. If successful, the strike would result in the biggest drug seizure in history.

The mission coordinator had often lectured them—"We don't exist. We do our job and move on. You won't get any awards or recognition for your work here, even if you disrupt a year supply of drugs."

"Check it out," Julian murmured, lifting his binoculars. A rain-scented wind blew through the gorge, ruffling the jungle canopy. The lower river was spanned by a table bridge, one that could be moved by means of a motor. Previous intel had not revealed that, and it meant the chopper was vulnerable on the beach a few miles to the north. They had set it down not knowing armed vehicles could reach it. Nor had the earlier reconnaissance detected the formidable array of antiaircraft weaponry. Through his scope, Julian saw guns and antiaircraft weaponry, including a rolling airframe missile, which he'd never even seen up close before. The thing was capable of tracking and correcting its own course, literally chasing an aircraft through the sky.

He reported the new intel to Angel.

"A bridge?" De Soto demanded. "A fucking bridge? How did we miss that? Hell, never mind, hurry your asses up."

A whirring sound drew his attention to Ramos. Julian looked over to see his partner plummeting down the rock face. Something had unclipped and he was in free fall, his hands grappling with the rope.

No, thought Julian. Nononononono... This couldn't be happening.

Ramos had dropped into the thick foliage at the base of the rock. To his credit, he'd not made a sound. Only the ominous *whir* of the rope could be heard, inevitably followed by the crunch of impact. Both Julian and Ramos were packing forty pounds of gear.

Julian was already descending as he radioed to report the mishap. De Soto, always known for his sangfroid, was completely silent for several heartbeats. For Julian, that hesitation underscored what he knew—this was bad. Really bad.

"Get to him and get out," de Soto ordered. "I'll alert the chopper. Over."

"I'm on it, over." Julian pictured the chopper, which had previously been used for fire control, waiting outside the compound, far enough away to avoid detection.

"And don't get killed."

"Roger that."

He silenced the radio and lowered himself to the jungle floor. Ramos lay bleeding on the brushy ground. A branch had ripped through his arm. The blood was bright red, spurting with every pulse of his heart—this meant it came from an artery.

Bleeding was always worse than it appeared, Julian knew that. However, one glance at Ramos's ashen face, his glazed eyes struggling to stay open, told him the wound was bad.

"I got you, Francisco," Julian said. "I'm here."

"Tried to stop the bleeding," Ramos said in a thin voice. "Hand's too slippery..."

"Aguanta," said Julian. "Hang in there." He applied direct pressure to the wound, praying the blood loss was not as bad as it looked. The human body contained twelve pints of blood. A person could tolerate losing a pint. Two

pints would send him into shock. Three… Julian pressed harder on the wound. With his other hand he pressed above the elbow, where he'd been taught the brachial artery was located. The bleeding slowed but didn't stop.

He took a second to look around, reconnoiter. There was no way they could climb back up, not with Ramos bleeding like this.

"We're inside the compound," Julian muttered, spotting a towering chain-link fence topped with razor wire. "Nobody's spotted us. Might as well wait here."

"Just us and the jaguars," Ramos said.

Julian managed a rough field dressing, securing it with his belt. He didn't want to apply a tourniquet because that would probably cause his friend to lose the limb. He made Ramos drink as much water as he could stand. In the surrounding forest, Crayola-colored birds swooped and chittered. Julian used silent code to relay their situation to the base. A satellite GPS would guide them to the chopper. He only hoped the wire cutters were stout enough to take on the chain link.

"Tell me about your family," he said, checking the supply of water in the canteen.

"You're only asking me that to keep me conscious."

"Just talk. Pretend we're at that cantina in Calle Roja, drinking longneck bottles of Bahia beer pulled straight out of the bins of ice."

"I've already told you everything."

"Tell me again."

Ramos sighed. "My parents wanted me to marry up, eh? Find some girl from a wealthy family, who would bring me up in the world. They never understood, the heart doesn't work that way. You can't go and find someone. Your heart takes you there, *sí?*"

"Yes," said Julian, thinking of all the times through the

years when he'd tried to talk himself out of loving Daisy. "You're smarter than you look, amigo."

"Rosalinda's family wanted the same for her. A rich boy, someone with prospects."

"You've got prospects," Julian pointed out.

"I have a beautiful wife and a home in Puerto Salgar. All I ever wanted was to run a river-fishing operation, a fine occupation in the outdoors, no? Something that would allow me to come home to my family each night. I thought serving in the air force would accelerate my dreams, eh? But Rosalinda, she is running out of patience. She has no idea what I'm doing, but she knows it's a risk."

Julian swallowed past a knot of guilt in his throat. There was the cover…and then there was the truth. The truth was, the team was so deeply secret, he wasn't even sure anyone but the top level Colombian hosts knew its true purpose. He wasn't even sure *he* knew its purpose.

"Look," he said, "you're doing this for your country and your family. If that's not worth taking a risk for, I don't know what is. You might even earn a special commendation after this."

"Not if I get discharged."

"For that?" Julian indicated the arm, hoping the bleeding had stopped. "A scratch. You'll heal."

"But perhaps not from this." Reaching down with his good hand, Ramos indicated his leg, above where the trouser was tucked into his boot. The angle was all wrong.

"Shit." Julian's stomach curdled at the sight of bone pressing against fabric. "Why didn't you say anything?"

"There is nothing to be done." Ramos was apologetic. "You're not equipped to dress a compound fracture. I cannot move or be moved."

"What the hell are we going to do then?" Julian demanded.

"I am considering my options."

Julian didn't like the tone of that. He radioed the base, and a medic explained what had to be done.

"Give him plenty of morphine," the medic advised, the digital message flowing across the tiny screen.

"Right, like I have that," Julian muttered in English. He looked at Ramos. "I'm going to immobilize the leg."

"Don't be an idiot. I'll scream like a coyote, and they'll shoot us both."

"You're not going to make a sound." Julian grabbed a thick length of webbing from the pack and handed it over. "Think of Rosalinda. Think of your two little kids. You've said it a thousand times, you would do anything for them. Anything."

With a shaking hand, Ramos took the webbing and clamped it between his teeth. Julian had nothing to use for disinfectant, so he emptied the canteen on the wound. Ramos made a hissing sound but held still.

"I'll be quick," Julian said. *"Aguanta."* As he applied a makeshift splint of wood, Ramos breathed fast and hard, and tears streamed down his face. Julian forced himself to keep going, wrapping the climbing rope to secure the splint. His friend Sayers would approve of his field dressing. "Maybe you'll pass out," he said. "Maybe that wouldn't be such a bad thing."

Ramos didn't pass out. He didn't make a sound. To Julian, it felt as if he was taking an eternity, but at last, he had a crude splint roped around the leg.

"I cannot walk," Ramos said.

"I'll carry you."

"Now you're really being an idiot."

"You'd do the same for me."

"Then we're both idiots. That is why we were chosen for this mission, eh?" With his good arm, Ramos swiped his brow. "Now there is nothing to do but wait until dark. Let me rest. I promise not to die."

Julian nodded. Falling asleep was probably not the best option for a guy in Ramos's state of shock, but it was a way to escape the pain. Julian tended to escape inside his head to cope with things. So much of an operation demanded nothing more than patience. In fact, mental techniques for times like this had been part of his training. As always, his mind went to Daisy. One day, when they were old and sitting on their rocking chairs on a porch somewhere, he would tell her everything. Until then, however, he was sworn to secrecy.

Email, online chatting and Skype calls were forbidden. In his letters home, he wrote about the weather and the landscape and life at the air base. Like the rest of the world, she believed it was a routine cooperative training venture with the Colombian Air Force.

Ramos awakened with a soft moan. Julian could only imagine the pain the guy was in. "How you doing?" he asked.

"Just peachy," Ramos said in English; he liked using the occasional phrase he heard from his training buddies. He waved a hand toward the fence. "It's nearly dark. Get over there and cut through the fence." His voice sounded weary and slurred by pain. Someone—a guard, probably—patrolled with a flashlight. They could see the light moving inexorably toward them. Spurred by a sense of urgency, Julian went to work.

The wire cutters were barely adequate against the stout fence. Every cut was a battle. He managed to pry an opening wide enough to crawl through. With Ramos's bad arm and useless leg, it was going to be a challenge. He'd need more space to get through. The flashlight beam swung across the area. Cussing under his breath, Julian went back to work. After another eternity, he returned to Ramos.

"Okay, amigo. Time to—" He broke off. Ramos was

gone. The progress of the guard with a flashlight had stopped. Beneath the damp, secret rustling of the jungle, Julian could hear crackling radios and guys talking. He crept forward to see Ramos lying in the glare of the flashlight.

Four armed men pointed their AK-47s at Ramos.

"No dispare," Ramos yelled, his voice hoarse with pain and desperation. *"Por favor, no dispare."* Don't shoot. *"Me rindo."* He said this several times in succession. *"Me rindo."* I surrender. He started to babble, asking for mercy and offering his cooperation.

Julian knew Ramos would never put the team in jeopardy. Moreover, he surely knew there was no way the two of them could make it safely away. Francisco had sacrificed himself, stalling for time, no doubt hoping Julian would disappear before the armed patrol went looking for him. He weighed his incredibly shitty options. He could surrender alongside Ramos and hope they wouldn't both be executed. He could come out shooting, one guy against four submachine guns. Or he could make a run for it. He had about three seconds to decide.

He grabbed his gear and dove through the hole in the fence. Darkness closed around him, and he had to rely on his GPS. Judging by the length of time he'd been running uphill, he was a mile away from the compound. Still running, he radioed the base.

"Just get to the chopper," de Soto ordered. "Just get there."

He headed west, knowing the team waited near the beach. Though it was too dark to see, he could hear the chopper. His beacon indicated he was only a couple hundred meters away.

His relief was short-lived. Someone else had found the bird, too. Thanks to the bridge, four Humvees and a couple of Blazers with guns mounted on the back were speeding along the beach. The chopper's blades whirled, gathering momentum. Julian raced ahead of the armed trucks. He kept his head down as he darted in and out of the vehicles' headlamps. A hail of small arms fire chased him, plowing up the grainy sand. He felt the wind of the chopper blades, flinging more sand against his goggles and stinging his face.

He piled into the chopper.

"Ramos?" asked Sergio.

"Not coming," Julian yelled.

The chopper lifted as the last boot left the ground. The firing continued, riddling the hull, but they were away, the bird sweeping up and out over the water. Except for Ramos, the team was intact—Rusty and Doc, Truesdale, Simon and José, and a few more guys he'd trained with from the Colombian militia. They'd have to come back undercover for Ramos.

The airframe vibrated and shuddered, oil spurting from somewhere. Julian heard a larger noise, a hollow thump so deep it reverberated in the belly—a rocket?

Then he saw it, a slender deadly rod crowned by a teardrop-shaped warhead, lying on the deck. "Grenade!" he yelled, grabbing the thing. His mind shut down, his conscious will receded. He simply acted. In a single swift movement, he scooped up the RPG and lunged for the hatch, hurling it out of the chopper.

The thing detonated in midair. The explosion rocked the bird like a child's toy. At the edge of the hatch, Julian lost his grip. He was flung like a stone from a sling. Beneath him, he felt nothing but sky.

Ten

Daisy gazed at herself in the mirror of the bridal salon. "This is it, then," she said, looking at her mother and then at Sonnet. They had both accompanied her to the final dress fitting. "This is the dress I'm getting married in."

Sonnet's eyes shone as she admired the gown. "You look amazing."

Daisy turned to study her reflection again. The dress she'd chosen was a froth of ivory tulle and antique lace, the sort she'd always secretly dreamed of wearing.

"It's lovely," said her mother. "Sweetheart, you're the prettiest bride I've ever seen."

"Spoken like a true mom." For a moment, she turned thoughtful, picturing her mother getting ready for her own wedding, long ago, to Daisy's father, Greg Bellamy. Sophie had been even younger than Daisy was now. She'd worn a designer gown, which she still had in storage. A few months ago, she'd offered it to Daisy. The gown was still beautiful and it fit, but it hadn't felt quite right. Daisy had not wanted to wear a dress from a marriage that hadn't worked out. Her mother understood completely. Instead, she'd urged Daisy to find her own perfect dress.

Yolanda Martinez, the shop owner, had done the alterations herself. The crystal beaded bodice hugged the torso, sweeping up to a glittering sweetheart neckline. Now Daisy turned to her. "The fit is perfect. I don't know how you do it."

Yolanda stood back, fluffing the skirt. "You chose well. And you didn't do that foolish bride thing of going on a crash diet at the last minute and getting too skinny. I'm glad you like the alterations."

A lot of the brides Daisy had photographed had bought their dresses here. Yolanda had a keen eye for fashion. She was a petite, industrious Latina woman who had opened the bridal shop in Avalon a couple of years before. She'd moved up from Texas so her son could be near his father, Bo Crutcher, who pitched for the Yankees. A single mother like Daisy, Yolanda was hardworking and determined to make good choices for her son. Daisy recognized a deep loneliness in Yolanda, though, because she used to feel that way too, all the time. The late nights, working alone, the determined cheerfulness and putting on a brave face—these were all too familiar to Daisy. She was incredibly grateful her life was about to change.

"Are you going to invite a doctor to the wedding?" Sonnet asked, eyeing her from head to toe.

"My stepfather's a vet. Why do you ask?"

"Because Julian's going to die when he sees you in this. He will absolutely die, so I figure he'll need CPR."

"Yeah? You think he'll like it?"

"He's so smitten with you that you could probably wear a gunnysack. But this dress…it's going to knock him flat. Julian's going to die when he sees you, completely die," Sonnet repeated.

Daisy smiled, closed her eyes and pictured Julian waiting at the altar, with his perfect military posture and that expression in his eyes…. There was nothing so handsome as an officer in full dress uniform on his wedding day. Sometimes when she thought of the upcoming day, she got dizzy. "He might not be the only one who'll keel over from happiness."

"Nobody's gonna die," Yolanda said. "And speaking of Julian, I have something to give you from him." She crowned Daisy with a veil held by silver combs. The gossamer lace fluttered with ghostly lightness over her shoulders. "Your *novio* paid me a visit before he left. He wanted to surprise you."

Daisy's heart melted. "I can't believe he did this."

"He is becoming one of my favorite grooms. You must be proud that he is so fluent in Spanish."

"That's so sweet of him," said Daisy's mom.

Daisy touched the edges of the veil. "I never thought about wearing one of these."

"Do you like it?" her mother asked.

"Most brides wear a veil, don't they?" Daisy mused.

"Is this how you want to look on your wedding day?" Sonnet asked.

"What do you think, Mom?" asked Daisy. She noticed her mother's stricken face in the mirror. "*Mom.* Not again."

"Sorry," said Sophie, dabbing at her eyes. "I'm having a moment." She stood behind Daisy and smoothed down the veil. "You look so lovely, I can't even stand it."

"Mom," said Daisy. "Don't start with the crying, or we'll never get done with this fitting."

"Speak for yourself," Sonnet said, her voice thick with emotion. "We're so happy for you, Daisy."

In spite of herself, Daisy felt the thick heat of tears gathering in her throat. She was so lucky to have people in her life who wanted nothing more than to see her happy. "I never thought I'd get to be the bride, you know. I figured I'd missed the bride boat. But now here I am, and

I can't believe this is all happening to me. I'm so happy, sometimes I'm almost scared."

"It's too late to change your mind now," Sophie said. "The dress is picked out, and the alterations are done. Oh, and it's paid for."

"Really? Mom—"

"I want to, okay?"

"Totally okay. Thank you." Her heart sped up; as the wedding day approached, things seemed more and more real. The plans were well under way. There would be a ceremony and reception at Camp Kioga, the place where their love had begun. All in all, it was a relentlessly traditional plan, but for some reason, Daisy found herself clinging to convention. She wanted to honor the occasion in every possible way—a lakeside ceremony, the solemn gathering of family and friends, the cake from Sky River Bakery, the toasts—all of them. For some reason, sticking to the tried and true seemed to add weight to the occasion.

"I'll be right back," Yolanda said. "I need to find the right garment bag for that dress." She headed through a curtained doorway.

Daisy raised herself up on tiptoe to gauge the heel height of her shoes. She lifted the hair off the back of her neck to simulate an updo. She looked at Sonnet and then her mother, and she was filled with a feeling of buoyant possibility.

I cannot wait, Julian, she silently exulted. I cannot wait to be your wife.

Through the shop window, she could see the occasional passerby pause to peek inside. People—even perfect strangers—always wanted to catch a glimpse of a bride. In the course of her work, she'd observed this over the years. It was rare, like seeing a shooting star or a four leaf clover. It made people feel lucky, privileged.

She spotted a familiar face outside and waved. "There's

Olivia," she said, motioning her cousin to come inside. "And Connor."

The two of them entered the shop and hurried toward Daisy.

"Hey there, future brother-in-law," she said to Connor. "I assume you know you're sworn to secrecy. This is the most top secret dress ever made, get it?"

"Daisy, listen." Olivia's voice wavered with a curious intensity Daisy didn't recognize. "We thought we'd find you here. I called Logan."

"Did something happen to Charlie?" Daisy asked.

"No," Olivia said quickly, "nothing like that." She looked so solemn, her eyes red and damp. This dress must really be something.

"Logan said we'd find you here." Olivia's knuckles were white as she gripped her handbag.

So far, Logan was being pretty great about everything, keeping Charlie when Daisy had things like dress fittings and cake tastings. Now, seeing her cousin's face, she said, "I'm sorry I didn't call you for the final fitting. I thought you'd be busy."

"Daisy." Connor cleared his throat. He was emotional, too, which touched her heart. She was going to love being his sister-in-law.

"You like?" she asked, twirling on tiptoe. "You think Julian will like it?"

"Daisy." Her mother's voice, low and taut, brought her up short. And then her mom stepped up beside her on the dais in front of the multifaceted mirror and put her arms around Daisy. The physical sensation of her mother's embrace enveloped her.

No. Daisy's mind seized on the thought. She didn't have any idea what she was saying no to, but the denial blasted through her, as powerful and irrational as a sudden storm. *No.*

"What is going on?" her mom asked Connor, still holding on.

More tears welled in his eyes. "You should sit, Daisy."

And that was when she knew. There was a strange, detached moment when she observed herself as if from a distance, as though this were happening to someone else. Stepping back from her mom's arms, she stood apart on the dais, still in view of the mirror.

She saw her mother with a look in her eyes Daisy had never seen before. And Sonnet, sinking to the floor and drawing her knees up to her chest, shaking her head in vigorous, futile denial.

Daisy saw herself, resplendent in the gorgeous gown, at least six of her in the multi-paneled mirror. The bride, who had looked so flushed and pretty a moment ago, was now a complete stranger, white-faced, eyes haunted by a horror she could not escape. Which Daisy was the real one? They were all doing the same thing—hand to heart, mouth open in a silent cry of anguish so deep it didn't even have a voice.

Eleven

Numbness enveloped Daisy like the gauzy layers of a cocoon. She could feel her family and friends swirling around her, treating her like the victim of a terrible accident. Her mother took her home, and Daisy asked for some time alone. She sobbed until she was sick, her stomach sore as if she'd done a thousand sit-ups. She placed a cold washcloth over her swollen eyes and cheeks, not wanting to worry Charlie by looking like a wreck.

When Logan brought Charlie home, he touched her arm lightly, as if she might break. "You going to be okay?" he asked in a low voice.

No, she thought. Never. Then she focused on Charlie, taking his hand and managing to nod to Logan.

"Let me know if you need anything."

She tried not to squeeze Charlie's hand too hard. "I have what I need."

After Logan took off, she sat down with her little boy, gathering him into her lap.

"Why are you sad?" he asked. Her son had grown so much these past months. No longer a baby, he was a talkative little boy. In a way, it made things even harder, because he was going to understand the horror and the hurt.

"I need to tell you something. It's about Julian."

"Daddy-boy's on a mission. It's a secret."

"That's right," she said.

"He'll be back when the leaves change."

"Yes." She fumbled through an explanation, trying to speak to Charlie in terms he could understand. "It's what he promised. But…something happened, Charlie, honey. His team was in a helicopter over the ocean, and it crashed." The details were sparse but chilling. Julian had gone down with a disabled transport helicopter, and the site of the crash, offshore, was deemed inaccessible and the aircraft unrecoverable. A ten-kilometer exclusion zone had been demarcated around the spot where the downed chopper was last recorded. Underwater robots, sent by a French oil company, had emerged from the depths with blurred photos that might be the wreckage of the helicopter fifty meters down, in a trench.

Connor had tried to get more details but had been told no covert actions or activities would be discussed. No bodies would ever be brought home. There was nothing to mourn but the memories.

"He's not coming back after all," she told Charlie, amazed she could get the words out.

"When is after all?"

"I mean he's never coming back. Do you know what 'never' means?"

"When is never?"

"Look, I need you to know. We're not going to see Julian again. That's why I'm sad."

"No more Daddy-boy?"

"That's right. No more Daddy-boy."

His face darkened. "I want him. I want to see him."

"Ah, baby." Tears boiled up again, searing her face. "We all want that, but we can't."

"Why can't we?"

"Because he's dead." It ripped at her heart to say it aloud.

"Like a dead bug?" He had found some desiccated bugs on his windowsill, only this morning. This morning, when she'd awakened full of excitement about the dress fitting, feeling one step closer to being Julian's bride.

"Um..." Oh, God. "Yes," she said quietly. "Kind of like that."

He offered her an odd little smile. "That's silly."

"Isn't it, though?"

"He's going to jump off the dock with me."

"You'll have to jump with someone else."

"I want to jump with Daddy-boy."

So do I, she thought. So do I.

She dreamed of Julian every night, so that all she wanted to do was sleep. She couldn't wait for bedtime because that was when she got to see him again, in her dreams. Her doctor and military family support group, her friends and family were all there for her, but mostly she wanted—needed—to retreat into the shadow world of sleep, where Julian was alive and vibrant, laughing and touching her, whispering secrets into her ear. Waking up was torture, because it forced her to face the bleak reality of a future without Julian.

She dragged herself through each day, struggling to find a smile or soft word for the sake of Charlie. If not for her son, she would have drowned in grief; at least he helped her tread water. People said the pain would fade, that she would find the joy in life again one day, but she couldn't imagine how to do that. She hadn't had enough time with Julian. The dreams meant they weren't done with their relationship. They would never be done, because love didn't die, did it? It couldn't be turned off like a light switch. Yet without Julian, she didn't know what to do with that love, so it froze into one huge ball of pain that wouldn't let her go.

Lieutenant Tanesha Sayers came to Daisy's house with a letter from Julian. Sayers talked about being in ROTC with him. Daisy felt a wild surge of envy. Lieutenant Sayers had spent more time with Julian than Daisy had. Yet she was grateful for every crumb she could learn about Julian, and so she listened and wept.

"I'll tell you something you already know," Sayers said as she was leaving. "He was the best of all of us. I'm… sorry, I'm destroyed. We all are."

After Sayers left, Daisy opened the letter with shaking hands.

> *My beautiful, beautiful Daisy, I'm sorry you're reading this. It feels surreal to be writing these words, because it means I'm gone. How does somebody who's gone talk to somebody who's still around? I'm going to make this short because it's pretty pointless. Of course, I'm coming back to you. However, they're making us do all this stuff. It's part of the drill. So here goes, the only true thing I can think of in all the chaos of getting ready to leave—Love never dies. I know, because of my dad. Even though he passed away, he is still with me, he still loves me. I carry him in my heart, every day. And if you're reading this, know that I'm with you. I always will be. You can go ahead with your life and do great things. Love other people, make art, watch Charlie grow, laugh and think of me—but not too much. Don't let this make you sad every day. Be happy for the time we had. Take care. I will always love you, wherever I am, Julian.*

"Mom! Help, Mom!"

Charlie's cry from the backyard startled Daisy into action. Without really thinking about it, she jumped up from the sofa, where she'd been sitting, staring at nothing, and raced out back to find her little boy.

"I'm stuck," he called from the gnarled apple tree against the back fence. "I can't get down."

"Oh, Charlie. What are you doing up there? You could break your neck." She bit her lip, regretting the choice of words.

"I climbed up all by myself."

"Then you can climb down." She positioned herself under him. "Slide your foot until you feel that branch."

"I can't see it. I can't look down."

"Just slide your foot, and you'll feel it. Trust me, I won't steer you wrong. Why did you climb up so high, anyway?"

"Grammy Jane said Daddy-boy's in heaven," Charlie explained as she carefully guided him back to earth, branch by branch. "I wanted to get a closer look."

The simple, childlike statement brought a fresh wave of grief sweeping over her, and she staggered a little. "I don't think it works that way, kiddo."

"How does it work?"

"I don't know," she said, unable to pretty it up for him. "I have no idea, because this is all so new. Tell you what, maybe we'll help each other figure out how to be closer to Julian."

When she could finally reach Charlie, she grabbed him around the waist and lowered him to the ground. "Oof, you're getting so big." She sank down to the grass and kept her arms around his warm, leaf-scented form. She held on tight because she was shaking, clinging to her son as if he was the one thing keeping her anchored to earth.

* * *

A hand-lettered cardboard sign hung on the doorknob of the community center: Grief Group. Daisy stared at it for a moment, then resolutely headed inside, awkwardly joining a dozen or so attendees her grandparents' age. They gave her tea and cookies and a stick-on name tag, and she bit her tongue to keep from saying, "I'm in the wrong place."

As she turned to gaze yearningly at the exit door, she spotted Blythe, the girl who had been widowed at the age of nineteen. Blythe took one look at Daisy and drew her into a hug. "I remember you from the family meeting—last spring, wasn't it? We were all so happy and excited."

Daisy nodded, then managed to stumble through an explanation.

"I can't tell you any words you haven't already heard," Blythe said. "Just know that you'll get through this. It doesn't seem like you ever will, but things will get better. You won't ever be the same as you were when he was alive, but…you'll be okay. Life will be good again, I promise. I still have my moments, but I survived, and so will you."

"I thought you moved on and fell in love again," Daisy said. She tried to imagine doing that. Impossible. Julian was so deeply embedded in her heart, there was no room for anything else.

"True," Blythe said, "I *am* in love again, but a part of me will always grieve for my first husband. You never really get over a loss like that. You have to live your life and find the joy."

"I have no idea how to start." Daisy tried to find a shred of inner resolution. "For my son's sake, I have to try."

"It won't happen overnight. Here's a bit of unsolicited advice. Getting over this kind of blow is not like having a flesh wound where you stick on a Band-Aid and wait for it to scab over. It's more like you were pulled mangled from a wreck. It's going to take hard work, therapy, medication, whatever works to get you back to yourself. Mostly, it will take time. Only time."

On the morning of the memorial service, Daisy stood in front of her closet, completely catatonic at the idea of choosing something to wear.

"Hey," said Sonnet, who had come up from the city for the service. "Can I help with something?"

"What the hell do you wear to bury an empty coffin?" Daisy asked dully.

"Anything you damn well please."

"You're supposed to wear black for a funeral, right? I've got plenty of black..."

"Here." Sonnet grabbed the yellow-and-white sundress Daisy had worn at Julian's commissioning ceremony. "I know it's out of season, but wear this."

"To a memorial?" She swallowed hard. He'd loved that dress. She could still picture the expression that had lit his face when he'd seen her in it. The memory lashed across her heart. "All right. But, Sonnet, I'm a wreck. I'm going to fall apart."

"So fall apart. People will understand."

"Charlie?"

"It won't mess with his head to see you fall apart...so long as he sees you heal."

"That's just it. I won't. I can't ever get past this."

"It seems like that now. I won't pretend I know what you're going through, but you're strong, Daisy. You're the strongest person I know. Look what you've done with yourself so far. You had a kid, launched a career, made a life for yourself. You can do this. You need to do this."

"I'm leaning on Charlie too much," she fretted. "It's

terrible of me to be so emotionally dependent on my little boy. But honestly, he's the only reason I take the next breath of air. If not for Charlie, I wouldn't bother."

Tears sparkled in Sonnet's eyes. "Aw, Daisy. Do us all a favor and keep breathing, okay?"

A police escort drove in front of the shiny black hearse, two cars ahead of Daisy. She was shocked to see the entire main street of Avalon lined with citizens holding flags, most of them strangers to her but all of them showing an attitude of deep respect. Although she hadn't brought her camera, she couldn't stop herself from framing the scene with a photographer's eye, seeing everything in heartbreaking detail. There were old men in lawn chairs, wearing veteran's medals. Teenagers held out cell phones to take photos. A clutch of bikers, helmets held under their arms, watched from the roadside. A mother held her toddler on top of a newspaper vending box, pointing out the flags on the hearse. Shopkeepers stood in front of their stores, and tourists spontaneously stopped and stood still. Many put their hands to their hearts as the cortege passed. The flags at the library and town hall flew at half mast.

"It's like a parade," Charlie said, pressing his hands to the window.

"Kind of," Sonnet agreed. She was driving and Daisy sat in the passenger seat, trying not to claw her way out of the car, burst past the crowd and escape.

"It's really sad," Charlie added. "I'm sad."

"We all are. The whole town is. They're showing respect for Julian, because he was brave and good." Sonnet's voice broke, and she cleared her throat. "I need a root beer barrel. You want a root beer barrel, Charlie?"

Daisy passed out the candies, taking one for herself, though she could hardly swallow past the lump in her throat. She loved the people of Avalon for the gesture. At the same time, she wanted to scream at them—What are you crying about? You didn't know him….

"Look, there's where Dad works," Charlie said. "And there's Dad. Hi, Dad!"

Logan's business was located next door to the radio station. The display window was painted with the slogan, O'Donnell Insurance Agency—You're Safe With Us. Logan stood in the doorway of the building. He didn't seem to see Charlie, waving from the backseat of the car. Logan's gaze was fixed on the hearse. He held his Yankees cap to his chest, and his expression was completely unreadable. Daisy had no idea how the news had affected him. He and Julian had been rivals, which was ridiculous, since there was no competition for her heart. She was loyal to Logan, who had been nothing but good to her and Charlie. But her heart had always been with Julian.

Mourners packed the Heart of the Mountains Church. Julian's mother, his aunt, uncle and cousin Remy were there. Remy wept openly, his huge size magnifying each shuddering sob. "He shouldn't have died," said Julian's cousin as everyone filed in. "I gave him a kit to survive, with matches and a compass. He shouldn't have died."

Julian's mother looked beautiful, perfectly dressed in a black sheath and veiled hat. From what Julian had told Daisy of his upbringing, she hadn't exactly been the model parent, but behind the veil, new lines etched her face.

Daisy sat one row from the front. She didn't really look around, simply sat frozen, trying not to shatter into a million tiny pieces on the floor. The pallbearers, perfectly uniformed and achingly somber, brought in the flag-draped coffin. All she could think about was that it was empty. There was no part of Julian left in the world.

She closed her ears to the music because every note chipped away at her heart. A poem was read—"Breathe soft, Ye winds, Ye waves in silence rest." She shut her eyes, trying not to picture the deep waters that had taken Julian away, trying not to wish she could somehow follow him. She cast a desperate glance at Charlie, in Sonnet's lap. He was her anchor, the one thing keeping her here.

"In our unit, we called him Jughead," said Lt. Tanesha Sayers, her voice shaking with emotion. "He was completely fearless and completely loyal. Though we'll never know what his last moments were like, we know he faced them with the same brave dignity with which he lived his life. Julian Gastineaux was an officer and a gentleman, with a warrior's spirit that will never die."

At the cemetery, the ceremony opened with the piercing strains of Taps. An officer in a fine beret, braids looping his shoulders, supervised the folding of the flag. It was handed over to Julian's mother, who hugged the officer and then stepped back, mascara-colored tears tracking down her face, triangular bundle clutched to her chest.

Daisy wanted that flag with a fierce, almost angry desire, but it was not hers to take. She hadn't been his wife. She wasn't his widow. There were no special provisions for a fiancée left behind. Except he had loved her with the same unwavering intensity with which she loved him. How could he be dead when she still loved him so much? How could he be dead?

Goodbye, she silently told him, her thumb worrying the band of her engagement ring. Goodbye. But it didn't feel like goodbye at all. It felt like falling down a deep well, into dark nothingness.

She grasped at Charlie again, reaching out to her son, her lifeline.

Part Two

Twelve

When the bride stepped in a pile of dog shit, Daisy was tempted to capture her expression of horror and disgust, freezing the moment for all eternity. Blair Walker was that kind of bride, difficult from day one. Daisy resisted the urge to snap a shot, however. Everybody had their moments.

"Get it off," Blair wailed, and with a kick, sent the shoe flying toward the groom's grandmother. "Get it off *now*."

Some had more of those moments than others.

Daisy rummaged in her bag, producing a container of baby wipes. She handed it off to the wedding planner's assistant. "I'll let you do the honors."

"Lucky me."

A few moments later, Daisy snapped the bride and groom in the midst of an affectionate hug. Except it wasn't a hug, it was a death grip. And Blair was not whispering sweet nothings into his ear; she was hissing a threat of dismemberment if he so much as looked at bridesmaid number two again.

The photo would show a sweet moment for the bridal couple, and no one would realize it was an illusion.

Daisy excelled at creating illusions. For her, it was a

survival skill. She needed, so desperately, to cultivate the illusion that life was good, and all the effort of living worthwhile. If she didn't convince herself of that, she'd curl into a fetal position and never come out.

The weather was unseasonably warm for April. The winter snows had melted early this year, emphasizing the inexorable passage of the seasons. Somehow the holidays had slipped by, barely noticed. She'd struggled to make it a joyous time for Charlie, but inside she was hollow, unable to escape the thought that she should have been married by then, a new bride….

"What a nightmare, eh?" muttered Zach, approaching her with video camera in hand. "I interviewed the best man, but it's so full of profanity I'll have to overdub with music."

"You'll figure out a way to edit it so everything sounds fine."

"One of the wedding guests hit on me," he added.

"Of course she did," Daisy said. "You're gorgeous."

"It wasn't a she."

"Okay then, you're equally gorgeous to men and women."

"You've got an answer for everything."

"Must be my unending quest to be right about something."

"Yeah? So how're you doing with that?"

She shrugged.

"More to the point, how are you holding up these days?"

"Now that, I wish I knew the answer to. I have no idea. Some days feel pretty normal. I'll be going about my business, at work or with Charlie or whatever, and things seem okay, and then boom. It's like somebody hit me in the back of the head with a hammer."

"Aw, Daisy. You've got a lot of people pulling for you."

"I know. I'm incredibly grateful for that. Thanks, Zach. Thanks for checking in. I know I haven't been a barrel of laughs, and you've been really patient."

He offered a sideways grin. "You're always good for a laugh. Anyway. I'd better go interview some more of these lovely folks before they get too drunk to talk."

She was glad the wedding was being held at the Inn at Willow Lake. The boutique hotel and grounds belonged to her dad and stepmom. The main inn was an elegant Edwardian-style building with a wraparound porch and a belvedere tower. The property featured an old-fashioned boathouse with quarters above and a sturdy dock. There was a gazebo on the grounds, too. Its storybook elements swept people away to another place and time, making it perfect for wedding photos.

The idyllic setting would go a long way toward making the bridezilla's photos look as beautiful as memories that had not actually happened.

That was how Daisy had come to regard Julian—a perfect memory that had never actually happened.

Julian. She could now think his name without sliding into some kind of catatonic state, so she was making progress. *Good for me.*

At first, she'd been so lost in her grief that she felt unstuck from the world. It was like being in a maze in the pitch-dark; she could find no way out. If she tried to grope her way to safety, she was pierced by thorns and lashed by overhanging branches. In the very early days, she'd felt quite certain she would die, too. Her heart had been ripped out. It was physically impossible to live without a heart.

She'd come a long way from those soul-freezing days. Through sheer will and determination, she had fought and clawed her way out of the darkness, a wildcat fighting free from a steel trap, gnawing off its own paw. Sure, she'd done herself some damage in the process, but she was alive. She had Charlie and her job, family and friends.

Recovering from the grief and shock had been a daily, sometimes moment-to-moment struggle. And she still wasn't there yet. She still woke up in the middle of the night, crying so hard she had to bury her face in a pillow to keep from waking Charlie.

In time, Julian faded from Charlie's memory; now he flickered in and out like a shadow in the wind. Charlie still remembered his name and the fact that he'd never quite dared to jump off the dock that day. The framed photo she'd taken that day—the shutter on timer, their arms around each other, the sun-gilt lake in the background—stayed on the bedside table, even though it was heartbreaking to look at. They had been so happy that day, so deeply in love. Hope for the future shone from their eyes, their smiles. Sometimes she fantasized about magically stepping into the photo, where she could feel the warmth of the sun on his skin and hear the sound of his voice, whispering in her ear. There were moments when the fantasy felt more real than life itself—and that was when she scared herself into fighting her way back to the real world.

Her chief motivation was Charlie. She learned so much from her small son. All her child-rearing books cast the parent in the role of teacher. Yet few of the books reminded readers to pay attention to the lessons a child could offer—the joys of living in the moment and a wide-eyed wonder at the world. The kid didn't need lessons in that sort of thing. Charlie had some kind of genetic code; he was hardwired for happiness.

She vowed to make sure that never changed. The quest was fierce and focused, working her way through the grief like a shipwreck survivor rowing to shore. Over time, she did start to get better. She could function. She could smile and laugh and love and enjoy life. She could pretend the huge gaping hole in her heart was not there. Julian would be proud of her.

"You're not fooling anybody, you know." Logan was helping her wash her car. She couldn't recall the last time she'd washed it and was in the middle of the chore when he stopped by. Charlie loved having his dad around, and Daisy had to admit it was nice, not having to do everything by herself. Charlie had helped with the fun part—the squirting hose, the soap bubbles—but now that they were down to rinsing and drying, he'd grown bored and was kicking a soccer ball around the yard with Blake.

"I don't know," she said to Logan. "Fooling who? About what?" A flutter in her stomach told her she was lying. She did know. Logan never talked about Julian, so this was something new.

She wrung out her chamois cloth and waited to hear what he'd say to that. Logan had been kind to her after Julian's death. He'd held her close and said, "I'm here for you. That will never change."

As good as his word, he helped take care of Charlie and had urged her to go to her support groups and appointments. He came around a lot, made himself available.

"What I meant," he said, "is that you're doing a great job getting through every day. I'm proud of you. Not everybody can survive a loss like that."

She squirted foam cleaner on a stubborn spot on the car hood, then scrubbed at the spot. "So then, why do you say I'm not fooling anyone?"

"Because you need to do more than survive. More than just get through the day. You're strong, Daisy. You're ready. You need to believe it."

She fell silent, methodically polishing the car in a steady rhythm. A black mayfly dive-bombed into the foam polish, ending its life in front of her face, *splat*. Wrinkling her nose, she plucked the fly out, then went back to polishing, methodical as ever.

Sonnet came for a rare weekend visit. She was working at UNESCO at the UN and had very little time to herself. She lived in a cramped studio on the east side of midtown and claimed to love everything about it. However, when she managed to steal away to Avalon, she relaxed visibly.

Although she could probably take her pick of any room at the Inn at Willow Lake, owned by her mom and Daisy's dad, she preferred to stay with Daisy. They usually made popcorn with too much butter and salt, and stayed up late watching chick flicks.

They put Charlie to bed with four stories. The number four was his current favorite. Then they had their showers, donned their most comfy pajamas and made the popcorn. Daisy poured too generous glasses of cheap, dry champagne—their favorite.

"To us," she said. "Especially to your brilliant career."

"And yours," Sonnet pointed out. She looked severely beautiful, almost exotic, with her wet hair twisted up in a towel, though the effect was spoiled by cowboy flannel pajamas and fuzzy slippers.

"Fine. To both our brilliant careers." They clinked glasses and drank. The movie started up, a repeat viewing of the best version of *Pride and Prejudice* in existence. Charming as it was, Daisy couldn't keep her mind on the film. "Logan says I haven't moved on," she blurted out.

Sonnet immediately hit the mute button. "Is he right?"

"I thought about it for a long time after he said it," Daisy mused, tossing her popcorn in the bowl to distribute the butter. "I think he might be right. And how weird is that, a guy being right?"

"Totally weird," Sonnet said.

"I don't cry myself to sleep anymore. I don't wake up in the middle of the night clutching my chest like some nightmare's after me. I don't have imaginary conversations with Julian every time I'm alone."

"All good. But…?"

"I want more than simply to exist. More than simply getting through the day. I want a full life. I don't want to be the girl whose fiancé was killed. I want to…live again. I want to be in love."

"So fall in love."

"You of all people know it's not that simple. It—"

There was a soft knock at the door. Blake started barking and swirled like a dervish.

Sonnet frowned. "Were you expecting someone?"

Daisy glanced down at her Yankees jersey and flip-flops. "The fashion police?" She hurried to the door. Through the glass pane, she saw Logan and Zach. "Hey," she said, letting them in. Sonnet stood up, touching the towel on her head. "Oh. Hi."

Zach grinned at her. "I heard you'd come up for the weekend. I wanted to see you." His gaze dropped from her toweled head to her bare legs and fuzzy slippers.

"You should have called first," she said, clearly flustered.

Daisy looked on, bemused. Sonnet and Zach were childhood friends, having met and bonded at the finger-painting table in preschool. Lately, though, there was a slightly different tone to the friendship.

"I smell popcorn," Logan said. "Mind if we hang out for a while?"

Daisy paused. With few exceptions, she spent every other Saturday night alone, reading, watching TV, loading photos from the day's shoot if there had been a wedding. Sometimes she stared guiltily at the box she'd set aside for the MoMA competition. She had missed last year's entry deadline while lost in the deep vortex of grief. This year, she thought she might pursue it again, but the box remained as empty as the file marked "MoMA" on her computer.

"Sure," she said. "We're having a *Pride and Prejudice* marathon." She gestured at the stack of DVDs on the coffee table, the silent people in costume on the screen. "The BBC version, with Colin Firth. Aka the *only* version."

Both Zach and Logan looked queasy.

Sonnet said, "Can you make us a better offer?"

"And it cannot involve a controller," Daisy said hastily. She'd never been a fan of video games.

"How about little wooden tiles on a board?" asked Zach.

"Scrabble." Sonnet clutched her chest. "Be still my heart."

"That settles it," said Daisy. "Company chooses."

"Winners get to pick the movie afterward," Logan suggested.

Knowing Sonnet's brain power, Daisy readily agreed. While the guys set up the board, she and Sonnet went to her room to make themselves a little more presentable. "I can't believe they didn't call first." Sonnet bent forward from the waist, freeing her masses of curls from the towel.

"I think it's cute, Zach wanting to see you so bad he'll go for a night of Scrabble."

"Knowing I'll destroy him," Sonnet added. "I wonder what's up with that."

"He's got a crush on you, idiot. He has ever since you got back from Germany."

"Zach? And me?" Sonnet snorted, but then she looked intrigued. "Really?"

Daisy pulled on her favorite pair of jeans. "Don't act so shocked. It's been a long time coming."

"Wait a minute." Sonnet leaned toward the mirror and applied some lip gloss. "How do you know this surprise visit is about Zach coming to see me? What about Logan and you?"

Daisy ignored a tug of tension in her stomach. "Logan and I see each other all the time. Because of Charlie," she added.

"Uh-huh."

"It'll never be more than that," Daisy hastened to add. "Too much has happened."

"There's no such thing as too much happening."

"I mean, there's too much baggage."

"Hey. Everybody has baggage. It's nice having someone to share the burden, eh?"

I wouldn't know, thought Daisy. "Come on," she said. "Let's go open a can of whup ass on that Scrabble board."

When she stepped out of the bedroom, she noticed that Logan had gone in to check on Charlie. He bent over the dinosaur bed and drew a blanket up under the little boy's chin.

Daisy stepped into the room. "He always kicks off his covers, doesn't he?"

Logan nodded. In the dimness of the night-light, she could see him smile. "I like bedtime," he said. "I wish I could be around for more of them."

"You're around plenty," she said. She understood, though, that this was not what he was talking about. "Let's put on the noise machine," she suggested. "That way, if we get too loud, we won't wake him." She turned the bedside device to "ocean waves."

As she and Logan exited the room, their bodies brushed together, and she was startled to feel the tingle of...something. And she found herself remembering what he'd said to her while washing the car. Live your life, Daisy. It's time.

A person didn't always end up with a life she'd planned

or expected. But turning her back on everything was no solution.

In the living room, Zach and Sonnet were arguing about whether or not "mofo" was an allowable word. "Fortunately," she said, holding out her iPhone, "there is an app for that."

"I can see I'm not going to get away with anything tonight," said Zach.

"Not even worth trying." Sonnet looked up. "You two ready?"

They delved into the popcorn and Scrabble like a group of college kids in a dorm. Sonnet and Zach got into the champagne. Daisy switched to ginger ale with Logan. He eyed the frosty glasses on the table. "You don't have to do that."

She shrugged. "No biggie." As a general rule, she avoided drinking alcohol around him. He always appeared to be secure in his sobriety, but it seemed prudent not to wave champagne in the guy's face. She didn't believe in tempting fate. Abstaining around Logan was a show of respect, too, in support of what she knew was an everyday struggle for him.

"Hey," said Sonnet. "You can't add 'alicious' to my word." She scowled at Zach.

"I just did, and I get a triple word score for the whole thing."

Daisy looked at the board. "Pupalicious?"

"Sure," he said, crossing his arms over his chest. "Just ask Blake. Right, Blake?"

On hearing her name, the dog thumped her tail.

"And I get a bonus for using up all my letters," said Zach.

"All eight of them."

"Yup."

"So," she said, removing the tiles one by one, "not only

are you illiterate, you're a cheat, as well. You're only allowed seven tiles on your rack. However, because I'm feeling generous, I'll let you stay in the game."

The competition was by turns silly and fierce. Some of the combinations—outgnaw, yabbo, vug—caused arguments, settled by checking a geeky internet site. Sonnet was determined to win, but Logan came from behind, using the prized Q on a double word score at the last minute.

"Sheqel?" Sonnet demanded. "Give me a break."

"It's an ancient unit of measure," he said. "Consider yourself schooled. And I'm picking the movie. Buh-bye, Mr. Pansy-Ass Darcy." He perused the DVD collection, his face registering dismay. "*Hope Floats? The Age of Innocence? Phantom?* Come on, you're holding out on us."

"Trust me, I don't have a spare copy of *Gladiator* or *300* stashed somewhere."

"How did you know my two favorite movies?"

"Aren't those every guy's two favorite movies?"

"They're mine," Zach admitted.

"We need a plan B," Logan said, grabbing the remote. He scrolled through some channels, then said, "Yes. Paydirt."

The four of them lined up on the sofa for an evening of live boxing. And in spite of herself, Daisy kind of got into it. She admired the technique, the raw power of a well-landed blow, the way the opponents sagged against each other in exhaustion, then started swinging again. Fueled by the champagne, Zach and Sonnet got rowdy, but the noise didn't wake Charlie.

Daisy felt happier and more relaxed than she had in months. It was so simple, hanging out with old friends and being silly. She needed to do stuff like this more often.

Another round started up. The announcer introduced the contenders, elongating the words in his circus ringmaster's voice. "Aaaand in this corner, we have newcomer Bullseye Tillis, fresh out of the air force!" The words *air force* came at her like a sneak attack, a slender blade slipped between her ribs, puncturing the bubble of happiness. The others didn't seem to notice as they laughed and talked and passed the popcorn. It occurred to Daisy that this syndrome—letting grief overwhelm her life—could be the end of her. Maybe not literally, but emotionally.

Her grief counselor had explained the debilitating effects of lingering in a grieving mode—exhaustion, sleeplessness, distraction, disconnection… It was only now, in this moment, that Daisy understood its impact.

The other thing she realized, sitting there with her laughing friends, was that the time had come to choose happiness. She hadn't felt anything but grief for ages. She needed to move on, or she would lose herself. She wanted happiness. She wanted to stop dragging herself through each day and crying in the night, clutching an old shirt of Julian's. He expected more from her; he would want her to live her life, not struggle through it. For you, Julian, she thought. And for me.

The next day dawned with a brilliant sunrise, the kind of day that made Daisy feel glad to be alive. She grabbed her camera bag and took one photo. She only needed the one, and she knew it. Some shots were just right.

She hurried to the computer and checked it out on the big screen. The shot was a close-up of a trumpet-shaped white blossom, beaded in dew. Every droplet on the flower created a convex mirror reflecting the sunrise, creating a complex mosaic of natural color. There was something special about the photo, a peculiar magic that touched her when she looked at it.

For the first time in a long time, she felt like an artist again. She saved the file and made a print and studied it.

Then on the back, she noted the date. She took a breath, feeling exhilarated, and slid the print into the tray that had been empty for far too long—the MoMA Emerging Artist competition.

It was a wild long shot, but she was going to do the work, even if it meant going without sleep. If the impossible happened and she was selected for the honor, it would be a miracle. Even if she didn't place, she would still wind up with a portfolio she could be proud of.

When Charlie woke up a bit later, she left him with Sonnet, making pancakes in the shape of dinosaurs. Taking her camera bag and a small notebook and pen, she started on a journey she had been mapping out in her head since the night before.

She drove up to Camp Kioga and walked to the communal fire pit by the lake there. No one was around. The remains of some charred logs lay in the pit, and the lake was like a sheet of glass where the light struck it. She found her angle, and instead of fighting the sun flare, took the shot she wanted, knowing the flare would add a mystical element to the photo.

"I was sitting right there the first time I met you," she said, speaking softly even though there was no one around to hear. "You were so different from anyone I'd ever met before. I tried to get you to smoke pot with me, like that was going to impress you or something. You said no, but you were really nice about it. And I knew then that I wanted to be friends. All my other friends only wanted to get high and party. I couldn't figure out what you were after, but I was definitely intrigued. Julian, you were everything to me. Losing you was like having a hole blown open in the middle of my chest. Somehow, I'm still alive, walking around and going through the motions of life, but all I've felt this past year is the pain of missing you. Nobody can live with that kind of pain.

"So today is about moving on. I'll never forget you. I'll never stop loving you. But starting now, I'm going to stop wishing for a life that can never be. I need to find another life, and I'm pretty sure that means finding another love." She took a deep breath. "Maybe it's a matter of accepting the love that's already in my life. I don't know. This is all so new and horrible. I only know it's time to say goodbye and move on. If you were here, you'd understand. You were more full of life than anyone. I learned so much from you. I haven't been loving my life and I intend to begin. Starting now."

She grabbed a canoe and paddled out to the spot where he had proposed to her. There were a few resort guests exploring the place, but she didn't mind. The shot that told the story was taken from ground level, two trees framed by an arch of the gazebo with the sky vast and marble hard as a backdrop. She squeezed the shutter as a bird took flight.

Through the rest of the day, she took her time, driving the back roads of the countryside, stopping at the places Julian had taken her to the day he'd proposed. She revisited all those old memories and made pictures and photographed them, and with each mile she traveled, she felt lighter. It was as if, at every stop, she unloaded the heavy rocks and relics of her grief.

The notebook filled up with thoughts from the heart. The photos were nature shots that told a deeper story. She hoped she was capturing the nuance she was after. She suspected she had. She could feel the shots; they were bringing something out in her. It felt new and kind of exciting, as if she had opened a door to a hidden world.

It was late afternoon by the time she returned to the little row house on Oak Street. She felt like…not a different person but maybe a better version of herself.

"I hope it's not a fluke," she muttered under her breath.

It wasn't. It felt like the real thing. Her thumb worried the base of her finger where the engagement ring used to be. She had finally taken it off because to feel it there, to see it, created a constant reminder of his absence. He'd had one word engraved inside the band: Forever.

What was it he'd once said? *I'm saving forever for you.*

She let herself in, calling out to Sonnet and Charlie.

"Mom!" her little boy came barreling into the front hall with Blake scrabbling along behind him. Charlie threw himself into her arms and said, "You're home."

She nuzzled him, inhaling his scent of maple syrup and little boy. "That's right, kiddo. I'm home."

Thirteen

Daisy felt a thrum of apprehension deep in her gut as she stood in front of the nicest boutique in town, Zuzu's Petals. She'd been in a boutique—a bridal shop—when she'd received the news of Julian's death and had not actually set foot in one since that day. With the grief counselor, Daisy had attempted to joke about the issue. "I must really be cracking up. In the history of psychology, has there ever been a female patient who is afraid to *shop?*"

"You'd be surprised," the counselor had said, and she'd advised Daisy to push past the fear.

Now Daisy was meeting her cousin Olivia at Zuzu's. The shop's owner had exquisite taste and a businesswoman's judgment. Her collection included an eclectic mix of styles, everything from pricey Vena Cava silk dresses to handcrafted sweaters from local artists and simple but delicate tops that looked perfect with a good pair of jeans.

Something New Is Always Blooming At Zuzu's read the slogan above the door, which fronted the town square. It was an idyllic shopping day, the temperature mild and cool, slightly overcast, the kind of weather that didn't make you yearn to be outside. As she stepped through the door of the cozy, pleasantly cluttered boutique, she breathed in the pleasant aroma of potpourri and new clothes.

Today's excursion had been Daisy's idea. Both cousins had left their kids with their respective dads.

"What's the occasion?" asked Olivia. "Something tells me this is not about having a bit of girl time."

"You're right," said Daisy. She felt oddly bashful about disclosing her purpose. "Couple of things. I got a nice bonus from a wedding shoot and it's burning a hole in my pocket."

"Excellent. This shop will definitely help you out of that little bind." Olivia plucked a fluttery scarf of watered silk from a display shelf and tossed it around Daisy's neck.

"Also, I need your impeccable style sense," Daisy added.

"Aw. I'm flattered."

"Don't be. It's the truth, and I need you."

Olivia's first career had been staging houses for real estate agents. She'd always had the best flair for fashion of anyone Daisy knew, and Daisy needed that expertise now.

"I'm ready to start looking good," she said.

"You always look good. You're gorgeous."

"I appreciate the loyalty, but I don't feel gorgeous. Since getting the news of Julian's death, I haven't felt like doing anything for myself. Now, I want to change. Not only for Charlie's sake but for my own. It's time to quit dragging myself through each day. And God help me, it's time to meet new people. You know, like, *guys*. I'm so sick of being alone. I mean, I have great friends and family, but I want to be special to someone again."

Olivia gave her a hug. "Good for you. I mean, really good." There were tears in her eyes. Daisy wondered if she was thinking about Connor. After the news of his brother's death, Connor had sunk into a black hole of rage and depression so deep that it scared everyone—including Connor. He battled the thing like a warrior, marshaling every weapon he could—counseling, support groups, medication, meditation, breathing exercises, even yoga. It was incongruous to picture Olivia's husband—a ringer for Paul Bunyan—twisting himself into yoga poses and chanting in Sanskrit, but he was determined to leave no stone unturned in trying to crawl out of his grief.

And the thing was, all his efforts paid off. He found a kind of peace and acceptance.

Daisy had taken a different, longer path. The day she'd revisited all the places that had been so special to her and Julian, she had made a series of stunning photos. It hurt to look at them but they were the best work she had ever done.

Finally, she was ready to focus on herself.

Olivia happily embraced the mission. Daisy could tell her cousin loved putting together the perfect outfit, and she left the shop with three ensembles, including some great pieces that would be the start of a new, improved wardrobe. When Daisy stressed out about what she was spending, Olivia kicked in for some accessories, refusing to take no for an answer.

"You're going to look amazing," Olivia assured her. "Let's see if they can take a drop-in at the salon."

"Yes." Daisy wanted to immediately. She couldn't remember the last time she'd gone in for a cut and style. "Great idea."

She had long thought she should cut her hair but kept putting it off. She wasn't sure why. Correction—she did know why. Julian had loved her long hair. But everything was different now, and that was what today was about.

Waist-length hair was nice in shampoo ads, but in real life, it simply said, "I'm neglecting myself." Not long ago she'd gone down to Windham to shoot a wedding, and someone had asked her if she was Pentecostal. Not that there was anything wrong with being Pentecostal, but the question had made her feel like an impostor. An impostor in her own life.

The Twisted Scissors salon was owned and operated by the three Dombrowski sisters who believed, with unwavering faith, in the power of pampering. Maybe, thought Daisy, that was the reason she'd stayed away from the place. Pampering and getting pretty hadn't seemed compatible with her grief.

When she walked through the doors of the salon and was hit by the fruity smells of high-end hair products, she realized what a fool she'd been.

This was a place of healing. Why hadn't she thought of that before?

The Twisted Scissors did more than hair. The youngest sister, Tina, offered the most beautiful manicures and pedicures. The middle sister, Leah, had gone to cosmetology school and was a genius with makeup. All the local brides used her. And the eldest sister, Maxine, was the hair stylist.

When Olivia and Daisy walked in, Maxine was with a client. "I can take you in about a half hour," she offered. "Get a mani-pedi while you wait."

"Really good idea," Olivia said.

"Why not?" Daisy was up for it. She should've done this a long time ago. "Er, that is, if you think we have time."

"Sure, we have time. The guys can watch the kids all the way through bath and bedtime if we want."

Daisy knew Logan would never complain about keeping Charlie. When he'd picked Charlie up and headed to Camp Kioga, he'd seemed fine with the proposed plan. The dads and kids were going on a hike and a swim if the day warmed up, then back to Connor's for videos and naps.

She nodded to her cousin. “I wonder if Logan feels weird, spending the day with Connor.”

“Why would he feel weird?”

“Let’s see, we’ve got the father of my child spending the day with the brother of my dead fiancé,” she said. “I’m wondering how the conversation will go.”

“They’ll talk about the kids. And sports. And work. They’ll make giant club sandwiches for lunch. We can always hope they’ll remember not to teach the kids any bad words or how to burp on command.”

Maxine lifted the dryer from her client’s head.

“Hey, Daphne,” Daisy said, surprised to recognize the receptionist from her mom’s law firm. “Good to see you. This is my cousin Olivia.”

Maxine settled Daphne in the chair and began methodically undoing her foils. The color of choice this time appeared to be electric magenta, which contrasted starkly with Daphne’s black hair. She also sported an interesting array of tattoos depicting anime characters.

“How have you been?” Daphne asked. Her tone was polite rather than friendly. She had never really seemed to like Daisy, and Daisy had no idea why.

“Better, thanks. Olivia and I went for some retail therapy. And now I’m here for a makeover. I’m ready to move on with my life.”

“Was something wrong with your old life?” asked Tina, adjusting her rolling stool across the manicure table from Daisy.

Daisy nodded and took a breath. By now, she was used to telling her story. In the grief group she’d attended, they’d advised her to practice. It was a peculiar process, explaining the most devastating incident of your life in a way that wouldn’t make the other person uncomfortable.

“My fiancé died last September,” she said. “He was

serving in the air force and he was killed while on a mission."

"Oh, no," said Tina, grabbing Daisy's hand and slathering it with warm lotion. "My word, that's terrible. Did you hear that, girls?" she asked. "This poor kid's fiancé was killed. Honey, we are so, *so* sorry."

"Thank you," said Daisy, relieved that she'd managed to stumble through the explanation. "There were days when I honestly did think my life was over, too, but that's no way to be, right? I have a beautiful young son and great friends and family."

"Oh, sweetie, you had his baby?"

"Um, it's a little complicated. My son isn't my fiancé's." From across the room, she could feel Daphne's keen attention. "Good lord, my life sounds like a telenovela."

"But in English," Olivia clarified.

"So who's the baby's daddy?" Leah wanted to know.

"A guy I've known all my life. We had a wild weekend in high school and ended up with Charlie." She was surprised at herself, sharing personal details with women she barely knew. That was the nature of a salon, though. It was a place where a woman felt safe giving up her secrets.

"The rat bastard. Knocked you up and—"

"Logan's okay," Daisy said quickly. "He's pretty great, actually. He's watching Charlie all day today, so I can do this."

"Well, then, there you go," Tina said. "There's your happy ending after all."

"Hey, Maxine, I need to get going. Meeting someone for a matinee," said Daphne. "I'm going to have to skip the comb-out today."

"You sure?"

"It'll be fine." She jumped out of the chair and peeled off her smock. At the front counter, she scribbled a check and headed for the door. "See you around, Daisy. And good luck with everything. Nice meeting you, Olivia."

"Was it something I said?" asked Daisy after she'd left.

"She has Sailor Moon on her checks," said Maxine. "You know, that anime character. Daphne is a little quirky, but great."

With her seashell-pink manicure still drying, Daisy went for the works on her hair—wash, condition, cut, style. She had not been to a salon since her wedding hair trial. Her cousin Dare, who had also been the wedding planner, had taken her to a specialty salon in Albany, and the day had been insanely fun. She had laughed and dreamed and imagined how her wedding would go, what she wanted Julian to see when he caught his first glimpse of her. The stylist had created a swirling updo, sprigged with fresh flowers and held in place by her grandmother's silver and mother-of-pearl clasp. She had looked in the mirror and glimpsed the bride she would be.

Now she leaned back over the shampooing sink, shut her eyes and imagined the agony of that memory flowing away, being rinsed off of her and washed down the drain. Enough, she thought. Enough pain.

"Go short," she said to Maxine after the wash.

"How short?"

"Like, a bob, maybe."

Maxine drew a wide-toothed comb through her long, wet hair. "You sure?"

"I am right now. Do it fast, before I change my mind."

"You won't regret it," Olivia said. "I always thought you'd look great with short hair."

The scissors snipped with crisp precision, rasping in Daisy's ears. She watched her long locks fall away in damp hanks, each one hitting the mat under the chair with a soft, wet slap.

"It's like a ritual shearing," she said, pretending not to be nervous.

"It *is* a ritual shearing," Olivia insisted. "The ritual being, you, my dear cousin, are going to step out of this salon a whole new woman."

"I'm cool with that," Daisy said, "but there's one problem."

"What problem?"

"The whole new woman is going to step back into her old life. Same job, same routine..."

"Maybe so, but you'll have a new attitude. Guys will pick up on that, and you'll start dating again."

"I never dated before. Went straight from high school to motherhood. I have no idea what to do."

"Honey, when we're done here, you won't need to know a thing except how to hold on tight while you get swept off your feet," Maxine assured her.

Daisy gulped as reality set in. This was what moving on was all about. "How do people even meet guys these days? Am I going to have to go online?"

"Maybe," said Olivia.

"I am so not ready for that."

"All right, then do it the old-fashioned way. Let your friends introduce you to people."

"Fine. Who are you going to introduce me to?"

Olivia hesitated a beat too long.

"See? You don't know any—"

"Ned Farkis!" Olivia said with a relieved smile. "He's my CPAs associate, and I know he's totally single because—"

"Ned Farkis? What kind of name is that?"

"Don't judge people by their names, for Pete's sake."

"I don't know anything else about him."

"Well, he seems very nice and smart."

"What does he look like?"

"He looks nice," she said, clearly evading now.

"And smart?" Daisy teased. "Does he look smart, too?"

"Okay, let's say he's kind of geek chic. And, um, he's got a little extra around the middle."

"Better and better."

"All right. Let's move on."

"Do you know Alvin, from the video store?" asked Leah. "He's cute. Shaggy hair, shy smile."

"Alvin Gourd?" asked Daisy. "I don't think so." Although she agreed he was cute in a John-Cusack-*High-Fidelity* way, he was definitely not her type, pale and retiring, a walking encyclopedia of movie trivia.

"Maybe we're going about this the wrong way," Olivia said. "You're smart, successful and fun. And you're turning more gorgeous by the moment. No need to worry about introducing you to guys. They're going to flock to you, mark my words. We will build it, and they will come."

The haircut turned out as amazing as Maxine had promised, a shiny bob that skimmed the tops of her shoulders. She tossed her head to and fro; the new style felt light and strange.

Leah did her makeup beautifully, and Olivia insisted she put on one of her new outfits.

"Seriously?" asked Daisy. "My plan for the rest of the day is to pick up Charlie and spend the evening at home."

"Oh, come on. Humor me."

In a back room of the salon, she changed into a new pair of dark-wash jeans, heeled sandals to show off her pedicure, and a flowy watercolor top with a scoop neck. Then she stood in front of the salon mirror and stared. "Well."

"Well is right."

"I look pretty good. I didn't think I was that bad before, but I look *good*."

"Everybody can do with a little change now and then."

* * *

Charlie took one look at her and plastered himself against his dad. "Mom!" yelled the little boy. "What did you do?"

"I cut my hair. Do you like it?"

"No. Put it back."

"Hey, buddy," said Logan. "None of that." He looked at Daisy, then did a double take, his gaze visibly warming. "It's outstanding."

"That's what I told her," said Olivia, bustling into the house. She and Connor had built the place together, and it had always seemed like a dream house to Daisy. It had everything from a river-rock fireplace to a storybook garden and a picket fence, and was sited perfectly on a slope above the Schuyler River, with a grand view of the lake in the distance.

"How did everything go today?" asked Daisy.

"Excellent," said Logan. "The kids got along great. The dogs, too, I guess. I don't think Barkis really likes Blake."

"Nonsense. Everybody likes Blake," said Daisy.

"Just ask Blake," said Logan, glowering at the little terrier. "You ready to head home?"

"Sure." She watched him go around the room, picking up Charlie's gear here and there. The look on Logan's face when he saw her had been gratifying. She smiled, finally feeling an inkling of hope for the future.

"Thanks for everything," she said to Olivia. "I had a great day."

"You're going to have a great life."

"Here's hoping."

At the door, Olivia grabbed her wrist and leaned toward her ear. "And just a thought—when you're looking for dating material, you might want to try close to home."

"What?"

"I saw how Logan reacted to the makeover," Olivia

said. “And it wasn’t only the way he was staring at you. It was the way you were staring at him.”

Daisy opened her mouth to protest, but Olivia stopped her, holding up a hand. “I’m just saying.”

Really? thought Daisy all the way home. Seriously? Logan?

No way. Getting involved with Logan was too obvious. Something so obvious could never work.

She sat quietly as he drove her and Charlie home. Neither seemed to notice her silence. They were singing an unbearably bad version of “We are the Champions” along with the radio and having a great time. They always had a great time together.

As they passed through the center of town, she said, pretty much without thinking, “How about we stop and pick up a pizza for dinner? I’m too glamorous to cook tonight.”

“Yay!” crowed Charlie from the backseat. “And Dad, too?”

“Of course Dad, too. It would be rude to get a pizza and not give him any.” She hesitated. “I mean, if you don’t have other plans.”

“I’m in,” said Logan. “Carminucci’s or Sir Lancelot’s?”

“Carminucci’s, for sure,” Daisy said, “superior crust.”

At the take-out counter, Logan ordered a large pizza, half cheese, half mushroom.

Daisy regarded him with bemusement. “How did you know I like mushroom pizza?”

“I always know what you like.”

“Hmm.”

“What’s that supposed to mean?”

“Just trying to decide if that’s thoughtful, or kind of stalkerish and creepy.”

“Thoughtful,” he said. “Trust me on that.”

While they waited for the pizza, they took Charlie over

to a huge fish tank that occupied one wall of the pizzeria. The little boy loved the colorful fish and worked hard to emulate their bugged out eyes and bubble-shaped mouths.

Daisy loved seeing the world through Charlie's eyes. He never failed to remind her to regard things with wonder and to believe in magic. Of all the cameras she had ever looked through, his was the freshest and most compelling. Sometimes when she was composing a shot, she tried to use what she termed the "Charlie filter." How would her little boy view the scene? It made for some interesting results.

"Look at that, Momdad," Charlie said, with his habit of running their names together. "A little man in the tank."

It was a ceramic scuba diver half-hidden in the colorful reeds, with a harpoon in one hand and an oxygen tank on his back.

"He's hunting for treasure," said Logan, pointing out the tiny pirate's chest overflowing with riches.

"That's cool," said Charlie. "But—oh. Look." He pointed out a small tropical fish lying on its side near the surface. Its blue and black markings were faded, its tiny gills frayed, and it was motionless except for the occasional shudder of movement from the current created by the pump. Charlie tapped his finger against the glass. "I think that fish is dead."

"I think you're right," Daisy agreed.

"So it's dead? Like, *dead* dead? It'll never swim again?"

"Doubtful."

"Will somebody take it out?" Charlie asked.

"I imagine someone will take it out next time they clean the fish tank."

"But what if they don't?"

"Then it will kind of…dissolve into smaller and smaller pieces until you can't see it anymore." Daisy was not loving this exchange. It was a little too close to the reality she had been dealing with in the past year.

When she'd first heard how Julian had died, she'd been haunted by questions that would never be answered, and grim images had disturbed her dreams. Had he been scared? Had he died in pain? Was there a struggle to stay alive, or was death instantaneous?

"Pizza's ready," Logan said, pulling out his wallet. "I'm starved. What about you two?"

"Starved," Charlie agreed.

Logan paid for the pizza and a six-pack of root beer.

Daisy sighed, inhaling the smell of freshly baked pizza as they got in the car.

"Something wrong?" asked Logan.

"Not at all. I'm wondering why people bother to eat anything else when there's pizza and root beer in the world."

"Thanks for keeping Charlie all day," Daisy said later as Logan eased out of Charlie's bed, where he'd spent the past half hour reading him to sleep. Charlie had outgrown the dinosaur bed and now had a regular bed with trendy sheets.

"No problem," said Logan, gently shutting the door. "Never a problem. You know that."

"Would you like another root beer?" she offered.

"Sure, thanks." He took the brown bottle from her. "I need to get going pretty soon."

"Oh—I didn't mean to stall you, if you have plans…" She'd been feeling slightly awkward all evening, and she knew exactly why. Olivia's whispered suggestion about Logan had planted a seed, and although nothing on the surface had changed, everything felt different all of a sudden.

"I definitely have plans," he assured her.

She was curious, but didn't ask. Their relationship had always been a strange dance of intimacy and distance. Due to Charlie, their lives were inextricably entwined, yet separate. She realized it was probably only a matter of time until he met someone special. He was young, successful and undeniably good-looking, with his deep russet-colored hair and leaf-green eyes, his athletic build and an infectious smile.

There was every chance that he would one day give Charlie a stepmother. And half siblings. It was strange to contemplate, but lately Daisy was inclined to face reality and look to the future.

She was dying to know what plans he had but had a horror of seeming nosy.

"I bet you're dying to know what my plans are," he said.

"I would never pry." She could tell he saw right through her. "Okay, I'm not *dying* to know, but I'm totally curious."

"I got a hot date."

Her heart sank. "Oh."

"With a church basement full of twelve-steppers."

Now she felt ridiculous for letting her thoughts run rampant about stepmothers and half siblings. "I see. Sorry if I seemed nosy."

"Not at all. I hope that's not a problem for you, the meetings, I mean."

"A problem? Are you kidding? Logan, I think your commitment to your program is amazing."

He polished off the root beer and emitted a long, satisfied belch.

"Charming," she said.

"Hey, a guy's got to cut loose somehow."

She laughed. "Right." Then she studied him for a long

moment. "Does it...bother you, being around people who are drinking and partying?"

"Yes and no. Maybe in the way it bothers a diabetic to walk into the Sky River Bakery when they're putting out the iced maple bars."

"Ouch."

"It's okay. I'm going be fine."

"For good?" She was curious about this program, which had caused him to do such a one-eighty in his life years ago.

"For one day at a time. That's how it works. You don't get any guarantees."

"Same as everything else," she said brightly. She put his bottle in the recycling bin.

"How about you?" he asked. "What are you up to tonight?"

"Nothing," she said. Pretty much what she did every night.

"Then what's with the hair and the new clothes?"

"Oh, this. I decided it was time for a change. For several changes, in fact. Nobody should spend her life being stressed out and sad all the time."

"Good point. I agree with you there."

"So I'm getting on with my life. And all this—" she gestured at the hair, the clothes "—is kind of symbolic."

"Okay, cool."

She hesitated. Should she tell him what else she'd decided? Probably so. If he was planning to see someone, she would want to know.

"I'm going to start dating," she said in a rush.

"Who?" he asked, just as quickly.

She laughed briefly. "I haven't thought that far ahead yet. But I have prospects," she assured him.

"I don't doubt it."

"And trust me, I will keep Charlie's needs first and foremost in my mind."

"I know you will." He studied her for a moment longer. She thought he might say more, but he didn't. "I better get going," he said.

She walked him to the door. "Thanks again, Logan. For today and dinner and…everything."

"You bet." He paused in the doorway. He was certainly staring at her oddly. His gaze slipped from her eyes to her mouth, and he was standing very close. For a wild moment, she thought he might touch her.

For an even crazier moment, she wanted him to.

Then the tension broke, and he headed off into the evening, leaving her alone with her new look.

Fourteen

Daisy was on a power walk with her friend Maureen Haven, the town librarian. Blake strained at her leash as she lunged toward every bird or squirrel that flitted or skittered across their path.

"Guess what I figured out?" she asked Maureen.

"What's that?"

"I hate dating."

Maureen laughed. "I hated it, too. Sometimes I think it's the main reason I got married, so I wouldn't have to worry about dating."

"A likely story. You married Eddie Haven because you fell madly in love with him."

"Okay, there's that."

"Why do I have to date?" Daisy whined. "Why can't I just fall in love?"

"As a general rule, one thing leads to the other. Let's work the problem, figure out what you need and where you want to be in your life. We could do some research—"

"Now you're going all librariany on me," Daisy complained. "Maybe I need to vent."

"No, you need answers. What is it you can't stand about dating?"

Daisy had to give her credit for persistence. "Let's see. The artificiality of the whole setup. The nervousness leading up to the actual event. The awkwardness. And—oh, yeah, the guys."

Maureen pumped her arms faster as she walked. "Where are you meeting these guys, anyway?"

"Just around. Through friends. That sort of thing."

"Have you tried online?"

"Everybody asks me that. No, I haven't tried online."

"Maybe you should."

"Or not."

"Give me a rundown of your dates so far."

Daisy picked up the pace, wishing she could somehow power walk away from her own life. "My cousin Olivia fixed me up with a guy named Mac. He's a physician's assistant who is planning to go to medical school."

"That sounds…promising. Was it awful?"

"Let's put it this way—he took me to a chain restaurant—"

"Strike one."

"And annoyingly modified everything he ordered—you know, like asking for his croutons on the side and an odd number of ice cubes in his Coke—"

"Strike two."

"And he spent the whole evening talking about how hard the life of a med student is, and how he'll never have time to do anything but study, sleep and work, and how this will go on for years if he wants a specialty."

"Strike three. He's out of there."

"Oh, and he tried to grope me in the parking lot when we said good-night."

"That's foul."

"Way foul."

"I take it you crossed him off your list," said Maureen. "What about the others?"

"Let's see. Then there was Dean from my degree program at school. A fellow photographer. He spent three hours telling me about all the competitions he enters and all the awards he's won. He has four shows a year in Manhattan. It's always great to hear about someone's accomplishments, don't get me wrong. But he has this way of doing it that makes me feel like a total failure."

"Not good. You need to be around people who leave you feeling better about yourself. Any others?"

"Jerome Cady. He's a teacher at the high school. He was brand-new when I was a senior. I remember lots of girls had a crush on him."

"Were you one of those girls?"

She shook her head, remembering the chaotic times. Getting pregnant meant she'd had to leave her exclusive Manhattan high school and move to Avalon, spending her second semester of senior year among strangers. The last thing on her mind had been crushes on teachers. "I was too busy gestating."

"Oh. Well, how is Jerome?"

Daisy sighed. "I think there's something wrong with me."

"Why would you say that?"

"Well, because he's pretty terrific. Still the best-looking teacher at the school. Teaches physics and coaches basketball. Volunteers at his church. What's not to like?"

"You didn't like him."

"I wanted to, Maureen. I really, really tried to. It all felt so forced. I kept telling myself, here's this guy. This great guy who seems really into me, and there must be something wrong with me because I wasn't feeling it."

"It's chemistry," Maureen said. "No one can explain it. And you can't manufacture it. You can make a list of all the things you want in a guy, but if the chemistry is not there, you're sunk."

"That's depressing."

"No, think about it. The chemistry is what helps you see past the surface things and tells you when something is right. In my experience, anyway. I hated dating, too, and I all but gave up. Then Eddie came along and everything about him was wrong for me. Completely wrong. Come on, a librarian and a recovering-alcoholic rock star?"

"You two are great together," Daisy pointed out, though she did realize they seemed an unlikely match. She didn't know Eddie well but had to admire the way he'd changed his life. He was Logan's sponsor in the recovery program and had probably helped Charlie's dad more than she would ever know.

"That's my point," Maureen said. "We're a complete mismatch, except with him, the magic is there."

"I'm not looking for magic. I'd settle for a guy to just be with, and have a good time with." *I'd settle.* Daisy's own words bothered her. No, the *truth* of them bothered her. And they were true, because the lonely ache that kept her awake at night made her realize that while she waited around to find some guy, life was marching on without her.

"Hang in there," Maureen said. "It'll happen. When you least expect it, maybe. Isn't life interesting?"

Daisy stepped into the foyer of the Apple Tree Inn, her stomach clenching with apprehension. She was a fool. She never should have let Olivia talk her into yet another setup. But Olivia had been persuasive. She had offered to take Charlie overnight so Daisy could stay out as late as she wanted. She had been positive this would be a good thing.

So not only was Daisy on another date. She was on another blind date.

She tried not to act nervous, waiting for her mystery man. She perused the foyer, admiring the art on display, etchings by a local artist. The Apple Tree Inn was the most elegant place in town. Located in a restored historic mansion, and overlooking Schuyler River, it was situated beside an orchard.

The decor was spare, with tables arranged around a smallish dance floor by the piano. The menu, hand-lettered in European script, was enticing, featuring local produce, fish and game. This was a place people came to for a celebration, or for pampering, or…for a surprise.

She was wearing a new dress she and Olivia had picked out together on their shopping spree day. Olivia's judgment had been spot on; the dress fit perfectly and had the kind of fluttery, feminine appeal that made it a perfect date dress.

When she'd shown it to Charlie, he had offered her a wide-eyed stare, a big grin and two thumbs-up. "I have the prettiest mom," he'd said.

After which she had done their special dance with him, something they'd made up while being silly one day. Accompanied by whatever happened to be on the radio, it was a mixture of ballroom and beat boy.

"I should cancel and hang out with you tonight," she'd said. "You're all I need."

"I want to go to Olivia's," he'd insisted. "I got my Clifford bag." He loved visiting Olivia and Connor, especially because of his cousin, Zoe. Sleepovers at her house were something special because there was a bunk bed that was exited by a slide, like evacuating an airplane.

Daisy smiled, thinking about her son. Why couldn't he be enough for her? What was she doing, looking for love when the she already had the love of her life?

Okay, I'm going to bail, she thought. Let Mr. Mystery Date make whatever he wanted of her absence. Her heart wasn't in it.

She was digging in her bag—chosen because it looked so good with her shoes—for the car keys when a shadow fell over her.

"Going somewhere?"

Her head snapped up. "Logan! What are you doing here?"

He smiled. "Same thing you are. I'm meeting a date."

Oh, wonderful. Now she really did need to get away. The last thing she wanted was to find herself in the same restaurant as Logan and whoever he was dating.

"You have fun," she said. "I have to go."

"I wish you wouldn't," said Logan.

He looked wonderful, she thought with a twinge. Like, really wonderful. Good without trying too hard, in a well-cut sport coat over a golf shirt and khakis. It looked as if he'd gotten a haircut, too, and the style made the most of his thick, reddish-brown waves.

She wondered who the lucky girl was. Then she squashed the thought and moved toward the door. None of her business.

He touched her arm. "What about our date?" he asked.

Daisy froze. She thought about her cousin's sneakiness in setting this up. Yes, this was definitely a setup. "You're kidding, right?" she asked.

He merely smiled.

"*You're* my mystery date?"

"Surprise."

"Oh, for Pete's sake." In spite of herself, she started to smile. In relief, mostly. Thank God, she thought. Thank God he's not some freak or head case or lech. Finally, a normal guy she actually knew.

"What is going on here, Logan?" she asked.

"Let's talk about it over dinner."

* * *

The salads were made of butter lettuce, fresh pears and walnuts. The pianist was playing quiet, unobtrusive songs, drifting through the consciousness like leaves in the stream, notes forgotten as soon as they were struck.

"You're being a good sport about the fruit in your salad," Daisy pointed out, well aware of his aversion, because he'd apparently passed that on to their son.

"Thanks for noticing. I'm a big believer in separation of fruit, salad and nuts. Tonight I'm making an exception."

"I've been reading *Peter Rabbit* to Charlie, hoping it'll motivate him to eat more salad. It could backfire, though. It might turn him paranoid that Mr. McGregor will come after him with a rake."

Logan regarded her across the table. The linens were white and crisp, the crystal glassware reflecting the glimmering candlelight. "Time," he said quietly.

"I beg your pardon."

"Time-out, I mean. I'm going to set one rule for tonight."

She felt an instant prickle of resistance. "What kind of rule?"

"No talk of Charlie, just for tonight."

"Nonsense. He's all we ever talk about."

"Exactly. That's why we should try talking about other stuff."

What other stuff? she wondered. "Why would you want to leave Charlie out of the conversation?"

He took a drink of his Pellegrino water, set down the glass with firm deliberation. "Because I don't want Charlie to be the only thing we have in common."

The reply startled her. "Okay," she said. "Then…how about you begin by explaining what all this is about." She gestured vaguely around the candlelit restaurant.

"You've dived into the dating pool."

"I said I was going to."

"So I wanted to take you out on a date," he said. "Is that so strange?"

"Then why the cloak-and-dagger stuff, getting Olivia to set us up and all that?"

"I was afraid you'd turn me down."

"Aw, Logan. Come on, what do you take me for?"

"Oh, now there's a loaded question."

"Do you honestly think I would've turned you down?" After as many disappointments as she'd had, she would have been relieved. No, more than that. *Pleased.*

"I don't know," he admitted. "At least this way, you're stuck with me."

"That's one way of putting it."

"I want to show you a good time."

She finished her salad and helped herself to a warm roll from the bread basket. "Well," she said, "honestly, I think it's working."

"Cool."

Their entrées were wonderful. Daisy ordered a terrine of layered roasted vegetables, and Logan had the pan-seared rainbow trout.

Over the course of the meal, Daisy discovered that they had plenty to talk about besides Charlie. She told Logan some of her choice work stories—the bride whose friends shaved off one eyebrow at her bachelorette party, the fainting groom, the canine ring bearer, and they laughed together. He talked about work as well, surprising her when he admitted his struggle to explain to his father that he didn't want to be in the family business.

"They don't get it," he said, referring to his fiercely proud, successful parents. "O'Donnell Industries was founded by my great-grandfather, and there's been an O'Donnell in charge every generation since. That business, though—international shipping—it's not for me."

"What don't you like about it?"

"God, where do I start? Just for example, deals are made in bars over tons of drinks. Not really my scene, I guess you know."

"I do know. I'm glad you know it, too." Sobriety, she realized, could be a fragile thing, and she was grateful Logan worked so hard to preserve it. "Did you ever say that to your dad?"

"Funny, that's something my sponsor asked me. My sponsor in AA."

"And?" she prompted.

"And my dad doesn't quite get it."

"Parents," she said. "Everybody has their share of problems with parents. Me included. Things are better with my folks, now that they're so busy with their new lives."

"Did you save room for dessert?" asked their waiter, coming to refill the water glasses.

"None for me, thanks," said Daisy.

"Just coffee for me," said Logan. "On second thought, bring the chocolate raspberry torte, and two forks."

"You're determined to corrupt me," she accused him, though she knew the dessert would be delicious.

When the plates were cleared, he stood and held out his hand, palm up. "Dance with me."

"Uh…sure." They joined the other slow-dancing couples. He held her gently and they swayed to a soft song. It occurred to her that she had never danced with Logan before. Strange to think they'd made a baby together, he had once impulsively proposed to her and been turned down, yet they'd never had a date and had never danced together.

She liked it so much that they continued for three more sets. It was easy. Comfortable. They seem to fit together.

"Thanks," she said as they sat down to share dessert. "You're a good sport about dancing."

He flashed her a grin. "Dancing's not really my thing. I like dancing with you, though."

"Yeah?"

"Yeah." He leaned in across the table and lowered his voice. "Maybe you're my thing."

The way he said it, the way he looked at her, made her pull back to study his face, trying to read his purpose.

"Don't act so surprised," he said.

"I'm your thing?" she asked, incredulous. She couldn't imagine how. Not only had she turned down his impulsive proposal, she'd gone abroad for half a year. How could she be his thing?

"Maybe you are," he said. "No, you definitely are. You have been for a long time. You simply haven't wanted to see it."

"But—"

"Tell you what. Let's dance again." The piano player glissandoed into another slow song and he caught her in his arms. "And just so you know, after tonight, I want to take you on another date. A real, actual date where I pick you up and we go out and I bring you home."

"Why?"

"Do you have to ask? We had a baby together—"

"We were kids—"

"We had this baby, and now he's our little boy, yet we've never been out on a date."

"That's because we don't like each other. In that way, I mean. People who don't like each other shouldn't date."

"I like you," he insisted, bringing her close against him. "I've always liked you. Even when I hated myself, I liked you."

She was touched by his stark honesty and by the gentleness of his embrace. "If this is how you like someone, I'd hate to see how you treat your enemies."

"I have an insurance agency," he said. "I have no enemies."

She laughed, and it felt so good to laugh with someone, even Logan, with whom her complicated relationship was about to get more complicated. She was willing to let it, though, to take this risk. Lifting her hand, she ran her fingers up the lapel of his jacket. "I believe it," she whispered.

"Good," he said. "I'm glad."

His hand at her waist hugged her in closer still, and what had started out as a dance hold became an embrace. And it felt so wonderful to be held. It had been way too long.

"What's that smile?" he asked.

"It feels nice to hold somebody who isn't smeared with peanut butter and jelly."

Daisy was still smiling when she got home much later, after a little more dancing and a lot more conversation. What a simple thing it was, to enjoy an evening out. She couldn't believe how buoyant it made her feel, to simply set aside stress and worry, to relax and be with Logan. Logan, of all people.

She sat in the car to hear the end of the song playing on the radio. Then she got out and pulled the garage door shut. Logan said he wanted to take her on an *actual* date. In the restaurant parking lot, they had almost kissed. She caught herself wondering what that would have been like.

The thud of a car door closing startled her. Peering through the darkness, she could make out the gleaming shape of Logan's SUV.

"Hey," she said, meeting him on the front walk. "Did you forget something?"

"You could say that, yeah." He pulled her into his arms and gave her a long, sweet kiss. "That's what I forgot."

For a moment, she couldn't speak. The kiss was a delicious surprise. "I'm glad you remembered," she told him.

"I can remember a lot of things, Daisy." He took the keys from her hand and went to the front door, unlocking it.

"I'm not sure this is such a good idea," she said.

"Then what do you say we find out? We've been together before."

"For one weekend, we were together. Not exactly something to build a future on."

"What about this?" he asked, kissing her deeply. "Can we build a future on this?"

Recovering from his kiss, she said, "That's not fair."

They barely got the door shut behind them. He pressed her against it and kissed her long and hard as she clung to him, reaching out to him with all the aching loneliness inside her. There was no further talking in the suddenly urgent race to shed their clothes. They hurried, as if by silent mutual agreement that they did not want to be talked out of this.

Daisy offered not one more breath of protest. She wanted this, too. She wanted the release and surrender of feeling him next to her, the welcome weight of him covering her, filling the empty spaces and holding her through the night.

It was the first time she'd ever spent the entire night with a man. She gave it mixed reviews. On the one hand, it was a heady delight to cuddle up to a large, warm body; she felt cocooned and fulfilled in a way she'd never experienced before. On the other hand, because he was large, he took up a lot of room, and because he was warm, he tended to kick off the covers. She finally understood why people invested in king-size beds.

But on balance, the delight won out. She was made for

this, for being held and caressed and kissed, deep into the night, and then for falling asleep from sweet exhaustion. She woke early, lying still while Logan slept on, breathing loudly but not quite snoring. Feeling a crick in her neck, she eased away from him.

"Not so fast," he muttered, snaking an arm around her midsection and drawing her close. "I'm not done with you. Not even close."

"I have to get going."

"Going where? It's the crack of dawn, Sunday morning."

"I need to take a shower before church."

"Skip the shower," he said, nuzzling the back of her neck. "Skip church."

To be honest, the idea appealed to her. There was something not quite right about heading off to church after a night of illicit sex. Or maybe the service was what she needed. "I have plans to meet Olivia at church and bring Charlie home."

"Let's shower together, then. And we'll go to church together, too."

She sat up, tucking the sheet under her armpits. "Whoa. I don't think we should do that."

"I'll wash your back," he said. "I'd do a really good job."

She couldn't deny a small thrill of excitement. Focus, Daisy. "I mean the church part. Not a good idea. Not today, anyhow."

"I don't know about you, but I'm not worried about coming out as a couple."

"How can we be a couple? Until last night in the lobby of the Apple Tree Inn, I didn't even know we were dating."

"Sweetheart. This has been a long time coming."

"We haven't even figured out what *this* is. How do we even define it?"

"Who says we have to? We're together, we have the greatest kid in the world and everything is fan-effing-tastic." He stretched luxuriously, knocking a file folder off the bedside table. "Sorry," he said, picking up the photo prints that spilled out. "Is this a work thing?"

She bit her lip, feeling nervous as he flipped through the photos. These were very personal shots, her good-bye project to Julian, taken the day she'd revisited all their special places. "It's sort of work. Not for the firm, though."

"I hope not. Jeez, they're depressing as hell," he said, frowning at a close-up of a leaf being washed downstream.

Really? When she looked at the shots, she saw layers of emotion, but not depression. "I was planning to submit them to a juried show at the MoMA. It's really competitive, but it's something I've always wanted to do."

"So even more people can be depressed? Honey, you don't need to run yourself ragged entering shows and taking downer pictures. Weren't you voted best wedding photographer in Ulster County this year? You should stick with what you're best at."

"I'll think about that while I'm in the shower." She slipped from the bed and felt instantly self-conscious, so she snatched up her robe and hurriedly pulled it on. "Oh, God, this is an awkward moment."

He lounged back on the pillows, grinning at her. "Not for me. An awkward moment never killed anyone."

"True."

"And they're over fast."

"That's why they're called moments," she said nervously. Lame, Daisy. She scurried to the bathroom. Just stop talking before you're so lame you can't even walk.

Since she had made the decision to date, she had to be conscious of many more things, like the tidiness of her bathroom. Personal grooming took on a new emphasis. Charlie never cared if she remembered to shave her legs, but now she was forced to attend to such details. Not this morning, though. This morning, she just wanted to be quick.

Hers was an older house, and the plumbing creaked and groaned when she turned on the shower. The tub was an antique claw-footed affair, which was great for baths, but who had time for a bath? The shower was a makeshift arrangement consisting of a spray nozzle and plastic curtain on a rickety metal rod. But the hot water felt heavenly as she worked the kinks out of her neck, gently rubbing her soapy hand over the area.

The curtains stirred, and suddenly Logan was there.

"Hey," she said.

"Hey, yourself. Hand me the soap, will you?"

"There's not enough room here for both of us," she said. "We don't fit."

He gently ran his hands over her neck and shoulders. "We'll make it work."

Despite the warmth of the water running over her, she felt a shiver of remembrance. He'd said those words to her before, long ago. He'd said them on the night they'd made Charlie.

Fifteen

November 2006

Daisy had lied through her teeth to get her parents to let her spend the weekend on Long Island. Her friend Frida, from school, would provide the cover. Frida's family had a beach house in Montauk—that much was true. Daisy begged her parents to let her spend the weekend there.

That was the lie.

The O'Donnells had a place in Montauk, too. Logan O'Donnell had let it be known through the school underground that he was planning a massive party. His parents were in Ireland. He and his friends would have the place all to themselves.

Daisy wasn't proud of the deception, but she had to get away. She had to. The house was like a funeral parlor, with unhappiness lurking in the corners, infesting the curtains and seeping up through the cracks in the floor. Her parents had told her and Max that yes, it was official. They were throwing in the towel. Their marriage was over. No more trial separations, no more pretending things were normal. Mom and Dad were splitting up. The Bellamys would never be a family again.

Max, her younger brother, actually took the news okay, better than he'd taken their marriage. Something about the strain of all those years of trying used to get to Max. He had tantrums and refused to learn to read, which drove their parents nuts. Once they resigned themselves to splitting up, however, Max actually started acting like a normal, happy kid, which probably meant that in the long term, this was the right thing to do.

Daisy was slower to come around. The shrink they took her to said she had to feel her feelings, whatever the hell that meant. She turned her pain and anger into a deep capacity for deception and won their permission to head out for the weekend. Probably they were being lenient because they felt so guilty about everything.

The promised weekend party was a full-blown crazyfest. It was exactly what she needed. Even before she entered the house, perched at the top end of Long Island, she could hear the deep belly pulse of the stereo, blasting Usher's latest hit. The place was a stone's throw from Bernie Madoff's, and he was, like, one of the richest guys in New York. She turned to her girlfriend Kayla and grinned. "I think we found it."

"After you," said Kayla. "Let's go. It's freezing out here."

It was a blustery day on the jagged edge of winter. Daisy went inside to find the downstairs crammed with kids from school. Every surface was covered with open bags of chips, bottles of wine and beer. A giant lobster pot stood on the counter, filled with Everclear punch. Okay, she thought. Sweet oblivion. She guzzled down a few cups of punch, wincing with every gulp. The sweetness failed to mask the sharp bite of the liquor. But it made her feel good, and she moved happily into a group of kids who were dancing in the dimly lit living room. An aroma of pot wafted through the air, the scent an evocative promise of forgetfulness.

Maybe she would smoke some pot later. Maybe she would bum a cigarette from someone.

No, not that. She'd sworn off cigarettes for good last summer. Last summer, with Julian Gastineaux. She had promised him.

It was funny how just thinking about him took her to a better place. She shut her eyes and swayed to the music, and within a few minutes, she was back to the summer, surrounded by warm breezes and majestic views of Camp Kioga.

If not for the renovation project at the summer camp, she and Julian never would have met. He was from a small industrial town east of L.A., while she came from Manhattan's Upper East Side.

Fate was funny that way.

Daisy and Julian had not had a summer romance. A summer romance only lasted for a season. The bond she felt with Julian, even now that he was three thousand miles away, was deeper and stronger than a single summer, stronger than anything she'd ever felt before.

Yet she and Julian had not done anything together all summer except become friends. They hadn't made out or fooled around, even though they'd both wanted to. Daisy had been too messed up. She needed a friend, not a boyfriend. She didn't want to blow it with him by turning things physical too soon. He was too important.

Then again, maybe they would never be more than friends. It was entirely likely they'd never see each other again. Still, she cherished what they had been to each other last summer. She was only sorry she couldn't be with him all the time. He made her know she was special, and maybe more importantly, he made her want to be a better person. More like him, honest and strong and able to deal with whatever the world hurled at him.

She was having trouble keeping her chin up through her parents' divorce, though. It was hard to be good when you felt so bad.

She finished her punch and decided to switch to white wine instead. A grown-up drink. The kind of stuff people drank when they were getting a divorce.

"Hey there, Daisy-Bell." A strong arm slid around her waist.

"Hey, yourself," she said. "Great party, Logan."

"It is, now that you're here." They grinned at one another.

She had known Logan O'Donnell since they were tiny, when she had accidentally bloodied his nose with a tetherball. It was the first time she could remember making someone bleed. She'd felt as though the world was coming to an end, crying louder and harder than Logan himself. She had vowed that day never to hurt anybody ever again.

Through the years, they had known each other with the comfort and familiar ease of old friends. This fall, Logan had started paying a different kind of attention to her. He was in a rare spot for Logan O'Donnell—between girlfriends. He'd been persistent in trying to get Daisy to go out with him. So far she had resisted. Studying him now, she wasn't sure why.

The last of the wine tasted overly sweet. "You're cute, you know that?"

"So people tell me. I bet they tell you that, too."

"I'm a mess. I'd rather be...interesting. Smart. Talented. Or at least, capable of filling out a college application form without feeling as though I'm lying."

He tightened his arm around her. "Tell me about it. My folks have been nagging me about college since preschool.

They want me to go to Columbia or Harvard or a good Jesuit school like Boston College. See? No pressure."

"Where do *you* want to go?"

He hugged her against his side. "Wherever life takes me." Lifting a longnecked bottle, he polished off the last of his beer. Then he took her hand. "Let's go to the beach."

She followed him outside. The night was cold, yet the air was sea-scented, a subtle reminder of warmer times.

The beach at Montauk was vast and timeless, a moonscape of whipped-cream dunes rimmed by the occasional erosion fence and tufted by dry grasses. The beach itself flattened out, disappearing into the late-autumn darkness. Tonight the moon was up, its light glinting in the rushing waves, infusing the foamy water with a bluish glow.

Seized by impulse, Daisy kicked off her sneakers and ran down to the breaking surf. "Come on!" she called.

"Right behind you," he said.

A moment later, they had their pants' legs rolled up and were knee-deep in the surf. The water actually felt warm in contrast to the air.

Daisy flung out her arms and offered up a wordless yell. Logan joined his voice to hers, and they ended up laughing until they were weak. She collapsed against his chest. "Hope we didn't wake the neighbors."

"Nobody's home, not at this time of year."

Indeed, the other houses had only security lights on. The O'Donnell place was ablaze with noise and light. A gut-level thunder of bass pulsed from the stereo. Through the windows, she could see little toy people bobbing around as they danced or talked.

"It's exactly what I needed," she said.

"Me, too," he said, then laughed. "So why are we outside, in the cold, getting soaking wet?"

"Because you're out of your gourd."

"And drunk."

"That, too." She gave his hand a tug and led him to dry sand, where they had a seat together, facing out at the moonlit sea.

"I wish I had my camera," she said. "I'd take a special picture of this night."

"All your pictures are special," Logan said. "Didn't you, like, get offered some big prize for photography?"

She nodded. "The Saloutos Photographic Arts Award last September. In the nature category." She'd entered a shot of Willow Lake at sunrise, one she'd taken last summer. She'd awakened at dawn on a clear day to do a series of sunrise shots. The winning picture had captured a moment when a loon was taking off toward the sky. A chain of water droplets streamed out behind, making the bird appear tethered to the lake by a slender golden thread that shone with a metallic gleam. The thin sweep of amber-tinged clouds created a dramatic backdrop. On hearing that she'd won, she had rushed home to tell her parents, only to find them locked in yet another argument about the same stuff they'd been fighting about forever. It hadn't seemed fair to tout her success at that moment, and her triumph deflated. She hadn't said anything, but put the news on her Facebook page.

"Maybe you can come out here again and bring your camera," Logan suggested.

"Maybe you'll be my model." She framed him with her hands. "You've got that Ralph Lauren vibe going on."

"Right. Let me show you a little leg." He peeled back his damp jeans and flexed his leg, burlesque style.

"What's that scar?" she asked, lowering her hands. The moonlight glinted off a thick zipperlike scar that curved around his knee.

"Old war wound," he said with a chuckle.

"Seriously."

"It's from when I blew out my knee playing soccer. My

dad didn't realize how bad it was and there was a title at stake, so he told me to keep playing. Which, like an idiot, I did, until my knee was so trashed they had to do this big procedure on me, replacing all kinds of stuff in there. We won the tournament, though, so that's something."

"My God," she said, outraged. "I can't believe parents sometimes. The stuff they make us do, I swear…if I ever have kids, I am not going to be like that."

"My old man didn't mean anything by it." Logan's tone was conciliatory. "And hey, the whole ordeal introduced me to my new friend, Oxy." He leaned back and dug a prescription pill bottle out of his pocket. "Ever try one of these? Here, give this a shot."

All the right words popped into her mind: Dangerous. Illegal. Addictive. But the word she spoke was, "Okay." She popped the pill into her mouth, telling herself adults always overstated the danger of things.

"What am I supposed to feel?" she asked.

"Nothing."

"Nothing sounds good to me."

"It's, like, a vacation for the mind. You'll see."

"Speaking of vacation…" She jumped up and peeled off her sweater, shirt and jeans, flinging them to the sand. "Last one in is a rotten egg," she yelled, and raced into the surf. The water felt wonderful, a warm liquid embrace.

Logan followed, wearing only his boxers. "You're crazy," he said, putting his arms around her. "Crazy Daisy."

"This is not going to work," she warned him, even as she leaned in, pressing her hands to his chest. "You and me, I mean. It's not going to work."

"We'll make it work."

And that was the night they made Charlie. Actually, it could have happened on any of several occasions. They did little else. They were into each other and they were careless, and the sex helped them escape their own lives. Neither thought about the fact that there would be permanent and irrevocable ramifications. Both of them believed—if they thought about it at all—their relationship was only temporary.

Sixteen

"We're sorry, Ms. Bellamy," said Mr. Jamieson, the director of the MoMA Emerging Artists program. "We won't be featuring your work this year. The competition was very, very fierce." He slid the packet of application materials and the portfolio of originals across the desk to Daisy.

Seated in the bright, cluttered office in midtown Manhattan, she tried to maintain her dignity. She'd known this was coming; the bad news had arrived via email the day before. Still, all the way down to Manhattan on the train, she had entertained a fantasy that the editorial board would change its mind. We've made a terrible mistake in judgment, they would say. There's no way we can conduct this year's show without your work.

She should have deleted the email and carried on. Instead, she'd decided to come and collect her portfolio in person and spend the day with Sonnet. She'd tried sharing her disappointment with Logan, but he simply didn't understand. "No big deal," he'd said. "Move on."

"Ms. Bellamy?" The director spoke kindly, drawing her back to the present. The sounds of Manhattan—honks, shouts, whistles, sirens—filled the air outside.

"I understand," she said, taking care to appear cool and professional. "I'm grateful for your consideration."

"You have many fans here, and you have ever since your original submission a few years back. It was a tough decision. You're very close."

Good to know, she mused. *Close.*

"I hope you'll submit again for next year's show. Persistence pays. It's trite, I know. In your case, it's true. Many of the artists accepted have gone through the submissions process multiple times."

"I'll certainly keep that in mind." Rejection was part of the process, Daisy told herself. She'd always known that. From her first Kodak Kids prize in the third grade, she'd been keenly aware that when you made art and put it out there, people judged you, and it was completely subjective.

Her entry had been a shot she'd taken of her friend's tabby cat, perfectly silhouetted on the windowsill, its tail a question mark echoed by the shape of a tree branch outside the window. It had placed second, and one judge had noted that many people were allergic to animals. The best shot in the world of a cat wasn't going to impress someone who didn't like cats.

"On a personal note, I want you to know, I'm one of those fans," said Mr. Jamieson. "I've seen quite a lot of growth in your work from the previous submission to this one. This portfolio is more mature, and the point of view is stronger. It's a good deal darker in tone."

Losing the love of your life will do that to a girl, she thought.

She met Sonnet by the UN, and they headed downtown on the subway for lunch in Chinatown.

"They're nuts," said Sonnet, when Daisy told her the results of this year's jury. "Completely batty. They ought to be begging you for material."

"Thanks," Daisy said. "I'm not going to let myself get depressed."

"Good for you. Next year's coming up before you know it."

Daisy tried not to think about all the hours and hours of work and focus and concentration it was going to take to put together another portfolio. Many people believed taking pictures was a matter of point and shoot. They didn't consider what it was like to wait in the freezing cold for the light to reach a certain quality, or to spend hours laboring over an image to elevate it into an expression of her art.

"I'll be okay," Daisy said. "Tell me something good. How's work? How's life?"

"Work is amazing," Sonnet said, and her face was filled with light. "Work is my life."

"Try to remember to have both, okay?"

"Easier said than done. My hours are insane and I never know what's happening next. I've made some great friends at work, and we go out when we can."

"Anybody special?"

"Oh, don't get me started on guys."

"I figured you'd be meeting all kinds of cool, exotic foreign guys at the UN."

Sonnet stabbed her fork at a kalamata olive. "I'm meeting them all the time. I don't know about 'exotic,' though. I'm still looking. I went out with a Finn who was gorgeous, but he was all over me after one drink. It did give me a chance to practice my self-defense skills and I'm happy to report that they work quite well."

"Really? Did you make a scene?"

"No. I have to watch myself, because of the job. My duties require me to 'demonstrate integrity by modeling the UN values and ethical standards,'" she recited. "Anyway, he was too embarrassed and he walked away.

A good outcome. Oh, and then I went out with this guy from Ghana but he had issues."

"What kind of issues?"

"OCD, I think. He was constantly cleaning his hands with disinfectant gel and knocking his fists on the table. And a guy from the Latvian delegation asked me out, but he looks like a troll and drinks like a fish. Where the hell are all the normal guys?"

"In fairy tales. Disney cartoons."

Sonnet heaved a sigh. "Exactly. There's a reason Disney's *Tarzan* is my favorite movie. So how about you? How's the dating going?"

"Surprisingly well."

Sonnet leaned forward. "Really? That's great. Anyone special?"

Daisy hesitated. "Actually, yes. I'm seeing Logan."

"Logan O'Donnell? Get *out*."

Sonnet had been in the loop from the start, ever since they were teenagers. She had seen Daisy arrive in Avalon, still dreaming about her summer with Julian. She'd been one of the first to learn Daisy's crushing news that she was pregnant. And she had witnessed the fallout from the Logan-versus-Julian smack down. Daisy had sworn after that incident that she was through with them, and probably with men in general. So much for keeping that vow. She'd gotten engaged to one guy and now was dating the other.

"We were set up," she explained. "By Olivia. She sent us on a blind date and it worked out…really well."

"How well?"

Daisy flushed and glanced away.

"Thank God," said Sonnet. "You're finally getting laid."

"Guilty as charged."

"That's a relief. I was worried you'd *never* get any action. So how's it going?"

"Well, it's…nice. Extremely nice."

The new relationship with Logan had been an awakening for Daisy. Finally she felt herself shedding the hurt and grief of the past, and when she looked to the future, the days ahead were colored by hope.

"What's going to happen?" Sonnet asked.

"I don't know. We're being really low-key about it because of Charlie. Don't want to give him weird mixed signals. Something's happening, though. And it feels good."

"Well. I hardly know what to say."

"You'll think of something."

"I've always respected Logan. I mean, you guys didn't exactly travel the standard route to starting a family, but he stepped up and took responsibility, and he's been a really good dad. I have to say, I'm liking this." Sonnet polished off her salad.

"Me, too."

They paid their tab and went for a walk in the city, wandering over to historic Orchard Street for the shops. "I love it here so much," Daisy said, inhaling the New York smells of exhaust, garbage, coffee and food from the street corner carts. The energetic bustle of pedestrians and the buzz of excitement in the air was such a contrast to the placid serenity of Avalon. There was a sense of things happening here, of life moving forward.

"You should visit more often," Sonnet said.

"I should. I'll try to do that."

They shopped the funky sidewalk markets and boutiques in search of something cheap but perfect. For Sonnet, it was a ruby-red fringed shawl that she said would be ideal for long meetings in the chilly glass-and-steel conference rooms of the UN. And for Daisy, a pair of delicate chandelier earrings that were completely impractical but so pretty she had to have them. At a book stall, Sonnet picked out a volume of Persian poetry, saying she had no time to read a novel or memoir. Daisy selected the latest by Robert Dugoni, her favorite thriller writer. Reading was her way to unwind and go to sleep at night. Perversely, the more disturbing the story, the better she slept.

Although, lately she had a new way of unwinding—making love with Logan and then falling asleep in his arms. Yet she still wasn't ready to commit to him and didn't want to confuse Charlie, so they had to sneak around as if they were still teenagers, and Logan had to slip out before dawn. Sometimes she wished he could stay, but she still hadn't decided what to tell Charlie.

"How is Zach these days?" Sonnet asked, her tone self-consciously casual.

"I wondered when you'd get around to asking." Daisy had always sensed the attraction between the two of them. They were both quick to deny it, but that didn't make them any less attracted to one another. "Zach is great," she said. "Same as always."

"Is he seeing anyone?"

"Not unless you count staring at your picture."

"Really? He stares at my picture?"

"Incessantly."

"Is it a good shot?"

"Not the same as seeing you in person," Daisy said. "You should come for a visit."

Seventeen

"I want to explain us to Charlie," Logan said to Daisy. It was something he'd been thinking about for a while. Things were going well with them and he wanted to take this—whatever it was—to the next level. "We've been together long enough to know this is not a fluke. It's time." He took care to speak in a reasonable tone. Not pushy or aggressive. He'd tried that with her in the past, and it never worked. When he pushed, Daisy pushed back.

Now she surprised him by saying, "I've been trying to figure out an explanation myself. He knows we've been, um, hanging out a lot."

Logan slipped his arm around her, his confidence lifting. "Not as much as I'd like. So how about we level with him over dinner tonight?"

"Tonight?"

"The sooner, the better. Once Charlie understands, we can finally come out as a couple."

She sighed. "That would be...great. Yes, I think we should tell him. It's been strange, trying to act as if nothing is going on."

Logan felt a wave of relief. This was going to go well.

It was something he had focused on for a long time, and finally he could see a future for them.

"Tell you what," he said. "We'll take him swimming at the park after work. We can explain it to him then."

Her eyes darted away, then returned to him. "All right. That will be the plan."

They met later at Blanchard Park, which had a busy swimming area with a beach and a dock. Charlie was overjoyed to go swimming. Kids were running around everywhere, chasing beach balls, playing tag, rushing out into the cool, clear lake water.

Daisy had brought along an old blanket and some towels and Blake on her leash. Logan and Blake had settled into a mode of mutual tolerance. Neither was terribly enamored with the other, but they were part of the same family, and they were about to get a lot closer. Daisy spread the blanket under a tree and tethered the dog. Blake trotted around as if patrolling the perimeter.

"Ready for a swim, my man?" Logan asked Charlie.

"Yes." Charlie peeled off his T-shirt.

"Hang on," Daisy said. "Sunscreen. Even though it's late in the day, you could still burn."

Charlie submitted, presenting his back to her and stretching out his arms like a martyr.

"Trust me," Logan said, "sunscreen is better than a sunburn. I once got a sunburn so bad it made blisters."

"Yikes," said Charlie, turning to Daisy and screwing up his face while she applied more cream.

"Yikes is right. You and I both have the same pale skin and believe me, it does not like the sun."

"Why do we have pale skin?"

"It's the Irish O'Donnell in us—white skin and freckles. Contributes to our manly appearance." He struck a body builder pose, which Charlie instantly emulated.

Charlie was big for his age, with a taut, strong body and plenty of physical coordination. With his fiery red hair and light spray of freckles across his nose, he was all O'Donnell. Logan was proud of the resemblance, but he tempered his pride with caution. Attaching all your pride and expectations to a kid could be toxic. He was proof of that, for sure, trashing his knee just so his dad could see him play in a damn high school soccer match. Glancing down at the sickle-shaped scar, he could still feel the blazing fountain of pain that had erupted from his knee. And still he'd managed to score the victory goal and savor the expression of blissful pride in his father's face. Had it been worth it?

A quiet, dysfunctional voice in his head whispered, *Yes.* He kind of hated it that making his dad happy trumped keeping his own freaking knee. The Oxy pills had made it all easier to bear—the fiery physical agony as well as the need to escape his father's emotional hold on him. And thus the cycle had gone, a cycle he was determined *not* to repeat with his own son.

Logan peeled off his golf shirt, feeling a twinge of self-consciousness about his thickening waistline. Damn desk job.

"Something wrong?" asked Daisy.

"Just thinking I need to get to the gym more often."

Her face softened and she slipped her arms around him. "Stop it. You're just right. You look like a young Russell Crowe to me."

"I assume that's a good thing?"

"A very good thing." Stepping back, she shrugged out of the oversized shirt she was wearing, and he forgot all his complaints. He forgot everything.

He must've made an involuntary sound, because she sent him a teasing grin. "Behave."

"Yes, ma'am."

"Ready?" Charlie asked, jumping up and down.

They each took hold of one of his hands and ran together into the water, Charlie squealing with delight.

"Watch, Momdad, watch me swim," Charlie ordered, gesturing for them to make room. He'd been in swimming lessons at the community aquatic center and had recently been promoted from pollywog to minnow. His strokes were squirmy and a little desperate, but he crossed the distance between his parents several times before getting winded.

"That's amazing, bud," Logan said. "You the man."

"Yeah, I'm the man." He beat his chest, caveman style, but nearly sank in the process.

"They haven't worked on treading water in his swim class," Daisy pointed out, grabbing his little white arm.

In the shallows, they chased each other and splashed around. This was the best part of having a kid—being able to cut loose and have fun, without a care in the world. Logan knew he'd become a father way too young, but he had grown into the role. He'd been clean and sober for years, and his biggest motivation was right here, this squirming, laughing, forty-pound ball of energy.

And things were going so damn well with Daisy. For the first time in a long time, Logan dared to believe they could be a family. He caught Daisy's eye, and they shared a smile that was full of promise.

Charlie slowed down a little to watch some kids running to the end of the dock and jumping in. Logan recognized the longing in the kid's expression.

"You want to do that?" he asked Charlie. "You want to jump off the dock?"

Charlie shook his head and grabbed Daisy's hand.

"Come on," Logan cajoled. "I can tell you want to."

Charlie shook his head more vigorously and clung harder.

What are you, a chicken shit? Logan's father's voice jeered in his head. *Quit being a baby.*

Logan shoved the nagging memory into a dark corner of his mind. That was his father's way, not his.

"We can go together," he said. "I'll hang on to you, buddy."

"No," said Charlie. "I'm going to wait for Daddy-boy."

The lake water turned to ice. That was how it felt to Logan, anyway. Daisy wore a look of such naked emotional pain that he felt it, too.

She quickly recovered and said, "I told you about Julian. He's not coming back."

"Then how will I ever jump?"

Logan couldn't believe the kid still remembered him. In Charlie's world, a week was an eternity, and Julian had been gone a lot longer than that.

Daisy offered a helpless shrug.

"Tell you what," Logan said, pushing past the tense moment, "let's talk about dinner."

"Dinner!" Charlie's face lit up.

"I was thinking the Tastee Freeze."

"Yes, yes, yes!" Charlie leapfrogged for joy in the shallows.

Daisy laughed. "Good job, Logan."

"Tell me you don't like the Tastee Freeze."

"Are you kidding? Everybody loves it. Charlie most of all."

"Let's get dried off and go."

One of the chief virtues of the place was that it was a drive-in. Totally old-school, with roller-skating carhops, trays that hooked onto the car windows. Each parking bay had an illustrated menu with buttons that lit up when you pushed them to order something.

And order they did—burgers, curly fries, milk shakes,

a dinosaur-themed kid's tray for Charlie, cones of soft-serve for dessert.

"Now this," Charlie declared, "is awesome."

Daisy and Logan laughed. It was cool to hear the kid talking like an adult.

"Promise me you won't get carsick on the way home," Logan said.

"Pinky swear," Charlie said, holding out his small, sticky hand.

Charlie told Logan he didn't understand why he needed a bath if he'd been swimming, but Logan coaxed him into the tub with the promise of a few minutes of Xbox before bed. Even while he gave the kid a bath, then hurried him into his Yankees pajamas, Logan could sense a peculiar tension in the house.

They still needed to tell Charlie about their new relationship. The conversation was long overdue. Daisy was going to do most of the talking.

Charlie stood on his step stool and brushed his teeth in a hurry. "Okay, I'm ready for Xbox."

"Sure," said Logan, carrying him piggyback into the living room. "Your mom and I want to tell you something first."

"Will it be quick?"

"I don't know. I guess it can be if you listen real well."

Daisy patted the sofa beside her. "Come here, you."

Charlie clambered up and Logan settled on his other side. Logan was surprised to feel a prickle of nervousness in his chest. What if the kid didn't like the idea of a guy horning in on his mom? Maybe there was something to this Freudian crap about boys being subconsciously jealous of their mothers. What if the kid brought up Julian again? What if—

"Hey, Charlie," Daisy said in a cheery voice. "You

know how much you like it when your dad comes around and does stuff with you?"

"Uh-huh. Like Xbox."

"And swimming and going for ice cream and being around the house. You seem to like that a lot."

"Yep."

"Well, it turns out I like it, too. I like being a family with you and your dad."

"Like the Three Bears," Charlie said.

"Right. And, um, I also like being with your dad even when you're not around. We are, uh, kind of like boyfriend and girlfriend. Do you know what that means?"

"Yup. Kissing and loooove." He started jiggling his foot with impatience.

"Wow. I guess you know more than I thought."

Logan jumped in, sensing Charlie was getting antsy. "We wanted to make sure that's all right with you, if your mom and I have some kissing and love."

"It's okay." He jiggled the other foot.

"And suppose we have a sleepover?" Logan said. "Is that okay, too?"

"I like sleepovers," said Charlie.

"I meant, the kind of sleepover where I sleep in the bed with your mom."

"Sometimes I sleep with Mom," Charlie said with a slight frown.

"You can still do that," Logan said. "Sometimes."

"Okay."

"So you're good with me and your dad being together," Daisy said.

"Okay. I'm ready for Xbox."

Logan grinned at Daisy over their son's head. It was hard to tell how much Charlie had taken in and how much he'd actually understood.

Time would tell.

Eighteen

Daisy hunkered down at her computer, laboring over a shot she was considering for her new portfolio. She'd decided to take her last rejection from the MoMA program as a personal challenge and was now trying hard to regain her confidence. Giving up was not an option.

Persistence had a price. She had to steal hours whenever she could, and sometimes she felt guilty, opting out of family time or social time in order to work.

The labor was absorbing, though, and the result was often its own reward. The image currently on her screen was a complex composition, one that had taken her days to capture and hours to edit it to perfection. She had wanted a particular view of the Avalon Free Library, a solid Greek-revival stone building surrounded by a park-like grove of giant horse chestnut trees.

When the sun was just so, and there were people and dogs in the park, it looked like an image out of a dream. An interesting dream at that, maybe something the artist Seurat might have painted. A patina of nostalgia overlay the picture, yet it didn't have a sheen of cheap sentiment. Instead, it seemed to capture the life of a community for a moment in time, expressing the story she wanted to tell.

She had such mixed feelings about Avalon. It was the place she called home, where she found support and connection to the friends and family she loved. Still, there was a part of her—a secret, reckless part—that sometimes yearned for a different life. Living in Germany with Charlie had been an incredible adventure, but instead of satisfying her wanderlust, the trip had left her hungry for more.

Something in her picture of Avalon expressed that subtle, inner restlessness, shaded by patient adjustments made with her editing program, and she had a sense that this shot was important to her as an artist.

The screen door snapped like a mousetrap, startling her.

"Hey, babe," Logan called, coming in from the backyard with Charlie. "My buddy here and I were talking about going to the Hornets game this afternoon. What do you say?"

"Yeah, Mom," Charlie chimed in. "Say yeah."

The prospect of an afternoon at the ballpark tapped into that same push-pull of conflict she'd been feeling. Family time with Charlie and his dad was priceless, yet her time for working on the portfolio was limited. She had a wedding to shoot tonight, meaning a tight turnaround between game and work. She'd have to ditch the portfolio for the rest of the day.

"Well," she said, "I was putting the finishing touches on these library shots." She gestured at the screen, curious to see what they thought.

"Nice," said Logan.

"Pretty, Mom," said Charlie. "So can we go?"

She regarded them both, so alike in their rusty haired, green-eyed adorableness and plaintive expressions. "Sure," she said. "I'll finish this some other time." She swiveled around in her chair to save her work, clicking "Yes" to the pop-up query on the screen.

The moment she did so, she realized her boneheaded mistake. The window had said "Discard all changes?" And she had just obliterated hours of painstaking, impossible-to-replicate work.

Her heart sank down to her churning stomach. There was nothing—*nothing*—quite so frustrating as knowing the work had been lost, along with the energy that had inspired it. "I can't believe I just did that. I discarded all my editing and I'm back to the raw file."

"Looks pretty much the same to me," Logan commented with a glance at the screen. "Come on, we'd better go."

She literally bit her tongue. It was not Logan's job to understand and commiserate over her costly blunder. If not for Logan, she wouldn't have had the entire Saturday morning to work, anyway. "So. A Hornets game." She forced brightness into her tone.

"It's George Bellamy Memorial day, according to the schedule," Logan reminded her.

"Oh, man," she said. "I'd totally forgotten about that. Of course I wouldn't miss it."

"Who is George Bellamy?" Charlie asked, putting on his beloved Hornets cap.

"Great-granddad's older brother. We never got to meet him because we were in Germany when he came to town."

"Will we see him today?"

"No, he died. A memorial means people will remember him, especially today." George had left a legacy to the city, funding the ballpark in perpetuity.

"I hate when people die," Charlie remarked.

Daisy winced at the bald truth of his statement. Time had blunted the searing sharpness of losing Julian, but every so often a reminder reared up and caught her unaware, stabbing her in an unseen place. "George was really old," she said. "And sick. Great-granddad is going to be really happy to see us at the ballpark today. We should get going."

She checked herself in the mirror. Legs recently shaved, hair washed this morning. Not bad. Since starting this new thing with Logan, she'd embraced her girly side again. Personal grooming took on new meaning. "Welcome back to the land of the living," she said to her reflection.

The Avalon Hornets were the town's pride and joy—a bona fide professional team in the Can-Am league. They were having a great season, too, and the club boasted a hot new pitcher named Danny Alvarado, so the crowd was substantial and parking scarce.

"Check it out," Logan said, regarding several rows of bleachers near the third base line. "It's like a Bellamy family reunion."

"Wow, I'm glad you reminded me to come," Daisy said. "Thanks, Logan."

"No prob." He slung his arm around her shoulders, drew her close.

Her dad and brother were there, along with her grandparents and a bunch of aunts, uncles and cousins. Within moments, they were seated in the midst of everyone she loved.

"Hey, you made it," her dad exclaimed, his face lighting up. "Get over here in the cheering section."

Daisy struggled to shake off her frustration with work. She sat back, determined to enjoy the company and the game.

"My goodness," her grandmother Jane murmured, settling next to her, "you two are quite smitten with each other these days, aren't you?" She indicated Logan, who was busy showing Charlie how to toss a piece of popcorn in the air and catch it in his mouth.

"I guess we are," Daisy agreed.

Her grandmother gave her hand a squeeze. "You seem happy. That makes me happy."

Daisy was learning, day by day, to redefine happiness for herself. It was no longer an effortless embrace of each day but a concerted choice. She tried to pay attention to the game. The plays were being called by a semi-celebrity, Kim Crutcher, a sports commentator whose husband pitched for the Yankees. But Daisy's focus kept coming back to Logan. She observed how naturally he fit in with her family, as though he was already one of them. He leaned toward her dad, saying something that made him laugh.

A vendor passed with a tray of cold beers for sale. Probably only Daisy could read the wistful yearning in Logan's face. He had his demons but kept them in check. She knew it wasn't easy, and hadn't been all through the college years, when the next party was only a dorm room away.

His chief motivation sat by his side, swinging his feet and eating popcorn. Charlie idolized his dad. As Daisy watched, they each sipped their root beer in unison and belched at the same time, celebrating their success with a fist bump.

"They're quite a pair," her grandmother observed.

"They sure are." She gave a little laugh. "Whoever thought Logan and I would date?"

"What's wrong with it?"

"We've done everything out of order—first the baby, then coparenting, and…now this." She and Logan were hard to define. The little family they'd made brought her a feeling of security, and after everything that had happened, she knew this was something to cherish.

Her grandmother smiled. "Life happens to us in as many ways as there are people. The important thing is that it happens."

"Charlie's so nuts about his dad. I love how the two of them are together."

"And you?"

"What about me?"

"How do you feel about Charlie's dad?"

"I…" It was the first time anyone had directly asked her that question. "He's been wonderful. He makes me feel lucky we're together. I'm pretty sure that this is meant to be."

Olivia, seated on her other side, leaned over and said, "Does that mean what I think it means?"

Daisy flushed. "Maybe it does." It did feel good to finally push away the heavy burden of grief, storing it in some shadowy corner where she wasn't compelled to feel it all the time. Heartache was not a good way to go through life. She was grateful to Logan for pulling her out of the darkness.

Sometimes, she reflected, love simply happened on its own, like a rainbow…or an accident. Or like Julian. Other times, she was learning, it was up to her to make love happen, to build it layer by layer. Watching Logan with her family, she knew she owed it to him—and to Charlie and herself—to try.

By August, they were talking about moving in together. Daisy wasn't sure who broached the topic first. Perhaps it had been Logan, jokingly referring to his house as a glorified place to check his email and pick up his laundry delivery, because he was never there anymore. Or it might have been Daisy, looking in her fridge one day and realizing the contents had changed entirely.

"It's full of man-food," she said one morning, rummaging around for the grapefruit juice.

"What do you mean, man-food?" Logan asked, glancing up from his iPhone.

"Just, you know, food guys eat."

"Like what?"

"Bacon, for one thing."

"Who doesn't like bacon?"

"That's not the point. I like bacon myself, but I never buy the stuff unless it's turkey bacon."

"Turkey bacon." He shuddered. "If you like bacon, you should buy bacon."

"And this," she said. "Five varieties of cold cuts. Flavors of mustard not found in nature. Whole milk. It's guy food."

"Okay, guilty as charged. What do you want me to do about it?"

"Nothing. I was making an observation."

"So what did you use to keep in your fridge?"

"Yogurt. Veggies. Soy milk."

"Girl food. No wonder Charlie wants me to live here."

Oh, God. "Did you bring it up with him?" she demanded, ready to panic.

"Come on, Daisy. What do you take me for? When we tell him, we'll tell him together."

"Of course," she said. "Sorry. I know you'd never do something like that."

"Good. So, about Charlie…when do you want to have that talk with him?"

"First we have to figure out what to tell him." The prospect made her stomach flutter, and she realized this talk was really more for her and Logan, not Charlie. She wished she could borrow some of Logan's ease with the whole situation.

"That's a no-brainer," he said. "We tell the kid we love

him and each other, and we want to be together all the time. He'll be down with that. You know he will."

Logan was right. Their son loved nothing better than having the three of them together. Truth be told, Daisy felt the same way. When she was with Logan and Charlie, she was in her right place in the world.

"He'll want specifics," she pointed out. "Like whose house we'll live in, and where he's going to put his stuff."

"I've been thinking about that," Logan said. "My place would work best. This is a rental, and it's pretty small. We'll all move to my house on Caliburn Ave."

Logan's house was in a gentrified neighborhood of older homes, with shade trees and sidewalks on both sides of the street. Daisy's rental was in a slightly funky, bohemian little area of town, filled with nice people who had more imagination than money. Logan's neighborhood was a haven for the upwardly mobile, which she found slightly ironic. He had been born to the O'Donnell shipping fortune. Had he stuck with his family's plan, he could live anywhere he wanted, but he had something to prove. He wanted to make it on his own.

She related to that entirely. Both her parents had been supportive of her from the moment she told them she was going to have a baby and would be a single mother by age nineteen. Either one of them would have gladly helped her in any way, providing whatever she needed.

She had opted for independence, getting her own place, balancing school and work and Charlie. It had been harder that way but ultimately the rewards were greater. Being a good mom to Charlie meant making a life on her own.

And now here was this new opportunity. To be a traditional family with Logan.

What a concept.

"All right. Let's figure out how and when to tell him."

He laughed and pulled her into a bear hug, picking her

up until her feet left the floor. "Sweetheart, that's the easy part. And I have a great idea."

She shut her eyes and let his laughter fill her up, knowing she was ready at last to go forward toward a future she'd never imagined.

Nineteen

Night pressed in around him, and his head was too heavy to lift. His arms and legs, also too heavy. Even his eyelids—glued shut. He tried to move his jaw. No success. Holy shit. Was he in a coma, then? He'd read of cases in which a person appeared to be in a coma, yet had enough cognitive function to be aware on some level.

No way, he thought. No freaking way would he let that be his fate.

A sound came from his throat. He was pretty sure the sound came from him. He couldn't form words but emitted a throaty rumble. Then he managed to open his eyes to slits, blurred by his lashes. The wheelchair that had been his home—his *hell* for the past year—slowly came into focus.

He tried his best to shake off the vestiges of the dream. The nightmare. But really, it was neither; it was the memory that haunted him, waking or sleeping. The dream, which looped over and over in his head, tortured him with a reminder that he had escaped death, only to find himself in hell.

His mind played through the events that had brought

him here. He hadn't made it out of Colombia. He'd been blasted out of the chopper, he'd fallen from the sky.

He had been so disoriented in those early hours after the incident. Lights had flashed in his eyes; a strange feeling of numbness claimed his body. He remembered trying to figure out where the hell he was. What about the unit? Were they looking for him?

When he'd first come to, he'd found himself in a white room. Whitewashed ceiling and walls, white blinds covering a single window. White sheets covering his unmoving legs. A white door swinging open, a guy in a white coat.

Yes, Julian had thought. He was in Medical.

"Move your feet for me," said the bored-looking doctor.

Why would the doctor talk to him in Spanish?

"Try, please. Move your feet," a voice had repeated, still in Spanish.

A guy in olive-drab fatigues had come into the room. He wore a flat cap and had a full beard, and was armed with a semiautomatic pistol and a belt heavy with clips. The stenciled webbing on his chest identified him as Palacio. A deputy of some sort. "He's awake, I see. Lucky dog, surviving a fall into the ocean like that. We'll see if his luck holds with Don Benito."

Slowly it had dawned on Julian that he wasn't with the good guys anymore. He was a prisoner, and the hospital was part of the drug lord's empire. Benito Gamboa was served by a private militia that was better funded than the state's military. Apparently Palacio was part of Gamboa's security force, and the doctor was probably on the payroll, too. Or maybe he wasn't a doctor at all. The white coat might mean he was a lab tech for the cocaine production operation. Or a torture specialist, maybe.

In those first hours of captivity, Julian had willed his feet to move, but they weren't there. He could see his bare legs and feet, livid with cuts and bruises, but they didn't even seem attached to him. "I cannot," he'd said.

"Try again."

His legs were useless. Not even numb. Just…gone. "I cannot."

The doctor took out a long-needled syringe. And then another. The mysterious injections went in. Then the doc had jabbed the needle into first one toe, then another. Then into Julian's ankle in its most tender spot; no sensation came through. He set his jaw, but his mind was screaming in wordless denial. He remembered his late father's ordeal, becoming paralyzed in a single second. It was a kind of death.

Somehow, he had managed to detach, going away in his head to a different place. To Willow Lake, its surface as still as glass. As still as Julian, who took himself away from the shock of waking up a prisoner, paralyzed. He was that lake water, unmoving, unruffled by the slightest breeze.

"Well?" asked the deputy.

"No function or feeling in the lower extremities."

"I'll make a note for the interrogators."

The statement had been chilling in its very matter-of-fact nature. Julian understood then that he would be tortured.

The doctor had cleared his throat, seeming uncomfortable. "The standard protocol is a course of physical therapy to restore whatever functionality we can."

"This is not a service offered to a prisoner. Maybe he is not as lucky as I thought. Don Benito will decide whether or not to keep him alive."

The doctor had said nothing. A week later, Julian had been manhandled into a wheelchair, blindfolded and transferred. In the ensuing months, he'd been moved repeatedly, treated in ways he couldn't even conjure up in his worst nightmares.

Long ago, he'd lost all hope of rescue or release. They were keeping his existence a secret, fearful of reprisals from U.S. or multinational forces. He wasn't sure why he was still alive, for what purpose. They were killing him slowly, with indifference and neglect, punctuated by torture sessions that left him breathless.

Julian closed his eyes again, praying the nightmares and memories would give way to the only thing that was keeping him alive—a dream of Daisy, and home.

Twenty

"One more time on Pirates of the Caribbean," Charlie begged, his face alight with enthusiasm. "Please."

The Technicolor chaos that was Disneyland swirled around Daisy's small son. She traded a glance with Logan, knowing they would both be in agreement. A trip to Disneyland didn't come around every day, and they were determined to make the most of it.

"Tell you what," she suggested. "You guys go together, and I'll take your picture."

"Cool," said Charlie. "Come on, Dad."

These were not the kind of pictures she usually took, but the wild activity, with its color and light and frenetic movement, inspired her. She captured both father and son laughing, their heads thrown back, the two of them completely overtaken by surprise and delight.

"Good call, Logan," she murmured under her breath, "this is a perfect way to celebrate Charlie's fifth birthday."

Logan had never been one for half measures. When Daisy agreed they should tell Charlie they were going to live together, Logan had suggested they deliver the news right after his birthday. They didn't want to tell him *on* his birthday. That might send the wrong message.

In his usual larger-than-life way, Logan had organized a three-day adventure. He insisted it had to be Disney-*land*, not Disney World, because nothing was ever as good as the original. While they were away, a local moving company would bring Daisy's belongings to Logan's house. Not all of them, she corrected herself. There was a box of things Julian had given her—mementos, pictures, little gifts, her engagement ring—she had stored at her mother's house. She couldn't let go of them, but neither could she bring them into her new life with Logan.

The comparisons had to stop. The loss of Julian would forever be an ache in her heart, and she would never replicate what they'd had. In a tiny corner of her heart, she recognized that she and Logan didn't share the grand and breathless passion she'd found with Julian. Theirs had been a once-in-a-lifetime love, and she knew better than to search for it with someone else. Her relationship with Logan was quiet and secure, a bond forged by their mutual love for Charlie. She had to stop thinking about what she'd lost and focus on what she could have. When they arrived home, they would all be living under the same roof. A family.

At last.

The prospect filled her with a sense of purpose. She had not agreed to this blindly or impulsively. She'd committed to it, and so had Logan, and they were both determined not only to make it work, but to find a new kind of happiness together, the three of them. Logan offered comfort, security, stability, safety. And relief—Lord, sweet relief from the dating. She'd known him all her life, and his friendship had helped her through her grief.

She could see a future with him. Logan would never break her heart...because he'd never owned her heart, not the way Julian had.

She and Logan were going into this with eyes wide-open. Neither of them assumed it would be a cakewalk. Starting a serious relationship felt a bit like moving to a foreign country. She had to learn a new language, a new culture. She was ready, though.

While waiting for them to finish being pirates, she photographed some of the details of Disneyland. The August day in Anaheim was blindingly hot, and the park was crowded with excited kids and families. There was a peculiar beauty in all the artifice—the pristine, geometrically laid-out gardens, the pinwheels of coordinated color everywhere she turned. Unsightly features were camouflaged by clever plantings and facades, rocks made of resin, and glossy, giant-headed characters.

There was one section of fence where the sprinkler system had apparently failed. The hedge there had died, leaving only the skeletal remains of a few shrubberies. Beyond that, she could see a chain-link fence and a parking lot crammed with touring coaches and marigold-colored school buses. As she watched, a bus pulled to the curb and disgorged a tumble of excited kids, mostly black- or brown-skinned, all of them wearing school T-shirts.

She zoomed in on a little girl who was so excited, she spun in pirouettes on the sidewalk, her multiple braids flying outward.

Then Daisy noticed the lettering on the side of the bus—Chino Valley Unified School District.

That was where Julian had gone to high school. He'd never had much to say about Chino, California, only that he'd gotten in trouble there, and it was nobody's fault but his own. He'd said this with a smile on his face, long ago, adding, "If I hadn't been a juvenile delinquent, I never would have been packed off to Camp Kioga that one summer. Never would have met you."

Thoughts of him often sneaked up on her like this, despite her resolve to focus on the future. Many times since he'd died, she been told by well-meaning friends, "At least you have your memories to cherish."

She did have memories, and she definitely cherished them, but they offered small comfort when she contemplated all that was lost at the bottom of the ocean. She and Julian simply hadn't had enough time together. They'd had shared dreams, fantasies, aspirations. Not enough time. Never enough time.

"Yo, Daisy-Mama," Logan yelled at her, using a pet name she wasn't completely in love with. He was carrying Charlie on his shoulders and grinning from ear to ear. "You wandered away. I thought we'd lost you."

She lifted the camera to her face and snapped their picture. "I'm right here," she said.

The airport in Anaheim didn't have a direct flight home, so they had a long layover in Las Vegas. To make matters worse, mechanical difficulties grounded the aircraft, and passengers were offered generous premiums for giving up their seats on subsequent overbooked flights.

"Let's do it," Logan said suddenly. "Let's give up our seats and have a night in Vegas."

"Yeah! Vegas, baby," Charlie said, though he clearly had no idea what the city was about.

Daisy hesitated. "But—"

"Please," they both said in unison.

She laughed at their pleading expressions. Then she called and left a message with Olivia, who was taking care of Blake. Afterward, she caught Zach at the studio.

"No worries," he said when she explained about the delay. "There's nothing on the schedule until Friday night."

"Thanks, Zach. Tell everyone I'll see them on Tuesday."

"Will do. Vegas, eh?"

"Yeah, we've got a day to explore the city. I've never been to Vegas before."

"I've heard you can get into a lot of trouble there."

She laughed. "We'll do our best. Right now we're working on getting a cab."

"Okay. Well, don't do anything too wild."

"*Moi?* Never."

Logan managed to corral a cab. They could have waited for a hotel shuttle, but it was sweltering hot, and Charlie was hungry and cranky.

In the taxi, Logan studied the voucher he'd been given by the airline. "Airporter Express," he muttered, crumpling up the slip of paper. "You know what? I've got a better idea."

"Now what?" She regarded him suspiciously.

"We've got one night in Vegas. We can do better than the Airporter Express."

"I don't understand."

He leaned forward to the driver. "Take us to the Bellagio."

"What's the Bellagio?" Charlie asked.

"It's kind of like Disneyland, only for grown-ups."

Logan hadn't been exaggerating. In fact, all the artifice of Disneyland dimmed in comparison to the incredible light show that was the Vegas strip. Charlie momentarily forgot his hunger as he stared out the window, slack-jawed with amazement.

"Hey, Momdad," he said. "Look at all the people." He pressed his face to the taxi window, watching street performers, winos, tourists and hookers against a backdrop of massive casino hotels. "What is this place?"

"I don't think we're in Kansas anymore, Toto," Daisy said.

"Cool."

“Does the hotel have a swimming pool?” Charlie asked, focusing on the only feature that mattered to him.

“I don’t know. Logan, is there a pool?”

Logan laughed. “Is there a pool?”

The Bellagio had much more than several pools. It also boasted a huge singing, dancing fountain that erupted in time with the music. They stood in front of the massive water feature, gaping like the tourists they were. People gathered at the figured concrete railing to watch. Logan bought hot dogs from a vendor for himself and Charlie, to hold them over until dinnertime. No fewer than three newlywed couples stopped for pictures. Daisy was not in work mode, but she appreciated the brides’ bubbly happiness and the way the water feature exemplified their soaring joy.

As one couple walked into the lobby ahead of them, she overheard the groom asking, “Now, what was your name again?”

“I want to wear my Mickey Mouse ears,” Charlie said. At Disneyland, a giant Mickey had shaken his hand. The ears had instantly become a sacred object to him.

“No problemo,” Logan said, and approached the front desk. While he registered, Daisy and Charlie explored the lobby. It was beautiful in an overly designed, aggressive way. There were fabulous art pieces, blown glass, paintings by old masters, sculptures in lit alcoves. Shops filled with sparkling jewelry, colorful fashions, sumptuous gifts, bags and luggage lined the hallway. The glittering artifice made Daisy feel as if she’d landed in some alternate universe. Faintly, behind everything, she could hear the sounds of the engine that drove the entire city—the electronic pings and burbles of the slot machines and games emanating from some unseen casino.

“It’s incredible,” she said to Logan in the elevator on the way up to their room. “I’m blown away.”

“Me, too,” said Charlie.

"We haven't seen the room yet," Logan pointed out.

It was on the top floor. Daisy held her breath as he opened it with the key card. He swung the door wide, and she gasped aloud. The room was flooded with sunlight filtered through the sheerest of drapes.

A balcony overlooked the heart of Vegas. There was a seating area with a bar and a wide-screen TV. The vast king-size bed was draped in rococo glory. Charlie raced to the window and pressed his nose against the glass. "I love Las Vegas," he declared.

Laughing, Logan hoisted him up. "We're going to make the most of our night here, okay?"

"Can we go swimming now?"

Logan nodded, and Charlie ran to his suitcase, digging for his swim trunks.

"I didn't pack with this layover in mind," Daisy said, retrieving his still-damp swimsuit from a plastic bag.

"It's okay, Mom," he said. "We'll get wet in the pool, anyway."

Wrinkling her nose, she said, "What's worse than putting on a clammy bathing suit?"

"I have a great idea. You go down to the lobby shops and buy a new swimsuit. And a dress, too. Buy a really nice dress for tonight."

"Oh. I don't think—"

"Come on, humor me. Look, they gave me a twenty-percent-off coupon at one of the lobby boutiques when I checked in."

"I don't need—"

"Go for it, Daisy. It'd make me happy. Charlie and I will meet you at the pool."

"Way to twist my arm," she said. "I'll make it quick."

The shop with the coupon was called Lola's, and the sign in the window bore the slogan, Whatever Lola Wants,

Lola Gets. The collection leaned toward tropical prints, gold lamé and plus sizes. The only other person around was the woman at the counter, who was middle-aged with skin that had seen too much sun, and her hair was dyed, fried and flipped to the side in a style that had gone out of fashion in the eighties.

"Welcome to Lola's," she said in a smoker's voice. She had a nice smile that didn't quite mask a kind of loneliness Daisy could relate to.

"Er, I came in to see if there was a swimsuit," she said, feeling a bit trapped by all the metallic fabrics.

"Ah. Your husband called me."

"My husband—"

"Mr. O'Donnell. Suite 3347."

Daisy immediately thought of Charlie. "Is something wrong?"

"Not at all. He wanted to make sure you get everything you need here, and that the bill goes to him."

Logan loved making grand gestures like that.

The shopkeeper chuckled, gesturing at the crammed racks. "You're a lucky woman. Go ahead, knock yourself out."

"Thanks," Daisy said, knowing now she would never get out of Lola's without buying something from the inventory of gypsy-colored garments. "So much to look at," she said diplomatically. "I really just need a swimsuit."

"Let me see what we have in your size. You're a bit smaller and younger than my usual clients. I probably shouldn't say that." With expert precision, she snapped through a rack. "These might be the only two I have in a small."

The options were a leopard-skin bikini and a shiny silver garment, more space suit than swimsuit. Daisy thought about her clammy red maillot and wished she'd settled for that.

She hadn't said a word, but the woman read her mind. "Let me see if we have anything in the back in your size."

Daisy contemplated making a break for it. How had a simple, single-layover flight home become so complicated?

Turning from a family of two into a family of three had its challenges, and she knew she would be discovering new ones every day. She reminded herself that it also had its rewards, and that was what she would stay focused on.

She flipped idly through the dresses to see if something jumped out at her. What did one wear to dinner in Vegas? Apparently, something made with feathers, metallic fabric or crushed velvet. A couple of the dresses had all three—a trifecta of bad taste.

She knew her suitcase would yield a more tempting option, even if that meant she had to iron something.

"Honey, I hit the jackpot, as we like to say in Sin City." The shop lady emerged from her cramped back room with some garments draped over her forearm. "These are going to look fabulous on you."

Daisy had already resigned herself to a mercy purchase, buying something for the sake of the saleslady, who was probably on commission. Smiling politely, she took the garments to the small curtained area in the corner.

"I don't wear much white," she said, shucking her jeans and tank top. "I've got a little boy who tends to get his grubby hands on everything— *oh*."

She tugged the white tankini in place and stared at herself in the mirror.

"How is it?" the woman asked.

Daisy parted the curtain and went to check herself out in the three-way mirror. "I like it. I never thought I'd like a white swimsuit."

"This one is lined to the hilt, so you don't have to worry about it being see-through, wet or dry. I've always liked the look of a blonde in white. It's very striking and classy."

Daisy conceded the point. There were touches of gold, but only in the piping that edged the neckline of the suit.

"Great," she said. "I'll take it."

"And try the dress. It's by the same designer. She's retro, but in a fun way, I think."

The dress was also white, with a halter-style bodice and a full, floaty skirt. When Daisy stepped out, the woman clasped her hands in delight.

"It's as pretty as I'd hoped. You look like Marilyn Monroe in that famous subway-grate shot. You can tell that dress was inspired by it."

Even though Marilyn Monroe was from her grandmother's era, Daisy was familiar with the iconic photo from *The Seven Year Itch*. The shot had made—no, *defined*—the career of photographer Sam Shaw. Even today, students of photography argued the pros and cons of having an entire body of work measured against a single famous image.

"Both pieces have been marked down," said the woman. "They're the last ones I have left."

Daisy surrendered. "Then I'd better get both."

"And these." The woman offered a pair of gold-heeled sandals embellished with crystal beads. "Shoes make the outfit."

The guys were already at the pool—one of the five Mediterranean-inspired pools—by the time Daisy made her purchases and joined them. Logan was swirling Charlie in circles as they both made motorboat sounds.

She located their stuff on a lounge chair and shrugged out of her terry-cloth robe. When Logan spotted her, he froze as if the pool water had turned to ice.

"Wow," he said, saying much more with his eyes.

"Mom!" Charlie grinned up at her. "There you are. We've been waiting and waiting forever."

She slipped into the pool, feeling a tiny bit self-conscious about the suit. "The water feels good, doesn't it?"

"Totally good." His eyelashes were spiked like the points of stars. He exuded happiness, and suddenly she was glad about the forced layover. He constantly reminded her that every day offered a new adventure.

Logan's gaze kept lingering on Daisy, and the heat in his eyes awakened another sort of reminder—she finally got to have a sex life. She'd been deprived for too long.

A flush of warmth coursed through her, and she dived beneath the surface of the clear water. The three of them played and splashed each other, lost in the pleasure of the unexpected vacation.

After a while, Charlie's attention meandered to a group of kids about his age, darting in and out of the gushing fountain in the shallow end.

"Can I go?" he asked.

"Sure," Logan said before Daisy could reply. "Your mom and I will keep an eye on you."

"Did you put sunscreen on him?" Daisy asked.

"Of course. The waterproof stuff in the blue bottle."

"Thanks. Sorry to be such a mother hen."

"Believe me, I don't want him getting burned, either. He'd fry like an egg in the sun." Logan leaned down, indicating his shoulder. "See the scarring there? It's from soccer camp when I was in sixth grade. I was on the no-shirt team, and I fried. Blistered, too, and puked all night from sun exposure."

"Poor guy." She bobbed up in the water and kissed his shoulders, first one and then the other. He was as handsome as ever, an Irish hunk. He'd grown husky, but it looked good on him, making him seem more substantial and mature, somehow.

Charlie had already joined in a game of keep-away with a beach ball and was in the thick of things, laughing and yelling as he lunged for the ball.

"He's great with other kids," Daisy observed. "I'm really proud of him for that. He used to be shy."

"He's getting over it."

She hesitated. "I think he's become more self-confident and independent since you and I got together."

Logan smiled hugely. "Yeah?"

"You're good for him. For *us*."

"Yeah, likewise." He slid his arm around her.

"Charlie is growing up so fast," Daisy observed. "And listen to me. I *do* sound like a mother hen, one with an empty nest. I'm too young to be an empty nester."

He leaned over and kissed her. "Then don't be."

"What's that supposed to mean?" She was almost afraid to hear his answer.

"Wait here a second." He hoisted himself out of the pool and went to the lounge chairs where their things were stashed. He returned a moment later with a glossy trifold brochure. "I was wondering if you had any plans tonight."

"What did you have in mind?"

His hand seemed to tremble a little as he showed her the brochure. "How about we get married?"

"I beg your pardon."

"You heard me." He took both her hands in his, right there, waist-deep in pool water. "Look, I'm not going to go down on one knee and ask you. I tried that once, and we both know how it turned out. My feelings haven't changed, though. I still want to make a life with you and Charlie. I'm no Julian. I'm no GI Joe out saving the world. But I'm the guy who's been there from day one, and I don't plan on going anywhere else."

Her heart sped up. Really? Was he really saying this?

Every word he'd said was true. From the moment she'd

told him she was pregnant—fully expecting him to deny responsibility and turn his back on her—he had been a steady presence in her and Charlie's lives. The day Charlie was born, Logan had brought her a pizza in the hospital and vowed he'd always be there for their son. So far, he'd kept his promise.

"But…marriage?" She backed up against the pool's edge, poised to hoist herself out of the water.

She didn't realize she'd spoken aloud until Logan said, "The Always and Forever Wedding Chapel is booked for six o'clock, followed by the best table at Le Cirque for the three of us."

"When did you do all this?"

"I bought the 'Romantic Impulse' bridal package at check-in. Including a pair of rings from the lobby jeweler."

She hesitated, half in and half out of the pool. Could he be serious? The notion made her feel…strange. Strangely happy. But…outmaneuvered.

On the other hand, without Logan, where would she be? Drifting, alone, in love with a ghost, unable to let go of memories. That wasn't healthy for her *or* Charlie.

One more heartbeat of hesitation passed. Then she lowered herself back into the water. With a laugh of abandon, she splashed Logan. "You're crazy," she said.

"Dearly beloved…"

Daisy stood in her Marilyn Monroe–style dress beside a slicked-down and surprisingly nervous Logan, while Charlie sat nearby in a molded plastic chair and looked on, agog. She had been given a bouquet of small pink daphnes, and the strong scent tickled her nose. Canned organ music emanated from speakers hidden behind the fake gilt-and-marble columns lining the Always and Forever Chapel. Between the notes, the sound of traffic from the Vegas strip could be heard.

The officiant was a young Asian man named Mr. Lee, who seemed to take his duties seriously. He read in mild, even tones from a pamphlet marked "Short Version."

Short. In a matter of minutes, she would be pronounced Mrs. Logan O'Donnell.

They faced each other, holding hands, and repeated their vows after the officiant. Despite the circumstances, the vows felt weighty and real.

Daisy could scarcely believe she'd agreed to the plan. On the one hand, doing this felt like the ultimate impulse. Married in Vegas? Seriously?

In a strange way, it felt inevitable. She and Logan had every reason to marry. They'd known each other forever and wanted to give Charlie a traditional family. They'd already committed to moving in together. This was part of the natural progression of things. Wasn't it?

While getting ready for the ceremony, she'd had a twinge of conscience. She had been tempted to call her mother and Sonnet, to get their blessing, and maybe to be told that this reckless impulse was bound to lead to something good. But she didn't call them. She wanted to feel confident in making this decision, uninfluenced by anyone.

And, okay, she didn't want them to blast her for cheating them out of the chance to put on a wedding for her. Sure, it would have been fun, but this was about her future, not about a one-day event.

It was a leap of faith, and she had to trust that marrying Logan would work out. In her experience, leaps of faith often did.

Of course, those that didn't were usually termed *mistakes.*

"Daisy..." Logan gave her hand a squeeze, prompting her to speak.

"Oh, sorry." She mentally regrouped. "Uh, yes. I do."

The matching bands Logan had bought were very pretty, gold etched with a Florentine texture. When he'd shown them to her earlier, she'd tried hers on. "It fits perfectly."

"I didn't think your ring size had changed since..." His voice had trailed off.

They both realized it probably wasn't the best idea to bring up that long-ago failed proposal, not now. It seemed so distant, something that had happened to a different person in a different life.

Now the new golden band glided onto her finger as Logan repeated the traditional vows. Daisy did the same, her hands trembling with the import of the symbolic act. From the corner of her eye, she could see Charlie fidgeting in his chair and swinging his feet.

Hang on, buddy, she thought. We're nearly done here.

The officiant obliged her with haste, concluding the ceremony quickly. "You may now kiss the bride."

Logan smiled down at her and placed a gentle, brief kiss on her mouth. "Welcome to the world, Mrs. O'Donnell," he whispered, stepping back and gazing down at her with a look of pride and triumph.

She smiled back, then turned and held out her hand to Charlie. "How about that?" she asked. "Your mom and dad are married."

He beamed at both of them. "Finally."

The curiously adult inflection broke the tension, and they had a laugh. Mr. Lee gestured at a round table with a fringed cloth. "We have to do a little paperwork, and you'll be on your way."

The certificate was signed all around and witnessed by Mr. Lee's assistant, who had been working the sound system. "Congratulations." He handed them the official packet. "I hope you'll be happy together."

Logan shook his hand. "That's the plan," he said.

Part Three

Twenty-One

Through slitted eyes, Julian stared at the wand of the cattle prod, hovering near his face. His heart raced with unnatural force, as though it possessed a will of its own, the will to escape his tormented body. He was strapped into a battered wheelchair that bore the scratches and dents of former users, including *Jesús me guarde* etched in the chipping black paint. His prison-issue clothes—a loose blouse and pantaloons made of rough burlap—had been wetted down to better conduct the current.

The *picana eléctrica* was an old-school torture device, first used by the gauchos of Argentina on their herds. Nowadays it was commonly applied to prisoners, a cheap and effective way to deliver agony and disorientation without killing the victim.

This particular interrogation team was new to him; whenever they moved his location, he faced a new team. From the start of his imprisonment, he had been moved, blindfolded and hooded, at least a dozen times. He suspected this was to keep him from mounting an escape. And it worked. There was simply no time to come up with a strategy.

The interrogator was a slender man in paramilitary

garb, who looked more like a fussy bureaucrat than a practiced torturer. He leaned toward Julian and spoke in English. "You give us nothing, we offer you everything. Freedom, escape, for the simple truth."

They wanted information about the cooperative operation. Julian could barely make his jaw function as he repeated the only information he was authorized to offer—his name and rank, social security number and date of birth. Each time he was moved to a different location, a new interrogator took over, but despite the beatings, the electrocutions, sleep deprivation and coercion, he gave up nothing. His training in SERE—survival, evasion, resistance, escape—had come into play from his first moment of captivity, and he held fast to its harsh lessons. In attempting escape, he would probably die. In staying put, he most certainly would die. There really was no other option.

"Again, to the temple," the interrogator instructed in Spanish.

Julian was a master at hiding things. He didn't know where this skill came from, but he used it every moment of every day. He pretended to have only a rudimentary grasp of Spanish; as a thick piece of rubber was inserted in his mouth, he gave no sign that he knew where the prod would touch.

He retreated in his mind, a technique he'd rehearsed during the mock interrogations of his training. He coaxed himself back to his earliest days, living in New Orleans with his bachelor father. His dad had been a brilliant man, gifted far beyond his humble roots in southern Louisiana. He had loved Julian in his distracted but sincere way, teaching him the principles of rocket science as a bonding activity.

Julian remembered the exact moment when he realized love made him brave. He'd been maybe six years old.

It was a steaming summer day, and the window units of their wood frame house were churning out cool, mildew-scented air. Their place was a small guest house, squeezed between mansions on Coralie Street, convenient to the university. His dad was in the cluttered dining room—which was never used for eating—laboring over some problem or theory. Julian, hot and bored, had decided to climb to the top of the fig tree in the backyard because that was where he'd find the ripest, sweetest fruit. The climb was wicked fun, and he'd reached from branch to branch until he felt as if he'd gone to the top of everything. Being aloft in the tree had been a revelation. The world below didn't appear so large and complicated and bewildering. Instead, it intrigued him; it was something he could understand and fit into, like a piece of a puzzle. Everything was in perspective. No wonder birds seemed to soar for the sheer joy of it. Who wouldn't want to be as high in the sky as possible?

"Dad," he yelled, hoping his father could hear him despite the chugging of the old dripping air conditioner wedged in the window. "Hey, Dad, look how high I am!"

The branch he'd been on bowed but did not break. It was almost graceful, the way it dropped him. He grabbed another branch to save himself, managing to hook on with one hand. He hung there briefly, stunned by the distance to the ground but oddly energized by the danger. He fought to hang on, all the while knowing he would lose this battle. Gravity would do what gravity always did. When your dad was a renowned physicist, you grew up with this understanding.

The smooth bark had offered no purchase, and the tree let him go. The second he was airborne, he had an immediate sensation of weightlessness. This had been rudely disrupted when he'd crashed down through a series of branches below him, then hit the ground with a *whump.*

He didn't remember crying out as he fell, but something must have alerted his dad. Maybe the sound of his long fall through the branches of the gnarled old tree had grabbed his dad's attention.

Everything had rushed out of Julian on impact. His next breath of air eluded him completely. Mute and wild-eyed with panic, he'd gazed up to see his father looming over him, as imposing as the Lord above. Julian's vision had focused, and he'd seen his father's terror, rimmed in stark white around his eyes.

His father never left his side while the ambulance guys came. He'd talked to Julian more than he'd ever talked to him before, speaking in reassuring tones, saying he loved him, praying Julian wasn't hurt.

At the emergency room, they'd examined everything about Julian, inside and out. They'd shone a light in his eyes, put headphones on him to check his hearing, listened to all his insides with stethoscopes and ultrasounds, had taken X-ray pictures of him and scanned his brain.

Julian had learned a couple of new words that day—*abrasions* and *contusions*. It was a fancy way of saying scrapes and bruises. He learned that, although even the minor ones hurt, things could have been worse. Lots worse. No matter how hard the doctors searched and prodded, that was all they could find wrong with him.

And throughout the tests and observations, his dad had been there, projecting worry and love and relief. It was the longest amount of time in Julian's memory that his dad had stayed focused solely on him. He had never felt so loved and secure.

All because he'd dared to climb to a high place.

"You're a very lucky young man," the doctor said, signing his name on a form.

Julian had felt a flood of warmth. "Yes, sir."

After that, he'd been brave about everything. He knew

he could be brave because his dad loved him. He was no idiot; he realized he wasn't invincible, but courage that came from confidence took him to new places. He was always pushing at the edges of safety, climbing trees and water towers, scaling walls, jumping from bridges and train trestles, riding a bike or skateboard in hair-raising places. No one scolded him. His dad believed, in the most scientific sense, that for every action there was a reaction, and this held true for growing boys. Everything a kid did had consequences, which made scolding unnecessary.

Julian, of course, found this out the hard way, having to face disgruntled property owners, highway patrolmen, traffic cops, schoolteachers. His dad had never judged him, but simply loved him in his distracted but sincere way.

And so, when Professor Gastineaux was in a wreck and ended up in a wheelchair, Julian had despaired and lost faith. Loving his father was not enough to heal him. Julian had felt stupid for ever believing otherwise.

"Don't you fret, honey," his dad had said, surrounded by all kinds of high-tech gear. "I'm safe now."

To Julian, it was beyond comprehension how someone could feel safe without the full use of his body. His dad said he could still think and theorize and teach, and those were the things that were important to him.

He had been sent to a rehab facility to be trained for his new life, and the training included personal stuff, everything from drinking a soda to going to the bathroom. During this process, eight-year-old Julian was sent to summer camp, where his much-older half brother Connor worked as a counselor.

Camp Kioga had given Julian a glimpse of a different life. He'd never really seen people who lived this way, their days revolving around organized activities, sing-alongs and home-cooked meals served family-style at long tables in an old-fashioned pavilion.

Sending him to Camp Kioga had turned out to be his father's final gift to Julian. For when he'd returned to New Orleans, he'd been told his father did not have much longer to live. "Not much longer" turned out to be a few years, during which Julian made it his mission to absorb every bit of knowledge and love his father offered. He learned the painful intimacy of caring for someone in a wheelchair, and he never resented his father's physical needs. Young as Julian was, something in him had recognized that when time was short, you made the most of it.

He had a mother he didn't know. Supposedly she'd tried to keep him after he was born, but within six months, she'd had enough and gave him to his dad to raise. She kept trying to launch an acting career, and she didn't pretend to be happy about bringing Julian back in her life. Unfortunately, when Julian's father quietly passed away one night, neither she nor Julian had a choice.

Seared by loneliness and grief, he'd been forced to move to California. There, he'd hurtled his way through adolescence, hell-bent on self-destruction. He'd careened recklessly through each day, taking risks and getting in trouble, always one incident away from juvey. After his junior year of high school, his exasperated mother had sent him to Camp Kioga once again, this time to help his brother renovate the summer place. If not for that summer, he probably would've gone off the rails long ago. Instead, it became the summer of Daisy Bellamy.

Reality came splashing back as a bucket of water was dumped over him. The odd smell of high voltage electricity—more a sensation than a smell, really—mingled with the harsh prison stench. A string of spittle pooled in a fold of his shirt.

"Ever wonder if paralysis can be cured with an electrical current?" asked the voltage operator. "I have seen a dead frog animated with a shock." He yanked at the waist tie of Julian's trousers, recoiling when he exposed the condom catheter that conducted urine into an attached bag. "Good God, what is that?"

"You will have to remove it if you intend to shock the genitals," said a laconic voice.

Julian thought he was hallucinating. Francisco Ramos? He didn't move or offer a sign of recognition. He wondered what Ramos, the partner who'd surrendered during the recon mission, had endured in order to become a part of this operation. Their gazes met for a fraction of a second.

"Disgusting," said the operator. "Forget it."

"He has no sensation anyway," Ramos said. "That is why he cannot take a piss on his own."

Toileting was the least of Julian's worries. His father, wheelchair bound from the time of his accident to the end of his life, had made such things seem routine to Julian.

So where the hell are you now, genius? he asked himself. Stuck in a hole in the jungle somewhere, a prisoner with no hope of justice. This was what he got for trying to be a good guy, minding his p's and q's, joining the military. Looking back, he figured he'd have been better off being a juvenile delinquent.

The thought filled him with dark amusement. Another survival tactic. If you can keep a sense of humor or at least irony, maybe you're not so far gone.

Another tactic was something called self-guided imagery, sending your mind on a trip to a better place. That was where Daisy came in. He had developed the ability to conjure her image in his mind in the minutest detail—the shadow of her eyelashes on her cheeks, the shape of her fingernails, the sound of her laughter, the way her smile lit him up when he walked into a room, the scent of her hair when she laid her head against his chest. He made sure he thought of her many times a day because he didn't want her to slip away, inch by inch.

She was the great love of his life. This was something he knew with gut-level certainty. He'd sensed it the first moment he'd laid eyes on her—beautiful and troubled, with a chip on her shoulder and a bad attitude. Even then, her sweetness had seeped out, as irrepressible as the rising sun.

Daisy. She was the whole reason he opened his eyes each morning. The reason he took the next breath of air. She was the reason he would find a way out of this hellhole.

He pictured her now in her favorite place, relaxing on a dock overlooking Willow Lake. He could see her sun-browned arms braced behind her, head tipped back as she lifted her face to the sun. Her corn-silk hair had always been long; she claimed she was too insecure to cut it short. He claimed she was too beautiful. It was a good argument to have. The prospect of a lifetime of arguing with her kept him sane and focused.

Sanity and focus, he reminded himself again and again. Sanity and focus. In this situation, they were mandatory.

Ramos had a distinctive gait, no doubt due to the leg injury that had caused him to surrender. Julian stayed completely still when he heard the footsteps outside his cell, giving no sign of recognition. "Take these in with his meal," Ramos said.

"Why should he be given something to read?" the guard demanded.

"Best to occupy his mind with fiction. It is better, anyway, than letting him lie around all day, contemplating rebellion."

Along with the day's rations—the usual stale, crumbling arepa bread and some beans in broth—were two battered paperback books in English. Julian suspected Ramos understood completely the irony of the subjects. There was a Penguin Classics edition of *The Count of Monte Cristo* and a copy of *Alice's Adventures in Wonderland,* its pages curled and yellowed. Julian devoured both books, combing the text for any sign of intel from Ramos. The only possible clues were a couple of dog-eared page in *Alice*—"So many out-of-the-way things had happened lately, that Alice had begun to think that very few things indeed were really impossible…."

Julian couldn't tell whether or not the passage had been marked by design or by happenstance.

He read both texts obsessively, absorbing the words, even memorizing whole passages. Each book was a particular sort of fantasy—a tale of injustice, endurance, escape and revenge. On the surface, Monte Cristo seemed to reflect Julian's situation—a man imprisoned and forgotten, bent on escape.

Yet he felt more of a kinship with Alice, trying to find a way back through the rabbit hole. He was a stranger in a strange land, filled with characters who bore him ill will or, at best, utter indifference. Some were as insane as the Mad Hatter, their brains fried on coke, their livers stewing in *aguardiente,* which more than lived up to its literal translation, "burning water."

Edmond Dantès was another kind of lifeline. Reading the frayed pages of *The Count of Monte Cristo*, Julian learned there was more power in forbearance than in an exploding temper. He never lost it, no matter how they tormented him. Poor Dantès had to wait seventeen years for success. That was another thing Julian had learned—things could always be worse. Always.

Alice was more puzzling, maybe because she was female. Another passage that may or may not have been marked by a crease in the page gave him much to contemplate: "Just at this moment Alice felt a very curious sensation, which puzzled her a good deal until she made out what it was: she was beginning to grow larger again, and she thought at first she would get up and leave the court; but on second thoughts she decided to remain where she was as long as there was room for her."

Twenty-Two

"Well, look at you." Sonnet breezed into Daisy's house to find Daisy hard at work, applying a maple-colored stain to the dining room baseboards.

"I'd rather not, thanks," said Daisy, blowing upward to chase a lock of hair out of her eyes. She was long overdue for a trim.

"You look so…domestic," Sonnet said. "Mrs. Happy Hands at Home."

"Right, that's me." The phrase had appeared in an outdated home economics textbook they'd been made to study in high school. Apparently the authors considered an idle wife to be the devil's instrument, and so keeping busy at all costs was advocated.

"What on earth are you doing? I'm up from the city to babysit for your first anniversary weekend and you're what, painting the woodwork?"

"Staining," Daisy corrected her. "I'm staining the woodwork because it needs doing."

"Well, I hope you've got some big plans for this weekend, seeing how the wedding itself was kind of a non-event."

Daisy sat back on her heels. "You're still bitter about that, aren't you?"

"*Moi?* Bitter? Why would I be bitter about my best friend and stepsister running off and getting married on the sly?"

"It wasn't like that. It was…spontaneous."

"You were my only hope of being a maid of honor, and it was snatched away by your insane Vegas impulse."

"I'll get out my tiny violin." Daisy used a rag to rub on more stain. She knew Sonnet had forgiven her long ago.

"Seriously, how's it going?" Sonnet asked. "And I don't mean the woodwork."

Daisy ducked her head and rubbed harder. "Great," she said, ignoring a secret tug in her gut. "We gave Charlie a family. It's what I've always wanted. I—"

The phone rang.

"Could you get that?" Daisy asked. "My hands are a mess."

Sonnet picked up. "Oh, hey, Logan. It's your stepsister-in-law. You know, the perfect one." She was quiet for a moment. "Okay, sure. I'll let her know."

She rang off. "He's going to be late tonight. Said not to hold up dinner."

Daisy nodded. It wasn't unusual for him to miss dinner. Business was good for Logan, but the downside was, he worked long hours. He was consumed with doing well. His schedule made for some lonely evenings, but she was determined not to complain.

"So it'll just be the three of us for dinner, then," said Sonnet.

"Call Zach," Daisy suggested, finishing the last of the baseboards. "He loves coming for dinner, and he always brings a pie from the bakery."

"You keep trying to play matchmaker."

"You know you like him. You always have."

"Zach? He drives me out of my mind."

"That's a good sign."

"Being out of my mind?"

"Right." Against her will, Daisy remembered feeling so in love with Julian she couldn't think straight. Even now, she could still recapture that feeling—a flutter of the heart, an all-consuming passion that did seem like a kind of insanity.

She reined in the thought. She was married to Logan now. To *Logan*. He was a good husband, and he'd stepped up, giving her this home, turning the three of them into a family.

"Call Zach," she said again.

"Fine, whatever." Sonnet dialed the phone. "Voice mail," she said. "Hey, it's me. Daisy wants you to come to dinner tonight. She says to bring a pie. And it wouldn't kill me if it was peach. Six o'clock, okay?"

Daisy had to smile. Just talking to his voice mail put a sparkle in Sonnet's eyes.

"Done," said Sonnet. "It's up to him now."

"And you were so gracious about it. I thought working at the UN would teach you diplomacy."

"I'm off duty."

Daisy stood up and surveyed her work. The dining room gleamed with the richness of the old wood, revived by the refinishing process. "Nice, huh?"

"The whole house looks great. Domesticity agrees with you."

"Hmm. I'm not sure I want it to. But I do like working on the place."

Daisy had always wanted a place on the lake, but Logan preferred this neighborhood, with its tree-lined avenues and proximity to town and schools. She felt an odd compulsion to make it beautiful. For reasons Daisy refused to examine, it was hugely important for her to create a lovely house and garden. It was more than pride of ownership. She wanted this house to look like the kind of place where a happy family lived and thrived.

Because that was what they were, she reminded herself.

Blake, her little dog, wandered in, sneezing as she caught a whiff of the stain. Logan had never really warmed up to the terrier, but he tolerated her for Charlie's sake. The boy and the dog were inseparable.

"Hey, girl." Sonnet got down on the floor, offering Blake some serious belly rubs. The terrier's eyes glazed over with bliss. "Life is so simple for a dog," Sonnet remarked.

"That's why it's nice, having her. She reminds me every day to keep things simple."

Blake flipped over, coming to attention, and her ears pricked up.

"Check this out," Daisy said. "She can hear the school bus a block away."

Tiny toenails scrabbling, the dog shot toward the front door. A few moments later, Charlie came tumbling in. He dived for the floor, lying down on the hall carpet while Blake covered him in kisses.

"Heya, kiddo," Sonnet said. "Don't I get a hug?" Charlie jumped up and went to her. Round-cheeked and red-haired, his green eyes alight, he was a baby no longer.

"Aunt Sonnet, I didn't know you were coming."

"I'm staying for dinner," she said. "And Zach is bringing pie for dessert."

"Awright."

"How is first grade treating you?" Sonnet asked.

"Good," he said quickly.

Sonnet probably didn't notice the flicker of uncertainty in his eyes, but Daisy caught it. She went over to him and planted a kiss on the top of his head.

"Hey, little man," she said.

"You smell funny." He wrinkled his nose.

"I've been staining the baseboards."

"You're always doing stuff to the house."

"That's because it's our house, and I want to make it nice."

"Boring," he said.

She picked up his backpack. "How was school?"

The flicker again.

"Charlie?"

"There's a note from Mrs. Jensen," he mumbled.

Her heart sank. She unzipped the backpack and fished out a long white envelope. Now what? she wondered, exchanging a glance with Sonnet as she unfolded the note. Even before reading it, she knew it was bad news. The school year had barely begun, yet the teacher was already seeing red flags.

"Charlie continues to act out inappropriately when he should be focusing on his lessons," the note read in even Palmer Method handwriting. Mrs. Jensen was old-school, preferring a handwritten note to email. "He is still quite behind in his reading skills. I would like to schedule a meeting at a mutually convenient time."

Charlie watched her, contrite. "Am I in trouble?"

She took a deep breath. "We'll talk about it when your father gets home. And I can't believe I said that. Good lord, Charlie, you're turning me into my mother."

"Huh?"

"Never mind. For now, we'll hang out with Sonnet."

"It's a beautiful day," Sonnet said. "Why don't we take Blake out in the backyard and have a game of catch?"

"Yeah!" As mercurial as his dad, Charlie switched from despondent to eager as he led the way out the back door.

"I need to get cleaned up," Daisy said. "I'll be down in a few."

She put away the painting supplies and went upstairs to scrub her hands and face and change clothes. Charlie's laughter wafted up through the open window, followed by Blake's barking.

Stepping into the bedroom, Daisy tried to shrug off her troubled feeling. The bedroom was supposed to be a sanctuary of tranquillity, right? Olivia had helped her decorate, picking out shades of subtle blue and white, everything carefully coordinated for this showcase of a house.

She put on some nicer jeans and a loose, flowy tank top. A happy family. They had their ups and downs, same as everyone, but at the end of the day, all was well.

Mostly.

Making marriage work was a process. She and Logan had to be patient and understanding with each other, same as they were with Charlie. Tomorrow night would be a great chance for some quality time. They had reservations at the Apple Tree Inn to celebrate their first year together.

She ran a brush through her hair, pausing with her arm lifted.

Great, the rash was back. For several months now, she'd been plagued by a weird skin rash that came and went without explanation. Maybe it was all those household chemicals, she thought, putting on a light sweater to cover the spot.

"You're too skinny," Sonnet said when she joined them in the yard.

"Who, me?"

"I don't see any other freakishly skinny people around here. I myself have the Romano fondness for pasta and bread, and Charlie takes after his dad. Husky as a dockworker."

"Yep," said Daisy.

"Who you calling husky?" Charlie demanded.

"Hey, it's a good thing. Husky means healthy," Sonnet

explained. He ran off with Blake, and she turned back to Daisy. "Are you okay?"

"I'm fine. And I'm not skinny."

"Just…take care of yourself."

Daisy watched her little boy, lost in exuberance as he kicked a soccer ball with the dog chasing along. "Always."

Twenty-Three

"'I could tell you my adventures—beginning from this morning,' said Alice a little timidly: 'but it's no use going back to yesterday, because I was a different person then.'"

Julian set aside his book and angled the wheelchair toward the pale slits of light that lay across the floor of his prison cell. When the wind blew just so, he could smell freedom through the louvered vent in the wall. It was the blue-green aroma of fresh ocean breezes blowing in from the west, tinged with the lighter scent of river water, the perfume of flowers and the harsh reek of chemicals used in cocaine production.

Occasionally, he caught a whiff of exhaust. That—the exhaust—was the scent that most compelled him. Combined with the lawn-mower whine of a small engine, it told him there was a float plane that came and went regularly from the compound. The plane came twice a week, on days Julian had designated Monday and Friday, though he didn't actually know. By the sound of it, the aircraft was too small to be used for drug transport. It was likely a means of transport for an individual, a high-level worker, perhaps.

Julian wished he could see outside. He pictured a dock

on a river, where cargo could be loaded on boats and taken out to sea.

In a training exercise that had seemed meaningless years ago in the ROTC program, they'd undergone sensory deprivation in a variety of situations. If deprived of sight, how could they use their other senses to evaluate their environment? In a pitch-dark room they'd been required to identify sounds, smells and textures in order to find a way out. Similar exercises had taught them to function without the ability to hear or speak. At the time, it had been hard to imagine how such a situation might arise.

Since his capture, he'd learned that anything could happen. He'd been moved around so much, he started to wonder how many places Don Benito Gamboa controlled. Surely there was a limit.

Julian himself had a limit. He had reached it. Could feel it in his bones. If he had to endure any more of this shit, he would lose his mind.

Sometimes he thought about Daisy so long and so hard, he was sure she must be able to sense his presence.

Not likely. Julian was a realist. Just because his mind was screaming, I'm alive, I'm coming home, didn't mean there was anyone on the other end to hear.

Flicking pebbles against the wall, he studied the crude small marks he had made in the plaster, marking off each day. It seemed important to keep a count. *Every single day matters*—that was going to be the key message of his wedding vow to Daisy. Before he'd left the States, the two of them had agreed to write their own vows. He'd been stymied, wondering how to cram everything he felt into a two-minute speech. Now he realized the message needed to be simple and clear: he wanted to go through life with her, celebrating every day being in the world together.

The thing to do, he told himself every day, was to get the hell out of this place, not become an embittered career prisoner like Dantès in the novel he'd read over and over again.

He had to plan with cold calculation, though. He would have the element of surprise only once.

His training had drilled a message into him. *There is always a way out.*

He clung to this notion like a lifeline.

Knowing the passage of time was a curious kind of torture. He had no idea what had been reported to his family. Missing in action? God forbid—killed in action? That wasn't out of the realm of possibility. But no. That wasn't how it worked.

Early on in his captivity, he had listened for any hint of a rescue unit—the thud of a chopper, the rustle of boots in the night, the soft crackle of a radio. He'd heard nothing. Either there was no rescue unit, or they hadn't been able to penetrate Gamboa's labyrinthine operation.

The cell was equipped with an iron bunk bolted to the floor, a thin mattress covered in stained ticking, a slop bucket for his waste, which he was required to deal with himself, because the guards were completely skeezed about it. Presumably anything else could be a potential weapon to use against the guards who attended him—not that they were too diligent about it.

Seated in the wheelchair or lying on the bunk, he had watched the entire life cycle of a large brown spider. There was a peculiar Zen in staring at her gossamer web, pinned in a corner, its evenly spaced strands waiting, soon to be a soft, sticky embrace to trap her next meal. She was both patient and selective, taking her time, choosing her battles. She would not tangle with a wasp, for example; nor would she eat a moth. Presumably one was too great an enemy; the other too poisonous.

Pick only the battles you can win.

Miguel Cuevas was on duty; Julian had memorized

the rotation. Cuevas wasn't too vigilant, and he worked on Friday, when the plane arrived at twilight. He talked about his girlfriend and his cat when he was bored, and he sent constant text messages on his cell phone. He was tall and big-shouldered, with a beard. That part would probably turn out to be important.

Julian hoped he wouldn't have to kill the guy. He'd do it, though, if it came to that.

Despite the guard's lackadaisical ways, there was a high probability of failure, which meant a high probability of death. Julian didn't love the odds.

Cuevas came with his tray as usual. *"Hola, amigo."*

"How are you today?" Julian asked.

"Very satisfied, if you must know. My *novia,* Celisse, she is a fine woman. A fine, fine woman." He preened a little.

It was a conversation they'd had many times, a routine exchange. Miguel was usually chatty before the weekend, and in no hurry to get after his other duties. And invariably, a text message came in. This was crucial.

Everybody knew you weren't supposed to turn your back on a prisoner, but Julian was no threat, bound in his wheelchair.

While Cuevas was busy with his texting, Julian made his move.

He shot up from the chair, hooked Cuevas from behind in a sleeper choke hold. The phone dropped from the guy's hand as he sank into unconsciousness. It would be safer to kill him, but Julian held off. He grabbed Cuevas's sidearm, then stuffed a strip of his undershirt in the guy's mouth and bound it in place.

Then he swapped clothes with the guy and put him to bed. He used more strips of fabric to tie him down, even binding his head to the cot to keep him from thrashing.

Cuevas started to come around as Julian was lacing

up the boots. He made a gagging sound and stared at Julian, who was balanced on one foot as he tugged on the borrowed fatigues.

"Surprise," he said. "Sorry you had to find out this way. No, who am I kidding? I'm not sorry." Damn, but it felt good to be in his body once again, to quit pretending. He'd kept his recovery a secret; his captors had made it easy by not putting him under a doctor's care. After that first day, when the infirmary doctor had given him a couple of injections and pronounced him a paraplegic, Julian had been on his own. The doctor had suggested a course of physical therapy, but no one had bothered to follow up on that.

Sensation had returned gradually, not long after his capture. First he'd noticed a twitch in his toe. Soon he'd been able to move his feet, bend his knees. He became his own physical therapist, working in secret, in the dead of night, building his strength with squats and calisthenics, then spending the days malingering in the chair, pissing in a bag and playing up his helplessness. Most guys wouldn't know the first thing about faking paraplegia, but Julian had firsthand knowledge of it. After his father's accident, the two of them had learned together to adapt. He knew what it looked like, what had to be done. When he asked for rectal suppositories and rubber gloves, his captors had asked no questions and merely provided them.

There was a small caliber pistol clipped inside Cuevas's belt. In addition to the pistol, the guy was equipped with a lock blade knife and a Leatherman tool, a pair of field glasses, a box of cigarillos and some wooden matches, some condoms, a small sum of cash and the ever-present bag of bazuco, a low-grade paste of preprocessed cocaine. It was plentiful in these parts, and guys liked to smoke it.

"You're a real Boy Scout, eh?" Julian muttered. He

helped himself to everything. He'd feel better if he had one of the submachine guns favored by the rebels, but Cuevas wasn't so equipped. Maybe Julian would have to take down a guard outside and could help himself to a more powerful weapon. He gave himself a haircut with the knife and covered his head with the guard's cap, made of army-green canvas with an oversize bill.

A couple more text messages appeared on Cuevas's phone. Julian hastened to put it on silent mode.

"She sent you a dirty picture," he informed his captive. "Don't worry, I didn't look. The subject line gives it away." He hesitated, wondering how Cuevas might respond to the incoming text. Immediately, that was how. Text messaging was like crack to the guy.

Julian scrolled through a few of the sent messages to get an idea of how the guy wrote. Text in Spanish slang was not his strongest area of expertise. He told the *novia* he was pulling extra duties to cover for someone's absence and would give her an appropriate reply later.

He would need to ditch the phone at some point in case it had a locator beacon. He checked the time—how weird to actually know the exact time, after so long without knowing—1900. Late in the day, then. The plane would be landing soon.

Time to venture outside. He hoped like hell he could keep a low profile once he left the cell.

Whenever he was taken anywhere, he would be blindfolded, so he had only the vaguest idea of what he was in for. He stepped out into the hallway, lit by a bare bulb, and locked the door behind him. There were several other doors, but he didn't avail himself of them. He headed toward some stairs leading up and out.

His hands were tense on the knife and gun. He stepped outside, blinking like Rip van Winkle just waking up. The light was dazzling gold, filtered through a thick canopy of vines and trees. An overgrown slope led down to a broad river or canal; he couldn't tell which.

He'd known, based on the noise outside, that this was probably a big operation. He wasn't prepared for how big, though. Bundles of cocaine were being loaded onto a barge—a freaking barge. It was like something at the Long Beach Waterfront in California. Along the flat roof of the compound, guys with scopes and guns kept watch. Workmen were using forklifts and a crane to move whole pallets of the stuff. There were machine guns mounted on beat-up Chevy Blazers. Row after row of barrels lined the dock, and the forklift was bringing in more. Julian used the field glasses to check them out. These were probably chemicals used in cocaine production—kerosene or gasoline, acetone, sulfuric acid. He couldn't read the lettering but spotted an unmistakable symbol—a skull and crossbones.

Excellent, he thought.

Footsteps crunched on a gravel path that traversed the front of the compound. Julian lifted the mobile phone to his ear, hunched his shoulders and headed down toward the water. Although his biracial looks made him seem vaguely Latino, he didn't much resemble Cuevas. Anyone who spotted him and gave him a moment of thought would know he was a stranger. He simply had to count on the idea that people were, for the most part, wrapped up in their own lives and not looking for trouble.

The guy on the gravel path barely glanced at him. Julian measured his paces, trying not to hurry.

A nasally whine signaled the arrival of the plane. It was expertly landed and motored to the docks. A worker helped moor it. The flimsy door opened, and a man in khakis and mirror-lens sunglasses stepped out. He exuded an air of authority as he strode along the quay next to the lined-up barrels and pallets of wrapped cocaine.

Business as usual. Still unremarked upon, Julian headed toward the plane. Assuming he managed to commandeer the aircraft, he would be flying with no notion of where he was. He could only hope the instruments would help him out. The main task was to get to it before the pilot exited. Everyone seemed focused on the passenger. It could be Don Benito himself. Julian didn't care. He simply wanted to get the hell out.

Soldiers were loading the wrapped kilos onto pallets for the barge. Emulating the other workers, he transferred a dozen of the bricks, stamped with a black spider logo, to a hand truck and headed down the slope to the quay, where another pallet awaited. He kept his head down, eyes watchful, fighting the urge to hurry. On the dock, a *jefe* was fussily organizing the parcels next to the barrels.

A preponderance of no-smoking signs marked the area. Close enough to see the labeled barrels, he realized they contained a slushy mixture of coca leaves steeped in kerosene. These would be dried and treated with sulfuric acid and other substances, and then the crude paste would be refined into cocaine hydrochloride, the white powder.

The rows of barrels provided a partial concealment between the dock and the staging area. Julian thought about the cigarillos and wooden matches. Some guys up above were smoking, but no one down here. Too risky. But hell, everything he was doing was too risky.

He paused in his labor, took out a slender brown cigarillo. He'd never been much good at smoking. His mom had caught him at it as a kid. Instead of punishing him, she had insisted on making him smoke menthol cigarettes, one after the other, until he grew dizzy and puked. Aversion therapy. It had worked like a charm on him.

He opened the box of matches and sparked one, lighting the cigarillo, puffing on it a few times to get a good ember. There wasn't much of a breeze; it wouldn't be long before someone noticed.

Months of boredom had prepared him well, perfecting his aim. How many times had his idle fingers flicked a stone or stick at a designated spot on the wall? With the ease of so much practice, he flicked the burning cigarillo at the barrels. The amber tip landed under the rim of a barrel. It would likely fizzle, but it was worth a try.

Now he headed with a purpose toward the plane, a single-engine craft he didn't recognize; it might be Russian. He offered a wave to the pilot, but the guy was on his phone. Julian swiftly untied the two mooring lines from the deck cleats. This was a crucial moment. If the pilot copped to what he was doing too soon, there would be trouble. If the door was locked—it wasn't locked. Julian pushed his way into the seat beside the pilot.

"Hola, amigo," he said, simultaneously jamming the handgun under the guy's jaw and snatching the mobile phone from his hand, turning it off. "Do as you're told and you'll be all right." These days, his Spanish was nearly perfect, and there was no chance the pilot misunderstood. Julian took the pilot's gun and knife. It was a good firearm, a long-range semiautomatic pistol. "Turn on the engine and head out for takeoff."

The pilot's face blanched. "Where? Who the hell are you?" He was a hefty guy, maybe forty, wearing the paramilitary fatigues everyone around here seemed to favor.

"Just do as you're told. Quickly."

"If they think I'm up to something, they'll shoot."

Julian didn't have to ask who "they" were—the guards on the roof and the patrols in the Blazers. All were armed heavily enough to take out the flimsy plane.

"Or," he said coolly, "you can try your chances with me. The difference is, I will shoot you *now*. No headset. Just turn over the engine."

The familiar buzz started up. Julian kept his eyes on the pilot, whose face now ran with sweat. Yet he sensed a shifting of focus. No doubt, people around the compound were noticing the plane.

"Hurry," he commanded.

The pilot obliged, cutting a wake to the middle of the channel. When they got about fifty meters away, Julian said, "Get out."

"But—"

"Now." He jabbed the pistol barrel deeper into the guy's jaw.

The pilot pushed open his door. Aided by the speed, he fell out of the aircraft. Julian managed to grab the flapping door and pull it shut. He didn't take the time to see if the pilot had made it.

A strafe of machine-gun fire stitched across the water. Shit. He'd hoped for more time. He pulled back and went aloft with barely enough speed to sustain him. Glancing at the port, he saw puffs of smoke blooming from the machine gun–mounted Blazer.

There was more firing. He couldn't hear it over the engine noise, but could see men racing down the slope to the dock, some of them with long-range rifles. *Shit.*

Julian used his knees to work the controls as he unlocked the safety of the pilot's semiautomatic. Opening the side window, he pumped every round at the barrels. At first it didn't appear anything would happen. There was a flash, followed by an explosion that spread first in slow motion, then in a lightning bolt of fire.

The force of the blast rolled across the water like a tidal wave. Julian raced the plane ahead of it, praying the speed would be enough.

"Come on," he said through gritted teeth. "Come on, come on, come on…"

The plane accelerated, rising above the now-churning

waves. Finally he gained altitude, barely clearing the tops of the trees. The explosion created a weird turbulence that wrestled with the plane, but he fought it, climbing as fast as he could.

Below, the thick canopy of the jungle rolled down to the ocean, seemingly endless. He checked his fuel and powered up the GPS, which would tell him where the hell he was. Looking down and to the right, he blinked at the destruction he'd left in his wake. The barge had caught fire. A fine dust mushroomed up from the rubble, and he realized it was cocaine.

Twenty-Four

The Apple Tree Inn, billed as the "most romantic restaurant in the Catskills," didn't have a table for Daisy and Logan on their anniversary.

"We can seat you in forty-five minutes to an hour," the host said.

Logan turned to Daisy. "You didn't make a reservation?"

She shook her head. "I thought you took care of it." A little embarrassed, she turned to the host. "I guess we had a miscommunication."

Delicious smells wafted from the elegant, wood-paneled dining room. Soft music, trills of laughter and murmurs of conversation mingled in the air. Forty-five minutes was not so long to wait, she thought. For her, dinner usually consisted of chicken nuggets, mac and cheese and cut up fruit, so she had been looking forward to this date all week.

"You could wait at the bar," the host suggested. "They're running a special on single malt Scotch—"

"Or we could take a walk along the river," Daisy was quick to suggest.

"No thanks," Logan said, crossing the foyer. "I'm starving. We'll come back another time."

She felt a nudge of annoyance as she followed him out. "So what's our plan B?"

"I didn't make one. Did you?"

"No. We could go up to Camp Kioga," she suggested. "There's always room for us at the pavilion." When her cousin Olivia had taken over the place a few years earlier, the camp's dining pavilion had been transformed into a mecca for foodies.

"I'd rather not. It's already getting late."

Since when, she wondered, was eight-thirty at night considered late?

"I'm wearing a new dress," she said, twirling to show off the silky outfit she'd splurged on for the occasion. "And my dancing shoes."

He pulled her against him and leaned her back in a dip. "And you are totally hot," he said. "Prettiest wife a guy ever had."

"You think?"

"I know." He headed toward the car. "You're giving me a complex about getting fat."

"You're not fat."

He patted his undeniably thick girth. "It's the O'Donnell curse. Look at my dad."

In middle age, Logan's father was definitely stout, but he was still a handsome man.

"I'm looking at you," she said, "and I think you're totally hot, too. I always have."

He chuckled as he left the parking lot. "Always?"

"Ever since we first met in Mrs. Laughlin's kindergarten." She leaned back against the headrest. "Wow. We've known each other forever."

"Forever is a long time," he said. "And it's not over yet."

"Don't look so grim when you say that." She tapped him playfully on the arm.

"Sorry. You know me. I get cranky when I'm hungry. Just like Charlie."

"So, what about dinner?" She went over the possibilities in her mind. Carminucci's had incredible pizza and pasta, but it was casual in the extreme. There was a good Thai place, although it was likely to be as crowded as as the Apple Tree.

"I have a kind of off-the-wall idea," he said.

"Sounds good to me." She didn't really care where they ate. The point was to spend the evening celebrating their first year as a married couple. "Surprise me," she said, and flicked on the radio. "Wonderful Tonight" by Eric Clapton was playing; she recognized it within three beats as the song that had been playing when Julian had proposed to her.

With lightning reflexes, she switched the station. Even now, she thought. Even now, dammit.

"Hey, I like that song," Logan said, oblivious to her turmoil. "Why did you change it?"

She shrugged and kept her gaze out the window as the Black Eyed Peas filled the car. "Just in the mood for something else," she said.

A short time later Daisy was still in the passenger seat, staring straight ahead. "This is your off-the-wall idea?"

"You said to surprise you. So are you surprised?" He took a big bite of his cheeseburger and a slurp of syrupy soda.

In front of them loomed the giant screen of a drive-in movie, one of the few left in the region. A host of menacing, CGI-enhanced warrior drones filled the sky.

"I'm surprised," she said, swirling a spoon in her root beer float.

The window-mounted speaker blasted sound effects at them. The movie involved a space-age mercenary fighting—what else?—an evil overlord in order to keep him from dominating the planet and making slaves of its people. Mostly, the movie was an excuse to dazzle the eye and assault the ear with digital special effects.

Logan was into it, she could tell. And why not? He represented the coveted target demographic—the eighteen-to-thirty-year-old male—sought after by movie marketers.

Daisy set aside her root beer as she felt a headache pushing at her temples. This was not exactly the anniversary date she had envisioned. Then again, this was not exactly the life she had envisioned. It was the life she had. Her fervent hope was to embrace it and feel grateful for it every day.

She reached over the console and took Logan's hand. He lifted hers and kissed the back of it, then turned to her. She lowered her eyelids, expecting a kiss.

"Are you going to finish your French fries?" he asked.

Laughing, she handed over the paper cone of fries. "You are such a hopeless romantic."

"That's me," he agreed.

The movie unfurled in all its preposterous glory. The hero endured torture at the hands of his enemies, escaped and was recaptured numerous times, and finally in one do-or-die push, he fled to freedom, leaving scorched earth in his wake.

"Ah," said Logan. "That gets two thumbs-up from me."

The closing credits were accompanied by a surprisingly good song. Daisy relaxed and listened, trying to get Eric Clapton out of her head while Logan threw away their trash. Cars began trundling out of the parking lot.

"Some anniversary, huh?" He slid into the driver's seat. "Sorry about the restaurant."

"At least this was memorable."

"Right. We'll always associate our first anniversary with mayhem and gore."

"And root beer floats and French fries. We'll do better next year." She reached into her bag and took out a wrapped parcel. "According to tradition, the first anniversary is celebrated by a gift of paper." She laughed at his expression. "Hey, I don't make the rules. Anyway, this is for you. A gift on paper."

He unwrapped the parcel, angling the picture toward the light. "It's great," he said. "Thanks. This is an awesome, awesome shot of Charlie."

"My favorite subject. I thought you'd like to have it at your office."

The photo showed Charlie at his happiest and most exuberant. He was in his peewee soccer clothes, practicing his moves in the backyard with Blake. He was laughing, and the sunshine glinted in his hair. With the little dog running at his side, she had captured a joyous moment of childhood.

"The frame is nice, too," Logan said. "Doesn't seem to be made of paper, though."

"I cheated, a little."

He reached into the console between them and took out a small, oblong box. "I cheated a little, too."

"Really?"

"Open it."

She eagerly peeled off the wrapper and opened the box. "Wow. Logan, these are beautiful." She lifted the strand of pearls, which emitted a bluish glow in the artificial light. In the center was a diamond pendant, glinting at her.

"I hoped you'd like it," he said.

She took hold of the clasp and put them on, the beads smooth and cool against her neck. It was a choker-style necklace that fit snugly around her neck. The pendant settled in the hollow of her throat. "It's too much," she said.

"Hey, you're worth it."

"A diamond? For our first anniversary?"

"I didn't buy the diamond, just repurposed it. That's what the jeweler said, anyway."

"Repurposed from—*oh.* You mean, this is…"

"That's right. The diamond from the first engagement ring I got you."

The one that sent her into a spiral of confusion, ultimately causing her to run away abroad for nearly a year.

"I mean, it was a nice stone," he continued. "Didn't want it to go to waste."

"Of course not," she said, trying to shrug off a feeling of discomfort. "It's lovely, and it's still too much."

"But classy. Very classy," he said.

"That's me." She leaned across the console and kissed his cheek. "Thank you, Logan."

"Happy anniversary."

The credits finished rolling and the screen went black. "We're the last ones here," she said.

"Yep."

"Maybe we should move to the backseat and make out."

He laughed, turning the key in the ignition. "The theater owner's a client of mine. We should save the make-out session for home."

"So responsible," she said.

"I'm working on it. Maybe one of these days I'll be a pillar of the community."

"Ooh, a pillar."

"Hey, don't knock it."

"I would never." Her fingers reached up and touched the collar of pearls.

On the way home, they passed the Hilltop Tavern. The sign outside announced that her favorite homegrown group, Inner Child, was playing tonight. Led by Eddie

Haven, who came from a popular show business family, their music was always something special.

She didn't suggest stopping in, though. It felt wrong to ask Logan to go to a tavern.

When they got home, she was already thinking about the promised make-out session and fantasizing about where it would lead. It had been too long, that was for sure. Their lives had become quite busy—she with work and Charlie and the house, and Logan with work, his twelve-step meetings and fatherhood.

She was looking forward to some downtime with Logan.

They entered the house quietly, so as not to wake Sonnet or Charlie. "I'll go check on the little rascal," Logan whispered.

"Give him a kiss for me," she whispered and headed for the bedroom, knowing exactly which nightgown she would pick.

Sex with Logan was quite good indeed. The frequency had diminished over time, but according to the self-help books and articles she found herself reading so often, a tapering off of newlywed lust was normal. The articles didn't tell her if it was normal to miss all that just-married sex.

She put away her dinner-and-dancing dress and slipped on her most scandalous nightgown, and nothing else. Except the pearls. She kept the pearl choker on.

On the iPod, she found a playlist of soft, romantic songs. Sometimes she listened to music while editing wedding photos and creating multimedia shows for clients. It helped put her in the mood. There was not a single Clapton song on the iPod, though. She made sure of that.

She turned down the bed and lay against the pillows to wait for Logan.

* * *

"Mom." Charlie's voice slipped into her consciousness. "Hey, Mom, wake up."

Daisy startled awake, clutching the sheets against her décolletage and blinking at the morning light filtering through the window. "Hey, kiddo. What's going down?" She glanced over her shoulder at Logan, who was still asleep. Her heart sank. She'd blown it. She had somehow managed to fall asleep while waiting for him to come to bed.

"Nothing's going down," Charlie said. "Can we go to the lake today?"

"Maybe. Church first," she reminded him.

"Rats."

"Hey, you like church."

"It's boring. They make us color stuff like lilies and doves."

"It's a special form of torture."

"And we have to sing songs."

"You like singing. You're half Irish. You're good at singing."

"Nuh-uh. You have to say that. You're my mom."

"Which means I ought to know."

"Is Aunt Sonnet going to church?"

"No, we're taking her to the train station on the way."

"Rats," he said again.

"Now, scoot. Go fix yourself a bowl of cereal and we'll be down in a bit."

"I'm turning on the TV," he said. He knew she didn't like him watching so much TV.

"Brat," she said. "I'll be down really soon."

When he was gone, she turned to Logan and found him blinking himself awake. A beard stubble softened his jawline. He smiled at her with his eyes. "Hey," he said.

"Hey yourself. Logan, I—"

"Daisy, I'm sorry about last night."

"I was about to say the same thing."

"I said it first. I meant to snuggle in bed with Charlie when I went to check on him, and I completely fell asleep. Sorry."

Oh. So he didn't even know she'd done the same exact thing. "Well, then," she said. "Maybe during cartoons—"

"Man, look at the time," Logan said, heaving himself up and out of bed.

"Where are you going?"

"I'm meeting someone at the gym."

Now she was thoroughly bewildered. "It's Sunday morning."

"Prime time at the gym." He seemed a little sheepish. "I'm going to start working with a personal trainer." He patted his sides. "Time to get rid of the love handles."

"Aww, Logan. Are you seriously choosing the gym over sex?"

"I'm sick of myself. Having a desk job has its downside." He headed into the bathroom.

She got up and pulled her ratty, comfortable robe over the scandalous nightie. Suddenly the pearl necklace bothered her, and she took it off.

Moving to the bathroom door, she said, "Just so you know, I still think you look amazing."

"Thanks, but I don't think these extra pounds are amazing."

"More of you to love," she pointed out. In high school and college, he'd been a star athlete, in peak form, handsome and fit. He did have a sweet tooth, though, and a hearty appetite that didn't change, even after he settled into his career.

"Don't get too attached. The spare tire is going bye-bye." He put on his gym clothes and grabbed his bag. As he reached the bottom of the stairs, Blake shot in front of him and Logan went down. “Jesus Christ,” he snapped. “That damn dog’s always underfoot.”

“She’s not a damn dog,” Charlie said, running into the foyer. “Are you, Blakey? Are you, girl?”

“Right,” Logan said peevishly, and opened the door.

“Hey,” said Daisy, “don’t let the dog—”

Blake shot into the front yard.

“Out,” she said, hurrying down the stairs.

“Damn dog,” Logan repeated. “Get back in the house, you.”

Blake spotted a squirrel across the street and took off in a blur of speed. A car came around the corner. The moments unfolded with the slow inevitability of a nightmare—the blare of a horn, the thump of brakes and the squeal of tires, the dog’s yelp of distress.

“Blake,” Daisy screamed, her heart turning to ice.

Charlie burst into hysterical tears.

Logan rushed out into the street, Daisy at his heels. On the other side of the car, Logan bent down and straightened up, the dog tucked under his arm. “She’s okay,” he called.

“Keep your dog out of the street, man,” the driver yelled, and continued on.

Daisy took Blake and hugged her to her chest. “She’s fine, Charlie,” she said. “See?”

Blake licked the little boy’s face. Charlie was gulping the air in panicked breaths. “Are you sure?”

“I’m sure. She’s just scared.” Daisy brought the dog back into the house and set her down. She couldn’t even look at Logan. It was an honest mistake, but terror lingered in a ball of ice in her stomach.

“Sorry, buddy,” Logan said to Charlie. “Calm down, okay?”

“You never liked her,” Charlie yelled. “You just pretend, but I know you never liked her." He ran from the room, the dog at his heels.

"I *told* you not to get a dog," Logan snapped at Daisy, and left the house.

Logan was late for church. He'd told Daisy he'd meet them there after the gym, but she hadn't spotted him yet. She'd taken Sonnet to the station and then had gone on to church with Charlie, taking her place with the ever-expanding Bellamy clan. Heart of the Mountains Church had been attended by her grandmother Jane since Grandma was a girl, so it all felt very steeped in tradition.

Although Logan had been raised Catholic, he usually attended church with Daisy and Charlie. Ten minutes into the service, he slid into the pew next to her, mouthing, "Sorry I'm late."

He looked flushed, his hair still damp from the shower. Tamping down the leftover anger from the Blake incident, she showed him the page they were on in the prayer book.

Charlie fidgeted between them, but did an admirable job of squirming quietly. He gave his halfhearted attention to the reading, then quickly abandoned it. The small print was too challenging for a fledgling reader, anyway.

He was behind in his reading, according to his teacher. Behind in his reading, in math, and he'd been acting out inappropriately. Daisy bit her lip, trying to give the problem up to the Lord. It bounced right back at her. The Lord was funny that way. He never gave anybody a free pass.

She hadn't brought up the latest teacher's note with Logan yet. She hadn't wanted to spoil their anniversary.

Turned out they'd done a fine job spoiling it on their own.

Snap out of it, she told herself, and put her heart into the Communion song, an old favorite—"Abide in My Heart." As the song went on, she glanced around, suffused with gratitude to be surrounded by so many familiar, beloved family members, friends and neighbors.

Yet deep in a secret place, she felt an unbidden but too-familiar twinge.

She and Logan…something wasn't quite right. The notion had been sneaking into her thoughts with increasing frequency, despite her efforts to crowd it out by staying busy and pretending the feeling didn't exist. But this morning with the dog, and here in church, she couldn't lie or hide from the truth.

Looking at other couples she knew—Olivia and Connor, Jenny and Rourke were perfect examples—Daisy sensed they had something she and Logan lacked. In addition to the ease and comfort that came of familiarity, there was also the sizzle of chemistry. She tried hard to cultivate that chemistry with Logan, but again and again, her efforts fell flat. She wondered if he noticed.

No. They'd known one another forever. They were parents to a beautiful little boy. They lived in a nice home and had everything to be grateful for.

God, she prayed, let me be thankful for all the blessings in my life. Let me not want more. Let this be enough.

Maybe, she thought, that was what love was supposed to be—feeling content in the knowledge that what you had was enough. Except…sometimes that feeling of contentment eluded her, too.

After the service, there was a gathering on the lawn behind the church, as usual. The day was brilliant and warm, summer's final flare before the leaves began to turn.

"How did your training go at the gym?" she asked.

"I worked like a mule. Now I'm starving." He grabbed a glazed donut from the refreshments table and wolfed it down.

She bit her lip, saying nothing. Maybe the trainer would give him some tips about diet.

"Hi, Grammy Jane." Charlie sped over to his great-grandparents. "Dad's taking me kayaking today, aren't you, Dad?"

"Sure, buddy," said Logan.

"That sounds like fun," said Daisy's grandmother.

Daisy greeted her grandparents with a hug. Charles and Jane Bellamy had been married fifty-seven years and still seemed to adore each other. They'd surely had moments of conflict and doubt, but to be together that long had to mean they'd started with something special.

She watched Logan return to the refreshments table. He helped himself to another doughnut and chatted with Daphne McDaniel, the receptionist at Daisy's mom's firm.

"...setting a date for the family reunion, would that be all right?" her grandmother was asking.

"I'm sorry," said Daisy, shaking off her thoughts. "What was that, Grandma?"

"The reunion. I need to know what days everyone is available so I can set the date."

"Oh, I see." The tradition of an annual Bellamy family reunion, held at Camp Kioga, had sprung from sadness. Granddad's long-lost brother George had returned to Avalon, and two estranged sides of the Bellamy family found each other again. Shortly afterward, George had died, leaving behind a few simple truths—life was too short to be lived by half measures. And if there was a chance to get together with family, the opportunity should be seized.

"I'll email you my dates," Daisy said.

"For heaven's sake, don't email your grandmother," Jane scolded.

"Yes, who does that?" Olivia asked, joining them. "Who emails her grandmother?"

Daisy laughed. "I bet people in Seattle do. And Silicon Valley."

"Don't get cheeky with me. Come for a visit, and I'll

take out my proper engagement calendar and we'll pick a date. I wanted to check with you early because of your work schedule."

"Thanks, Grandma." The wedding photography business wreaked havoc on her free time, eating up entire weekends. "I'm sure we'll find a conflict-free weekend."

"Speaking of conflict..." Olivia patted Daisy's shoulder and gestured at the playground.

Charlie and another boy were yelling at each other, Charlie red-faced, his jaw jutting out. He gave the boy a shove, and the kid shoved back. Daisy hurried toward them, pulling Logan away from his conversation with Daphne.

"Hey," he said. "What the—"

"It's Charlie."

They reached the squabbling kids before the shoving escalated into blows. Logan bodily picked up Charlie and carried him away.

"What the hell was that about?" Logan demanded.

"He started it." Charlie's face was redder than ever.

"Let's go have a talk," Daisy said.

They found a spot under a shade tree. Horse chestnuts scattered the ground, encased in green, prickly pods. Charlie picked one up and flung it, hard.

"Hey," said Logan, "simmer down."

"What's going on, Charlie?" Daisy asked.

"He started it."

"That's not what I saw," Daisy said. "I saw the two of you yelling, and then you shoved him."

Charlie's cheeks puffed out. "But he started it."

"Back up a little," Logan suggested. "Who is he, and what did he start?"

"Brandon Wilkes and he's in my class at school."

Great, thought Daisy. Misha Wilkes's kid. Misha was in charge of everything at the school—president of the

PTA, chairman of the book fair, head of the Schools for Excellence committee, and probably a bunch of committees Daisy had never heard of. Misha Wilkes was exactly the kind of woman you didn't want for an enemy.

"And what did Brandon start with you?" Daisy asked.

"He called me a retard," Charlie blurted out. His chin trembled. Daisy could see his anger melt visibly into hurt.

"That's a completely inappropriate word," she said. "We don't even use that word in our family."

"Brandon said it about me."

"It's just a stupid word." Logan seemed completely confused by the situation. "Seriously, you can walk away from that sh—stuff."

"He said it a bunch of times," Charlie reported. "He said I'm the dumbest one in class and I'm going to flunk out and I'll have to go to a special school. He kept saying it and saying it."

Daisy's heart sank. She thought about the notes from the teacher. Had there been fighting at school, too?

"Well, it doesn't matter how many times he said it," Logan told Charlie. "You still have to ignore it and walk away."

"Then he would call me a chicken," said Charlie.

"They're just words, buddy. You got to let them roll off you. If this was a soccer game, you'd get a penalty."

"So here's the good news," Daisy said before they strayed too far from the issue. "The good news is, I'm not giving you a time-out or putting you on restriction."

Charlie's eyes widened. That was her typical response to many infractions.

"But here's the bad news," she added. "It's not bad, but you're going to have to be a really big boy about it."

"What do you mean?" A scowl of suspicion creased his brow.

"We're going to go find Brandon right now so you can

apologize and shake his hand." She looked to Logan for concurrence. He raised his eyebrows.

"No way," said Charlie, his face flushing again. "I can't."

"You can, and you will."

"No. He started it. I'm not sorry I pushed him. I should've punched him in the nose." He jiggled from one foot to the other.

"Tell you what," Logan suggested. "This kid Brandon, he sounds like a real rat's ass to me."

Charlie's eyes widened with delight. "He is. He is a rat's ass."

"Hey," Daisy objected.

"Anyway," Logan went on, "there's a way to deal with a kid like that. You go up to him and make a real nice apology and shake his hand, like your mom said. And then you'll see. It'll make him nuts, and the whole world will see he's a total rat's ass."

"I can't," Charlie said, though the protest sounded weaker now.

"If you're big enough to pick a fight, you're big enough to end it. He's over there with his mother." Daisy took Charlie's hand and held it firmly, towing him along. "Brandon," she called. "Hey, Charlie has something he wants to say to you."

Brandon's mother, Misha, turned to them. She was an older mom, with a successful career in advertising behind her. In her impeccable St. John's suit and with every hair in place, she exuded class...and chilly disdain.

"Go ahead," Logan said, nudging him toward Brandon.

Charlie stared at the ground. He mumbled something.

"You need to say it again," Daisy said, "and look him in the eye and speak up."

Charlie was trembling. His voice was quiet but clear

as he stared at the other boy and said, "I'm sorry I yelled at you and pushed you for calling me a retard."

Okay, so not quite the generous apology she might have wanted, but the words "I'm sorry" had been said.

Unprompted, Charlie stuck out his hand. Brandon, a boy with an angelic face and frosty blue eyes, took a step back. His mother nudged him forward. The boys' hands joined for one brief shake, then separated as though they'd each touched a hot stove.

"Fair enough," said Logan. "Let's go, Charlie. See you around, Mrs. Wilkes."

Daisy took note of Misha Wilkes's stiff posture and expression of startled contempt. "Hmm, have a nice day," she muttered, and followed Logan to the car.

At home, she sent Charlie upstairs to change. In the meantime, she showed Logan the note from the teacher.

"They want to schedule a meeting. It's not just his progress. She says he's aggressive and combative with other students. I guess we saw that after church this morning."

"That little shit provoked him," Logan pointed out. "Calling him a retard? Seriously?"

"I want Charlie to learn to walk away from things like that." She sat down at the kitchen table as a wave of nausea came over her. "Oh, God."

"You all right?"

"I'm fine. I had the weirdest flash of déjà vu."

"What do you mean?"

"My brother, Max," she said. "He struggled all the way through grade school. He would fly into these rages, and nothing could get through to him. My parents hired tutors and psychologists galore. He never actually learned to read until he was around ten years old. Then he learned over the course of one summer."

"Something must've clicked for him, then."

She paused, thinking back across the years. "That was the summer our parents split up," she said quietly.

"Believe me, a kid can learn to read without breaking up his family," Logan pointed out.

"I'm not saying…" Her voice trailed off. "I suppose it had to do with stress. Anyway, back to Charlie. The library opens at noon today. Let's take him to pick out some books, and—"

"Sorry, I've got plans today," Logan said. "League soccer."

"Oh." She bit her tongue, torn between saying to hell with soccer and telling him to enjoy his game. "God, Logan. You always do this."

"Do what?"

As if he didn't know. "Find a reason to take off when there's a problem."

"That's bullshit, and you know it."

"Then stick around and help me."

"I'll tell you what'll help. Back off and leave the kid be, for Chrissake. He'll come around. I'll read a book to him tonight."

Easy, she told herself. Logan worked hard all week, and he lived for the guy time with his soccer league. Then she thought of something else. "Isn't this a meeting night for you?" His Sunday night twelve-step meeting took place with invariable regularity.

"Yes, and I don't want to miss it," he said with a shrug. "Don't worry, I'll make some time to read with Charlie."

She already knew the time would not magically materialize. Sometimes when Logan went off to his meeting, she would feel a twinge of irritation, immediately followed by a stab of guilt. He needed the fellowship to keep himself clean and sober. His very life depended on it. She sometimes wondered what he said there, what went on. And then she backed off the thought.

"I need to go get changed now." He headed upstairs.

Daisy exchanged her dress shoes for flip-flops and exhaled a long sigh. A vague unsettling shifted through her, and she tried to figure out what that feeling was. Discontent? Frustration?

Life was confusing. Marriage was confusing. How was it possible to have exactly the life you thought you wanted and still feel pangs of yearning for something else?

She wandered over to the small nook off the kitchen that served as her home office, and woke up her computer. Somewhere along the way, she'd stopped feeling a surge of excitement at the prospect of work. She had security and predictability with Wendela's Wedding Wonders. She'd learned a lot. But there was no denying, the wedding photography had consumed all her time and creative energy.

The calendar indicated several upcoming wedding shoots. There was a shaded box in the middle of the week. "Shoot," she said under her breath.

"What's the matter?" Logan came back, dressed for soccer now in shorts, league shirt and shin guards, carrying his spikes in one hand. For a second, he resembled the guy he'd been in high school, cocky and sure of himself, a ladies' man.

"The deadline for the MoMA photo competition is this week. I haven't worked on my portfolio, and it's not even close to ready." She slumped back in her chair, deflated with disappointment.

"Isn't that the competition that already rejected you?" he asked.

"Well, when you put it that way..."

"I don't mean anything by it. Just seems like you go

to a lot of trouble to put your pictures together, and for what?"

"For...the possibility, I guess. I'm getting better every year. I like to think I am, anyway. The shows and competitions are a way of measuring that, and MoMA is the biggest one of all."

"Doesn't seem worth all the stress and extra work."

"It does to me."

"Maybe if you spent a little less time messing with those photos and more with Charlie, he'd behave better."

"You are not suggesting my work is causing his problems." A cold knot formed in her stomach.

"Your work?" He glared skeptically at the screen, then leaned forward and opened a folder to display all her portfolios from past years. He clicked on a series of portraits she'd done of Julian right after he'd asked her to marry him. "You call this work?" Logan demanded.

"Hey—"

"You're still stuck on him."

"He's dead, Logan," she said, resenting him for making her say so aloud.

"Like I don't know that."

"Then don't accuse me of being 'stuck' on him."

"Just telling it like it is. You don't love me the way you loved him. I can't compete with a ghost." He made an impatient gesture at the computer screen. "He's perfect. He'll never hurt you or disappoint you, never screw up, never get old or fat."

"He's a *memory,* Logan. You're my husband."

"Yeah, well, lately I feel like your roommate," he snapped.

"And whose fault is that?" she snapped back.

"Why are you fighting?" Charlie said, coming into the room. "You're always fighting."

"Ah, Christ," Logan said peevishly, "nobody's fighting."

"Watch your language," she said before she could stop herself.

"When you talk mean, that's fighting," Charlie stated. He put his arms around Blake and glared at them both. "You were more fun *before*." He stomped away, the dog at his heels.

"Whatever," said Logan. "I'm out of here."

She watched him go, feeling her jaw clench in frustration. *Before*. They could never talk about Julian without both of them getting all bent out of shape. For that matter, they could never talk about their deepest feelings without quickly backing away from each other.

Her stomach churning, she opened another file on her computer, containing shots she had been thinking about submitting. It was a very small collection, and none had been edited to her satisfaction. If she wanted to make the deadline, she would need to work practically around-the-clock.

And for what? In order to get rejected again, as Logan had bluntly pointed out.

What Logan didn't get—what no one seemed to get—was her passion. This was not merely a job to her. It was a huge part of her life. She wanted to grow as an artist, to tell her stories through the camera's eye, to have the validation that came from showing her work, garnering reviews good and bad.

Still smarting from Logan's words, she clicked back to the Julian file. He was still alive on her hard drive, vibrant and intense, exuding a passion for life, for adventure, for her. The pain of losing him had subsided to a dull ache, yet seeing his face, the light in his eyes, the shine of his spirit, brought him back to her in fresh waves of remembrance.

She had been wrong, earlier, when she'd told herself no one seemed to get her passion. Julian had from day one. He was the reason she had pursued photography in the first place. Back when they were teenagers, she had regarded it as a hobby. Julian had insisted it was deeper, as if he'd glimpsed something in her that she had not even recognized in herself.

"Thank you," she mouthed, studying a shot she had taken of him their first summer at Willow Lake. He had been fascinating to her, unlike anyone she'd ever met. She had captured him at the top of the diving platform that towered over the lake, about to jump. His hair was a ropey mass of long dreadlocks, and his eyes were on fire with excitement.

Sweet lord, she missed him. For as long as she lived she would never stop—

"Who's that in the picture?" Charlie asked, coming back into the kitchen. He regarded the big computer screen.

"You don't recognize this guy?"

Charlie shrugged. "His hair is weird. He looks like a lion."

"He kind of does. It's Julian, before he went into ROTC and shaved off all his hair."

"Oh. I like him better with no hair. Can I have something to eat? Please," Charlie added quickly.

She closed the file, feeling a now-familiar sense of restlessness. What dreams she'd had of her life with Julian. What beautiful, high-flown dreams she'd had of the three of them together, making their way from one adventure to the next.

Charlie had so few memories of Julian. Did he remember how Julian used to make him laugh? Did he remember that he used to call him Daddy-boy and beg Julian to show him how to jump off the end of the dock?

Charlie never asked to jump off the dock these days. He just quietly lowered himself into the water.

Twenty-Five

"This doesn't feel weird anymore," Daisy said to her mother, Sophie, when they encountered each other at Avalon Elementary School at carpool time. They had decided to let their kids play together on the school playground for a while, to unwind after the final bell, and to give themselves some mother-daughter time. "Maybe that in itself is weird."

Her mom smiled. "Life is funny that way. I never thought I'd end up with five kids, the younger three being in the same age group as my grandson. All right, now you have *me* thinking it's weird." Though Sophie was Charlie's proud grandmother, she certainly didn't look grandmotherly. She had an innate fashion sense that stuck with her through her career in international law to her current role as fourth-grade room mother.

"But in a good way, right?" Daisy asked, bending down to peek into the stroller where her baby brother slept. Noah Jr. was known as the miracle baby. Daisy's mom had been told she couldn't have more children, and so Noah and Sophie had adopted from overseas. Then one day, Sophie discovered she was pregnant. Now Daisy had a half brother who was younger than Charlie.

"In a really good way," Sophie said.

Daisy felt an intimacy that had not always existed between them. Back when her parents were struggling with their marriage, she had turned on Sophie, blaming her for the family's unhappiness. Now she saw the situation more clearly. Her mom had simply been in the wrong relationship, living the wrong life, despite doing her best to make it work.

Now Sophie was living the *right* life. She had a kind of serenity about her, a glow of contentment that shone through, no matter how busy she was. Daisy was one of the few people who knew how hard that had been for her to achieve.

"How's Charlie?" Sophie asked.

Daisy felt her stomach tighten. "I've got to set up another meeting with his teacher. He's not doing any better with his schoolwork." Or his behavior, but she didn't bring that up. Her mom had enough on her plate without being saddled with worries about Charlie.

"I'm sorry. Anything I can do?"

"We're working on the situation. Charlie struggles, and he seems like he wants to nail this problem, but then he shuts down."

"What do you mean, he shuts down?"

"Folds his arms, sits back. His eyes glaze over like he goes somewhere else in his head, you know?"

Sophie was quiet for too long.

"Mom?"

"I know that look. I know it all too well. It sounds like Max at that age."

"That's what I thought, too, when this first started going on. All that trouble Max had learning to read."

Daisy remembered feeling hopeless and lost as a little girl because she couldn't figure out how to fix what was wrong between her parents. She'd tried being perfect and it hadn't helped. She'd tried rebelling and not only had it failed to help; it had turned her into a teenaged mom.

The family dynamic had been even more destructive to Max. He'd lagged behind in school, particularly in reading. He'd had trouble controlling his temper. Nothing seemed to help until Greg and Sophie had taken a break from their marriage, one summer at Willow Lake. That was the summer everything had changed for the Bellamys, she recalled with a shiver of premonition. Max had experienced a complete turnaround. Something clicked and his reading had come up to grade level. He'd stopped picking fights and losing his temper. It had been an incredible summer of growth for Max. For their parents, it had led to a heart-wrenching decision to divorce.

More silence from Sophie. Then she asked, "How are you and Logan doing?"

"What?"

"As a couple, I mean. And the three of you as a family?"

"Charlie couldn't be happier about us being a family. Logan is a good dad."

"I'm glad to hear that. But you do know, you didn't answer the other part of the question. How are you and Logan doing?"

"Fine, I guess." Daisy bit her lip, looked away, then back at Sophie. This was her mother, for Pete's sake. She could tell her mother anything. "I know it's lame to say fine. I'd love to say it's one big, long string of wedded bliss."

"And I'd love to hear that," her mom said. "But I'm not hearing it, am I?"

"We're…in a bad place. Don't get me wrong, we're not in a fight or anything. It's just that, this doesn't feel the way I thought it would feel. I thought it would feel like…

a marriage. Instead, it's like a friendship. Or a project, I guess, like…remodeling the house."

She did not want to repeat her parents' mistakes. But wasn't that what she was doing? Enduring a strained marriage for the sake of the family?

She stiffened her spine. No. She and Logan were going to deal with this. She was not going to put Charlie through the kind of stuff she and Max had faced as kids.

"Does Logan know you're feeling this way?"

"We're seeing someone—a couples counselor. Logan doesn't have much to say except he likes being a family. I barely see him," she confessed. "He works long hours, and when he gets home, he's on the computer until bedtime. On weekends, he's all about whatever sport Charlie happens to be involved in or his own soccer league. Logan's been talking to his sponsor a lot. His AA sponsor, a guy who's in the program." Her mom probably knew it was Eddie Haven, who was in a band with Noah.

"I hope he'll talk with you, too. Even if you're not fighting, Charlie could be picking up on the tension. Kids have an incredible radar for things like that."

Daisy said nothing, testing the validity of her mom's words by imagining what things were like for Charlie. "So do you think he could be having trouble because of me and Logan?"

"Every situation is unique, and I'm hardly the poster woman for marital perfection. I'm sure it's quite complicated," her mother said. "Seeking counseling is a good move. Give this the time and attention it needs, Daisy. Your little boy is worth it. *You're* worth it."

"Mama," yelled Aisha, her little braids flying as she raced across the playground. "Can you push me on the swing?"

"Go ahead," Daisy urged her. "I'll stay here." She put her hand on the handle of the baby stroller. As she watched the children at play, memories nagged at her. Growing up, she and her brother Max had ringside seats at their parents' marriage, which had gone round after round for years and ultimately ended in defeat.

Daisy had no specific memory of discovering that things were awry. There was a sense of knowing but not knowing. It had felt like a tug of discomfort in her stomach. Her parents rarely fought. There was no yelling, just a pervasive sadness that could not be hidden, yet would not be acknowledged. The invisible force had proven to be toxic for the Bellamys.

She had developed an early obsession with family photographs. She'd spent hours collecting shots of her family, smiling for the camera, as though to convince the world—and herself most of all—that everything was fine. Capturing those happy moments eventually led to her passion for photography.

Her art was illusion. The images on paper showed a life her family didn't have.

She shivered again, despite the warmth of the day.

"Jogging sucks," Logan said to Eddie Haven, his longtime sponsor in AA.

"Hey, this was your idea," Eddie reminded him.

"Doesn't mean it was a good one. I'm dying here, and we haven't even gone a mile."

"One step at a time," Eddie said. "We'll get this done."

"That slogan sucks, too," Logan said, but he grinned as he spoke and forged ahead, glad to have company. Dealing with alcohol and drug addiction was a daily struggle, and having a mentor to help him work the steps was a key element of recovery. The two of them were fellow survivors and now fast friends. You'd never look at Eddie Haven and think, "recovering alcoholic." These days, he was a happily married man, with clean-cut, all-

American looks, an open and honest face, like one of the Beach Boys, with a shock of straight hair and surfer shorts. He didn't seem like a guy with a hidden dark past. He did have one, though; Logan had heard him speak of it in meetings.

Everybody had their secrets, he thought. Everybody.

After he'd convinced Daisy to marry him, Logan had felt as though he'd finally reached a goal. The feeling of triumph didn't quite cover up the fact that something wasn't right. They shared a deep regard for one another, they both adored their son, but the marriage itself had never been right, and it was getting harder to pretend. Logan never fully understood his feelings for Daisy. It seemed obvious that he *should* love her, and he'd convinced himself to do exactly that.

He scanned the trail ahead, marked with paving stones every tenth of a mile. Jogging was part of his self-imposed fitness regimen. To Logan's acute dismay, looking fit was no longer a no-brainer. With a desk job and settled lifestyle, he'd stopped paying attention to his physique. He cut out the Sky River Bakery *kolaches* for his midmorning coffee break and replaced his lunch hour with a daily jog. Eddie, self-employed as a songwriter, had agreed to join him, both for the fitness and the fellowship.

"Keep talking," Eddie advised him now. "It'll get your mind off the pain."

"Or shift it to another kind of pain," Logan said. With Eddie, he could be starkly honest, even when it was not much fun. "I never thought I'd be saying this, but my marriage is…it's not turning out the way I thought it would. And it's not just in my head. Daisy knows something's up, too. It's the elephant in the room."

"You've been saying that for a while. You been working on it?"

"We don't talk about it. I bet we're both thinking if we don't bring it up, then it won't be real."

"Magical thinking, my friend."

"True. So now we're in couples counseling."

Daisy's idea. The counselor asked hard questions. The hardest of all was the first thing he'd asked: When did you first fall in love with Daisy? To his extreme discomfiture, he could not answer this. The first time they'd had sex? Hardly. They'd both been too young, too stupid and too wasted to feel anything. When they found out Daisy was pregnant? Again, no. Horror, not love, had been his reaction. At Charlie's birth? Ah, the love had come over him like a warm wave—but now he knew that was all about Charlie.

"We're talking openly," he said to Eddie, "but instead of bringing us closer, it's making us both wonder if getting together was a mistake we can't fix." They passed a couple who were power walking together, laughing and talking, as if being a couple was the easiest thing in the world. "I pushed so hard for marrying her. Focused on it like a laser. I was convinced we belonged together. And you know me—I've never been one to take no for an answer."

"You also know the value of surrender," Eddie reminded him.

"That doesn't make me a fan. I wake up every day and tell myself I have everything I wanted. A job of my own making. I'm married to the gorgeous mother of my child. We live in a nice house..."

"I feel you leading up to one giant 'however,'" Eddie remarked.

Despite all Logan's efforts to ignore what his heart was telling him, the painful truth asserted itself. Something was missing. Some essential, elusive elements had gone missing, or maybe they had never existed in the first place. The dream of being a family with Charlie and Daisy had been powerful enough to fuel him. But reality kept nudging its way in.

"Do you ever get the feeling your marriage was a mistake?" he asked Eddie.

"To Maureen? Hell, no. I made all my mistakes before I married her. We're talking major screwups here."

"At first, I thought I'd finally done what I always wanted to do—give Charlie a real family. It's a sense of accomplishment, which is different from feeling, I don't know, marital love, I guess."

"That's when the real work of being in a marriage starts," Eddie observed. "It's supposed to be a labor of love."

"Daisy and I… It's different. We've known each other since kindergarten. We had Charlie together. We were raising him together. We love each other, but never really had that honeymoon stage. We're a family."

"And how's that working for you?"

"Charlie was thrilled when we first got together. It's all he's ever wanted, for us to be a family. Now that we are, the dream is better than the reality. He's having trouble in school and getting in fights."

"Why do you suppose that is?"

"Kids act out for any reason, or no reason at all."

"Is he the main reason you're together?" Eddie asked.

"There's no answer to that. It's a chicken and egg question."

"Let me put it another way. Do you love Daisy because she's the mother of your child, or do you love her because you can't help yourself?"

"Shit. I don't have an answer. We've been moving apart. Our only point of intersection most days is Charlie." There. He'd said it. The notion had been in the back of his mind for a long time.

"Is that what she thinks, too?"

"I'm not sure."

"Have you asked her?"

"Not in those exact words. What the hell am I going to say? 'Hey, hon, are you with me because you love me or because of Charlie?' She'd freak."

"Or not," Eddie said.

They were coming to the end of their run. Eddie slowed to a cool-down pace. "Could be the two of you are thinking the same thing but neither wants to bring it up. And believe me when I tell you, holding things in and pretending everything's fine is not good for any relationship, particularly when one's an addict. Don't look at me like that. You know what I'm saying."

Logan did know. He had some soul-searching to do, not exactly a comfortable process for a guy like him, a guy who had done so much damage back in his drinking and drugging days. The best thing he'd ever accomplished, by far, was Charlie.

He cringed, thinking about telling Charlie that things were not going so hot with Daisy. That maybe he and Daisy were going to take a break, a trial separation, one that might become permanent. It was tempting to keep pretending.

Charlie was no dummy, though. The kid could sniff out trouble like a bloodhound.

"Jogging sucks," he reminded Eddie.

Twenty-Six

Julian sat alone in the briefing room, deep within the confines of the Pentagon. He had only been to the Pentagon one other time. From this perspective, it felt like any other government building, chilly and utilitarian.

His head throbbed. His stomach was in knots. His mind shifted crazily from one disjointed thought to the next. He knew he was still not quite grasping the idea that he was a free man.

There was a writing desk against one wall, with a lamp on it, a pad of paper and a pen. In the center of the room stood a long conference table furnished with a few sweating pitchers of water. He had already swilled several glasses. In captivity, fresh water had been hard to come by.

In captivity.

The clock on the wall read 1647. Seventy-two hours before, he had been a prisoner in Colombia.

He now wore the plainest of civilian clothes—dark slacks that were a tad too short for his long legs. A crisp white shirt. Shoes that pinched a little. He was clean, though. Showered, shaved and fed in a way he hadn't been in twenty-four months. It felt so damn good. Probably half the world's problems would disappear if people were allowed to eat and shower to their hearts' content.

He got up and paced the room, pausing to read the captions under all the portraits on the walls. This was one of his least favorite aspects of military life—hurry up and wait. No matter what the situation, if the military was involved, you could be sure they'd keep you waiting. During his imprisonment, he'd learned a lot about waiting. One of the reasons he was alive today was attributed to the patience and forbearance he had forced himself to cultivate during those dark, lost months.

An ivory-colored phone without a dial hung on the wall. He was wondering what his chances were of getting an outside line when at last there was a knock at the door, and it opened.

A short, stout officer entered. Her black hair was slicked into a neat bun.

"Holy mother of God," she said. "Jughead."

"Sayers?" He laughed with joy and opened his arms.

She fell into them, sturdy as he remembered her. Just as quickly, she stepped back, wearing her bossy face as she checked him out. "Damn. Where the hell have you been, boy?"

"That's a good guess," he conceded. "I've been in hell."

Her eyes shone with tears, and the bossy face softened. "I can't believe this. We were *all* in hell, the whole detachment, when we got the news you'd been killed. They said you escaped by faking paralysis."

"I wasn't faking at first. The docs at Palanquero said it was probably a spinal cord concussion. Temporary paresis or spinal shock, something like that. Then when I felt myself recovering, I didn't say anything. Figured I needed the element of surprise."

"How the hell did you keep up the charade for so long?"

"My dad was in a wheelchair. I knew all the drills, and trust me, the guards didn't want to know too much about, er, personal habits. They pretty much left me alone."

She squeezed his hand. "You're going to be all right," she said. It was not a question.

"Of course," he assured her. Yet he was painfully happy to feel her hand in his. In addition to everything else, he'd been entirely deprived of human contact and hadn't until this moment realized how much he'd missed a simple touch.

"I'm sorry about your team," Sayers added.

Julian nodded, the words frozen in his throat. Until he had walked onto the base at Palanquero, hands in the air, prison garb flapping in tatters around his gaunt form, he had not known the helicopter had gone down at sea and was never recovered. That explained why both he and Ramos had been reported killed, along with the rest of them, and why no rescue unit was ever deployed. He had briefed his commanders about how Ramos had sacrificed himself and had been forced into Gamboa's operation. The mission to defeat the drug lord was still ongoing. The destruction Julian had caused during his escape had turned out to be a huge break for the joint special forces, but he couldn't really take much satisfaction in that, because he was still trying to get his mind around the enormous loss of his comrades.

Rusty and Doc, Truesdale, Simon and José, guys he'd trained with from the Colombian militia. He hadn't known any of them for long, but their bond was like no other. They'd put their lives in each other's hands, the ultimate act of trust. And now they were all…gone. Never mind that it had happened two years ago. He'd just found out, and the wound was as fresh as yesterday.

"Jughead?" prompted Sayers. "What's going on in that fool head of yours?"

"I feel like a ghost," he said.

"Go easy on yourself. You're not *that* skinny. Speaking of which, you're going to get the full treatment," she assured him. "I want you to promise me you'll take full advantage of everything they offer you, not only the physical, but the mental health counseling."

"No problem," he said.

She snapped to attention as three men entered the room—an undersecretary of the air force, an official from the State Department and a public affairs officer. Salutes were exchanged.

"At ease," said Colonel Garland, the undersecretary. "Lieutenant Gastineaux, welcome home."

"Thank you, sir." He shook hands with each of them in turn.

They sat at the table for a debriefing, his third in as many days. Paulson, the official from the State Department, ran the meeting.

"Lieutenant Gastineaux, we owe you too much respect to pussyfoot around. You've been part of a deep covert operation, one that is ongoing. Your oath of confidentiality is still in effect."

"I understand, sir." What did they think, that he was going to sell his story to the tabloids? What story? His story sucked.

"Excellent, because it's a critical matter."

"Yes, sir." Julian tried to figure out what he was getting at.

"We're going to require you to be circumspect, bearing in mind the many lives dependent on your discretion."

Jeez, how many ways were they going to say this? "Of course."

"We've prepared a statement for release," said Rankin, the public affairs officer. "You'll want to familiarize yourself with it."

Julian went over the few printed paragraphs. The bare facts were all there, although the mission was characterized as a routine training exercise. No mention of the team's mission, Gamboa or the fact that, in making his escape, Julian had taken out the largest cocaine production facility in western Colombia.

"Sounds good to me," he said.

"And here are your papers outlining a long-term medical leave of absence."

"I'm being put on leave." He had not expected that.

"It's necessary. You continue to qualify for all benefits, and—"

"Why am I being put on leave?"

"It's all there in the paperwork. When you've been on a remote and gone MIA, it's standard."

"Not so sure I'm okay with that, sir." A leave? For what? In the space of a moment he was forced to realign his life. His future.

"It's necessary," the undersecretary repeated.

Julian caught Sayers's eye, and despite the passage of time, he could read her like a book. She was telling him to keep his mouth shut, save his arguments for someone who could actually do something about his situation.

"All right. Sure. Whatever," he said.

"You'll need to sign another confidentiality agreement, extending the current one. There can be no discussion of the incident at the level of press."

Julian was quiet. He met Sayers's gaze again. "I really am a ghost, then."

They let Sayers stay with him after the officials left. They probably would've had to pry her off with a crowbar if they'd refused.

"I need to call my fiancée," he said, still reeling from

the explanation of what had gone on after his disappearance. "God, I can't believe she was told I died."

"Everyone on the transport died," Sayers pointed out. "All the families got the call."

He winced, imagining the pain Daisy had suffered. I'm sorry, baby, he thought. I'm coming home to you now.

"I can't even imagine how she's going to feel," said Sayers. "But…Jughead? Maybe you should call your next of kin first."

"My mother?" He shook his head. "She'll get hysterical. Maybe even blab to the press. Why would I call her first?"

"This fiancée—"

"Daisy." He couldn't believe he was only hours from seeing her again.

"Have you thought about—shoot, Jugs. This is hard. I'm just saying, maybe she's moved on, you know?"

The suggestion was patently ridiculous. Incomprehensible. He was about to tell her so when a cold spike of apprehension lodged in his gut. She'd been told he was dead. He was a fool if he thought she'd still be sitting around, grieving for him. Yes, she loved him, but he could not expect her to spend her days pining after a dead guy. She had a kid to raise. A life to live.

Sayers read the expression on his face. "I'm probably completely off base. What I'd love is for you to fit right back into your life as if you'd never left."

"And we both know that's not going to happen. I'm still trying to get my mind around the idea that the world considered me dead." He steepled his fingers together. "One of my favorite scenes in *Huckleberry Finn* was always the one where Tom and Huck attend their own funeral," he said. "Wonder what mine was like."

"Total sobfest. We were on our knees, I swear."

"You went?"

"Hell, yeah, I went. Chipped in fifty bucks for the funeral spray, too. I ought to ask for my money back."

"I owe you," he said. "Listen, I'm going to call my brother, Connor. He is the least likely to go into meltdown when he hears from me."

"Good plan," she said, handing him a phone.

He dialed the number from memory and listened to the rings. Shit, what if it went to voice mail? What the hell was he going to say to voice mail? *Oh, hey, Con. It's me, Jules. Listen, good news....*

"Davis Construction. Connor speaking."

Julian took a deep breath. "It's me, Julian. It really is. Your brother."

"What the hell—"

"Just listen, Con, okay? Damn, it's good to hear your voice. There was a huge mistake about my death, man. It was misreported, and...don't freak out."

He held the phone away from his ear as a loud yell came across the line.

"He's freaking out," Sayers observed, beaming.

"He's freaking out," Julian agreed.

After Connor calmed down enough to listen, and Julian convinced him that this was not a hoax, he said, "I'm not sure how to go about getting the word out. You're the first person I called."

"So, uh, you haven't spoken to Daisy."

It was the "uh" that tipped Julian off. That tiny verbal hesitation spoke volumes. He and his brother had always been straight with one another.

Julian asked, "Is she okay? What's going on?"

"She took it hard when we got the news about you," Connor explained. "Real hard. Went around like a zombie for months."

Julian's heart constricted as he imagined Daisy's hurt.

And he could imagine it because it was the same hurt he knew he would feel if he ever lost her.

He felt a glimmer of that pain even before Connor finished his explanation. Somehow, Julian already sensed what was coming. He steeled himself.

"About a year ago, she and Logan O'Donnell got married," Connor told him, the words rushing out fast, as if he wanted to get this over with.

Julian felt everything drain out of him.

"Jules?" Connor said into the silence. "Man, I'm sorry. And I have to be honest, I know this sucks for you, but I'm so damn glad you're alive that I'm still smiling."

"I need a favor," Julian said, his mind racing.

"Anything."

"Go see her in person and tell her. Just, you know, so she's prepared."

Sayers was watching him with mounting concern.

"I can do that," Connor said. "Olivia and I will find her right away."

"Good. Okay." Julian wanted to call Daisy himself, but he was in an impossible position now. She was married. *Married.* Boundaries were up. Regardless of how he wanted things to be, he had to respect those boundaries.

"I don't know what's going to happen in the future," Connor said, "but you're here. You're alive. And I can't wait to see you."

"Same here."

"When?"

Julian's gaze flicked to Sayers. She made a gesture as if to say, We're done here.

"Tonight," Julian said.

"Seriously?"

"Looks that way." Julian held the phone away from his ear.

"He still freaking out?" asked Sayers.

"Still freaking out," Julian confirmed.

Twenty-Seven

"Well," Daisy said with a happy smile. "This is a treat. I don't usually get a follow-up visit with my clients." It was hard to believe she had shot their wedding more than two years ago.

Andrea Hubble and her husband Brian exchanged a look that glowed with fondness. "You did such a beautiful job on our wedding photos that I couldn't think of anyone better to take pictures of our new baby."

Daisy looked around the sun-drenched porch of their new home, a modest frame house on the lake. The railed porch was hung with a late-blooming vine, its delicate white flowers exuding a beautiful fragrance.

"You don't need an expert to make this little sweetheart look good," she pointed out.

"I was thinking more about the mom and dad," Andrea said. "All these night feedings are cutting into my beauty rest, big-time."

"The three of you are going to look amazing," Daisy promised. "We'll get started as soon as Zach arrives with the rest of the gear."

She picked out her favorite lens and scouted around for some good settings—a nice old porch swing, a patch of six-foot hollyhocks, an overgrown meadow sloping down to the lake, a rowboat in the water, tied to the weathered dock.

"How have you been?" she asked the Hubbles. "I mean, apart from the obvious."

Andrea and Brian exchanged a glance. "It's been… everything. We've gone from newly wedded bliss to the honeymoon-is-over rage, and all the stages in between. We're great, though, right?" She nudged her husband. "Am I right?"

"You're right. And those have become my two favorite words in the English language."

Daisy was beginning to feel inspired. She loved it when the energy of the subject was so warm and positive. Andrea and Brian leaned in toward each other, regarding their baby son with a pride that shone so brightly, it was palpable.

Andrea leaned sweetly against her husband's shoulder. "It's been a process, and that's not a bad thing. I went from being swept off my feet to loving Brian like a habit, like breathing, if that makes sense."

"Perfect sense," Daisy murmured. She should work on that with Logan, yet caught herself wondering why it seemed so impossible to get into the habit of love.

"And it's not cheesy?" Andrea asked.

"The truth is never cheesy," Daisy assured her. "I'm really happy for the two of you." The Hubbles seemed to have a rhythm together, subtle, but the camera found it. Daisy wondered if she and Logan had a rhythm. They tended to go their separate ways—he with work and soccer league on the weekends, meetings with his group and sponsor. And she stayed busy with her own career and with friends and family.

Every couple was different. Andrea and Brian were passionate about each other, and the chemistry flowed from every cell of their bodies. Daisy had seen it while doing their wedding shoot; she sensed now that it was more powerful than ever. And it seemed effortless. Maybe for some couples, love *was* effortless. Others had to work harder at it.

She had never been one to shy from hard work. If that was what it took—and their couples counselor assured them that it did—then she would go the distance.

Checking a sunny corner of the garden with her light meter, she made a mental note to do something nice for Logan today. Fix salmon for dinner, his favorite. Maybe offer to go to the gym with him, if one of her parents was free to watch Charlie.

The last time she'd offered, Logan had declined.

"It's not exactly quality time, doing weight training across the room from each other," he'd pointed out.

She kept waiting for this awkwardness between them to melt away, but it constantly cropped up, like weeds in a garden. Sometimes she lay awake at night, praying, Please don't let us repeat my parents' mistakes.

And that, of course, begged the question—had her parents been mistaken in trying to stay together as long as they had? Or was their greatest mistake in calling it quits?

She heard the sound of a car door slamming and dragged her thoughts into the present.

"There's Zach," she said. "We'll get started in a few minutes. Hey, Zach," she called over her shoulder. "I'm going to need both the strobe and the ambient right away. Could you—" She turned to him and broke off in surprise. "Hey, Olivia. Connor. What are you guys doing here?"

"Sorry to interrupt you at work," Olivia said, with an apologetic nod at the Hubbles. "Zach told us we could find you here."

Daisy made hasty introductions; then Olivia and Connor took her aside. "What's up?" Daisy asked. "Is everything all right?"

"It's Julian," Connor said.

Even now, the sound of his name, spoken aloud, was like a fist to the solar plexus. "Why would you bring him up?" she asked, hurt and mystified.

Olivia put her arms around Daisy. "It's good news," she said, "but you might want to sit down."

Daisy wobbled in confusion, but said, "I'll stand, thanks. Just tell me what's going on."

"So this is totally freaky, but amazing. I had a call, completely out of the blue," Connor said. "He's alive, Daisy. He wasn't killed when the helicopter went down. He's been a prisoner in Colombia, and he finally escaped, and he's back."

Daisy swayed against her cousin as she tried to make sense of the words. They seemed to echo in her head without meaning. Julian…alive. Alive. *Impossible.* She moved her mouth, but no words came out.

"I spoke to him less than an hour ago."

Daisy choked, managed to summon her voice. "He's… you mean…you're *sure?*"

"He's in Washington and will be here tonight." Connor's voice shook, and Olivia took his hand.

Daisy broke away from Olivia. She couldn't figure out what to do with herself. She sank down on the grass and wrapped her arms around her knees. Julian. Alive. On his way here.

Tears of disbelief and gratitude spilled down her face, and her breath caught painfully in her chest. She was trembling hard, so hard she couldn't see straight.

"I'm going to tell your clients you'll need to reschedule this shoot." Connor went over to talk to the Hubbles, and Daisy didn't bother to object. Talk about blowing her concentration.

Olivia sat down cross-legged next to Daisy. "It's so incredible," she said. "Like a dream come true. Connor's been—he's a mess, ever since that phone call. But a happy mess."

Julian. "I still can't believe it."

"It'll feel more real when we see him in person tonight. He'll be here in time for dinner." Olivia's voice trembled with wonder. "I know you're happy, but I guess it's super awkward for you. I can't imagine what this must feel like."

Tonight. How could that be? Daisy had been thinking about going to the gym with Logan and fixing salmon for supper, and…and now this. How could Julian go from being dead one moment to sitting down to dinner the next? With every cell of her body, she wanted to leave the world behind, run to him and fling herself into his arms. But that, of course, was impossible.

"He didn't call me," she said, a curl of apprehension tightening in her stomach. "My number hasn't changed. Why didn't he call me?"

"Connor did explain to him that you—your circumstances have changed."

"He told Julian I'm married to Logan, you mean."

"He couldn't very well have said anything else."

"I know. I understand. But…oh, God. I hate that he found out like this, even though I love it so much that he's still in the world." Daisy lowered her head to her arms. With no effort at all, she could conjure up his scent and the way his hands felt on her, the sound of his voice and the taste of his kisses. The jumble of emotions inside her kept growing until it felt like a fountain she couldn't contain. She thought she understood what her life would be, but now this…it changed everything. No, she thought. This desire she had to see him again, to touch him and open her heart to him again had to be a secret.

"This must be such a shock," Olivia said. "How *are* you doing?"

"Still trying to get my head around this," Daisy admitted. "And I know this situation is about to get extremely complicated. However, right now I can't feel anything but grateful. I never knew happiness could hurt so much. Oh, God. I don't know what to do. I don't know what to say."

"No one does. This is not exactly the kind of thing that happens every day." Olivia took out her mobile phone and turned the screen toward Daisy. "Connor made him send a picture."

Daisy's breath caught. Her heart seemed to leap toward the photo on the palm-size screen. "Julian," she whispered. "He's so skinny. But…he's smiling." She'd seen that face in her dreams, night after night. She used to think the dreams came to her because she was not done with the relationship. He had been taken from her with brutal swiftness.

"He has a lot to smile about, wouldn't you say?" Olivia pointed out.

Daisy gazed down at the image. Even now, she recognized that smile. It was the one she used to be able to feel from the crown of her head all the way down to her toes.

Twenty-Eight

The Hubbles had been understanding about rescheduling their photo shoot with Daisy. There could be no way to concentrate and focus on work, not with this cataclysmic news buzzing in her head.

Besides, she had to find Logan and tell him, and the sooner the better. She wanted him to hear it from her first.

And dear God, she wanted for it not to be a problem between them. They had created enough of those on their own.

She pulled up to his office, in an old brick building facing the town square. Located next to the local radio station and dangerously close to the Sky River Bakery, the agency seemed to fit right into the bustle of Avalon's small but colorful downtown. The large front window was painted with the company logo and O'Donnell Insurance Agency—You're Safe With Us.

The logo—an heraldic shield—was not the most original choice. However, given the success of the company, it was probably the *right* choice. The brand consultant Logan had hired when he'd taken over the agency insisted that the symbol be instantly recognizable.

She sat in the car for a few minutes, trying to collect

her thoughts. The news about Julian was still so fresh, it was burning in her chest. Deep breath, she told herself. Deep breath. There was no way to make this less startling than it was, though she resolved to choose her words carefully. She even rehearsed a few attempts.

"I just got the most incredible news…."

No, then he might instantly think she was pregnant. Not a good topic for them, not at all.

"Logan, there's something I need to tell you right away…"

He'd probably think she wanted to talk about their marriage yet again. Of late, they'd had a number of fruitless conversations that circled around and never seemed to resolve the unsettled feelings that kept cropping up between them.

"Hey, guess what? The love of my life came back from the dead."

That made her press her hand to her mouth. Good lord.

"Just be honest," she admonished herself, getting out of the car. "Just tell the truth."

She stepped into the office, setting off a small bell over the door. "Hey, Brandi," she said, greeting Logan's assistant. Brandi had been the manager and engineer next door at the radio station, and Logan had lured her away. Sometimes she played electric bass in the same band as Daisy's stepdad, Noah. Brandi was loyal and reliable.

She was also drop-dead gorgeous and favored incredibly cute clothes.

Daisy had never been bothered by this. She never even wondered why this didn't bother her. The answer might be a little too revealing.

"Is Logan busy?" she asked.

Brandi glanced at the phone. "Nope, go right ahead."

Logan's private office had an old-fashioned door with a wavy glass pane and his name in the same lettering as the front sign. She took a deep breath, arranged her face into an expression she hoped would hide her nerves, and opened the door.

"Hi, Logan," she said brightly.

"Hey." He closed his computer's browser with a click of the mouse.

She wondered if he closed it too hastily. Then she reminded herself why she was here. "Sorry to interrupt your day."

"Don't worry about it. I was thinking about you, too. About us, actually."

"What about us?"

He regarded her solemnly. "I've been doing some thinking."

Now? she thought. *Now?*

"You know," he continued, "like we're supposed to do for our counseling session."

"Logan—"

"Look, I'll never be sorry I married you because of Charlie, but maybe—"

"Please, this can't wait."

"You think this shit is easy?" he asked. "The least you could do is listen—"

"It's Julian," she blurted out.

Logan's eyes narrowed. He leaned back in his chair, steepling his fingers. "Great. Now what?"

"He's been found. He's back." She struggled to keep her voice from breaking on a surge of joy and wonder.

He shifted his weight forward, planting his elbows on the desk. "What do you mean? His body was found?"

"No…but…yes. Sorry, I'm flustered. I just found out myself. Connor got the call from Julian. He wasn't on the chopper when it went down. He…I don't know any details. He was taken by some group in Colombia—a paramilitary group that served a drug lord, and he's been a prisoner this whole time. But he escaped, and he called his brother from Washington today. And he's on his way to Avalon. He'll be here by dinnertime."

Logan sat very still. His gaze moved over her with steady deliberation. "Wow," he said. "Pretty amazing news."

"A miracle," she said. "I never dreamed something like this could happen. Nobody did." The instant she said it, she heard her own lie. She had dreamed of this, for Julian to somehow be alive, hundreds of times since the terrible news had arrived. Watching Logan, she suspected he was more clued in to her than she'd ever imagined.

"So what's next?" he asked. "His ascent into heaven?"

"Logan."

He got up, pacing restlessly around the office. "Don't get me wrong, I never wanted the guy to be dead, but you'll excuse me if I don't break out the champagne and cigars."

She winced at his tone. "Connor explained to him on the phone that you and I are together now." Her stomach clenched even as she spoke. *I'm sorry, Julian. I'm so sorry. How could I have known?*

Logan played a hand through his hair, roughening the red locks. "I'm glad for the guy, and I feel bad for him at the same time."

"Fair enough," she said quietly. Later, she knew she would wonder about those lost months. What had he endured? How had he suffered?

"What does this mean for us?" Logan asked bluntly.

She hesitated. There was a part of her—a very big part—that yearned to turn back the clock, back to a time when she was Julian's fiancée, dreaming of their life together. However, the reality was, she had done the only thing that made sense and saved her sanity after getting the dreaded news. She had picked up the shattered pieces of her heart and put them back together as well as she could. Then she'd moved ahead with her life.

"This news is like five minutes old," she said. "It's barely sunk in."

"Just answer the question," Logan said. "Are you going to dump me now so you can go back to your old boyfriend?"

She caught her breath, feeling her heart speed up. "I'm married to you," she said. "I made a commitment to you, and I don't take that lightly."

"That doesn't exactly answer the question."

She understood his hostile tone. For him, this news was more than a surprise. It was a threat. She studied him for a moment. "I need to see him," she said. "Can you understand that I need to see him? Tonight, if he's willing…"

"Why wouldn't he be?"

"He didn't come back here expecting to find me married," she said. "He might not be too keen on seeing me."

"That's his problem."

Daisy decided both she and Logan needed more time to digest this news, so she picked up her bag and turned toward the door. She paused before leaving. "Sorry, I interrupted you when I first got here. What was it you were going to say to me earlier?"

"Never mind. It wasn't important."

Twenty-Nine

On his way home from work, Logan passed the Hilltop Tavern, same as he did every day. The only difference was that today, he was nearly overwhelmed by a raging desire to stop at the bar. He could practically taste the cold bite of just-tapped beer going down so smoothly. At the bottom of the pitcher was sweet nothingness to carry him away on a raft of oblivion.

He caught himself salivating like one of Pavlov's dogs. "Jesus, get a grip," he said aloud, reaching for his mobile phone. He thumbed in his sponsor's number and hit Send.

"Eddie Haven," said a voice on the other end of the line.

"Hey, it's Logan. Is this a good time?"

"Sure. I was headed to the gym. Maureen's dead asleep after a long day."

"She all right?"

"Other than feeling like she's been pregnant for years rather than months, she's fine," Eddie said. "We just learned it's a boy. We're going to name him Jabez. You know Maureen, she's a planner. It's the librarian in her."

"Yeah, that's great," Logan said, trying to sound interested.

"Sounds like something's on your mind. How about you meet me at the gym?"

"You got it." Logan glanced down at his midsection as he waited at a stoplight. The pounds were not exactly melting off. Daisy had always been kind about it when he brought the subject up. "More of you to love," she liked to say. Or maybe she didn't like saying it and was only trying to be nice.

Nice. That was exactly what Daisy was. A nice person. She was so freaking nice, it drove him wacko sometimes. She never said a word when his sweet tooth got the better of him and he went for a second bowl of ice cream or a stack of Fig Newtons that spanned from his thumb to his little finger. She was too freaking *nice* to nag.

Or maybe she didn't give a shit.

He thrust the dark thought away and changed into his gym clothes. He'd already started bench-pressing when Eddie showed up.

"What's up, bud?" Eddie asked, doing warm-ups on a nearby mat.

"My wife's fiancé came back from the dead," said Logan.

"Very funny."

Logan pressed the bar upward, barely feeling the weight. "Do you see me laughing?" As succinctly as he could, he related the sequence of events.

"Man," said Eddie. "*Man*. That is unbelievable."

"Tell me about it."

"I got a better idea. You tell *me* about it."

"I've been antsy all day," Logan admitted. "I usually don't even think about wanting a drink or popping an Oxy. Today it was all I could do to keep driving past the Hilltop Tavern. That's when I called you."

"You're smarter than you look."

Logan added more weights to the bar and settled back again. "Sometimes."

"So what is it that's making you so antsy, besides the general freakiness of the situation?"

He thought about that for a minute. "She and this guy—Julian Gastineaux—they were like, totally in love."

"What's your worst fear? That Daisy will leave you for Gastineaux?"

Logan pressed up again, welcoming the strain of the extra weight. He was about to say no, but he thought about it for a while. In his mind's eye, he could still see Daisy's face as she related the miraculous news of Julian's survival. In that moment, she'd seemed more alive than she had in months.

He increased his weight load again. Press up. Press down. "My worst fear is that she'll spend the rest of her life wishing she could be with him." The admission came from Logan with a wrenching honesty.

"Then again," he added, "it's kind of ironic. Before she dropped the Julian bomb, I was going to tell her maybe being married wasn't the best thing for us after all."

Eddie went to the bench next to Logan and threaded some weights on a bar. After a while, he said, "You've been saying some things about your marriage for a long time. Since before Gastineaux showed up again."

"Yeah. But now that this has happened—this Julian business—there's no way to talk about our problems with the marriage."

"What do you mean?"

"If I tell Daisy now, she'll go running straight to him."

"And how would you feel about that?"

"Like shit, man. How do you think? And what kind of message would it send to Charlie? To bail at the first sign of trouble?"

"Hell, Logan. You got more questions than me," said Eddie.

"And no answers. Not yet, anyway."

Every single night of his captivity, Julian had imagined his own homecoming. It was one of the mental exercises he'd done regularly to keep himself from ending up crazier than a shit-house rat. He had developed a habit of picturing the longed-for scene in his mind's eye down to the last detail. He saw himself getting off the train. He'd be in his BDUs, a duffel bag slung over his shoulder.

The second he spotted Daisy, the duffel would drop with a thud.

She would fly into his arms, literally, fly, in a blur of speed. He could feel her slender strong legs clasped at his waist, her arms clinging around his neck. *Yes.*

She had the best way of laughing when she got emotional. In his mind, he'd heard that special, broken laughter every day. And he could feel the warm silk of her hair and inhale her scent—fruity shampoo—and taste her mouth as he set her down and bent to kiss her.

Yeah, without that dream of home, he really might have gone bat-shit insane.

The reality, his actual homecoming, was different.

He sat alone on the train on the final leg of his journey. Connor had offered to drive up to the airport at Albany, but Julian opted for the train instead. He wore the civilian clothes they'd given him.

The staff psychiatrist had advised him not to make any big changes in his life. He was supposed to step back and let the readjustment take its own pace. Julian was pretty sure that would be impossible for him, but he agreed to give it a try.

The world outside streaked past the window. Albany and its outskirts were dull with industry, strip malls and big-box stores and depressing housing developments. Soon, however, the colors outside shifted to the intense green and gold of the Catskills. The scenery changed to lakes and rivers, neatly laid-out farms and towns, time-worn hills and cliffs rising to the west.

The approach to Avalon was just as he'd pictured it so many times in his mind. It was nearly dark, but he spotted the covered bridge spanning the river, and Willow Lake in the distance, rimmed by forestland and the occasional cottage.

The train clanked and hissed to a halt. He shouldered his bag, which still bore its tag—Second Lieutenant J. Gastineaux—and headed outside, feeling the coolness of the upstate wilderness in the breeze on his face. Avalon was an ordinary small town, like so many others all across the country. It looked so damn good to him. So…normal.

He reminded himself it wouldn't be the welcome he'd held in his heart for so long. But there was his brother, standing with arms open wide. They came together in a clash of joy, and in the midst of the fierce hug, Julian lost it, choking on sobs. He finally felt completely safe. During his ordeal, he'd forgotten that sensation.

"I can't believe it," Connor said. "I can't believe you're here."

"Me, neither." Julian dragged his sleeve across his face. "I thought this day would never come."

Connor picked up his bag. "Let's go home. Lolly's got a feast prepared. And wait till you see your niece." They got in the truck and started driving.

"Zoe was a baby when I left."

"Now she's a little kid with all the answers."

Julian remembered Charlie at three, a happy kid, in love with the world. What was he like now?

"I'm glad she has all the answers," he said to Connor, "because I got all kinds of questions."

"We all do, my brother."

"Everything around here looks pretty much the same," said Julian. "But I know it can't be."

"You still have your friends and family," Connor assured him. "We were all demolished when you were reported dead. And we never stopped thinking of you and missing you, not for a minute."

"I'm—I guess I don't know what to say to that. Thanks for not forgetting me?"

"Say anything," Connor advised him. "You get a free pass."

Julian understood that this was an opening for him to start talking about what had happened. In his debriefing, he had been strongly advised to seek further counseling, and he fully intended to do that. For now, he just wanted to be with his brother.

"I appreciate it," he said. "One of these days, I'll take you up on it."

"I need to ask you something else about tonight," Connor said. "About Daisy, actually."

Julian flinched at the sound of her name but covered his reaction. "What about her?"

"First of all, I hated telling you what I told you on the phone."

"There's not really a good way to break news like that," said Julian. He'd been playing the conversation over and over in his head. Sayers had advised him to take his time digesting the news. What she'd meant was that she didn't want him to go tearing off in a rage, howling about the injustice of it all.

And if he was being honest with himself, there was a part of him that was inches from doing just that.

"I'm glad I called you first," Julian said. "I'm glad you're my next of kin."

Connor pulled into the driveway. "Speaking of which, have you called our mother?"

"Not yet. I've had enough drama for one day."

"Then you'd better brace yourself," Connor said as they got out of the truck.

Olivia flew out of the house, her aging mutt, Barkis, at her heels, and flung her arms around him. "Welcome home," she said, her voice breaking. "Come inside. Are you hungry? I made all your favorites."

"That's not possible," Julian said. "Everything is my favorite." They went inside and he greeted his little niece, Zoe. She acted shy, hugging her dad's leg and peering up at him.

"I remember you," Julian said gently, hunkering down to her level. "You used to have a pink blanket you took everywhere."

She nodded, offered a smile. "I colored something for you. For a present." She scurried off to get it. Julian smiled after her. It felt so…normal, being here.

"Daisy wants to see you," Olivia said.

He flinched. "When?"

"That's up to you."

Best to get it over with sooner rather than later. "See if she can come over after dinner."

Following the phone call from her cousin Olivia, Daisy had fixed something for supper. For the life of her, she couldn't remember what it was. She rinsed the plates, and by the time everything went down the garbage disposal, she'd forgotten what she had served.

Her mind was a million miles away. No, that wasn't quite right. Her mind was miles away, firmly entrenched at her cousin's house, where Julian waited.

"Jeremiah Butler has a gun," Charlie announced, scooting a toy soldier along the edge of the counter.

"Is that the name of a song?" asked Logan. Before Charlie could answer, he checked his phone for an incoming text message. His hair was damp from the gym.

"It's the name of a kid," Charlie said. "Jeez."

"A kid who has a gun." With lightning fingers, Logan sent a text back.

"Yeah, he got it for his birthday." Charlie's soldier used a piece of string to rappel down the side of the cabinet. "His dad took him to the shooting gallery."

"The…range," Logan said. "The shooting range."

"Can you take me to the shooting range?" Charlie crawled on his belly, commando-style, toward the family room.

"Maybe," Logan said. "One of these days."

"You always say that," Charlie pointed out. "Which one of these days?"

"The one that fits our schedule."

"Mom says you make time for what's important to you," Charlie informed him.

Daisy put soap in the dishwasher and straightened up. "I said that?"

"Yep."

"I'm pretty smart. However, I'm not so sure about boys shooting guns."

"I knew you'd say that." Charlie hunkered down and backed into the family room. "Dad."

"One of these days," Logan repeated.

"Tell you what," Daisy suggested. "I'll give you an extra half hour of TV tonight because you did an awesome job cleaning your plate at dinner."

Charlie's eyes widened. "Yes." He scurried away before she changed her mind. Since his struggles in school had begun, she had restricted him to one hour of TV per day, so extra time was a huge bonus to him.

Logan went back to texting. She sat down across the table from him.

"I need to ask you something."

"Okay, just a sec." He finished his message and put down the phone. "Work stuff," he said. "It never ends."

"Julian's at his brother's house," Daisy said baldly, knowing of no way to ease into the topic. "He wants to see me."

Logan grabbed a leftover piece of bread from the basket on the table and slathered it with butter. "And?"

"And I would like to go see him."

"When?" Logan bit off a hunk of the bread.

"Tonight. Like, in the next hour or so." Every time she thought about the miracle that had happened, her heart nearly flew out of her chest.

Logan finished chewing and was quiet for a couple of minutes. Daisy forced herself to wait. With every fiber of her being, she wanted to bolt for the door and speed over to Olivia's house. She wouldn't, though. She was not the only one enmeshed in this situation. So much was at stake here. There were so many ways for this miraculous occurrence to turn painful.

"We'll all go," Logan said, his chair scraping loudly as he pushed back from the table.

No. The denial leapt up inside her, but she stifled it. She did desperately crave a private reunion with Julian. However, that didn't mean she was entitled to one. Her status was different now than it had been the last time she'd seen Julian. She wasn't his fiancée anymore. She was someone else's wife. Welcoming Julian home would be an entirely different experience from the one she had imagined so long ago when they'd said goodbye.

"I'll get Charlie," she said.

"Have you told him?" Logan asked.

She was startled to hear a waver of uncertainty in his

voice. Of course he was uncertain. Who wouldn't be, under the circumstances?

"I'll explain to him as best I can right now," she said. "And Logan?"

"Yeah."

"Just so you know—I meant what I said at the office, earlier. I'm married to you now."

She saw his shoulders tense up and wondered why he didn't seem reassured. "We'll be ready in ten minutes," she said and hurried to find Charlie.

Logan grabbed another piece of bread from the basket on the table.

In the family room, she switched off the TV.

"Hey," Charlie protested.

"Hey yourself. There's been a change of plans. That was a rerun anyway."

"It's my fave."

"I can think of something you'll like better. Come upstairs, and I'll tell you about it while we get ready."

He was intrigued enough to follow along.

Daisy had no idea what to wear. She didn't want to look dressed up, or as if she was trying too hard. On the other hand, she didn't want to look as if she didn't care.

Of course she cared. She cared with every inch of her heart.

"What do you remember about Julian?" she asked her son.

"When I was little, I called him Daddy-boy. You were going to get married to him but he got killed in the air force."

Daisy could not for the life of her figure out why this kid kept failing in school. He had a mind like a steel trap.

"Everybody believed that's what happened," she said. "I believed it, and so did the air force and his brother, Connor."

She culled through the rack in her closet. Maybe the aqua-colored top. No, that had been a gift from Logan, who had surprisingly good taste in women's clothes.

The coral-colored one, then, she decided, with the fluttery sleeves. She stepped into the bathroom and slipped it on, then grabbed her makeup bag from a drawer. Charlie was lining up the framed family pictures on the big bureau.

"We found out today that there was a terrible mistake. Julian didn't get killed after all. He survived, and now he's home in Avalon."

Charlie blinked, but didn't seem shocked at all. "Where is he?"

"At my cousin Olivia's house. We've been invited to go see him right away. Is that okay with you?"

"Will he remember me?"

"Of course. You were a lot smaller last time he saw you." She sat down at the vanity and unzipped her makeup bag. Go light on the makeup, she reminded herself. She brushed on powder, added a hint of blush. Mascara and lip gloss. She brushed her hair, then stood up.

"You got all dressed up," Charlie said. "Do I have to dress up?"

"I'm not dressed up. It seems fitting to look nice for a guy who—"

A horn sounded.

"Your dad's ready to go," she said.

After dinner, during which Julian had shoved down three helpings of everything, he went through a storage box he'd left in Connor's garage before shipping out.

The contents were mundane—photographs and keepsakes, civilian clothes, some favorite books, a baseball mitt, other sports equipment.

"Thanks for not getting rid of my stuff," he said to his brother.

"Thanks for coming back for it," said Connor with a grin.

In the guest room where he would sleep that night, Julian changed into some jeans from the storage box, a softly faded Cornell sweatshirt and a pair of sneakers. The jeans fit loosely, but it was good to wear his own clothes at last. It made him feel more like himself.

There was a shoe box full of cards, postcards, pictures and letters from Daisy, a correspondence that dated back to high school. He studiously avoided that box. He'd probably never throw it out, but he would never look at it, either.

Hearing the slam of the car door, he looked out the window to see that she had arrived. His heart tried to pound its way out of his chest. God, she looked so beautiful. There were a lot of things that were different about her—the short haircut, clothes he didn't recognize—to remind him of how much time had passed. Then again, certain things about her were timeless, like the way she walked and the tilt of her head as she headed toward the house. And that face, those eyes… He'd seen them in his dreams, every night. Her face looked older—more mature.

Then someone else got out of the car—Logan. Her husband. He exited the late-model SUV, followed by Charlie and Blake, the dog. They were a family now. It was obvious.

Charlie patted his thigh and called to the dog.

Charlie. Could that half-grown boy be Charlie? Julian's heart expanded almost painfully as he hurried down the stairs and out onto the porch. He tried to pull himself up short, but his aching arms, with a mind of their own, grabbed Daisy and swept her into a hug. He nearly came undone at the smell of her hair and the feel of her in his embrace. Somewhere in the back of his mind, he became aware that this could—and should—be the last time they touched. The girl was married now. Married.

He let go and stepped back. In spite of everything, he could not stave off a smile. "Surprise," he said.

"Yes, surprise." She was crying—hard, between gulps of laughter—but he could see her taking deep breaths, trying to hold herself together. Julian turned to Logan and stuck out his hand. "Hey, good to see you," he said.

"Yeah, welcome back," Logan replied.

They used to be arch enemies. Rivals for Daisy's affections. Now the enmity was gone because Logan had already won. Besides, compared to the things Julian had endured over the past two years, the fight with Logan was a cakewalk. Since that time, Julian had learned a thing or two about patience and forbearance.

"Hey, Charlie," he said. "Remember me?"

The kid eyed him bashfully, though a smile flickered on his lips. He was still really cute, but he was definitely a boy, not a baby.

"I remember," he said. "You gave us Blake."

At the sound of her name, the dog pranced around.

"Come on inside," Olivia called from the porch. "I have cherry pie for dessert."

"You like cherry pie?" Julian asked Charlie.

"Everybody likes cherry pie." Charlie's smile appeared again and this time stayed in place long enough for Julian to spot a missing front tooth.

They all headed inside. Blake trotted over and tried to get Barkis to play, but the older dog growled and ignored her. Zoe had better luck with Charlie. "Come sit by me for pie," she crowed, regarding him as though he'd invented sunshine.

Julian tried not to be too obvious about watching Daisy, but he couldn't keep his eyes off her. She appeared to be having the same problem because their gazes kept meeting, glancing away, meeting again.

"I can't believe you're here," she said.

"Feels like I've been away forever," he said, "down a rabbit hole somewhere while the world went on without me. I know for sure they didn't have cherry pie where I was."

"The pie is from the Sky River Bakery," Zoe said.

"No wonder it's so good."

"Where were you, Julian?" Charlie asked.

"Yeah, where were you?" Zoe echoed.

"Far away in a place called Colombia. I was lost for a long time, but now I'm back."

The situation felt almost mundane. It seemed both normal and strange to Julian, sitting around the kitchen table, eating pie. He kept feeling Daisy's attention like a physical touch. It both bothered and excited him. Married, he kept telling himself. The girl is married. Some lines were not to be crossed.

He got up to take the dishes away, and Daisy jumped up to help.

"How about a game of war?" Olivia asked, naming a favorite card game.

"Yeah!" Charlie said, punching the air. "You be on my team, Dad."

"You betcha," said Logan.

"I'll get the cards," Olivia said.

"Let's go outside," Daisy murmured to Julian. "Okay?"

He didn't say a word but headed out to the back porch. Olivia and Connor had a beautiful place. They had designed the house to fit into the landscape beside the river that rushed down from the hills to the lake. The back porch faced an upward slope with meadows and sugar maples, bisected by a cold spring. Julian used to spend hours imagining his life with Daisy, and it had looked a lot like this. It was fully dark, though the moon was so bright that the trees cast shadows across the lawn.

"I told Logan I would need some time with you. He understands."

No, he doesn't, thought Julian, but he didn't say so aloud. What he wants is for me to still be dead. And I don't blame the guy. Nobody in his right mind would want his wife's dead fiancé back in the picture.

Daisy stood with her back to the porch railing. "You're a miracle," she said. "A miracle man."

"I wish you wouldn't say that. Too much of a reputation to live up to. Like, what would I do for an encore, walk on water?"

"Don't do anything," she said. "Just be safe."

"I'm safe now."

She nodded, inhaled shakily. He could sense she was teetering on the brink of tears again. He still knew her well enough to tell.

"Don't go crying on me now," he warned, gripping the porch rail to stop himself from touching her.

"I'm trying not to," she said. "Lord knows, I've cried a river for you, Julian Gastineaux."

"Until I found my way back to Palanquero Air Base last Thursday, I didn't know what you'd been told. I had no idea the chopper went down. I feel bad that you had to go through thinking I'd died with the rest of the crew."

He tried to imagine what it might be like, getting the news that the love of your life, the person you'd planned on marrying, was dead.

"I'm sorry about the crew," she said. "Were you close?"

"Like brothers." There was so much more he wished he could tell her, but he held back. He wasn't at liberty to share his heart with her, not now.

"I'm so sorry, Julian. It's horrible. Just know…you'll heal. You'll never be the same, but you'll heal."

"That's the plan," he said quietly. "How about yourself? How are you?"

"No one could make it less horrible, but everyone was really kind and thoughtful to me," she said.

And was Logan kind and thoughtful? Julian wondered. How long did he wait before making his move?

"I loved you so much," she whispered. "And that didn't simply stop when they told me you'd been killed. I came to believe that love never dies. I'll always have you in my heart, no matter what else happens. That's what finally led me out of the fog. For Charlie's sake, for my own sanity, I had to quit grieving and start living my life."

"I know that, Daisy. I do. I respect it. And now I need you to listen, because I'm only going to say this once. You have to understand, all this time, I loved you more every single day. Most days, the thought of seeing you again was the one thing that kept me alive. I survived because you gave me something to come home to."

She gasped softly, her face showing a terrible mixture of hopelessness and joy. "I understand. But while you were doing that, I was grieving. And it was hell for me. Finally I had to put myself together. I *buried* you, Julian. There was nothing else I could do."

He winced and wished he didn't hear the hurt in her voice. Before he'd left, they had talked about it. They'd had the hard conversation every soldier was required to hold with his loved ones before deployment. He'd told her to live her life, find joy and love. He'd written her that letter, to be delivered in the event of his death, urging her to move on. Yet it had all been so theoretical, abstract, something he couldn't imagine actually coming to pass.

"I can't take back a decision I made when I believed you were gone forever," she said in a voice thick with tears.

"True," he conceded. "I'd never ask you to."

"I'm sorry," she said, the words seeming wrenched from her. "I'm so sorry. From the first time I met you, all I ever wanted was to be with you. And yet I kept screwing things up. I got pregnant and my life did a one-eighty away from you. We went down different paths. And then, when it finally looked as if we were going to get it right, I lost you again."

"There's nothing I can say to that. We both did what we did. Nobody's at fault here."

"I want to know what happened to you," she said. "That is, if you can talk about it. I mean, if you want to..."

"It's a long story. Grim in parts." He said no more but wished he could.

"I'm a good listener," she prompted. "You know I am."

"I do know. But it's not going to happen."

"What do you mean? I can handle it, Julian." Something—irritation?—edged her voice. "If I can survive the news of your death, I can probably deal with the story of your survival."

"No doubt," he said, trying to find a way to explain himself. "Listen, when you were going to be my wife, I would have felt okay, burdening you with my shit."

"I wouldn't be burdened."

"Just hear me out, okay? We don't have each other anymore. Now that you're..." He didn't know what she was. His ex? His former widow? "Now that everything's changed, we can't be having conversations like that. Or even ones like this."

She swiped the back of her hand across her cheek. With every cell of his body, he wanted to draw her close, to whisper that everything was going to be okay. He couldn't. He had no guarantee that *any*thing was going to be okay.

They stood quietly together in the dark. He could see the others through the window. They were gathered around the kitchen table, laughing over their game of cards. Logan and his son looked so alike, grinning at each other.

Daisy had made a family for herself. He didn't blame her, didn't begrudge her the happiness she had found. He wished it didn't hurt so damn much. What hurt most of all was that, when he looked into her eyes, he could see something he probably shouldn't be seeing—love and longing, every bit as powerful as it had been the day he'd left her.

Thirty

Logan was alone in the house on a Saturday, a rare state of affairs. Daisy had a bat mitzvah to shoot in Phoenicia and would be staying there overnight rather than driving home in the wee hours. Charlie had gone on a campout with his Tiger Cubs troop. For the first time in a long time, Logan was by himself.

He kind of liked it.

Sure, he had wanted to be a family with Charlie and Daisy, but the one thing he hadn't quite been prepared for was how…constant it was, having them around. Unrelenting. He was on call 24/7, no breaks allowed. Although he knew it was his destiny to be a family man, he didn't mind a day of downtime.

It didn't take long for him to realize downtime had a downside—he started thinking too much. Feeling restless, he did a bit of yard work, mainly to stay busy.

"Hey, neighbor. How's life treating you?" The guy next door, who had recently moved to the neighborhood, greeted him across the fence.

"Sending me too many weeds. How about yourself, Bart? You settling into your new place?"

"Yeah, it's great here. The wife ditched me for the

weekend, though. She went antiques-hunting with her ladies' club." He grinned. "Women seem to have a club for everything."

Logan chuckled, easing into camaraderie with his new neighbor. Bart and Sally Jericho seemed to be a fun, cheerful pair who wanted to make friends with Logan and Daisy.

"Hey, I've been ditched, too," Logan said. "Daisy had a work thing, and my kid is on a campout."

"And look at us, a couple of chumps doing yard work. We ought to be kicking back on the patio, guzzling cold ones and telling dirty jokes."

Logan had an instant visceral reaction to the idea of guzzling a cold one. The craving still took hold like a seductive mistress. With no effort at all, he could hear the click and airy hiss of the bottle opening, could feel the cold bubbles alive and dancing on his tongue, slipping down his throat and spreading sweet oblivion to every cell in his body.

"No rest for the wicked," he said to Bart with a laugh, and turned on his weed whacker.

Logan's folks were still amazed that he did things like yard work and household chores. He'd been raised differently, by people who mixed a shaker of martinis and called a contractor just to change a lightbulb.

Logan had made a different life for himself. His family didn't understand why he'd want to settle in a small town and set himself up in business. Sometimes even he didn't understand it. After he'd graduated from college and moved to Avalon, he had been focused on being a good dad. He thought that meant marrying Charlie's mother. Not long after the impulse-driven move he'd made in Vegas, he'd found himself reexamining that decision. Even before the miraculous resurrection of Julian Gastineaux, Logan had realized something was missing for him and Daisy. He hadn't expected this feeling of ambivalence. As far as he could tell, neither had she.

They both acted as though everything was all right, but the distance between them kept widening. The strain was starting to wear on him.

He heaved a sigh and went to shower off the sweat and grass clippings of yard work. Afterward, he sat down at the computer to check his email. The computer was a Mac, with all the bells and whistles Daisy needed for her photography work. Logan found it to be a pain in the ass. He should have brought his laptop home from the office.

His email queue was short. He dispatched the work stuff, feeling a small tug of satisfaction as he dealt with clients. Business, for him, was a simple matter. Marriage, not so much.

There was a note from his mother—"How was Charlie's soccer game? When are you going to bring him to see us? Montauk is so beautiful this time of year…"

Montauk. The place where Charlie had been conceived by a pair of reckless teenagers on a weekend of drunken revelry.

He hit Reply and opened a picture file to insert an action shot of Charlie playing soccer. One great thing about Daisy being a world-class photographer was that she documented Charlie's life superbly. He found a picture of the kid leaping into the air after a soccer ball and sent it to his mother.

Daisy was totally organized with her photos, labeling them with dates, names and events. Logan scrolled through the Charlie file, a pictorial chronicle of his son's life. The shots of the two of them together made Logan smile. Through the years he'd been a good dad. He was confident of that. He felt sure of himself in this role.

He spotted another file labeled *Julian*. Still hanging around like a virus on the hard drive. Some propensity for self-torture made Logan look. There was Gastineaux in all his glory, from a dreadlocked punk to the day he'd left on his save-the-world mission. Logan forced himself to look past the obvious—the guy was cut like a body-building ad—and imagine Daisy's state of mind when she took the photos. A good photographer could speak her heart through the pictures she took. And Daisy was a good photographer. What Logan detected in these pictures was a kind of passion unique to this guy, a passion that didn't exist for anyone else.

Not even her own husband.

"Yo, neighbor. You in there?" Bart Jericho called through the screen door at the back porch. He'd cleaned himself up, changed into a loud Hawaiian print shirt.

"Come on in," Logan called, shutting down the computer and pushing back from the desk.

Bart looked around the big, sunny kitchen, with its archway open to the dining room, living room and study. "Nice place," he said.

"Thanks. We remodeled the shit out of it."

"It's a stunner. Nothing like an old house."

"Thanks." Logan and Daisy had both thrown themselves into sprucing up the place. Now the house looked exactly like the illusion their new neighbor was seeing—a beautiful home. The kind of place that sheltered a happy family.

"Say, listen, I had a great idea. Since we're both wifeless for the afternoon, let's go grab some burgers."

Logan had planned on hitting the gym and then an AA meeting, but suddenly a burger with his new buddy sounded more appealing. "Cool. Did you have someplace in mind?"

"That's the other part of my great idea," said Bart. "Our membership at the country club was just approved, and new members are entitled to a special discount. So it's my treat."

Logan grinned, thinking about a juicy burger. "Even better."

The Avalon Meadows Country Club was old-school, with a gated entry and a broad avenue sweeping up to the grand Edwardian-style clubhouse. Lush lawns and tennis courts, a swimming pool and golf course surrounded the place. The moment they drove onto the premises, Logan felt a warm pulse of familiarity. This was a world he knew. The Bellamys were longtime members here, but Daisy never wanted to come. She claimed she shot so many weddings here, it felt like a place of work rather than relaxation.

Not Logan. He appreciated the quiet elegance of the clubhouse, with its view of golfers and their caddies hiking in and out of the afternoon shadows. Even the sounds were familiar and soothing—the *thwock* of tennis ball volleys and the laughter of children splashing in the pool, the smooth, discreet waiters with trays of drinks, the murmur of conversation and occasional bursts of laughter, the clink of ice cubes against fine crystal. The whole scene on the sunny deck took him back to simpler times when he was a kid, and everything in the world was a possibility.

"This is the life, eh?" said Bart, settling back in a deck chair and surveying the scene.

Logan nodded. A burst of little-girl squeals came from the pool area below. One of them appeared to be having a birthday party down there.

Bart studied the tent card on the table. "Hey, there's a drink called the Bellamy Hammer, didja know that? Isn't your wife a Bellamy?"

"Yep, that's right."

"Any relation to the Bellamy Hammer?" asked Bart with a chuckle.

"Some days I think she *is* the Bellamy Hammer." It just slipped out.

"Oh. Trouble in paradise?"

Logan shrugged. "The drink was named after some old uncle of hers, a geezer named George Bellamy who passed away. Having a drink named after him was one of those do-before-you-die things." He pushed the tent card away.

The waiter came for their drink order. He presented each of them with a printed card. "Good afternoon, gentlemen. Today's drink special is a rare single barrel bourbon. Highly recommended."

"I can't say I know exactly what that is," said Bart, "but count me in."

"I know exactly what it is," Logan began, "however—"

"Then count my buddy in, too," Bart said expansively. "Make them doubles, too. It'll save you a trip."

Logan took a breath. Opened his mouth to retract the order, but the waiter was quicker, heading off to the bar. Within moments, he'd returned with the drinks. The amber liquid looked beautiful in the sparkling crystal highball glasses. A silver bucket of ice and a carafe of water were set in the middle of the table.

Logan was flooded with longing. The daily battle that was his recovery was forgotten, entirely. Nothing existed except that perfect, beautiful glass of whiskey. Vaguely, he became aware of the guy across the table—his new friend, who didn't know Logan was damaged, one drink away from spinning out of control.

Bullshit, he thought, picking up the heavy cut-crystal glass. It was all bullshit. He wasn't a stupid kid anymore. He could have this one drink with Bart, and that would be the end of it.

"Cheers, neighbor," said Bart, clinking glasses with him. "Down the hatch."

The gorgeous, piney scent of the fine bourbon wafted on the country-club breeze, nearly bringing tears to Logan's eyes. On the pool deck, childish shrieks of excitement filled the air, mingling with grown-up laughter and conversation. He touched the glass to his bottom lip. Then, with a casual tip of his wrist, he took his first, glorious sip.

As the fire raced through him, he felt a dark, defiant glee.

Julian wasn't quite sure what to get his four-year-old niece for her birthday, and he was running late for her party at the country club, so he got her one of everything. Okay, that was overstating it. A local toy store, Queen Guinevere's Castle, was crammed floor to ceiling with stuff. He found a corner where everything was pink and filled his arms with everything a little girl would like—a stuffed poodle, a magic wand, a talking mirror, a pop-up book of princesses…

"Whoa, slow down there," said an amused voice. "You're not much for browsing, are you?"

He turned to see the shopgirl regarding him with a slightly teasing grin. She was cute, in her twenties, probably, like him. A black girl, something not so common in Avalon. "I'm in a hurry," he said. "On my way to a birthday party."

She eyed the armload of toys. "For how many kids?"

"Just my niece."

"Okay, big guy." The shopgirl methodically took back and reshelved each toy. "Tell me about your niece, and I'll help you pick out the perfect gift."

"Thanks. Her name is Zoe."

"And what does she call you?"

"Sometimes Unkie," he said, cringing a little. "Sometimes Julian. Does it matter?"

The girl's eyes seemed to shine even brighter. "It does to me. I wanted to find out your name."

That made him laugh a little. "Julian Gastineaux," he said. "That's me. And you are?"

"Guinevere Johnson."

"So is this your store?"

"No, I was named after the store. My mom has owned the place since before I was born. Is it weird, do you think, that it's named after a known adulteress?"

"Most people probably don't think of that," he said.

"All right, then. Let's talk about Zoe. Does she like to dress up or is she more of a tomboy?"

"Dress up, for sure. The kid's room looks like a burlesque dressing room, with feather boas and…those crown things."

"Tiaras."

"Yeah, that's, like, her basic gear. Her birthday's at the country club. A swimming party."

"And does she prefer playing sports or playing with dolls?"

"Dolls, I guess. This sounds like a compatibility test."

"Just doing my due diligence."

Eventually they settled on the idea of a baby doll with several clothing changes. Guinevere reached for a dark-skinned baby, but he stopped her. "I think she'd go for a white doll. Zoe's lily-white."

"Really."

"I have a very diverse family."

"Cool." She insisted on gift-wrapping it for him. She seemed to take her time, chatting away as she worked. "So do you live here in Avalon?"

"For the time being. I'm on an extended leave from the air force."

"Really? I've never met anyone in the air force. What's that like?"

"It's…interesting. I put in for pilot training. Waiting to hear back on that."

"Well, that's very impressive. I'd love to hear more about it." Their hands touched as she gave him back his credit card.

By then there was no question—she was flirting with him. This cute, funny girl was flirting, and he'd be an idiot to ignore her. He *was* an idiot. Everything about this girl was completely appealing, but loving Daisy wasn't something he could shed or have his psychiatrist explain away. Loving her was part of his blood and bone. Scary thought. Had she ruined him for all other women?

As Julian turned and passed through the wrought-iron gates of the country club, past the plaster jockeys holding their lamps, he reflected that there had been a time—not all that long ago—when a guy who looked like him would be arriving via the service entry, rather than through the main entrance as an invited guest.

Change was good, he reminded himself. It was good to be in a world where every possibility was open to him.

Every possibility except one.

He and Daisy were doing a good job avoiding one another, so that was something. She held true to her word to stick with her marriage. He had no choice but to respect her decision.

His medical team—physician, shrink, physical therapist—kept urging him to be patient with himself and take time to adjust, but he really wanted to wake up one morning and be over her. He was doing his best to focus on getting better and going on to the next phase of his career.

Zoe's party was set up at a shaded outdoor table by the pool. When she spotted him, she ran over and gave him a wet hug. Her swimsuit had fins and a shiny fish tale, and her goggles were studded with rhinestones.

As she scampered off to join the other kids at the wading pool, he wandered over to visit with his brother and sister-in-law. Connor and Olivia had been good to him since he'd returned, giving him a place to live indefinitely while he figured out the direction of his future.

"Mermaid juice?" Olivia offered, gesturing at a pitcher filled with a glowing green fluid.

"Thanks, I'll pass."

"There's a bar for the grown-ups." She indicated a deck overlooking the pool, accessed by a side stairway.

"A beer sounds good. Do you need anything?"

"I'll take a beer, too," said Connor.

"Be right back." He headed toward the bar. Halfway up the stairs, he paused and looked around, something he'd taken to doing since his escape. Never again would he take anything for granted, not even the chance to spend a few seconds breathing the air and taking in the scenery. He listened to the sounds of people splashing in the pool, the hollow click of a golf club hitting a ball, the cool jazz murmuring from hidden speakers. This was not his world, but he felt comfortable here. Considering the places he'd been, he knew how to fit in anywhere.

As he approached the outdoor bar, he heard a crash, followed by raucous male laughter.

"Whoa there," someone said. "That dude is starting to party early."

Julian looked over and saw some drunk guy picking himself up off the deck amid an upended tray and broken glasses. The drunk's companion, a guy in a Hawaiian print shirt and khaki pants, stood back, his eyes shifting as though he wanted to hide.

Julian's gut tightened as he walked over to the drunk

guy, who had fallen again. The red hair and husky build were unmistakable. Great.

Bending down, he grabbed Logan's arm. "Okay, my man, party's over."

"Is he a friend of yours?" asked his companion.

Logan glared at Julian, wobbled a little. "Yeah, we go way back, old Jules and Logan."

"How much has he had?" Julian asked.

"A few," the guy admitted. "Er, several. Doubles. Christ, my tab's going to be sky-high."

"I'm good for it," Logan said thickly. "Less get another round, my treat."

Julian kind of hated the guy in that moment. He'd never had any love for Logan, but up to this point, he'd admired his commitment to staying sober and his devotion to his kid. He hadn't even blamed Logan for marrying Daisy once it appeared Julian was out of the picture.

The swaying, bleary-eyed guy before him now seemed like a different person.

"I'm going to give him a ride home," Julian told the guy, then turned to the furious waiter Logan had collided with. "Sorry. We're out of here."

"The hell we are," Logan said. "It's single barrel bourbon day."

"Right." Julian didn't bother arguing. He kept hold of Logan's arm and led the way around the side of the building to avoid marching him through the clubhouse.

"I've always had a problem with you," Logan said, stumbling.

Julian moved in to keep Logan from falling again. "I'm the least of your problems."

Logan turned belligerent in the car. "This is none of your damn business."

"I'm making it my business. Is Daisy at your house? What about Charlie?"

"She's on the job, where else would she be on the weekend? Charlie's at a campout. And in case you didn't hear me the first time, s'none of your business."

Julian considered taking the guy home, depositing him on his doorstep or maybe throwing him in the shower fully clothed. That didn't seem like such a great idea. Logan might get a notion to drive somewhere or do something equally foolish.

"Pull in here," Logan ordered, jerking his thumb toward a package store on the right. "I need to pick up something."

"I got a better idea," said Julian, making a sharp left into Blanchard Park. "Let's pull in here." He passed a latte stand and parked by the lake. Jumping out, he went around, unbuckled Logan and yanked him from his seat.

"What the—" Logan flailed but was too uncoordinated to defend himself.

Julian turkey-walked him to the end of the dock and unceremoniously shoved him over the edge. Logan hit the water with a splash and came up sputtering. "Son of a bitch," he roared.

"Yeah, that's me," Julian said. "Do yourself a favor and sober up."

"You're insane. You're trying to drown me." He gasped, inhaled water and choked repeatedly.

"If I was trying to drown you," Julian stated, "you'd already be sleeping with the fishes."

The guy's eyes were looking a little clearer. Nothing like a shock of cold lake water to bring a person to his senses. "Fuck you," he said, his enunciation crisp now.

Julian had heard far worse from his brothers in the military. He regarded Logan coolly. "Get out of the water. I got a birthday party to go to."

"Ask me if I care. Christ, Gastineaux, what the hell do

you want from me? Why the hell do you care if I have a couple drinks?"

"As I understand it, you're not supposed to have even one drink, not even a sip."

"Did Daisy tell you that?"

"Of course not."

"You think it's easy dealing with all this shit?"

At that, Julian couldn't keep in a bark of laughter. "You think you're God's special drunk? You think nobody's ever been like you before? Well, guess what, buddy? We're all like you. And you're like all of us. Except you've got more to lose. Don't you see how good you have it? You've got everything I want—I mean, everything *you* want."

Logan swam awkwardly to the wooden ladder. "You're a real dick, you know that?" He grabbed the ladder and tried to hoist himself up. He slipped and fell back, going under again. He stayed under long enough for Julian to experience a flicker of worry. Then he reappeared, choking again. "Dammit, give me a hand," he demanded.

The moment Julian reached down, he realized his mistake. Logan grabbed him, hauling him into the water. It was cold enough to steal his breath. He resurfaced in a fury.

Logan tried to tackle him and drag him under. Although he had the advantage of outweighing Julian, it ended there. Julian was trained in every sort of fighting, including aquatic.

"Okay, wise guy," he said. "You picked my favorite combat technique." He easily took the upper hand, imprisoning Logan's arms and pulling them up and back to force his face into the water. Then he pulled back, hearing Logan gasp for breath.

"How often do you go on a bender like this?" he demanded, wondering how much Daisy had suffered through.

"None of your—"

Julian shoved his face in the water again and brought him back up. "You're a stupid SOB, aren't you?"

"Fuck off, Gastin—"

Julian plunged him under a third time, held him down, then hauled him up. "What the hell is your problem? You ended up with everything you wanted," he said. "And now you're pissing that away."

"Like I said, none of your business, dickhead."

Julian held him under another time. It occurred to him that he could finish this right here, right now. It was the most fleeting of thoughts, but the darkness of it worried him so he pulled up again.

"Just shut up and listen," he said. "We can go at this all day if you want. If you're ready for it to stop, keep your mouth shut. I don't care whose business it is, and frankly I don't care if you drink yourself into a coma. But I do care what happens to Daisy and Charlie, and they don't deserve to put up with a drunk."

"Who the hell are you to judge—"

One last plunge. Julian had to indulge himself. He quickly relented. Keeping Logan in a half nelson hold, he made his way to shore. He dragged Logan like a prisoner to the car. Their clothes and shoes squished with every step.

Julian went around to the driver's side and started the engine.

"You're going to ruin the upholstery, genius," Logan grumbled.

"Yeah, I'm real worried about that." The car was his old beater from college, nothing a little lake water would hurt. He pulled up to the latte stand and ordered a large coffee, black, fishing his wallet out of his soggy pants and paying for it with a damp bill and some pocket change. The barista regarded him with raised eyebrows but took the money.

"Drink it," said Julian. "Try not to scald yourself."

"Screw you." Logan took a sip and glared straight ahead. After a few more sips, he dug an iPhone out of his pocket and swore. "Ruined. You ruined it."

Julian didn't argue. "You need to make a phone call?"

"No. I need a damn phone." He drank some more coffee, then leaned back against the headrest and shut his eyes.

"You're not calling Daisy," Julian said through gritted teeth.

"I need to call my fucking sponsor, dumb ass."

Julian read a tinge of remorse in Logan's anger. "Who is he, and where does he live?"

A few minutes later, he drove up to a lakeside bungalow with flower boxes under the windows and birdhouses hanging from the trees. Julian went to the door. A guy with shaggy hair, in a T-shirt and jeans, answered, not even raising an eyebrow as he regarded Julian's wet clothes. Julian introduced himself and stepped aside, gesturing at the car. "I brought a friend to see you. Hope this isn't a bad time."

Eddie took one look at Logan. He didn't ask questions. "It's not a bad time."

Thirty-One

Summer ended in a haze of gold. Flowers bloomed riotously and with abandon, having no knowledge that they would soon fade away. There was something to be said for not knowing what came next, Daisy reflected. Use up everything you've got, all at once.

"How come Dad's not with us?" Charlie asked from the backseat.

"He'll catch up a little later," she said.

"Why do they call it the Bellamy Family Ruin?" he asked.

"Reunion," she corrected him. "It means a special time when we all get together and have fun being a family. Remember last year?"

"No."

"Sure you do. Aunt Sonnet got stung by a bee and had to stab herself with her Epipen because she's allergic."

"Yeah, that was cool."

"And it was a fun day, right?"

"Yeah. Why do we have a reunion?"

"To make sure we stay in touch, as a family, no matter where we are in the world." Not for the first time, she felt a barely acknowledged yearning to see and experience new things. She hadn't been anywhere since Vegas.

Stop it, she thought, and reminded herself to be grateful for the life she had and the good times the reunion would bring. Bellamys were coming from as far away as Japan and South Africa, Seattle and Santa Barbara, just to spend the weekend at Camp Kioga. The festivities would start this evening with a barbecue and a bonfire by the lake. Tomorrow would bring a picnic, games and boating or sitting around and catching up with one another.

"When's Dad coming?" Charlie asked again.

"I don't know what time, exactly. Tell you what. When we get to Camp Kioga, you can send him a text message from my phone."

Charlie was silent.

"Okay?" she prodded.

"Dad has to catch up with us later because he's at a meeting," Charlie said, proving once again that he missed very little.

"That's right." She kept her tone even, but she suspected her son could see right through the calm exterior. Since Logan's relapse, she'd come to realize that her son understood a lot more than she'd ever suspected.

The relapse felt like a turning point for them as a couple. Not that it was some unforgivable offense—far from it. But the crisis had the effect of forcing them to deal with things they'd been studiously ignoring, practically from the day they'd impulsively married. It made her wonder who she and Logan thought they were fooling.

Logan's slip had come as a total surprise, though it probably shouldn't have. She had returned home from an overnight assignment last Sunday to find him waiting for her, freshly showered and shaved, looking pale and deeply contrite. Oddly fragile.

"I got drunk last night," he'd said, and the whole story

had rushed out of him—the new neighbor, the country club… Julian's role. God. *Julian*. It was a terrible, splendid irony that he'd been involved, playing the role of rescuer.

Later that Sunday, when Charlie had come home from his campout, Logan had taken him to the backyard, where the two of them had kicked a soccer ball back and forth. When they came in, Charlie seemed thoughtful and subdued. He'd had nothing to say until now, with his observation that Logan was at a meeting.

"I hope it's okay with you," she said, "that your dad goes to meetings."

He shrugged. "They help him so he won't drink alcohol."

"Right." She parked near the main pavilion. There was plenty of room, because for this weekend only, the resort was closed to the public.

"Want to send a text message?" she asked, handing him her phone.

"Nah, he knows where to find me." Charlie had spotted the cluster of people around the main pavilion, and his eyes lit with excitement. He tumbled out of the car and went to find the kids to play with down by the lake. Four generations of Bellamys were present, from Daisy's grandfather Charles, the patriarch, to the youngest, a babe in arms recently born to Jenny and Rourke McKnight, their second.

Daisy headed to the reception area to greet and reacquaint herself with relatives from near and far. She was particularly taken with a second cousin she hadn't known that long—Ivy Bellamy, who worked as an artist in Santa Barbara. On the surface, the two of them didn't seem to have much in common, but Daisy had an odd sense that Ivy was the person Daisy would be if she'd made different choices in the past. Ivy was single, childless, fiercely artistic and joyfully carefree. She lived on the beach in

Southern California and seemed to be the kind of person who squeezed all the juice out of every day of her life. Daisy sometimes found herself wishing she had time to do some squeezing of her own.

"Welcome back," she said to Ivy. "I was hoping you'd come to the reunion."

"I wouldn't miss it." Ivy gazed out the window at the lake. "I love it here. It's always bittersweet, though. Makes me miss my granddad, but I feel closer to him here than I do anywhere else."

Ivy's grandfather was George Bellamy, who had spent his final days right here at Willow Lake, in a cabin known as the Summer Hideaway. Daisy veered her mind away from thoughts of losing a grandparent, or losing anyone. "I'm sorry," she said to Ivy. "Are you going to be all right?"

"Maybe after a few tequila slammers. Join me?"

Daisy was tempted. However, due to Logan's situation, she had made a private vow to abstain. "I'll stick with lemonade," she said. "My grandmother made her special kind, flavored with lavender." She helped herself to some from a frosty glass dispenser while Ivy made a quick trip to the bar.

"Tell me everything," she said, rejoining Daisy and clinking glasses. "You were a newlywed last time I saw you. How's married life treating you?"

"I'm fine," Daisy said, pasting on a bright smile. Later, maybe, when they had some private time—like hours and hours—she would go into detail about the emotional roller coaster she'd been on since Julian's return. "I want to hear about you and your fabulous life as a kinetic sculptor."

"What can I say? It's fabulous. I have some juried shows coming up so I'm insanely busy. In a good way, that is. There's something about the whooshing sound of an upcoming deadline that squeezes my best work out of me. I bet you're the same."

Daisy didn't reply, because she wasn't sure it was the same for her at all.

Ivy sipped her margarita. "Ahh. And what about you? How's work? Last time we talked, you were getting a portfolio ready for a spot in a big exhibition."

The MoMA show—again. To Daisy, it was like the rock to Sisyphus; she'd never get there. She felt a small flutter of guilt. Once again, she was allowing life to get in the way of what she really wanted to do. "The wedding stuff is steady. I'm mad at myself for not taking the time I need for studio work."

"Go easy on yourself. When the time is right, you'll get it done. Life is long and every day is precious."

Daisy grinned. "I like the way you think. Must be all that California sunshine. I've only been to California once—Disneyland." Ah, the fateful trip with Logan.

"Disneyland doesn't count. Come see me in Santa Barbara. I promise, you'll be seduced."

"Sounds good to me. Sometimes I wish I could live someplace seductive like that. Or, not even seductive. Just…different." Daisy was surprised to hear the words come out of her.

"What the hell? You can." Ivy lifted her glass and finished it off. "Excuse me. I spotted Ross and Claire. I haven't seen them yet."

"Go ahead. I'll catch up with you in a bit."

Ross and Claire were an intensely gorgeous couple. They'd had the most dramatic of Bellamy romances, one that had ultimately turned out well for them. He rested his hand easily at the back of her waist, and she tucked herself against him, looking secure and contented. Though they'd been married for a couple of years, they still had that honeymooners' glow when they gazed at each other.

Daisy caught herself wondering if she and Logan had that glow, if they'd ever had it. No, she ordered herself. Stop it. Don't compare.

Turning away from Ross and Claire, she brought herself up short. Julian had just walked in with his brother.

Though she fought the feeling, something inside Daisy caught fire when she saw him. She reminded herself of her marriage. She and Julian were done. They'd missed their chance. This had been clear to her on his first night back, when he'd refused to discuss the intimate details of his imprisonment, his ordeal in South America. She was unable to imagine the nightmares he'd endured. She didn't expect him to tell her, though. She couldn't share his pain and his deepest secrets. That role wasn't open to her now. She wasn't his wife. She wasn't allowed to love him and carry his burdens. It made her wonder, who did he have to lean on? Was he looking for someone else?

Choose me, she thought, her heart crying out against her will. On the heels of the thought came a painful mixture of guilt and longing. She'd expected to be able to handle this—seeing him but keeping her distance. Yet instead of getting easier, the encounters were harder each time. She hadn't crossed any lines, though, and was determined not to. She and Julian had not had a private conversation since the night of his return. After she told him she was committed to staying with Logan, there was nothing more to say. Particularly now, in the wake of Logan's relapse, she couldn't imagine abandoning him when he was at his most fragile and needy. Yet a curious thing was happening with Logan. He didn't *seem* so fragile and needy after the episode. Something in him was getting stronger. Still, that didn't mean she was free to turn her back on her commitment.

Best to get the uncomfortable greeting over with. "Hey," she said, approaching him.

His eyes lit when he saw her, but she could see him dim the reaction. "Hey," he said.

She studied his face, his strong hands and tall frame. He bore scars that hadn't been there when he'd left. There was so much she wanted to say to him but couldn't.

And honestly, she didn't have to. She and Julian could say more with a single look than a long conversation. They'd always been that way. Maybe in time the connection would weaken, but today it was powerful, filling her with yearning and forbidden heat.

"I…uh, wanted to say thank you for helping Logan out. He told me, you know, that you were there for him." It felt easy and right to say these things to him. She was deeply grateful to him for rescuing Logan that terrible day. He could have looked the other way, let Logan crash and burn at the country club. But that wasn't Julian's way. When he saw someone who needed rescuing, he stepped up. Even if it meant helping out his rival.

Good lord, this was awkward. How could she be so awkward with him when all she wanted to do was—no. She couldn't let her mind go there.

"No problem," he said. "He doing all right?"

She nodded. "He slipped. It happens. He's back with the program."

"How about you? Are you doing all right?"

"Sure," she said, quickly, brightly. "I'm great. Work is good. Busy. Charlie is good, too." When he's not getting in trouble with school. "He's going to be excited to see you."

"I'll go find him in a minute. Daisy—"

"So how are you?" she broke in, wanting to change the subject.

"Hoping to get to the end of this medical leave. I've got more rounds of physical therapy and psych evaluations, more hoops to jump through."

She was dying to ask him about his plans for the future, but she couldn't let his future matter to her. "I hope it goes well for you." The tension was extreme, prickling over her scalp. "Julian?"

"Yeah?"

"I—" She broke off as Logan strode through the door, lifting his hand when he spotted her.

"There's my wayward wife." He slipped his arm around her, drawing her close.

She smiled up at him. "*Moi?* Wayward?"

"Hey, Logan." Julian shook hands with him. "I was about to head outside. See you around." He sauntered away at an unhurried pace, though Daisy sensed he wasn't eager to linger.

Logan dropped his arm and stepped back. "How's our man Julian?"

"Fine, I guess."

"Were the two of you discussing my screwup?"

She winced. "I thanked him for helping out, that's all."

"Yeah, he's a real prince."

His comment unleashed an anger she'd been holding in for days. She'd been trying her best to do the right thing, but each day, her marriage seemed more and more untenable. Inches from losing it, right here in the middle of the family reunion, she took a deep breath and said, "Well. On that note…" She didn't let herself finish, knowing the conversation would lead to nowhere good. Turning on her heel, she went and grabbed her camera bag to take some pictures.

"Don't walk away from me," he said.

She could see an impending fight seething in his eyes. "This isn't the right time."

"It's never going to be right," he said.

She paused, taking in his words. "We'll talk," she said at last.

"Right. Catch you later."

She stood for a moment watching him go, wishing she felt more connected to him. But ever since the relapse, the unease that existed silently between them had grown more pronounced. It was as if he'd gone to a foreign country and come home a different person. Troubled, she stayed busy taking pictures, comfortable with her eyes obscured by the camera as she captured the laughter and sentiment in the faces of her cousins, uncles, aunts and immediate family. With her lens focused on couples, family groups, children and grandparents, it struck her how many paths love could take—even for her own parents, whose beginnings as a couple were eerily similar to hers and Logan's. They'd married for the sake of a child. And they'd gritted their teeth and endured it for years. She remembered something her dad once said to her. It wasn't the divorce that was so painful. The real hurt came from the failed marriage that preceded it.

As a child, had she noticed the sadness in her parents? Not consciously, no. She'd focused like a camera lens on the happier moments and maybe her brother had done the same. But both of them had ended up as collateral damage—she with her reckless behavior and Max with his school troubles.

Now she turned her fastest portrait lens on her dad as he and his wife, Nina, participated in a fierce match of bocce balls on the lawn, their opponents her uncle Philip and his second wife, Laura. Both her dad and his brother were blissfully remarried. Neither got it right until the second time around.

Feeling weirdly guilty about her own thoughts, she returned to the banquet area, capturing a shot of little Zoe carefully mounding whipped cream onto a serving of berry cobbler. In the background was Logan, chatting up Max as they both helped themselves to seconds.

"I like a man with a hearty appetite," said a voice behind her.

"Grandma." Daisy set aside the camera and gave her a hug.

"It's a glorious day, isn't it? Perfect weather for the reunion. Come sit with me. I need to get off my feet for a few minutes." They retreated to a pair of luxurious club chairs in the deserted reception area. "Now," said her grandmother, "tell me what's troubling you."

Daisy gave a short laugh. "Direct as ever."

"Dearie, when you're my age, you learn to get to the point."

"Why do you think something's troubling me?"

"I know that look."

"What look?"

"The one you were wearing just now, when you were taking a picture of your husband."

Daisy drew a deep breath, reminding herself that Grandma was safe to talk to. She was one of the most beloved and trusted people in Daisy's life. "Logan and I are in a weird place."

"Darling, marriage is a weird place, make no mistake. Sometimes I wonder why it was ever invented."

"Grandma!"

"So speak. Tell me about this metaphorical weird place."

"Logan and I…it's not working out the way we'd envisioned. And don't get me wrong, I didn't romanticize things or expect the impossible."

"There's your first mistake. Sometimes the only way to get through the rough patches is to over-romanticize and expect the moon. You have to take each other's most annoying traits and turn them into virtues. I recall spending the whole of 1967 pretending to love the hippie beard your grandfather grew."

Daisy laughed, trying to picture her buttoned-down granddad with a beard. Then she shook her head and laughter gave way to a painful hiccup of tears. "I'm afraid…all the pretending in the world only magnifies the fact that we're pretending. This past year, I kept thinking things would get better. We acted as if everything was fine, but it keeps getting harder and more strained." She swallowed past the thick despair in her throat. "A few months ago, both of us were thinking that getting married might have been a huge mistake. We were moving toward a really difficult conversation—about splitting up. Then Julian came home, and…it didn't seem right."

"You didn't want to dump your husband just because your ex-fiancé showed up," her grandmother said bluntly.

"That's part of it," Daisy admitted. "Only part. I'm so scared of repeating my parents' mistakes."

"Daisy, what do you want to do?"

"I want to be madly, passionately in love with my husband." Willfully she drove away a flash of fantasy that had nothing to do with Logan. "I want him to feel that way about me. But I'm beginning to wonder if that's possible with *any*one."

Her grandmother's eyes grew misty as she gazed out across Willow Lake. Daisy had the sense that Grandma was reliving something in the distant past. "Oh, yes," her grandmother said quietly. "It most certainly is."

"I ask myself that every day. I started asking long before Julian returned. And I have a feeling Logan's been asking himself the same thing. Neither of us has a satisfactory answer."

"Nor do I."

"I'm working on it. I really am."

Jane hesitated, then turned her pale eyes back to Daisy. "Sometimes we don't get what we want no matter how hard we try. Dear, listen to me. I'm not perfect but I've learned a thing or two in my time. Most important of all, listen to your heart. What is your heart telling you?"

Daisy bit her lip. "That I'm a terrible person because I got married for the wrong reasons, and now Charlie is feeling the effect. And that…Julian never really left my heart, even when he was presumed dead." She said the last on a broken note of pain. "I *am* terrible."

"You're not. You're human and flawed, and beating yourself up over it will get you nowhere." Grandma took her hand. "I wish I were as wise as I am old, but unfortunately, I'm human, too. I can only tell you this—live your life and be happy. That's all you can do."

Thirty-Two

Daisy allowed Charlie and Blake both to spend the reunion weekend at Camp Kioga, in one of the vintage bunkhouses with an assortment of cousins. She pictured them staying up until all hours, giggling and telling ghost stories, sneaking to the kitchen for a midnight feast. Like all kids, Charlie was happiest when he was unplugged and in the fresh outdoors. She knew he'd come home grubby and exhausted but filled with memories.

She pulled up to the house, parked and got out. Twilight was coming on, gilding the neighborhood with a soft glow. It really was a lovely house; people commented on it all the time. Logan had been fixing it up for years. She still remembered the day she'd driven up in time to see him slide off the roof. The memory would always make her cringe in fear for him. People were so fragile. He'd survived the fall, though, and now the house was their home.

She'd done her share of work, getting every room just so and turning the garden into a riot of flowers. And yes, the white picket fence was a cliché, but it looked perfect there at the front boundary of the lawn. Soon, the sugar maples would be turning, and the colors would change.

She could already smell the autumn coming, when the wind shifted just so.

As she gathered her things from the car, the neighbors, Bart and Sally Jericho, drove up and waved. They didn't linger to visit. Daisy had nurtured high hopes that they'd become friends, but since Bart had witnessed Logan's scene at the country club, there was a distinct chill that hadn't existed before.

Shouldering her big straw tote bag and camera bag, she headed inside. The house was too quiet, and an indistinct smell hung in the air. For some reason, the atmosphere depressed her. It depressed her to see the walls and baseboards and furniture she'd labored over in a vain attempt to find the joy in her life with Logan. Staying busy was no substitute for true happiness.

She turned on the radio for a little background noise. The thud of a car door alerted her that Logan was home. He came inside, his attention glued to the screen of his iPhone.

"Hey," she said.

"Hey."

"How'd you like the reunion?" she asked.

"It was fine. Good to catch up with all your folks. Charlie seemed pretty happy with it all."

"Yes." She hesitated. "It's still pretty early. Want to see what's playing at the Palace?"

"No, thanks. I've got some stuff to do on my computer. Then I thought I'd turn in early."

"All right. Logan—"

"Daisy—"

They both spoke at once, interrupting each other. "You first," she said. Every muscle in her body felt tense, as though bracing for a blow.

"I'm sorry as hell about the slip," said Logan. "And today, too. I wasn't in the best of moods."

"Don't worry about it. I'm glad you're back in the program. And I owe you an apology, too. I stopped remembering how hard sobriety is for you because you make it look so easy. I breezed out of here and went along to work. I wish—"

"Daisy. We need to talk."

No good conversation had ever started with those four words: *We need to talk.*

In the ensuing pause, she was tempted to do the old-Daisy thing, jump in and reassure them both that everything was fine, just fine. She always avoided upsetting him, not wanting him to ever have a reason to take a drink. Now she knew that was not her job. Only he could keep himself sober.

She sensed they were on the verge of having the most honest conversation they'd ever had. A cold lump formed in her throat. "Tell me what you're thinking," she said.

He grabbed a cream soda from the fridge and offered it to her. She shook her head, so he opened it and took a slug. "I'm thinking it's time to face facts."

"Facts about…us?" she asked, her voice wavering.

He set aside the soda bottle. "Neither one of us is doing anything wrong. We're not bad people."

"Did anyone say we were?"

"No, just listen, okay? We made a mistake. I made a mistake."

"About us, you mean." She felt light-headed, slightly nauseous.

He nodded. "All along, for years, I've thought you were the love of my life, but it was your life I loved."

Understanding glimmered in Daisy, giving way to a deep sense of defeat. "My life," she said, "was not exactly a huge party."

"I know, but I wanted to be part of it because you had this great kid who happened to be mine, and a great family that totally accepted me, and all of that was incredibly attractive to me. So much so that I carried a torch for you, and when you were practically destroyed by the report of Julian's death, I was there for you. When we first got married, I felt like I'd won something—the girl, the kid, the life. It didn't quite cover up the fact that you and I…hell. We made a great kid together, but we don't make a great couple."

She stood frozen on the spot, almost forgetting to breathe. She'd wanted honesty; now he was bludgeoning her with it. He was saying things she herself had thought, yet she'd buried them so deep, she never voiced them. But now she felt the painful truth of it. She and Logan shared a deep regard for one another, they both adored their son, but the marriage wasn't right, and every day it got harder to pretend. Julian's return had not caused this situation, but it was forcing them to face it.

Logan gestured around the kitchen, the café curtains perfectly aligned, the furniture painstakingly arranged. "We've been completely focused on making a family for Charlie, not making a life with each other."

She dropped her head, stared at the warm oak floor. "I hate the idea that we failed."

"Then let's not fail. You're the mother of my child and I'll always love that about you. What I've figured out, what we both know, is that being his parents will always be a bond between us, but it's not a strong enough foundation to build a life on."

"Oh, Logan." She couldn't say any more past the lump in her throat.

"Charlie knows it, too. Maybe not specifically but he knows something's not right, and it's not good for him. We're seeing that in his behavior at school. It's not good for any of us."

"Do you think there's a chance we could fix this?"

"There's always a chance. But what if we spend the next twenty or forty or fifty years trying, and it never works for us?" he asked.

She squirmed inwardly, not wanting to think about the answer. When it came to marriage, how long was long enough? "I hate that this is happening," she said, hugging her midsection against a pain she couldn't escape. "How did we get here?"

"One thing I can finally admit—it's not because of Julian's resurrection and the way it shook everything up. We were already in trouble."

"Yes," she shakily admitted.

"I thought you needed me."

"I did. I do—"

"You need—I don't know. I didn't see this coming, back when we got together. I saw somebody I made Charlie with, and it seemed like the right thing to do. Maybe it was, back then. But it didn't last. We went into this for the wrong reasons, and it's not working. You know that, Daisy. You *know*."

Tears tracked down her cheeks. "So now what?" she asked in a heavy whisper.

"Now we both get real. It'd be good to come up with some kind a plan before Charlie gets home." A *plan*.

"You're breaking up with me?"

He poured out the bottle of cream soda into the sink, then turned back to her. "Daisy-Bell. We're breaking up with each other."

The divorce was horrible, as divorces always had to be, even when both parties agreed to part ways. They told Charlie together, and he cried, and Daisy and Logan cried and said all the right things—they both loved him, they would always be a family, they would make their new life work, somehow. Eventually, Charlie came to a quiet acceptance. Daisy took him and Blake to live at the Inn at Willow Lake in the boathouse on the property. In the shadow of her father's quiet worry, she dedicated herself to helping Charlie heal.

When she went to tell Julian, it was with a sense of defeat, not joy. "I need time," she said. "I have to focus on Charlie. And…I'm not ready to talk about this."

"I understand," he told her, but she wasn't sure he did. How did a man who had been imprisoned and tortured empathize with someone like her? He took her hands in his. It was the first time they'd touched since his return, and she almost cried from the sweetness of it.

"I have to go away for a while," he said.

She took her hands from his. "Away…where?" No, she thought. The air force couldn't take him from her again. Then she reminded herself that she didn't have him.

"It's got a fancy name—the Haven Behavioral War Heroes Hospital. They treat military personnel with combat stress injuries and PTSD."

Her throat tightened with fear. His recovery had been so swift, and he looked like the picture of health. But inside, he was still bleeding somewhere from secret wounds. She'd been an idiot to assume he'd simply pick up his life where he'd left off. There were some things, she thought, that even love couldn't fix.

"Oh, Julian. Of course you have to go." She slipped her hands into his again.

"Doctor's orders."

"Yes."

"But, Daisy—do me a favor."

"Anything."

He flashed her the special smile that used to melt her heart. It still did. "Wait for me."

"As long as it takes," she said softly. She didn't know what else to say. They were both so damaged by all that had happened. She prayed that once they both healed, they could find their way back to one another.

The days melted into weeks and then months. Daisy found a place of her own, needing to break away from her father and stepmother, because it was too tempting to ease back into dependence on them. She felt in her bones that splitting up with Logan was the right thing to do, yet guilt and sadness still haunted her. Daily phone calls from Julian offered a splash of hope. Still, she knew she had to find a away to be on her own before she could even think of being with someone else—even Julian.

"There's something so…defeating about this," Daisy told Sonnet, who came up one weekend to help her move. "It's like, I made this giant mistake and—"

"Whoa, hold it right there." Sonnet set down a basket of clothes she'd brought into the new house. Daisy had found a rental cottage on the lake, with a dog run and a small dock. It was sweet, but didn't feel like home. She didn't know what home was anymore.

Sonnet turned to her. "You made the best choice you could under the circumstances and it was not a mistake."

"But Charlie—"

"Is going to be all right. He still has a mom and dad who love him. He feels secure and he knows life is good. That's all a kid needs. Believe me, I know."

Daisy paused, regarding Sonnet—her stepsister, her best friend—with a wave of gratitude. She was a veritable poster girl for growing up with a single parent. "You do know. I'm sorry, here I am fretting about my situation, and you've actually lived it, and you're spectacular." It was true. Sonnet's parents—her mother, Nina, and her father, an ambitious, African-American West Point cadet, had never been together. Yet Sonnet had managed to grow up happy and healthy. As an adult, she'd made a successful, remarkable life for herself.

"Just know you and Charlie are going to be fine," Sonnet told her.

"Sometimes I can totally believe it. Other times, I wonder what the hell I'm doing with my life."

"The good news is, you don't have to think about any of that right now. Just settle into your new house, take a deep breath, and take your time."

"Listen to you, going all wise woman on us," said Zach, backing into the house with a hand truck stacked with boxes.

"You got any better advice?" Sonnet asked. "Because if you do, we might forgive you for eavesdropping."

"I wasn't eavesdropping," he said. "I was listening to the conversation openly."

"How is that different from eavesdropping?"

Their bickering made Daisy smile. She knew—she'd always known—what was beneath it.

"Where's Charlie?" asked Zach.

"With his dad. I'll go pick him up tomorrow."

"How's that going?" asked Sonnet.

"I was a single mom until he was five. This is not so different, except that Charlie's older and he asks more questions."

She didn't let herself speculate on the impact of this transition on her son. It was too easy to focus on the process, and the kid had an uncanny radar for tension.

The family therapist they were now seeing cautioned her to relax, be honest and forgive both Logan and herself.

Alongside Sonnet and Zach, she worked steadily, organizing the house. Blake seemed happy enough to sniff and explore every corner of the place. Every so often, Daisy would pause to look out at the lake, its surface ruffled by a stiff breeze, a bank of brooding clouds pushing in from the west. There was something calming about this view, even in turbulent weather. Willow Lake had always been a special place to her. Its vastness, the arc of trees along the shore, the quality of the light glancing off the surface, took her away somewhere, to a place of clarity and simplicity.

For whole moments at a time, if she was lucky.

A brief whir and the sputter of an engine signaled the arrival of the mail. Blake gave a woof, but obeyed when Daisy commanded the dog to stay on the porch while she hiked up the driveway to the mailbox and brought in the stack of letters and catalogs. It was the usual detritus—catalogs filled with things she didn't need, solicitations from credit cards to spend money she didn't have, a thank you note from a grateful bride: "Thank you for capturing the happiness Matt and I will enjoy for the rest of our lives."

Hope so, Daisy thought.

"I guess I officially live here," she said, returning to the house. "I got my first electric bill. And—" She broke off, and bit her lip. There, sandwiched between a deck of coupons and the power bill was a crisp white envelope from the county court. Her stomach rolled over. Her hand was steady as she unfolded the document.

Her divorce was final.

She stared at it for a while. The damn thing was so… stark, the blunt words in black and white. Couldn't they have included a cover letter, maybe? Of course, that would be weird. What would such a letter say?

"We are pleased to inform you…"

"Congratulations! You're a free woman!"

Maybe, to defray mailing costs, there could be a little ad insert like the ones in a credit card bill: "Never reach for a cobweb again with the Bilko telescoping duster!"

Or a newsy tip sheet like those the power company included. "Ten ways to save your sanity." Or, "What to do when people ask awkward questions."

At least they could have made it prettier, she thought, folding the thing up and putting it in an empty Chock Full o' Nuts coffee can on the counter.

"And?" Sonnet prompted her.

"And as of yesterday, I am officially divorced." There it was. She tried to figure out if she felt different. The weirdness mingled with a giddy sense of freedom. What had changed, and what was the same? Her surname hadn't changed. While married to Logan, she'd kept her maiden name. She wasn't a big name, professionally. She wasn't any kind of name. But "Daisy O'Donnell" sounded weirdly fake, or as if she might be related to an outspoken talk show host.

"Well," said Sonnet. "I'm not quite sure what to say to that. In the Tongan delegation they might say something like—" She mouthed a string of words that sounded wholly unfamiliar.

"May the blessings of the moment outshine the abscesses of the past," said a deep voice from the doorway.

"Julian!" Daisy's heart flipped over as she turned to the door. Blake went nuts, leaping up and barking in greeting. He had returned to Avalon at summer's end, a new person after his time at the hospital in Colorado. Now he was staying with his brother again, awaiting the official end of his medical leave.

"Not abscesses, smarty-pants," said Sonnet.

"We can't all be polyglots," he said with a grin.

"Who're you calling a polyglot?"

"What are you doing here?" Daisy asked him.

"A little bird told me you might need some help with the moving." He nodded in Sonnet's direction.

Thank you, Sonnet, thought Daisy. No way would she have asked him herself. "Well…thanks." She wondered if he had any clue what she and her stepsister had just been talking about.

"How about I organize the kitchen?" Sonnet suggested. "You know I'm way better at that than you."

"Sure," said Daisy. "Thanks."

"Zach can help me," Sonnet added.

She was being way too obvious, but Daisy didn't care.

"Where do you want these?" asked Julian, indicating a stack of photo archive boxes. Each was marked with the year and subject.

Each box represented that year's unfinished projects. Her fine art photography always took a backseat to the paying gigs and the general busyness of life.

She and Julian found themselves together in the postage stamp–size study, setting up her workstation.

"You're in luck," Julian declared. "One of the main components of my training has been to turn me into an übergeek. I'll get you up and running."

"Thanks. There is no life without internet."

"So I found out," he said.

"How are you?" she asked, conveying with her tone that she meant more than a simple inquiry.

"Doing all right. I'm waiting for a decision on a pilot training program."

"Oh. Well, I hope it works out for you." She did. If he made pilot training, it would mean he was truly better, that he'd survived his ordeal. What it meant for her…she refused to contemplate right now.

"Yeah, me, too."

By happenstance or more probably by design, Sonnet and Zach had gone outside to sit on the dock. She could see them out there, huddled against the wind. Zach slipped a protective arm around Sonnet. The simple touch reminded Daisy of what she'd lost when she and Logan had parted ways—the comfort of ease with someone else.

This was the first time she'd been alone with Julian since his return. Contrary to people's expectations, she had not rushed into his arms in the wake of the divorce. He wasn't the cause of her breakup with Logan; he wasn't even the catalyst. But he was here now.

"How about yourself?" he asked. "For what it's worth, I'm sorry about what you're going through."

"Thank you. I wanted to say something, but I couldn't. It didn't seem right to dump my troubles with Logan on you."

"Damn, girl. There are some things about you I will never get."

"Think about it, Julian. Confessing my marriage woes to my formerly dead ex-fiancé? How would that help anyone?"

He didn't answer, but finished getting her computer hooked up. "There you go. Home office operational."

"Thanks." She still felt bashful around him, which was weird. At one point he had been the keeper of all her dreams, the one person she could say anything to. Now, the paths they had taken had turned them into strangers in some ways.

The screen saver kicked in, displaying a slide show of her best shots.

"Those are really something," he said quietly.

"Thanks." A haunting image of the lake in a storm drifted by. "I keep having this idea that I'll get my work into a juried show, but there's never time to get my portfolio ready."

"It's not a lack of time," he said bluntly, arranging the boxes on a shelf. "What's really keeping you from working on them?"

She hesitated. "No one's ever asked me that."

"I'm asking."

"I'm not sure I have an answer. It's so easy, so comfortable, to stick with what I know." She stopped, listening to her own words. Wasn't that what had driven so many of her decisions? Sticking with safety? She knew a huge part of her choice to marry Logan had been that he was familiar to her, a safe choice. And look how that turned out, she thought, exasperated. After becoming an unwed mother, she had stopped taking chances.

"Promise me something," Julian said.

His command made her melt a little. "Depends on what you're asking."

"Promise me you'll get back to it. You're a genius with the pictures. I know what it means to you."

Could she make such a promise? And if she did, could she keep it?

"All right," she said. "It's a deal."

"And not whenever. Start now. Tomorrow. Or at least, this week."

"Yes, sir." She offered a mock salute.

"Cool." He opened a large box. "Sheets and towels," he said. "Where do they go?"

"Bedroom." She led the way across the hall. The bed was set up, the mattress bare. When she turned around, she saw that he was pulling sheets from the box. "You don't have to—"

"Are you kidding? You're not seriously going to pass up the chance to learn from a master of military bed making."

"Silly me."

He demonstrated how to fit the sheets, forming a square corner so crisp it resembled a cardboard box. He explained the placement of the blanket and the symmetry of pillows. When they were nearly done, Daisy gazed at the bed in wonder. "It's a thing of beauty."

"And for this I incurred years of service."

"There's one thing missing." She extracted a yellow-

and-white striped duvet from the box. “How would the military deal with this?”

“What the hell is it?”

“A duvet.”

“A do-what?”

“A comforter.” She got him to help her fit the duvet into the cover.

The irony and suggestiveness of making the bed with Julian did not escape her. When her eyes met his, she could tell it hadn’t escaped him, either.

“Okay, this is awkward,” she said.

“Just say what’s on your mind, and it won’t be awkward.”

“You have no idea.”

“Try me.”

He asked for it. “Everybody thinks I’m going to go running into your arms,” she said.

“Is that what you want to do?”

A part of her wanted to leap up and yell, yes! It’s all I’ve ever wanted! But she shook her head. She didn’t want him to be the reason for her failed marriage. His arrival had simply coincided with the inevitable end of her and Logan. Charlie needed more time to adjust, and Daisy had to figure out what she really wanted. “I’ve got to heal from this, and who knows how long that will take? And who knows if you’ll even have me?”

“Try me,” he said again.

She shook her head. “You’ve been hurt by everything that’s happened, too. I don’t have any right to expect that your heart is still in the same place.”

He didn’t say anything to that. She was both relieved and disappointed. To set up a dynamic or expectations between them now would be foolhardy. They had both survived dramatic events in their lives, and they both needed to deal with everything before they could go looking for what had been lost between them.

She feared finding out. It was possible that through all of this, their love had changed, perhaps didn't exist anymore. The idea made her shudder.

They finished making up the bed. She plumped the pillows and stepped back. "Home, sweet home. For the time being, anyway."

They both bent at the same time to smooth a wrinkle. Their hands brushed, and she felt the instant heat of connection. She quickly recoiled, but the fleeting touch reminded her that time and distance didn't always matter.

She dared to meet his gaze, seeing a mirror of her own yearning in his eyes.

"I've been in counseling," she blurted out. "You know, to help Charlie and me work through this transition."

"That's probably a good idea."

"It does help. Surprisingly, it does. I'm learning ways to forgive myself and move ahead. And what I've learned… about another relationship is that I need to take my time. Like, a lot of time. Because the person I am right now is bound to change."

Thirty-Three

"She said that?" Connor asked Julian that night. "She actually said that bullshit about waiting and changing?"

"Yeah, and how do you argue with the advice of a mental health professional?"

"By telling them they're full of shit."

"Yeah, about that. I have to give the professionals their due. I was one sick puppy when I got home." It was true; he now realized the air force had made the right call in ordering his extended leave. He'd returned full of rage and raw need, not exactly the best combo for reentry into his life. "If not for Dr. Abernathy," he told Connor, "I'd probably be in some psych ward, strumming my lips. If I'd gone straight to Daisy—and believe me, I would have done exactly that if it had been an option—we'd probably have destroyed each other by now."

"Okay, point taken." Connor more than anyone else had watched Julian's journey from the brink of despair to balance and clarity. He knew about the nightmares and flashbacks; he'd had a ringside seat at Julian's daily fight to make sense of what had happened to him and move forward with his life. "I'm frustrated for you. You and

Daisy had something special. You always have. I'd hate to see you walk away from that now."

"I didn't say I was going to walk away. But we can't pick up where we left off, not after everything that's happened."

"What do *you* want to do?" Connor asked.

Julian wasn't ready to answer that, not for his brother or even for himself. He knew a little something about waiting around and being patient. A lengthy stint in a Colombian prison tended to do that for a guy. Yet he also knew the limits of endurance.

"I'm waiting for the doc's final report to the air force, certifying that I'm no longer damaged goods," he said.

"You never were, bro. Ever."

Charlie came in from the bus on a hot afternoon. Indian summer was having a last fling before winter's darkness and cold. As usual, Charlie was tackled by an ecstatic Blake, who greeted him as if she hadn't seen him in years. The two of them rolled around on the living room floor and giggled, enacting their everyday ritual. Daisy saved her work on the computer and went to see him.

"Hey, kiddo." She ruffled his hair and picked up his backpack. "How was your day?"

He was quiet for a moment. Then he said, "There's a note from my teacher."

Her stomach clenched. A note from the teacher had never been good news. "In here?" She indicated the backpack.

He nodded, gathering Blake into his lap.

She found the note, slipping it from the standard envelope stamped with, "Please sign and date to acknowledge receipt."

"'Dear Ms. Bellamy,'" she read aloud. "'I'm writing to

give you an update on Charlie's behavior and academic progress…'"

Great. She'd thought he was doing better.

"'I'm pleased to report that we've seen a marked improvement in both.'" Daisy nearly choked on the words.

Charlie flashed a smile. "Keep reading."

She did, her heart filling with relief and pride as the teacher enumerated examples of improvement. "'I am delighted with the progress Charlie has made. Thanks to you and Charlie both for all your efforts.'"

Daisy beamed at him as she stuck the note to the fridge with a magnet. "Way to go, Charlie. Come here and give me a hug." She held on—not too long; he was a boy, after all—absorbing the squirmy warmth of his body, inhaling the smell of him, a combination of fresh air, dog and youthful sweat.

One of the worst things about being single was the lack of physical connection—someone to simply put your arms around and hug. She was grateful for many things about Charlie; maybe this topped the list.

She let go at the slightest sign of impatience. "Let's celebrate. You can have any dinner you want tonight. We can go out or eat in. Your choice."

"Yes," he said. "And you know I want to stay home."

"Let me guess. You want breakfast for dinner."

"Breakfast for dinner! Pancakes, scrambled eggs, bacon, juice." Acting as though he'd won the lottery, he raced around the room, then headed out the back door with the dog.

Daisy stood at the kitchen window, watching them play, listening to Charlie's laughter and the dog barking. The two of them were inseparable. Sometimes she wished Charlie had siblings. He might, one day, but she would not think about that now.

Her spirits were high; she had finally come to the realization that she was doing better. She'd survived the divorce and the world had not come to an end.

Logan seemed to be doing better, too. He looked well, having finally shed the extra pounds gained during their marriage. Whatever he was doing seemed to be working.

For her part, she'd surrounded herself with family and friends, and buried herself in work. She no longer faced each day with a knot in her stomach and a buzz of unanswerable questions in her mind.

Lately she felt more relaxed, and the questions in her mind quieted. She still had no answers to the tough ones—Am I doing the right thing? Is this what's best for Charlie? But she'd come to the realization that there were no right answers. With the perspective of time and distance, she understood what had happened in her marriage—and to Charlie. She and Logan had spent most of their time avoiding each other and consequently Charlie. Now their son got more attention from both of them, and once again, he was blossoming.

What this whole ordeal had taught her—what life had taught her—was that you made the choices you made and lived the life you had with as much love and joy as you could find. Glancing at the phone, she considered calling someone to share Charlie's good news. But who? Logan? They weren't like that anymore. Her mother? Sonnet?

She went to her computer, determined to put in an hour of work before dinner. She had three different events to process, and the clients were impatient.

The amount of work was never-ending. Bride after beautiful bride paraded across her screen. She didn't care for the job she'd done on the most recent wedding. One reason she was so in demand was her artistry. For these pictures, it had deserted her. The images looked flat and uninspired to her.

Restless, she swiveled in her chair—and stopped.

There, stuck to the corkboard above the desk, was a glossy brochure announcing this year's MoMA competition. She had found it in her mailbox a few days ago, with Julian's bold handwriting across the top: *Go for it.*

He knew her well. He always had. She'd admitted to him that she had been avoiding the competition, skirting the deadlines, missing them. She could put her recalcitrance down to other factors—lack of time, other obligations, inability to focus, life's upheavals—but those were all excuses. The fact was, she had been avoiding this work out of fear, pure and simple.

A guy like Julian didn't understand fear. Or maybe he understood it too well.

"No fear," she said aloud, closing the work photos. She opened the folder marked "MoMA" and was shocked to realize she had not accessed the files in months. This was her art, she thought. Her passion. Yet she'd neglected it.

How easy it was to ignore the things that were most important. Funny how that worked.

When she revisited the images, she was surprised to see how good they were. She hadn't remembered that. Of course it was a long road from a good shot to a viable entry.

She didn't have long to work, but by the time she finished, she had a plan. She knew what she wanted to submit to the competition. No more excuses. She just had to go for it.

Brushing her hand over Julian's message, she spoke to him aloud, as if he were there with her in the room. "You're good for me. You always have been." He had returned from his ordeal a changed man. But the essence of him was the same. She loved his exuberance for life and his capacity for risk. She loved everything about him, and she had never stopped, not even when she'd received news of his death.

Yet once again, they'd managed to fall victim to bad timing. Whenever it seemed they were getting closer, whenever it seemed they might have a shot, something got in their way. Then Julian had been ripped away from her as swiftly and cruelly as an amputation.

Now, finally, it looked as if they might have a shot again. So much had happened, but she still felt that love like a steady flame in her heart. She was not naive enough to think everything would magically fall into place, but so what? The past few years had proved to her that she was stronger than she'd imagined she could be. She was resourceful and sometimes even smart.

It's too soon, her common sense told her. She'd just left a failed marriage, and getting involved with Julian now might be a huge mistake. People would shake their heads and say, "Of course her marriage didn't stand a chance once Julian came back..."

On the other hand, she thought, what did she care what people said? Furthermore, there was no harm in simply *seeing* him. They needed to spend time together.

What was she afraid of? She used to always ask friends and family what she should do. After scandalizing the Bellamys with her unwed pregnancy, she'd grown afraid; she'd never again allowed herself to color outside the lines. All her choices had been made in the interest of playing it safe and sensible for Charlie's sake. It was time to stretch her wings.

After everything that had happened, she was uncertain of Julian's affection, but that shouldn't stop her. Neither should rules or conventions. It was ridiculous to wait for some self-imposed deadline, like a fluttery Victorian miss in mourning. When it came to Julian, Daisy knew her own heart. She'd always known. Now, more than ever, she felt an almost painful love for him. He had endured captivity and torture, yet he hadn't broken. He'd served his country with honor in ways that could never be acknowledged, and he'd returned even stronger and more loving than ever. What in heaven's name was she waiting for?

She grabbed for the phone, the words already on her lips. "I love you. I'm a mess but I love you and I want to be with you."

Okay, maybe not that.

She dialed his number and he picked up right away.

"How do you feel about breakfast for dinner?" she asked.

"If it's food, I'm up for it."

"Charlie's choice. Would you like to come to dinner?"

There was a pause, during which every doubt she had reared up. Her heart tripped. "I mean," she said, "you don't have to. I know it's last minute—"

"Dinner would be fine," he said.

Daisy caught herself pacing the kitchen, a bowl of pancake batter under one arm, the other beating the mixture way too hard. It was ridiculous to feel nervous about Julian, wasn't it? He was Julian, for heaven's sake, whom she'd known and loved for so long. There was no reason to feel nervous. None. Nada.

She watched Julian and Charlie through the kitchen window as she was fixing the promised dinner of pancakes, scrambled eggs and bacon. Julian and Charlie were on the dock, skipping stones into the still water. The evening was unseasonably hot. After the stone skipping, they lay facedown on the wooden planks, probably watching the schools of minnows congregating in the shadows. Through the screen window, she could hear their voices but not their words. The sound of their laughter made her smile.

Charlie loved being with Julian. She could tell. The

boy adored his dad, of course, and missed having him around. But Charlie had always been an adaptable kid.

She kept going over what she wanted to say to Julian tonight, after Charlie was in bed. She wanted to tell him she was ready to move ahead. Even though the divorce was still a fresh wound, she wanted Julian to know her love for him was intact. It was a risk, though. She would be opening herself to hurt, and they had been apart so long, she didn't know if he still felt the same way about her. It was safer to keep her thoughts to herself for sure. They'd never found a way to be together in the past. Life kept getting in the way. Could be, they simply weren't meant to be together. No, she thought. The heat and tension, the constant yearning—these things could not be wrong.

A splashing war erupted between the two of them out on the dock, their laughter crescendoing. It was on the tip of her tongue to call out a warning, but she stopped herself. Charlie could take a bath later. Julian was a grown man, and Lord knew, worse things had happened to him than a soaking.

She got her camera and stepped outside to take a few shots of them playing.

She wished there were some sign, a kind of guidance from beyond to tell her what to do. If the universe wanted her to confess to Julian that she still loved him, maybe a sign would come. Yes, a sign would be nice.

Instead, the lake stayed calm and placid. Nothing changed.

Then as she watched, Charlie and Julian stood up and took hold of each other's hands. Before she knew what was happening, the two of them raced full tilt to the end of the dock.

"What—"

They jumped together, hands still joined, their bodies

frozen in midair for a split second. Almost by reflex, she lifted her camera and took the shot. They hit the water with a huge splash. Charlie immediately bobbed to the surface.

"Again!" he yelled. "Let's jump again!"

Daisy checked the camera's playback. She'd caught them in midair. Jumping off the dock, the thing Charlie had sworn he would never do.

"Maybe that's your sign," she said.

She watched the two of them go flying into the lake a few more times and took more pictures before grabbing some towels and heading down to the dock.

"You're a pair of crazies," she said, though she smiled as she spoke. "It's nowhere near warm enough to swim."

"Did you see, Mom? Did you see me jump?" Charlie yelled, bobbing in the water. "Me and Julian jumped off the dock. It was like flying."

"I saw. Now I'm seeing you get hypothermia."

"One more time," Charlie begged. "Watch us one more time. Please."

"All right, but that's it," she said.

Julian hoisted himself out of the water. She couldn't help staring at the way his clothes molded to his body, outlining the sinews of muscle. It was a stark reminder that her new life was lacking in several very important areas.

He turned and gave Charlie a hand.

"Ready," Charlie called. "One, two…"

"Wait." Daisy ran forward and grabbed his free hand. "Now we're ready."

They had dinner, Charlie fell asleep as soon as his head hit the pillow, and Julian and Daisy sat together in the living room, she in jersey pajamas, he in a borrowed bathrobe several sizes too small.

"That was nice," she said. "Nicest evening I've had since…in a long time."

"Glad to be of service, ma'am."

She tried to shake off her nervousness. But this mattered so much. "I can't take you seriously in my pink robe," she said.

"This robe is awesome," he said.

She stroked the lapel. "It's chenille. It's my favorite."

"I could say the same," he said, untying the belt.

And just like that, her nervousness disappeared. "You're here," she said. "You're here." She touched his arms, his shoulders. His neck and cheekbones and chin. She touched him everywhere, her fingers marveling. He was here. He was *here*.

Their lovemaking was different this time; they were different people, no longer young adults on the brink of their future but survivors, each in their own way. His every caress seared her with new emotions—love and elation, yes, but there were flashes of desperation, too. When he covered her body with his, she grasped him as if she'd never let him go. He sank down and took her swiftly, with an intensity that bordered on violence, and it was exactly what she needed, a sealing of the love that had survived the unthinkable. It was an ecstasy she never could have imagined, and she wept with the joy and emotional pain of it.

"Hey," he whispered, "it's okay now. It's okay."

"Yes," she said, and then, "No. You shattered my heart, Julian Gastineaux. I still hurt from that, do you understand? I'll never get over the feeling of losing you. Never."

"You will," he assured her, dropping to her side, pressing her against the length of him. "I swear, we both will."

"Promise me," she said. "Promise you'll never put me through that again."

He kissed her tears away. "What are the chances of something like that happening again? I promise."

Thirty-Four

Julian stared at the letter in his hands. There it was, in stark black and white—his acceptance into pilot training. The culmination of a dream that had been born at the top of a fig tree in New Orleans, in the heart of the kid who'd discovered that danger felt like love.

Pilot training. Upon returning from Colombia, he had rededicated himself to the dream. Finally, the powers that be had accepted him into pilot training. He'd be spending fifty-four weeks pursuing his dreams at last, preparing to fly high-altitude supersonic aircraft that would take him closer to heaven than most people went while still alive.

The one thing that wasn't perfect about the offer was geography. Vance AFB was in Oklahoma. He had nothing against Oklahoma, but once again, his career aspirations were leading him away from Daisy, and at the worst possible time. She was fresh out of a failed marriage. She was in no shape to take on another relationship and make another commitment, particularly one that would take her thousands of miles away from her family. He had no right to ask that of her.

In a perfect world, he would have time to properly court her, to find his way back into her heart by being close, whiling away the hours simply holding her, talking, making love…. Such simple things should not be so out of reach, but his world was not perfect. It never had been. There were challenges to face. Obligations to be met.

Dreams to be fulfilled.

This wasn't simply a case of bad timing, though. He realized that. When he'd first asked her to marry him, the danger of his job had been theoretical. Sure, they'd done the military's drill of writing the letters and filling out the forms. He barely remembered signing off on his benefits, because the possibility had seemed so remote. It was merely another form he'd filled out.

But then his capture and the report of his death had shown Daisy exactly what she was signing up for.

Could he ask her to take that risk again?

Daisy scrolled through a few missed calls on her mobile phone while driving home from a meeting with her clients, Andrea and Brian Hubble, to show them their new-baby portrait shots. Their *second* child. It was hard to believe nearly a year had passed when the session with their firstborn had been interrupted by the stunning news that Julian was alive. Since then, her life had taken twists and turns she never could have imagined.

She hoped they hadn't noticed her distracted state during the meeting, but there was a lot on her mind. She hadn't planned to sleep with Julian the night he'd come over for dinner. Dreamed of it, maybe. But she definitely hadn't planned on it. It defied all common sense to plunge into something with Julian, yet at the same time, it felt exactly right. It did. In the midst of recent events, she had forgotten what it felt like to follow her heart.

She stopped scrolling and pulled over to the side of the road when she came to a 212 area code. It wasn't Sonnet, but… Her heart sped up as she listened to the message. "It's Mr. Jamieson from the Emerging Artists program at the Museum of Modern Art. I wanted to let you know your work has been selected to appear in this year's exhibit..."

Finally, she thought. *Finally.* After trying for years, she had made the cut at last. Turning off the phone, she set it aside and stared out the car window at Willow Lake. From the shoulder of the road, she had a view of the lake and the town of Avalon, but the panorama blurred with unexpected tears. Finally, she thought again.

It was a sign. It had to be. Julian was the one who had pushed her to keep at it; he of all people understood what this meant to her. She grabbed the phone to call him, then changed her mind. This was huge. She wanted to tell him in person.

Driving through town en route to Connor's house, she sang along with the radio—an ancient song by Cream, "I Feel Free."

Every street and building of Avalon was familiar to her—the shops and restaurants, Logan's agency and the radio station, the library. It was a place where nothing seemed to change. Except... As she waited at a light, she spotted Logan coming out of the agency. He looked good, better than he had in ages. He was in fine shape, striding with athletic grace toward a woman who had parked in front of his place.

Daisy couldn't help staring as he put his arm around the woman. Daphne McDaniel, thought Daisy with a jolt of surprise. Logan was with Daphne McDaniel. So this was new. Also startling. Daphne was so very different from Logan, a girl who favored body art and hair colors not found in nature, ripped tights and Dr. Martens shoes. As a couple, they looked odd. But oddly compatible as they held hands and strolled together down the sidewalk.

Daisy tried to figure out how she felt, seeing them together. Logan was moving on. He was seeing someone. It seemed…appropriate, somehow.

The car behind her tapped its horn to point out that the light had changed. She rolled forward, glanced in the rearview mirror and saw Logan hug Daphne next to him as they walked, laughing together. Daisy couldn't remember ever walking with him like that, entwined and lost in each other.

Turning onto the lakeshore road, she shifted her thoughts to Julian. She couldn't wait to tell him her news.

He came out of the house as she parked in the drive and got out of her car. Good heavenly lord, he was a beautiful man, she thought with a flood of remembered pleasure.

"I have news," she said, running up to the porch and flinging her arms around him. The remembered pleasure intensified. "My work's going to be on exhibit at MoMA."

He picked her up and swung her around while she laughed for joy. Then he set her down with a kiss. "Of course it is. Your work is genius. It's about time they noticed. Really proud of you, Daze."

"You're the first one I've told. Julian, I was this close to throwing in the towel, probably would have if you hadn't pushed me."

"Yeah?" He pulled her close again.

"Yeah," she said against his mouth, before she kissed him. And just like that, any awkwardness they might have felt about their impulsive night together melted away. "I'll have to think of some ways to thank you." With that, she lifted herself and wrapped her legs around his waist, and he held her as if she weighed nothing. Craning her neck, she peered through the open door of the house. "Are you here alone?"

"Yes, ma'am," he assured her.

"Then maybe—" She broke off, peeling herself away from him. "Julian, what's all this?" But she knew, even before he explained. His duffel bag sat inside the open door. On the hall table were several thick envelopes from the Department of the Air Force. All the elation drained out of her, replaced by the chill of reality.

"My orders came."

A ball of ice formed in her stomach. "I see."

"There was hardly any notice. That's the military for you."

"Where?" she asked, fighting to keep her voice from breaking.

"Vance Air Force Base. It's in Enid, Oklahoma."

She lowered herself to the porch swing. Oklahoma. Okla-frigging-homa.

He sat down next to her, let out a huge sigh. "I'm going to miss you so damn much."

"Then..." *Don't go.* She wouldn't let herself say it. This was his dream, his duty, his life. He had to go. Still, she couldn't shake the notion that their lifestyles were never going to mesh. "We're not going to make it," she whispered, fighting tears. "Are we?"

He cupped her cheek in his hand, skimmed his thumb across her lips. "That's up to us."

She pulled back, unable to bear his touch, and folded her arms across her middle. "When you first proposed to me, I didn't know the monster lurking around the corner. Now I do. You said you'd come back to me and you didn't. I'll never forget that day, Julian. Ever. I still can't go into the bridal shop where I heard the news. Forgive me if I'm resistant to having my heart destroyed again."

"We were both destroyed by what happened. I've spent

the past year processing that," he reminded her. "We came through it. We survived the worst, losing each other, finding each other again. We can do this. I know we can. Please… Christ just love me enough to say you'll try."

Love me enough. Could she? Did she? "Why does it have to be so hard? Why can't anything be simple for us?"

"Because we never settle. That's not who we are. Look at you. Your work's going to be on display at the Museum of Modern Art. That didn't just happen, Daisy. You made it happen because you dared to go for it. And me, I'm…I have to do this. I'm asking you to respect that. It's my dream, but it won't happen unless we make it happen together."

"Why does that sound like an ultimatum to me?"

"It's not. It's me saying I love you. It's me asking you to take a leap of faith. Again, Daisy."

She put her hand in his. "I want us to be together." It was the most honest thing she could think of to say.

"I want that, too. But listen, if I've figured out anything through all of this, it's that you deserve to know what you're signing up for, wanting to be with me. It's not just a career, but who I am. I thought I showed you that, but maybe I never did," Julian said. "Not my forte, sorry."

"I know who you are. I've always known."

He took her hand in his, lifted it to his mouth.

"Why do we keep screwing this up? Why can't we get it together?" she asked, taking her hand back.

"We're both in different places. What you went through when you thought I'd been killed—it's a hazard of this career, and I don't feel right asking you to take that risk again."

She turned to him. The breeze off the lake lifted her hair, bringing with it the scent of autumn. "Julian, I'm telling you now—ask me."

"What?"

"You heard what I said. *Ask me.*"

A smile glinted in his eyes. He slipped his arms around her and drew her close, dropped his lips to her forehead and inhaled deeply. "I'm asking. Marry me, Daisy Bellamy."

Epilogue

The bridegroom was so handsome, Daisy Bellamy's heart nearly melted at the sight of him. Please, she thought. Oh, please let's get it right this time.

He offered her a brief, nervous smile. He was a storybook prince in his dress uniform, every hair in place, adoration beaming from every pore. He stared intently into her eyes and, in a voice that broke with sincerity, said, "I love you."

In that moment, she felt a wave of certainty—they *were* going to get it right this time. The autumn wedding took place in Avalon, on the grounds of Camp Kioga, where Charles and Jane Bellamy had been married more than half a century before. Daisy's family wouldn't have it any other way. The day was clear and bright, with a comforting breeze sweeping gently across Willow Lake, creating swirls of color with the fallen leaves.

This time around, there would be no impulsive ceremony in the wrong city, in the wrong dress, to the wrong guy. This time around, she was the bride she'd always dreamed of being, in the sparkling ball gown she'd chosen so long ago and the flowing gossamer veil Julian had bought for her. She was no longer that naive, hopeful girl, and Julian was no longer the idealistic young officer. Life had thrown them struggles beyond imagining, yet one thing had never changed—the deep, unwavering love she'd felt for him since their first summer together at Willow Lake. Now, at the conclusion of the emotional ceremony, she felt the echo of his whispered words, and her heart was so full of love she thought it might burst.

Their kiss-the-bride moment elicited audible sighs from the surrounding female attendants—Sonnet, Olivia, Dare and Ivy. When Daisy and Julian turned in triumph to their friends and family, a shower of white petals fluttered over them like confetti.

Through a haze of happiness, she saw her mother put her hand to her heart and her father blow her a kiss. Charlie beamed at them, her beautiful son, and then he laughed with joy, waving excitedly as they started down the aisle. He would be a boy with two dads and two homes now, and challenges of his own to face, but all of them—Daisy, Julian, Logan—were committed to being the best parents they could to this precious child. She, Charlie and Julian were Oklahoma-bound, and after that was anyone's guess. But she would always come back to Avalon and Willow Lake, so much a part of the person she'd become. Life was taking her elsewhere now, and her heart's home belonged in the strong and steady hands of her husband.

Holding fast together, the two of them ducked beneath the ceremonial arch of swords held aloft by uniformed air force saber bearers, coming through on the other side, bursting toward the future.

* * * * *

Acknowledgments

I owe a very special thank you to the real Andrea and Brian Hubble, and to Kay Fritchman and her furry family for their generous contributions.

When it comes to some books, the author is in need of a literary "pit crew" to keep everything in proper working order right up until the final lap. This book's pit crew included (but wasn't limited to) my friends and fellow writers—Anjali Banerjee, Kate Breslin, Sheila Roberts and Elsa Watson; Margaret O'Neill Marbury and Adam Wilson of MIRA Books; Meg Ruley and Annelise Robey of the Jane Rotrosen Agency.

Dear Reader,

You and I have been with Daisy since she first reared her rebellious head as a troubled teen in *Summer at Willow Lake*. Creating this young woman's journey through romance, heartache, tragedy and triumph has been a labor of love for me. The support and affection with which readers have embraced this story and all the Lakeshore Chronicles means more to me than you could know.

Starlight on Willow Lake, the latest installment in the Lakeshore Chronicles, will be published next month, and I can't wait for you to read it. This novel features the elements closest to my heart—mismatched lovers, glorious scenery by a magical lake, the bonds of friends and family, and as always, the incredible power of love to give life its deepest meaning.

This novel is drawn from a heartfelt, personal event in my own life—caring for my beloved, elderly dad. The main character, Faith, was inspired by the caregivers who work so selflessly for the people they look after. I often wonder what their lives are like at the end of a long, arduous day, when they've exhausted every bit of their patience, tenderness, compassion and sweat labor. What do they go home to? Who cares for *them*?

These questions are at the heart of *Starlight on Willow Lake*. And as I wrote this novel, the answers surprised even me. The unlikely pairing of international financier Mason Bellamy and the lonely young woman in charge of his mother's care compelled me from beginning to end. Their instant, sizzling chemistry set the tone for a passionate, funny, heartbreaking and ultimately uplifting love story.

I'd love to hear from you online. Please join the conversation at facebook.com/susanwiggs.

Happy reading,

Susan Wiggs

SusanWiggs.com

Turn the page for a sneak peek at
STARLIGHT ON WILLOW LAKE,
the newest addition to Susan Wiggs's bestselling
LAKESHORE CHRONICLES *series,*
available soon from MIRA Books.

Mason Bellamy stared up at the face of the mountain that had killed his father. The mountain's name was innocent enough—Cloud Piercer. The rich afternoon light of the New Zealand winter cast a spell over the moment. Snow-clad slopes glowed with the impossible pink and amethyst of a rare jewel. The stunning backdrop of the Southern Alps created a panorama of craggy peaks veined with granite and glacial ice against a sky so clear it caused the eyes to smart.

The bony white structure of a cell phone tower, its discs grabbing signals from outer space, rose from a nearby peak. The only other intrusion into the natural beauty was located at the top of the slope—a black-and-yellow gate marked Experts Only and a round dial designating Avalanche Danger—Moderate.

He wondered if someone came all the way up here each day to move the needle on the dial. Maybe his father had wondered the same thing last year. Maybe it had been the last thought to go through his head before he was buried by two hundred thousand cubic meters of snow.

According to witnesses in the nearest town, at the base of the mountain, it had been a dry snow avalanche with a powder cloud that had been visible to any resident of Hillside Township who happened to look up. The incident report stated that there had been a delay before the noise came. Then everyone for miles around had heard the sonic boom.

The Maori in the region had legends about this mountain. The natives respected its threatening beauty as well as its lethal nature, their myths filled with cautionary tales of humans being swallowed to appease the gods. For generations, the lofty crag, with its year-round cloak of snow, had challenged the world's most adventurous skiers, and its gleaming north face had been Trevor Bellamy's favorite run. It had also been his final run.

Trevor's final wish, spelled out in his last will and testament, had brought Mason halfway around the world, and down into the Southern Hemisphere's winter. At the moment he felt anything but cold. He unzipped his parka, having worked up a major sweat climbing to the peak. This run was accessible only to those willing to be helicoptered to a landing pad at three thousand meters, and then willing to climb another few hundred meters on all-terrain skis outfitted with nonslip skins. He peeled the Velcro-like skins from the underside of his skis, stowed them in his backpack and put his skis back on. Then he studied the mountain's face again and felt a sweet rush of adrenaline.

When it came to skiing in dangerous places, he was his father's son.

A rhythmic sliding sound drew Mason's attention to the trail he'd just climbed. He glanced over and lifted his ski pole in a wave. "Over here, bro."

Adam Bellamy came over the crest of the trail, shading his eyes against the afternoon light. "You said you'd kick my ass, and you did," he called. His voice echoed across the empty, frozen terrain.

Mason grinned at his younger brother. "I'm a man

of my word. But look at you. You haven't even broken a sweat."

"Mets. We get tested for metabolic conditioning every three months for work." Adam was a firefighter, built to haul eighty pounds of gear up multiple flights of stairs.

"Cool. My only conditioning program involves running to catch the subway."

"The tough life of an international financier," said Adam. "Hold everything while I get out my tiny violin."

"Who says I'm complaining?" Mason took off his goggles to apply some defogger. "Is Ivy close? Or did our little sister stop to hire a team of mountain guides to carry her up the hill so she doesn't have to climb it on her skis?"

"She's close enough to hear you," said Ivy, appearing at the top of the ridge. "And aren't the guides on strike?" She wore a dazzling turquoise parka and white ski pants, Gucci sunglasses and white leather gloves. Her blond hair was wild and wind-tossed, streaming from beneath her helmet.

Mason flashed on an image of their mother. Ivy looked so much like her. He felt a lurch of guilt when he thought about Alice Bellamy. Her last ski run had been right here on this mountain face, too. But unlike Trevor, she had survived. Although some would say that what had happened to her was worse than dying.

Ivy slogged over to her brothers on her AT skis. "Listen, you two. I want to go on record to say that when I leave these earthly bonds, I will not require my adult children to risk their lives in order to scatter my remains. Just leave my ashes on the jewelry counter at Neiman Marcus. I'd be fine with that."

"Make sure you put your request in writing," Mason said.

"How do you know I haven't already?" She gestured

at Adam. "Help me get these skins off, will you?" She lifted each ski in turn, planting them upright in the snow.

Adam expertly peeled the fabric skins from the bottoms of her skis, then removed his own, stuffing them into his backpack. "It's crazy steep, just the way Dad used to describe it."

"Chicken?" asked Ivy, fastening the chin strap of her crash helmet.

"Have you ever known me to shy away from a ski run?" Adam asked. "I'm going to take it easy, though. No crazy tricks."

The three of them stood gazing at the beautiful slope, now a perfect picture of serenity in the late-afternoon glow. It was the first time any of them had come to this particular spot. As a family, they had skied together in many places, but not here. This particular mountain had been the special domain of their father and mother alone.

They were lined up in birth order—Mason, the first-born, the one who knew their father best. Adam, three years younger, had been closest to Trevor. Ivy, still in her twenties, was the quintessential baby of the family—adored, entitled, seemingly fragile, yet with the heart of a lioness. She had owned their father's affections as surely as the sun owns the dawn, in the way only a daughter can.

Mason wondered if his siblings would ever learn the things about their father that he knew. And if they did, would it change the way they felt about him?

They stood together, their collective silence as powerful as any conversation they might have had.

"It's incredible," Ivy said after a long pause. "The pictures didn't do it justice. Maybe Dad's last request wasn't so nutty, after all. This might be the prettiest mountain ever, and I get to see it with my two best guys." Then she sighed. "I wish Mom could be here. She loves skiing so much. It's so sad that she'll never ski again."

"Adam will get the whole thing on camera," Mason said. "We can all watch it together when we get back to Avalon next week."

A year after the accident, their mother was adjusting to a new life in a new place—a small Catskills town on the shores of Willow Lake. Mason was pretty sure it wasn't the life Alice Bellamy had imagined for herself.

"Do you have him?" Adam asked.

Mason slapped his forehead. "Damn, I forgot. Why don't the two of you wait right here while I ski to the bottom, grab the ashes, helicopter back up to the rendezvous and make the final climb again?"

"Very funny," said Adam.

"Of course I have him." Mason shrugged out of his backpack and dug inside. He pulled out an object bundled in a navy blue bandanna. He unwrapped it and handed the bandanna to Adam.

"A beer stein?" asked Ivy.

"It's all I could find," said Mason. The stein was classic kitsch, acquired at a frat party during Mason's college days. There was a scene with a laughing Falstaff painted on the sides, and the mug had a hinged lid made of pewter. "The damned urn they delivered him in was huge. No way would it fit in my luggage."

He didn't explain to his sister and brother that a good half of the ashes had ended up on the living room floor of his Manhattan apartment. Getting Trevor Bellamy from the urn to the beer stein had been trickier than Mason had thought. Slightly freaked out by the idea of his father embedded in his carpet fibers, he had vacuumed up the spilled ashes, wincing at the sound of the larger bits being sucked into the bag.

Then he'd felt bad about emptying the vacuum bag down the garbage chute, so he'd gone out on the balcony and sprinkled the remains over Avenue of the Americas.

There had been a breeze that day, and his fussiest neighbor in the high-rise co-op had stuck her head out, shaking her fist and threatening to call the super to report the transgression. Most of the ashes blew back onto the balcony, and Mason ended up waiting until the wind died down; then he'd swept the area with a broom.

So only half of Trevor Bellamy had made it into the beer stein. That was appropriate, Mason decided. Their father had been only half there while he was alive, too.

"This is cool with me," said Adam. "Dad always did like his beer."

Mason held the mug high, its silhouette stark against the deepening light of the afternoon sky.

"Ein prosit," said Adam.

"Santé," Mason said in the French their father had spoken like a native.

"Cin cin." Ivy, the artist in the family, favored Italian.

"Take your protein pill and put your helmet on," Mason said, riffing on the David Bowie song. "Let's do this thing."

"Should we say a few words?" asked Ivy.

"If I say no, will that stop you?" Mason removed the duct tape from the lid of the beer stein.

Ivy stuck out her tongue at him, shifting into bratty-sister mode. Then she looked up at Adam and spoke to the camera. "Hey, Mom. We were just wishing you could be here with us to say goodbye to Daddy. We all made it to the summit of Cloud Piercer, just like he wanted. It's kind of surreal, finding winter here when the summer is just beginning where you are, at Willow Lake. It feels somehow like...I don't know...like we're unstuck in time."

Ivy's voice wavered with emotion. "Anyway, so here I am with my two big brothers. Daddy always loved it when the three of us were together, skiing and having fun."

Adam moved his head to let the camera record the majestic scenery all around them. The sculpted crags of the Southern Alps, which ran the entire length of New Zealand's south island, were sharply silhouetted against the sky. Mason wondered what the day had been like when his parents had skiied this mountain, their last run together. Was the sky so blue that it hurt the eyes? Did the sharp cold air stab their lungs? Was the silence this deep? Had there been any inkling that the entire face of the mountain was about to bury them?

"Are we ready?" he asked.

Adam and Ivy nodded. He studied his little sister's face, now soft with the sadness of missing her father. She'd had a special closeness with him, and she'd taken his death hard—maybe even harder than their mother had.

"Who's going first?" asked Adam.

"It can't be me," said Mason. "You, um, don't want to get caught in the blowback, if you know what I mean." He gestured with the beer stein.

"Oh, right," said Ivy. "You go last, then."

Adam twisted the camera so it faced uphill. "Let's take it one at a time, okay? So we don't cause another avalanche."

It was a known safety procedure that in an avalanche zone, only one person at a time should go down the mountain. Mason wondered if his father had been aware of the precaution. He wondered if his father had violated the rule. He doubted he would ever ask his mother for a detail like that. Whatever had happened on this mountain a year ago couldn't be changed now.

Ivy took off her shades, leaned over and kissed the beer stein. "Bye, Daddy. Fly into eternity, okay? But don't forget how much you were loved here on earth. I'll keep you safe in my heart." She started to cry. "I thought I'd used up all my tears, but I guess not. I'll always shed a tear for you, Daddy."

Adam waggled his gloved fingers in front of the camera. "Yo, Dad. You were the best. I couldn't have asked for anything more. Except for more time with you. Later, dude."

Each one of them had known a different Trevor Bellamy. Mason could only wish the father he'd known was the one who had inspired Ivy's tenderness and loyalty or Adam's hero worship. Mason knew another side to their father, but he would never be the one to shatter his siblings' memories.

Adam pushed through the warning gate and started down the mountain, the camera on his helmet rolling.

Ivy waited, then followed at a safe distance behind. Thanks to Adam, the cautious one of the three, each of them wore gear equipped with beacons and avalanche airbags, designed to detonate automatically in the event of a slide.

Their mother had been wearing one the day of the incident. Their father had not.

Adam skied with competence and control, navigating the steep slope with ease and carving a sinuous curve in the untouched powder. Ivy followed gracefully, turning his S-curves into a double-helix pattern.

The lightest of breezes stirred the icy air. Mason decided he had worked too hard to climb the damned mountain only to take the conservative route down. Always the most reckless of the three, he decided to take the slope the way his father probably had, with joyous abandon.

"Here goes," he said to the clear, empty air, and he thumbed open the lid of the beer stein. The cold air must have weakened the pottery, because a shard broke loose, cutting through his glove and slicing into his thumb. *Ouch.* He ignored the cut and focused on the task at hand.

Did any essence of their father remain? Was Trevor Bellamy's spirit somehow trapped within the humble-looking detritus, waiting to be set free on the mountaintop?

He had lived his life. Left a legacy of secrets behind. He'd paid the ultimate price for his freedom, leaving his burden on someone else's shoulders—Mason's.

"Godspeed, Dad," he said. With his ski poles in one hand and the beer stein in the other, he raised his arm high and plunged down the steep slope. The ashes created a cloud in his wake, rising on an updraft of wind and dispersing across the face of Trevor's beloved, deadly mountain. The things we love most can kill us. Mason might have heard the saying somewhere. Or he had just made it up.

The faster Mason went, the less he was bothered by something so inconvenient as a thought. That was the beauty of skiing in dangerous places. Filled with the thrill of the ride, he was only vaguely aware of Adam pointing the camera at him. He couldn't resist showing off, making a trail in a fresh expanse of untouched powder, like a snake slithering down the mountain. Spotting a rugged granite cliff, perfectly formed and perfectly covered for jumping, he raced toward it, aimed his skis straight down the fall line and launched himself off the edge. For several seconds he was airborne, the wind flapping through his parka, turning him momentarily into a human kite. The steep pitch of the landing raced up to meet him with breathtaking speed. He wobbled on contact but didn't wipe out, managing to come out of the landing with the mug still held aloft.

He gave a short laugh and brayed the Olympics theme song at the top of his lungs. Then, as the slope flattened and his speed naturally slowed, he realized Ivy was waving her arms frantically.

Now what?

He raced toward them and saw that Adam had his mobile phone out.

"What's up?" he asked. "Was my epic run not pretty enough? Or are you posting a Tweet about it already?"

Despite the chill air, Ivy's face was pale. "It's Mom."

"On the phone? Tell her I said hi."

"No, dipshit, something happened to Mom."